Charles Tomlinson

Rudimentary Mechanics

being a concise exposition of the general principles of mechanical science and their

applications

Charles Tomlinson

Rudimentary Mechanics
being a concise exposition of the general principles of mechanical science and their applications

ISBN/EAN: 9783337387327

Printed in Europe, USA, Canada, Australia, Japan

Cover: Foto ©Andreas Hilbeck / pixelio.de

More available books at **www.hansebooks.com**

RUDIMENTARY

MECHANICS

BEING

A CONCISE EXPOSITION

OF THE

General Principles of Mechanical Science

AND THEIR APPLICATIONS

By CHARLES TOMLINSON

LECTURER ON NATURAL SCIENCE IN KING'S COLLEGE SCHOOL, LONDON

TWELFTH EDITION, CORRECTED

Capio Lumen

LONDON
CROSBY LOCKWOOD & CO.
STATIONERS' HALL COURT, LUDGATE HILL
1878

PREFACE.

No department of science has probably received more attention from scientific writers than Mechanics. There are numerous treatises on this subject in all the languages of the civilised world, adapted, apparently, to suit the intellectual and pecuniary means of all classes, and including the costly quarto and bulky octavo for the advanced mathematical student, as well as the sixpenny catechism for the use of children. Between these two extremes, books on the subject are innumerable. In adding one more to the number, the writer does not feel any apology to be necessary, because, in the first place, he is not aware that any other treatise, with the same quantity and exactitude of matter, and with so many engravings, is to be had at so low a price; and, secondly, if he has approached his subject with a proper appreciation of the *principles* upon which mechanical science is based, he can scarcely fail to convey to the diligent and attentive reader some idea of their grandeur, generality, and importance.

In every scientific work where principles are fairly enunciated, the reader can supply facts and illustrations for himself; and he may take it as the test of his progress, if, while thinking of the principle, facts rise spontaneously in his mind to illustrate it; or if, while examining facts, he clearly perceive the operation of the governing principle.

The sale of the previous Editions of this Work, consisting each of 7,000 copies, within a limited period, is a sufficient proof that a demand has long existed for a cheap popular treatise on Mechanics, in which the peculiar difficulties of the subject should be fairly met instead of being slurred over; and, as far as could be done with the merest elements of Mathematics, made intelligible to the non-professional reader.

The third and fourth parts, devoted to Hydrostatics and Hydrodynamics, are very brief. This could only have been remedied by one of two methods:—either by encroaching on the space devoted to the consideration of Statics and Dynamics, or by extending this volume beyond seven sheets, thereby enhancing the price. The writer considers that the adoption of either of these methods would have greatly injured the utility of the work.

The work has been carefully read for this Edition. It is hoped that no material errors will be found in it to detract in the slightest degree from that success which has attended the previous editions.

C. T.

CONTENTS.

PART I.—STATICS.

I.—ON STATICAL FORCES OR PRESSURES.

PART II.—DYNAMICS.

PART III.—HYDROSTATICS.

PART IV.—HYDRODYNAMICS.

MECHANICS.

PART I.—STATICS.

I. ON STATICAL FORCES OR PRESSURES.

1. A BODY is said to be in equilibrium when the force which act upon it mutually counterbalance each other, or when they are counterbalanced by some passive force or resistance. Thus a body suspended from the end of a thread is in equilibrium, because the attraction of gravitation, which would cause it to fall, is counterbalanced by the resistance of the thread, and by that of the point of suspension. A body may be in equilibrium without any apparent resistance. Thus a fish may be in equilibrium in the water, a balloon in the air; but in such cases the weight which would cause the fish to sink, or the balloon to fall, is exactly counterbalanced by other forces, which will be considered hereafter. We may, however, regard all bodies which appear to us to be *at rest*, as being actually in a state of *equilibrium*, or equally balanced between or among forces which destroy each other.

2. The conditions of equilibrium are determined by the science of *Statics*,* as regards solids; and by *Hydrostatics*,† as regards fluids. The laws which determine the motions of solids, form the science of *Dynamics*;‡ while the laws of fluids in motion belong to *Hydrodynamics*. These fou divisions form the science of MECHANICS§ in its widest sense; that is, the science of *forces*, producing either *rest or motion*.

* From στατὸς, standing still. † From ὕδωρ, water, and στατὸς.
‡ From δύναμις, force. § From μηχανὴ, a machine.

Mechanics.

3. Forces that are balanced, so as to produce *rest*, are called *statical forces* or *pressures*, to distinguish them from *moving, deflecting, accelerating*, or *retarding* forces; *i. e.* such as are producing *motion*, or a *change* in the direction or velocity of motion. This distinction being wholly artificial, and made for the purpose of facilitating study, must not mislead the student into the idea that these are different *kinds* of forces; for the same force may act in any of these modes; it may sometimes be a statical, and sometimes an accelerating force; but as the consideration of forces when balanced, is much more simple than that of forces in motion, it is convenient to separate the former, and to confine our attention in the first instance to them, or rather, to regard all forces in a statical point of view.

4. Statical forces or pressures can, of course (like other quantities or magnitudes), be compared only with each other, but the ratio between any two quantities may be represented by the ratio between two other quantities, however different in kind from the first two; thus, two pressures may have the same ratio as two lines, or two surfaces, or two bulks, or two times, or two numbers; and these last are found the most convenient class of magnitudes by which to represent the ratios of all others. Now, when we represent magnitudes of any kind by numbers, we in fact compare them with some fixed or standard magnitude of the same kind, which we represent by the number 1: thus, the units commonly used for comparing *lengths*, are *inches, feet, miles*, &c.; and so also the units of *pressure* are *ounces, pounds, tons*, &c.*

* In strictness, however, these terms do not properly express units of *pressure*, but of *mass* (or quantity of matter); and they are used as standards of pressure, simply because the earth's attraction on a given quantity of matter is always the same *at the same place*, and differs but slightly in different places. But we must not forget that the same mass, in a different situation (as regards latitude, or level), would gravitate with a rather greater or less pressure. (See *Introduction to the Study of Natural Philosophy*, p. 67.) We must not therefore confound *mass* with *weight*, because the same names are applied to the units of both; for, in fact, the units of pressure are quite distinct from, though founded

5. Forces may also (like any other magnitudes) be represented by lines of definite lengths. A unit of length being taken to represent the unit of pressure, the length of the line represents the *magnitude* of the force; but the line has this great advantage over a number,—its direction represents the *direction* of the force; and its commencement or extremity, the point at which the force acts, or its point of application : thus, by a line, the force is completely defined in all its three elements; while a number can only represent *one* of them, viz., its *magnitude*.

Agreeing, therefore, to represent a force by a number or by a line, a double force would be represented by a double number, or by a line of double length, and so on. In this way forces can be brought under the domain of mathematical science, geometry serving to investigate their various relations by means of lines, arithmetic by means of numbers, and algebra and trigonometry by the properties common to directions and magnitudes of all kinds.

6. If two forces be in equilibrium at a point, they must be equal in magnitude, and opposite in direction. Two equal forces acting together, in the same direction, produce a double force ; three equal forces, a triple force, and so on. But whatever number of forces may act upon a point, and whatever their directions, they can only impart one single motion in one certain direction. We may, therefore, incor-

on those of mass ; just as the latter are derived from those of *length*, and all of them from that of *time;* the connection being as follows :—

1. A *pound pressure* means, that amount of pressure which is exerted towards the earth, in the latitude of London and at the level of the sea, by the quantity of matter called *a pound.*

2. A *pound of matter* means a quantity equal to that quantity of pure water which, at the temperature of 62 deg. Fahrenheit, would occupy 27·727 cubic inches

3. A *cubic inch* is that cube whose side taken 39·1393 times would measure the effective length of a London seconds pendulum.

4. A *seconds* pendulum is that which, by the unassisted and unopposed effect of its own gravity, would make 86,400 vibrations in an artificial solar day, or 86163·09 in a natural sidereal day.

porate all these single forces into one force, or *resultant*, capable of producing the same mechanical effect as the forces themselves, which are called the *components*. It is evident, that if to a system of forces a new force be added equal to the resultant, and acting in a contrary direction, equilibrium would be maintained.

If, for example, a boat be moving by the force of the current, by the force of the wind, and by the oars, we may imagine a single force, such as a strong rope, to be attached to the boat, and drawn in such a direction, and with such a force, as the three forces together would produce. The current, the wind, and the oars ceasing to act, this rope would supply their place, and constitute their resultant. Now it is evident that to this resultant we may oppose another force; a rope, for example, acting or resisting with the same power, and in an opposite direction. The boat would in such case be as completely at rest as if it were at anchor. It could neither go forwards, nor backwards, nor move to either side, until some new force should act upon it, or some change should take place in the existing forces.

When any number of forces act at a point in the same straight line, and in the same direction, the resultant is equal to their sum; if the forces act in opposite directions, the resultant is equal to their difference. For example, let a point be pressed *upwards* with a force of 7 pounds, and *downwards* with a force of 4 pounds, the resultant is an upward pressure of 3 pounds. Let it receive pressures from the *east* of 3 pounds, 6 pounds, and 10 pounds; and from the *west*, of 2 and 3 pounds. The resultant is, of course, a westward pressure of $3 + 6 + 10 - 2 - 3 = 14$ lbs. If the forces in opposite directions be denoted by the opposite signs $+$ and $-$, then the resultant is in all cases their algebraical sum; so that, having taken the arithmetical sum of the forces acting in one direction, and also of those acting in the contrary direction, the difference of these sums is the resultant force, and it acts in the direction of the forces which form the larger sum. When the resultant = 0, the forces balance each other.

Hence we may add equal and opposite forces at any point, without affecting a system of statical forces. This is called the *superposition* of equilibrium. So also we may remove from any point in a system those forces which are equal and opposite, without disturbing equilibrium thereby.

7. When two forces act upon a point in different directions, the resultant is found more easily by the geometrical method. It is obvious, in the first place, that the line representing the resultant must lie in the same plane which contains the directions of the two forces: for if not, on which side of the plane should it lie? There is evidently nothing to determine it to one side more than the other. For the same reason, when the forces are *equal*, the resultant must bisect the angle between their directions, for it cannot be nearer one than the other.* Moreover, in all cases, whether equal or not, we naturally expect that the nearer they coincide in direction, the greater will be the resultant, and *vice versâ;* and as their exact coincidence makes it equal their *sum*, while their exact opposition makes it equal their *difference*, we conclude that in all intermediate positions it will be less than their sum, and greater than their difference. But it is doubtful whether elementary mathematics will carry us further than this without the aid of experiment,† which teaches us the following beautiful law.

Let the point P (Fig. 1) be acted on by two forces, pressing in the directions P A and P B. From the point P, upon

---

* This kind of proof, by what is called the *principle of sufficient reason*, is of very extensive use in Mechanics.

† The first experiments for this purpose were made by Galileo, in some boats, at Venice, about the year 1592. This was the first step in inductive (or natural) science, or the first direct question put to nature, at least since the time of Archimedes. But although this point was first determined by experiment, it must be classed among abstract or necessary truths, being deducible from the simple principle above mentioned. The proof is too long to be given here.

the line P A, measure off any length P *a;* and from tho
point P, upon the line P B, take a length P *b* bearing the samc
ratio to P *a* that the force B bears to the force A.   The easiest
way to do this is to make the lines P *a*, P *b*, contain respectively, as many units of length (inches or feet, for example),

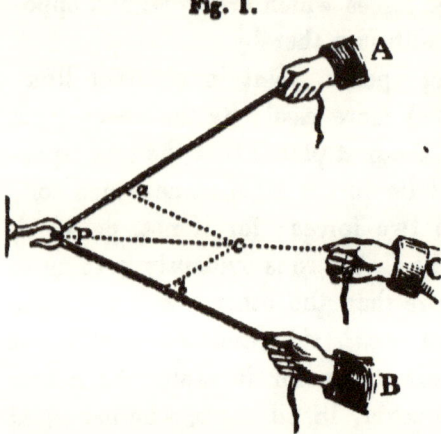

Fig. 1.

as the forces A B contain
units of force (ounces or
pounds, for example).
Through *a* draw a line
parallel to P B, and
through *b* draw a line
parallel to P A, and sup-
pose these lines to meet
at *c*.   We thus get a parallelogram, P *a c b;* and
the line P *c*, called its
diagonal, will represent

a single force acting in the direction P C, and consisting of as
many units of force as the line P *c* contains units of length ;
and this force will produce upon the point P the same effect as
the two forces A and B produce acting together.

      This method of finding an equivalent, or the resultant of
two forces, is called the *parallelogram of forces*, and is
thus concisely expressed :—If two forces be represented, in
magnitude and direction, by the sides of a parallelogram, an
equivalent force will be represented, in magnitude and direction, by its diagonal.—The two forces are called the *components* of the resultant.

      8. Any number of forces, acting at one point, can be com-
pounded by the same rule.   For instance, let the body *x*
(Fig. 2) be pressed at once by the three forces, whose directions are expressed by the arrows A, B, C, and their magnitudes
by the lengths *x a*, *x b*, *x c*.   We may first compound any
two of them (such as A and B), by completing the parallelogram *x a d b*, by which we find that the direction of their
resultant is *x d*, and that its magnitude is to their magnitudes

as the length $x\,d$ is to the lengths $x\,a,\,x\,b.$ We may then compound this resultant with the remaining force $x\,c$, by completing the parallelogram $x\,d\,e\,c$, the diagonal of which, viz. $x\,e$, will represent both the magnitude and direction of the general re-

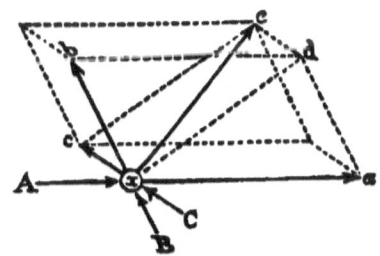

Fig. 2.

sultant of all three forces ; so that a force of the magnitude expressed by this length $x\,e$, and acting in the direction $e\,x$, would balance those three forces. Of course, the resultant of any greater number of pressures might have been found in the same way, by combining two at a time.

In this problem, it matters not whether the directions of the forces lie all in the same plane or in different planes. In the latter case, the three lines $x\,a,\,x\,b,\,x\,c$, would form the three edges that meet at one solid angle of a *parallelopiped;* aud by completing this solid figure (as shown by the outer dotted lines of Fig. 2), its diagonal $x\,e$ will represent the re-sultant. Hence, whether we regard the lines of this figure as they really lie flat on the paper, or as the projection or pic-ture of a solid parallelopiped, the law is equally true. The same process is of course capable of being extended to any number of forces in different planes.

9. The problem of the *composition of forces*, which is thus solved with so much ease by construction (or drawing on vaper), often becomes extremely complex in calculation, especially when in dynamics the element of *time* is added, and the forces are of constantly-varying magnitude. In fact, it would scarcely be possible to arrive at some of the simplest results of its application to every branch of physics, if re-course were not constantly had to the inverse problem of the *resolution* of forces. It is constantly necessary to consider a force (however simple its origin) as capable of being resolved into two or three distinct forces, having different directions;

for it is evident that we may substitute for any given force, any number of other forces, having any given directions (not opposite to each other) ; for we may make the line *s e* the diagonal of any number of parallelograms, or parallelopipeds, having their sides running in any proposed directions. When their directions are decided on, their lengths will be discoverable ; and thus we shall know both the directions and magnitudes of the forces into which, for convenience sake, the whole, or *resultant* force, has been resolved.

10. Examples of the composition of pressure are of constant occurrence, as in the exertions of our limbs, the action of the various tools and implements which we employ, and the external actions in which we participate. It is frequently of importance to consider whether the component forces are employed so as to produce the best resultant; that is, one acting in a direction most available for the object intended to be accomplished, and with as small an expenditure of force as possible.

Fig. 3.

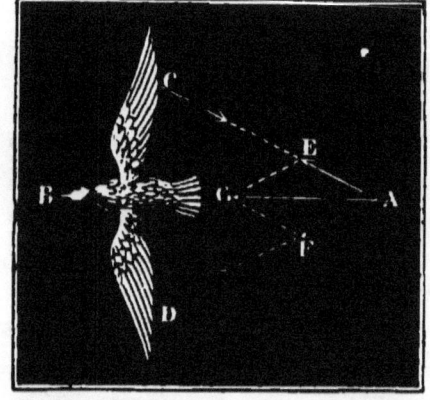

Birds have a figure symmetrical with respect to a vertical plane, A B (Fig. 3), which passes through the body. When they fly, their wings execute symmetrical movements, and strike the air with equal pressures. The resistance of the air to the pressure of the wings is perpendicular to their surface. Hence the direction of the resultant will be found by the parallelogram of forces, for which purpose draw C A and D A perpendicular to the surfaces of the two wings, these lines representing the directions of the forces by which the bird presses backward with each wing ; or, in other words, A C and A D are the directions of the resistances exerted by the air against the two wings; and neither of these pressures (when the wings are in this position) tends to impel the bird straight forward; but their *resultant* does so; for if the wings be similarly extended, and act with equal force, the lines A C and A D will make equal angles with the line A B, passing through the centre of the bird; and two lines representing the intensities of the two pressures, as A E and A F, being equal, the diagonal A G will coincide with that line, and the motion of the bird will be directly forward.

A man in swimming impels himself in directions perpendicular to the soles of his feet and the palms of his hands. If these forces be equal on either side of his body, the resultant is a line passing through the centre of his body.

The motion of a boat rowed by oars is evidently similar to the cases already noticed, where the forces are symmetrical on either side of a central vertical plane: but when sails are acted on by the wind, and the force thereby transmitted to the keel is modified by the action of the rudder, various problems arise, which are too complex to be studied here. We may, however, take a case, where the sail is supposed to be stretched so as to form a plane surface; and, neglecting the action of the rudder, as well as that of any tide or current in the water, let us consider the force of the wind only. Let *a b* (Fig. 4) be the length or keel of a sailing vessel, and let the right line *m n* represent the projection of a sail, supported at *o* against a mast. Let *o p* represent in magnitude and direction the force w, with which the wind acts upon the sail. Construct the parallelogram *o c p d*, of which *o p* is the diagonal. This force *o p* is evidently decomposable into two other forces; the first, *o c* in the direction of the plane of the canvas, and producing no effect in advancing the vessel; the second, *o d*, perpendicular to the sail, which is the only force which presses on the sail and gives motion to the vessel. But *o d* may also be decomposed into two other forces; the one *o E* in the direction of the keel or length of the vessel, and which tends to advance it in the direction of the arrow; the other *o f* acting at right angles to the length of the vessel, so as to urge it sideways. The form of the vessel enables it to offer a great resistance to the latter force, and very little to the former, so that it proceeds with considerable velocity in the direction *o* E of its keel, and

Fig. 4.

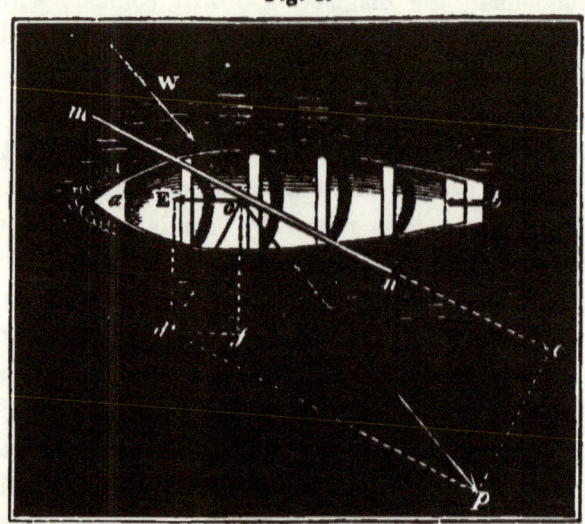

makes very little *lee-way*, as the sideward direction *o f* is called.* Thus some idea may be formed of the manner in which a wind, which is sometimes within five points (or $56\frac{1}{4}°$) of being *opposed* to the course of the vessel, may, with the aid of sails judiciously applied, be made to impel it.

* If this do not seem satisfactory, it must be remembered, that our present business is not with *motions*, but with *pressures*, and that we must consider, not what proportion the head-way bears to the lee-way (*i. e.* what proportion exists between the *velocity* of the vessel in the direction *o* E, and that in the direction *o f*), for statics has nothing to do with *velocities*; but we must reduce the problem to its statical form, by imagining the introduction of such a force or forces as would produce equilibrium. Now this would (in the present case) require a greater force in the direction opposed to the lee-way, than in that opposed to the head-way; for though the vessel *moves* faster forwards than sideways, yet she *presses* more in the latter direction than in the former, in the proportion that *o f* exceeds *o* E.

In the flying of a boy's kite we may study similar effects. To counteract (permanently) the force of gravity which would bring it to the ground, two other forces at least are required—viz. the wind, and the resistance of the string or of the point where it is fixed or held. The wind alone would keep it suspended, but only for a time—viz. until the kite had either turned its edge to the wind (so as to be pressed no more on the under than on the upper side), or else had become vertical, so as to be pressed only horizontally, and not upwards. If the kite had no tail, the former effect would rapidly ensue, and with a tail the latter would be equally certain. It is necessary, therefore, that the kite be *inclined*, and this is effected by the string being attached at such a point as to leave more surface (and therefore, a greater pressure of wind) below the point of attachment than above it. This excess of pressure on the lower half drives it to leeward, but only to a certain extent, where it is counterbalanced by the weight of the tail; but the maintenance of the inclined position depends on laws which will be explained further on. It is sufficient for the present to observe, that the horizontal force of the wind w (Fig. 5), the intensity of which may be represented by the line *o w*, must (like every other force that impinges obliquely on a surface, as on the sail in the last example) be resolved into two portions, one parallel, and the other perpendicular to the surface. The former portion *o a* has no effect; the kite is pressed only by the other portion, in the direction *o b*, in which direction it would move, if it maintained its inclined position, and were subject to no other force than the wind. But we have to consider two other forces,—the string and gravity. Supposing the string to pull in the direction *o s*, we shall find the intensity of this force by resolving the whole effect of the wind on the kite, represented by *o b*, into two portions, *o d* perpendicular to the string (and therefore not resisted by it), and *o c*, which must be balanced by an equal and opposite force in the string, which will accordingly be represented by *o s*. The action of the string and of the wind would therefore be to urge the kite in the diagonal $o\ d$ of the parallelogram $o\ b\ d\ s$; but with this we must further compound the force of gravity, which (the

Fig. 5.

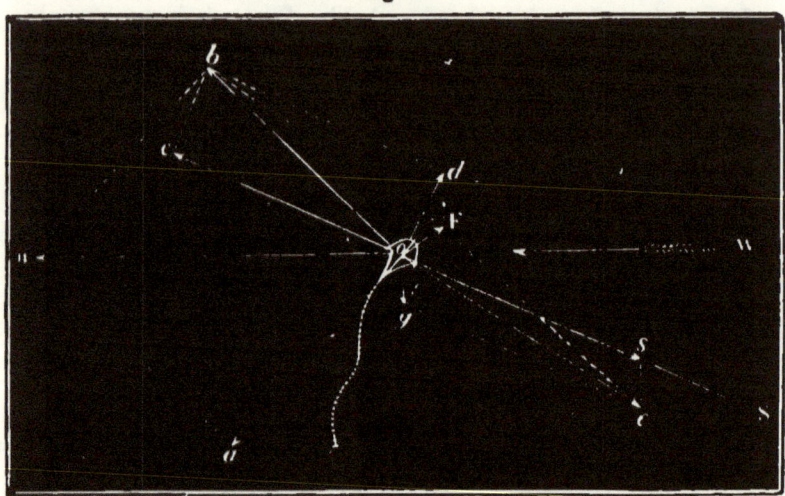

kite being very light) we will represent by the short line $o\ g$, and this, compounded with $o\ d$, gives the resultant o F, in which direction the kite will rise when subject to all three forces, in the degrees here supposed. Supposing the wind suddenly to cease, we shall find the resultant of the string and of gravity by compounding $o\ s$ with $o\ g$, which gives $o\ e$ as the direction in which the kite would then be pulled; and this compounded with the *effective* portion of the wind's force, viz. $o\ b$, will give o F as before. In this direction, the kite will, under these circumstances, rise till it has attained a position where the three forces $o\ b$, $o\ s$, and $o\ g$ are in equilibrium, *i. e.* where each is equal and opposite to the resultant of the other two, in which case we should on our construction find o F $= 0$, or the point F would coincide with o.*

* In order to raise the kite to its greatest altitude, the most advantageous angle for the kite to form with the horizon is 54° 44'; which is the same as the rudder of a ship should make with the keel, in order that the vessel may be turned with the greatest facility, supposing the current to have a direction parallel with the keel; and the same that the sails of a

11. The property of a system of statical or balanced forces acting on a point, that each is exactly equal and opposite to the resultant of all the rest, whatever may be their number, leads to a very simple and elegant theorem, called *the Polygon of Forces*. By this, any number of statical forces are represented in direction and magnitude by the sides of a polygon, taken in order; and they will, when applied to one point, produce equilibrium; or, in other words, in order that the forces may form a polygon, they must be in equilibrium.

In Fig. 6, let P^1 P^2 P^3 P^4 P^5 be forces in equilibrium acting on a point A, and represented in magnitude as well as in direction by the lines A P^1, A P^2, A P^3, A P^4, A P^5.

Fig. 6.

To find the resultant of P^1 and P^2, complete the parallelogram A P^1 C P^2, A C will represent this resultant. Compounding this resultant with the force P^3, by means of the parallelogram A C D P^3, we see that A D represents their resultant, or the resultant of P^1, P^2, and P^3. Compounding this last resultant with the force P^4, by the parallelogram A P^4 E D, we see that their resultant is represented by the line A E, opposite in direction to the last force P^5, and equal to A P^5. This line completes the polygon A P^1 C D E A, of which the sides A P^1, P^1 C, C D, D E, E A represent severally, in magnitude and direction, the forces P^1, P^2, P^3, P^4, P^5.

It is not necessary that the forces should all lie in one plane: but we may, perhaps, make this theorem clearer by attaching a number of pulleys to a vertical plane, such as an windmill, and the vanes of a smoke-jack, or of a screw-propeller, should make with the plane of their rotation. The reason cannot be shown in this elementary work.

upright board, and carrying over them the lines which represent the forces, and attaching weights to their extremities,

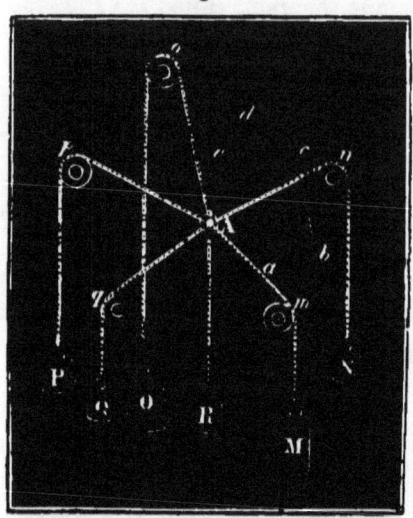

Fig. 7.

as in Fig. 7. Then take any part A *a* on the string A *m*, and from *a* on the board, draw a line parallel to the string A *n*, and take a part *a b* upon that parallel, such that A *a* is to *a b*, as M is to N. Again, through *b* draw a parallel to the string A *o*, and on that parallel take a part *b c* such that *a b* is to *b c* as N is to O. In like manner, draw *c d* parallel to A *p*, and such that *b c : c d* :: O : P; and draw *d e* parallel with A *q*, and bearing the same relation to the other lines that Q bears to the other weights. Finally, join the points *e* and A by a right line. A single force R, acting in the direction of the line *e* A, and having the same ratio to each of the other forces as the line *e* A has to the side of the polygon, which is parallel to that other force, will produce a pressure on the fixed point A, equivalent and opposite to the combined actions of the forces M, N, O, P, Q. This may be proved by attaching any weights at random to the various strings, and (when they have settled in equilibrium) making the construction above described, beginning with any side of the polygon, and making all its sides, except one, parallel with their respective strings, and with lengths proportional to their respective weights. The remaining side will then be found to lie always in a straight line with the remaining string, and to have the exact length proportioned to the remaining weight.

12. *Parallel Forces.*—It is evident that forces may be made

to act side by side with quite as much effect as in the same straight line. Two horses drawing a cart may of course be placed side by side, or one before the other, and the effect will be the same. Hence, the resultant of two parallel forces, acting in the same direction, is equal to their sum; it has the same direction with them, and when they are *equal*, is applied at a point midway between their points of application. All this is obvious from the principle of sufficient reason : but when they are *unequal*, their resultant, though still parallel with them and equal to their sum, does not act midway between them, as we shall presently see. And when they are equal, but act in contrary directions, they have *no* simple resultant, for they tend to produce *rotation*, and this tendency cannot be counterbalanced by any single force. But let us here confine our attention to the simple case of such parallel forces as are equal, and have the same direction.

The resultant of a number of parallel forces is obtained by a principle which is called the *equality of moments*, on which we shall enter shortly. It will be found that the *point of application* of this resultant will depend solely on the *points of application* and the intensities of the components, and will not be affected by any change in their *directions*, so long as they retain their parallelism and equality to each other.

II. THE CENTRE OF GRAVITY.

13. The forces with which the particles of a body at the earth's surface tend to descend, or, in other words, their *weights* or gravitating forces, may be considered as parallel to one another, since they converge towards a point, the earth's centre, the distance of which may be regarded as infinite, compared with the size of the body. Now all these equal and parallel forces, infinite in number as they are in a body of any size, may be replaced by a single force applied to a certain point ; and this point of application is called the *centre of gravity* of a body, or the centre of parallel and equal forces. It is a characteristic property of the centre of gravity, that it is a fixed

point in the interior of solids, and does not change, whatever position these bodies may be placed in, with respect to gravity. Thus the point G (Fig. 8) is the centre of gravity of the body A B C, whether the point C be upwards or downwards, or in any other position ; for, as we have already stated, the point of

Fig. 8.

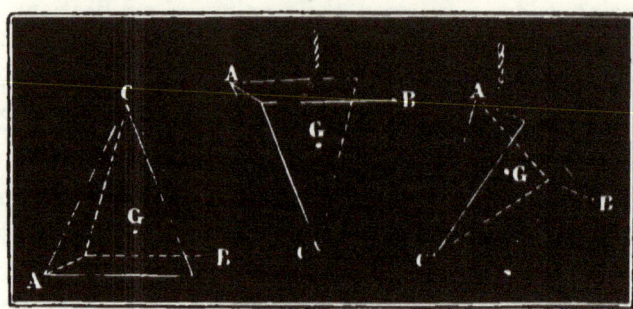

application of the resultant of parallel forces is independent of the direction of these forces.

14. In order that a heavy and perfectly rigid body* be in equilibrium, there is only one condition to be fulfilled, namely, that its centre of gravity be supported. Consequently, if the centre of gravity be fixed, we may turn the body about in all directions, and it will always rest in whatever position it may be placed, because it will always be in equilibrium. When a body is supported at a fixed point, which is not the centre of gravity, equilibrium can be main-

* That is, a body supposed to be totally incapable of any change of form. In Mechanics, it is constantly necessary to abstract or omit the consideration of certain properties of bodies, in order to reduce a problem to its simplest form ; for these complicating circumstances can always be added afterwards, one by one, though it would be impossible to encounter them all at the outset. Hence it is necessary at first to assume a perfection not found in any natural body ; and as in geometry we must consider lines without breadth, and surface without thickness ; so in Mechanics we must assume imaginary solids, fluids, and airs, which are not the solids, fluids, or airs of nature. The solids must be perfectly inelastic, or else perfectly elastic, the levers without flexibility, cords without rigidity, liquids without compressibility or viscosity, and airs must have their density and elasticity always proportional.

tained only when the centre of gravity is in the vertical of the fixed point, either above or below. This consideration affords an experimental means of finding the centre of gravity in a body. Suppose we have to fix a handle to a sextant A (Fig. 9) in the best position for holding it steadily. This position will be at its centre of gravity. It must be suspended, as at A, by means of a thread from some point of its surface, as c; and when at rest, we mark, as accurately as possible, the point m, or the point at which the thread would come out if it had proceeded

Fig. 9.

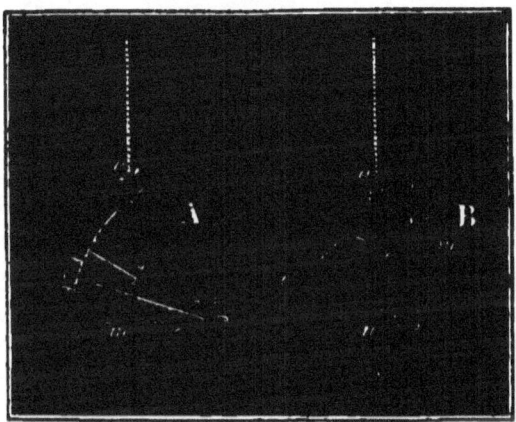

in its straight course through the body. From what has been said, it is evident that the centre of gravity must be situated somewhere in this line c m. The centre is exactly found by suspending the body from some other point, as at B, and marking the vertical continuation of the thread, as at n. The centre of gravity is also in this line, d n, and *must* therefore be at the point where the lines c m and d n cross each other.

With heavy bodies the experiment is made by turning them on their sides, or placing them upon narrow supports; but for bodies whose forms are regular, and the substance homogeneous, or of uniform density throughout, the centre of gravity is determined by certain geometrical rules. Thus, the centre of gravity of a cylinder is evidently the middle of its axis ; and whenever a body possesses a *centre of figure*, *i.e.* a point so situated that every plane which can be conceived to pass through it must bisect the body, this point is the centre of gravity (supposing the body to be of uniform density). Moreover, whenever a body has an *axis* of figure, that is, a *line*, every plane passing through which bisects the body, then the centre of gravity must be somewhere in that line. Consequently, when the body has more than one such axis, the centre must be found at their intersection. In other cases, however, and especially when the body is not homogeneous, the deduction of the centre of gravity becomes too complex to be useful, considering how easily it can always be found by experiment.*

The centre of gravity is not necessarily *in the body*, but may be in some adjoining space. This is obviously the case with a *ring*, an *empty box*, and, in general, any hollow vessel.

In Theoretical Mechanics, the principle already noticed, of *abstraction*, or considering certain properties of matter apart from others, has often to be carried so far, as to assume bulk without weight, or weight without bulk. Hence an imaginary *heavy line*, or *heavy surface*, may have its centre of gravity found ; and if the line or surface be *curved*, it is obvious that this centre must in general lie *out of* the line or surface itself.

15. *Centrobaryc theorem*, or *Method of Guldinus.*—These centres of gravity of lines or surfaces (which can be found approximately by experiments on thin wires or plates) afford an easy means of solving certain useful problems in mensuration,

---

* The following rules may, however, be useful. Every *pyramid* or *cone* has its centre of gravity at $\frac{1}{4}$ of its height, from the base,—every *paraboloid* at $\frac{1}{3}$ of its height,—every *hemisphere* or *hemispheroid* at $\frac{3}{8}$, —a *hemicylinder* at ·4244 of its radius from the axis of the cylinder. To find the distance of the centre of gravity of any *segment* of a *disc* or *cylinder*, from the axis. divide the cube of the chord by twelve times the area of the segment. To find the same in a *sector*, multiply twice the chord by the radius and divide by three times the arc.

the solution of which deductively (or by pure mathematics) would be extremely difficult, if not impossible. For instance, any *solid of revolution*, however complex or irregular its outline, may have both its solidity and its superficial contents found by the following very simple methods. Let A (Fig. 10) be the solid, and *a b c* its half section, or that plane figure which, in

Fig. 10.

revolving round the line *a c* as an axis, would require a space equal and similar to the solid—or, as it is commonly expressed, would *generate the solid*. Cut out this figure in some thin substance of uniform thickness, and by suspending it as above described (Fig. 9) find its centre of gravity, which we will suppose to be *g*. Now the volume of this solid is equal to the product of the area *a b c* × into the circumference described by the point *g* (which circumference will of course be found by applying the well-known multiplier, 3·14159, &c. to twice the distance of *g* from the axis, or twice *d g*). Again, to find the *surface* of the solid or of any portion of it, as formed by the revolution of the whole or any portion of the curve *a b c*, bend a wire into the form of that portion required. Let this wire be *e f*, and suppose that (by suspension) we find its centre of gravity to be at *g'*; then the surface generated by the revolution of *e f* = its length × the path described by its centre of gravity, which path is found, of course, by multiplying its radius *g' h* by twice 3·14159, &c.

Among other useful deductions from the properties of the centre of gravity, we may observe that the force expended in erecting a building, or lifting all its materials from the ground to their places, is the same as would be required to lift them all to the height of the centre of gravity of the building.

16. It has been said that the only condition of equilibrium in a solid body is, that its centre of gravity be supported. There are, however, various ways in which this condition is fulfilled, according as the body is suspended from fixed points, or placed upon supports. If the hand of a clock moved

Fig. 11.

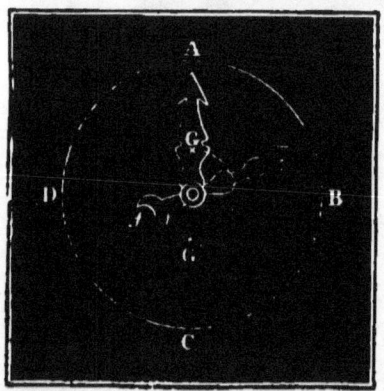

freely upon its axis on a vertical dial, A B C D (Fig. 11), in order that its centre of gravity be supported, it must be in a vertical plane passing through the axis; and this can only take place when G, the centre of gravity, is below or above the axis, as at G' and G, which gives two positions of equilibrium; one of which, when the hand is below the axis, is called *stable equilibrium*, because, in drawing the hand aside and letting it fall, it will oscillate a few times, and then settle in this position, G'. On the other hand, when G is above the axis, the equilibrium is said to be *unstable*, because, on moving the hand aside, it would not return to its previous position. Between these two positions, equilibrium is impossible; and although, in the case of a clock, the hand is retained in all positions by its friction against the axis, yet there is a constant tendency in the hand to drag the axis into a position of stable equilibrium, and the more so in proportion as the centre of gravity is removed from the vertical. Thus, with a heavy clock hand, in which the centre of gravity is far removed from the axis, the clock would gain from 12 to 6 A.M., and lose from 6 A.M. to 12, were it not for the counterweight usually attached in large clocks, as shown at *f*.

17. A body placed upon a horizontal surface, touching it only at one point, may assume various positions of equilibrium, some of which are stable, and some unstable; and there are other positions which are said to be *indifferent*, because when the body is disturbed therefrom it does not tend either to regain its former position, or to increase the disturbance, but simply remains in the new position. If from the centre of gravity of a body, rays are produced to every part of its surface, the greater number of these rays are oblique to such surface; but there are always some which are perpendicular, or *normal* thereto, whatever be the external form of the body: there is, in general, a maximum ray among them, and a minimum ray, both normal to the surface. There are also other rays which are maximum or minimum among the surrounding rays, and which are essentially normal. It is evident, then, that if the body touch the horizontal plane by the extremity of one of these normal rays, the centre of gravity is in the vertical of the point of contact, and there is equilibrium. If, on the contrary, the body touch the plane at the extremity of an oblique ray, the centre of gravity is not sustained, since it is no longer in the vertical of the point of contact.*

18. If the ray of the point of contact be normal, but not maximum nor minimum, but simply equal to the neighbouring rays, the equilibrium is indifferent. Such is the case when a sphere is placed on a horizontal plane ; it is in equilibrium in every position, and consequently in indifferent equilibrium, for the centre of gravity can fall no lower than it is. Now, if a portion of the upper part be removed (as

---

* It may be stated generally that a body is in the position of stable equilibrium when the centre of gravity is the lowest possible, because in a body free to move in any direction, the centre of gravity always assumes the lowest possible position.

by making a hole there), the equilibrium becomes *stable*, because the centre of gravity is brought below the centre of figure, there being in such case more matter below the centre of figure than above it. Now, in this case it is easy to see that the ray from the centre of gravity to the point opposite the hole is a *minimum* ray; but let the hole be filled up, by inserting a small cylinder long enough to project beyond the surface; it is now plain that the centre of gravity being nearer this projection than the opposite point, a ray drawn to the latter will be a *maximum* ray, so that the balance thereon will be *unstable*, because any motion sideways tends

Fig. 12.

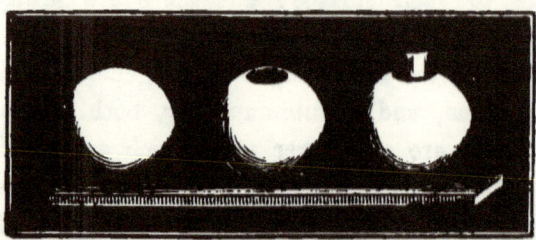

to *lower* the centre of gravity, and to enable it to fall still lower; whereas, when a body rests on a minimum ray, any rocking must *raise* the centre of gravity, so that it will *fall back* to its previous position. If the normal ray of the point of contact be only the minimum among several other neighbouring rays, equilibrium is stable only as far as these rays extend; and lastly, if the ray is in one direction equal to adjacent rays, whilst it is in other directions a minimum, equilibrium is indifferent in the one direction, and stable in the other directions. This is the case with an egg placed on its side.

An egg on one end is resting on a maximum ray, and is therefore in unstable equilibrium, so that it cannot in general remain thus poised for a moment. There are two modes, however, by which this feat is sometimes accomplished, both of which afford good illustrations of the above principles. If we neglect the difference between the two ends, and regard the egg as having a centre of figure (14), this would also be its centre of gravity if it were of uniform density. Although the yolk is denser than the white, yet if they be concentric, as in Fig. 13, A, the centre of gravity will still be at their common centre a, and the ray a will plainly be longer than b b, &c., rendering the equilibrium unstable in every direction. But if the egg be shaken, so as to break the membrane that encloses the yolk, and allow that fluid to sink to the lower end, as in Fig. 13, B, the centre of gravity is lowered, and may in some cases be

Fig. 13.

below a', the centre of curvature of the surface at the point of contact; in which case the ray a' will become a minimum with regard to b' b', &c., and the equilibrium will be *stable*. This is more likely to happen, the shorter or more spherical the egg; but it is also more probable at the *small* end than at the *large*, because the latter contains a cavity full of air, which must throw the centre of gravity towards the small end. The other method (commonly ascribed to Columbus) consists in scraping off a little of the shell, so as to flatten a small extent of surface (Fig. 13, c), when (the centre of gravity remaining at a″) the ray a″ becomes a minimum among all those drawn to this small surface (all those between b″ and b″ for instance), so that if the egg be not disturbed beyond this extent, it will stand.

19. When a body is supported on a plane by two points, the vertical, let fall from the centre of gravity, ought to fall upon the line which connects these two points. Thus, in two-wheeled carriages, the vertical of the centre of gravity ought to fall between the wheels, and upon the line which unites their point of contact with the ground. If it fall either in advance or in the rear, the carriage is too much loaded in front or behind. When carriages go down hill, they are liable to upset, if the centre of gravity fall out of the line of contact of the wheels, but this is less likely to happen with large wheels and a heavy load placed low down.

20. When a body rests upon a base more or less extended, equilibrium obtains only when the vertical of the centre of gravity falls within the area of the base. It matters little whether this base be continuous or not; the base of a square table, supported on four legs, is formed by the square of which the four legs form the four corners. In proportion as the base is extensive, the centre of gravity may be disturbed, without deranging the support of the body.

21. A variety of toys, and feats of posturing, &c., depend upon the dexterity with which the vertical of the centre of gravity is supported on a very narrow base. In some toys, the base is fixed, but exceedingly narrow; and on this base are placed the hind legs of the figure of a prancing horse, and the figure rocks backwards and forwards in an apparently impossible position, by means of a leaden weight attached to the further end of a bent wire, proceeding from the lower part of the figure, the effect of which is to throw the centre of gravity *below* the centre of motion; in which case, equilibrium is always stable, because every disturbance must raise the centre of gravity above its natural (or lowest) position, to which it will therefore return, as is the case with a pendulum, or any hanging body. In balancing rods on the hand, chin, &c., the base is in constant motion, and the art is to keep this base under the centre of gravity. The tight-rope dancer has the double disadvantage of a narrow

and also a moveable base. He is greatly assisted by holding in his hands a heavy pole, the effect of which is to remove the centre of gravity from his body into the centre of the pole; or rather, the centre of gravity of the dancer and of the pole taken together is situated near the centre of the pole, so that, as has been well observed, the dancer may be said to hold in his hands the point on the position of which the facility of his feats depends. Without the aid of the pole, the centre of gravity would be within the trunk of the body; and those performers who dispense with the pole may astonish more, but their motions are far less graceful, because they are unable to modify the position of the centre of gravity with ease and rapidity.

III. PARALLEL FORCES—MOMENTS OF FORCE—THE PRINCIPLE OF VIRTUAL VELOCITIES.

22. WE have seen that when the centre of gravity of a body is supported, there is equilibrium, and that if a rigid line or *axis* be passed through the centre of gravity, as in Fig. 11, the body will rest indifferently in any position.

The centre of gravity, then, in any body may be regarded as the centre of any set of equal and parallel forces acting in the same direction on all the particles of the body; that is to say, it matters not in what direction these parallel forces act, provided they act all in *the same* direction, their resultant will always pass through this point.

23. We have seen that the resultant of two parallel and *equal* forces is a parallel line lying midway between them; but we have now to observe that when they are *unequal*, the resultant is no longer half-way between them, but so situated that its distances from them shall be inversely as their intensities. The property of the centre of gravity enables us to prove this in the following manner. Let A B (Fig. 14) represent a rigid bar of equal thickness and density throughout its length. It may obviously be balanced on a single point at its centre C, so that all its weight acts as if it were concen-

trated at this one point. The same would be true of any other such bar; for instance, if we suppose the bar to be divided into two bars of unequal lengths A D and D B, the former might be balanced on its centre E, and the latter on its centre F. Hence we see that two parallel and unequal forces (viz. the weight of A D and the weight of D B), acting at the points E and F, have not their resultant passing through the centre between E and F, but through C, which is nearer E than F in the exact ratio that the force at E exceeds that at F; for the

Fig. 14.

weights of the two bars A D and D B are as their lengths, and it is easily seen that E C equals half the length of D B, and that F C equals half the length of A D; so that the distance E C is to the distance F C *inversely* as the weight whose centre is at E is to the weight whose centre is at F. To test the truth of this conclusion, suspend from these points E and F two additional weights, bearing the same ratio to each other as the weights of A D and D B, so that the ratio of the whole force at E to the whole force at F, may remain unchanged; and we shall find the balance of the bar continues undisturbed, though there is manifestly more weight on one side the fulcrum C than on the other.

24. Hence we learn, that when two parallel but unequal forces are supported or balanced by a third, this third force

Fig. 15.

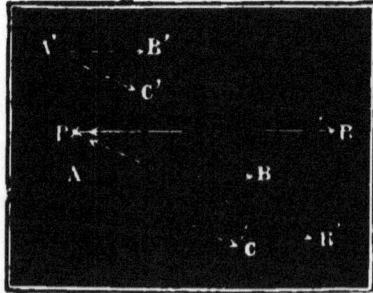

must be equal to the sum of the other two; it must act in the contrary direction, and must be applied at a point nearer the greater force than the less, its distances from them being inversely as their intensities. Thus, in Fig. 15, any two parallel forces acting at A A', and having their intensities expressed by the lengths A B and A′ B′, will be balanced by a force whose intensity is expressed by the length R P = A B + A′ B′, provided it act at a point P, so situated that P A : P A : : A B : A′ B′. And it matters not what may be the common direction of the three lines representing these forces, provided they be all parallel; so that if A′ B′ and A B move into the positions A′ C′ and A C, without any change of intensity, then R P must be moved into the position R′ P, and the equilibrium will remain undisturbed.

When therefore a force, applied to any point of an inflexible bar, supports two other forces applied in the contrary direction to two other points of the bar, the above conditions must apply. Thus, in Fig. 16, when the three forces at B, A′ and *a* are in equilibrium, B : A : : the distance A *a* : the distance B *a*. In its present position, the figure may represent a steelyard, B and A the weights pulling down its two ends, and *a* the upward reaction

Fig. 16.

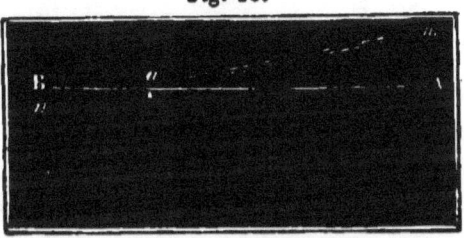

of the point of support; but if we turn the figure upside down, then it may represent a pole, by which two porters are carrying a load, the weight of which acts at *a*. In such case B and A will be the upward forces which the porters must exert in order to support it; and it is thus evident that the burthen is not shared equally between them, unless its centre of gravity be over or under the middle of the pole. In its present position, B has to support more than A, in the proportion that A *a* exceeds B *a*.

25. When one point of a rigid body is supposed to be immoveably fixed, the effect of any forces applied to that body can only be to turn it round the fixed point, as a centre of motion; and when two points are fixed, the motion can only be round the line joining them, which thus becomes an *axis*. Now it is plain from what has been said above, that, in these cases, two forces which tend to turn the body in contrary

directions will be in equilibrium if their intensities are inversely as their distances from the centre or axis; that is, if A : B :: the distance of B from the axis, or a B : the distance of A from the axis, or a A. But in every proportion, the product of the first and last terms is equal to the product of the second and third; or, as it is commonly said, the product of the extremes = that of the means. Thus, instead of saying that the forces A and B are inversely as the distances a A and a B, we may express the same thing by saying that the product of the force A × the distance a A = the product of the force B × the distance a B. That is, if both forces be measured by the same unit of pressure (both in ounces or both in pounds, for example), and if both distances be measured by the same unit of length (both in inches, or both in feet, for example), then, the number that represents each force being multiplied by the number that expresses its distance from the axis, the product will be the same in each case. Thus, if a straight bar be balanced (as in Fig. 16), and, at the distance of one foot from its fulcrum, or point of support, a weight of 12 pounds be suspended, it will be found that this weight will be balanced by a weight of 6 pounds, distant 2 feet on the other side of the fulcrum; or by a weight of 4 pounds at the distance of 3 feet; or by a weight of 3 pounds at the distance of 4 feet. Now by multiplying these weights by the number of units (feet) representing the distances from the centre, we get in each case 12; thus, 6 pounds at 2 feet = 12 pounds placed at 1 foot; or, $6 \times 2 = 12 \times 1$. In like manner, 4 pounds at 3 feet, or $4 \times 3 = 12$; and 3 pounds at 4 feet, or $3 \times 4 = 12$.

These products are called the *moments* of the force, and it is important to observe that any two forces applied to a body supported on an axis, and tending to turn it round, will be in equilibrium when the moments of the two forces are the same. In like manner if the moment be doubled or halved, or increased or decreased in any proportion, the efficacy of the force in turning the body round the axle is doubled or halved, or increased or decreased, in exactly the same proportion. For example, if the weight of 12 pounds in the last example, situated at 1 foot from the axis, be brought 6 inches nearer that axis, its moment is reduced one half, and to produce equilibrium, the moment of the weight of 6 pounds on the other side of the axis must be halved also, either by bringing it to *one* foot from the axis, or by reducing its weight to *three* pounds; or if the counterbalancing weight be at 3 feet, it will be 2 pounds; or if at 4 feet, it will now be $1\frac{1}{2}$; and it will be found that each of these weights, multiplied into the distance, will equal 6, as the weight on the other side (12 pounds) × its distance ($\frac{1}{2}$ a foot) = 6.

26. It may be evident also from what has been said, that by increasing the number of forces on each side of the axis, the body will be in equilibrium, provided the sum of the moments on one side of the axis equal the sum of the moments on the other side of the axis. For instance, suppose that on one side of the axis we have three weights, A, B, C; A of 2 pounds, at the distance of 2 inches; B of 3 pounds, at the distance of 3 inches; and C of 3 pounds, at the distance of 5 inches.

The moment of A is $2 \times 2 = 4$
The moment of B is $3 \times 3 = 9$
The moment of C is $3 \times 5 = 15$
___

Then the sum of the moments on one side of the axis . . . . $\left.\right\} = 28$

Now, suppose that on the other side of the axis we have two weights: D, of 4 pounds, at the distance of 4 inches; and E, of 2 pounds, at the distance of 6 inches. Then

the moment of D is $4 \times 4 = 16$
and the moment of E is $2 \times 6 = 12$
___

and the sum of the moments on the other side of the axis . . $\left.\right\} = 28$

Hence, if several forces tend to turn a body round its axis, they will be in equilibrium if the sum of the moments of those forces which tend to turn it round in one direction, be equal to the sum of the moments of the forces which tend to turn it round in the other direction.*

27. As the principle which we are now illustrating is the most important in the whole range of mechanical science, and may indeed be considered as the basis of mechanical science, it is desirable to illustrate it by another method. If two weights in equilibrium, as in Fig. 16, at the extremities A and B of a bar supported on an axis a, passing through its centre of gravity, be made to oscillate gently through a small space, it is evident that the spaces moved through by the two ends of the bar will be directly as their distances from the axis; for, the angles A a m and B a n being equal, the arcs A m and B n, are as their radii a A and a B. For instance, if the weight B be 12 pounds, suspended at 3 inches from a, its moment may be expressed by the number 36; and it will be balanced by a weight of 6 pounds, 6 inches from a, because its moment is also 36. Now if these two weights be made to oscillate through a small space, such as B m, for the weight which descends, and A n, for the weight which ascends, the latter space will be only half the former, because it bears the same ratio to a B (or 3 inches) that A m bears to a A (or six inches).

Hence, if B n be one inch, A m will be two inches, and the products of these two quantities, with their respective weights, will be equal to each other; that is, the effect of 12 pounds moving through 1 inch, or of 6 pounds moving through 2 inches of space, is the same. And though we are not now concerned with motions, but with *pressures*, the same principle applies to them. Any two pressures, however unequal (a pressure of one pound and one of 1,000 pounds, for instance), will balance each other, if they are so applied that the motion of the first through 1,000 inches would be necessarily accompanied by a motion of the second through *one* inch, and *vice versâ*. Any means by which this connection between the two pressures is effected, is called a *machine*.

of the body, and then the distances of the forces being measured from this imaginary axis by perpendiculars let fall from it upon their respective directions, the principle of the equality of moments obtains in respect to those forces about that imaginary axis.

28. The principle which has thus been illustrated (27), is known under the name of the principle of *virtual velocities*, and is that which regulates the action and constitutes the efficacy of every machine in which power is employed to overcome weight or resistance. In the composition of machines, it is usual to speak of *six mechanical powers ;** namely, the *lever*, the *wheel and axle*, the *pulley*, the *inclined plane*, the *wedge*, and the *screw;* although in reality these contrivances are but applications of the principle of virtual velocities, whereby a small force acting through a large space is converted into a great force acting through a small space. But in this there is no gain of power, neither is there any loss ; the advantage is in its application. Every pressure acting with a certain velocity, or through a certain space, is convertible into greater pressure, acting with a less velocity, or through a smaller space ; but the quantity of mechanical force is not altered by the transformation, and all that the mechanical powers can accomplish is to effect this transformation.

29. Before proceeding further with our subject, it may be as well to notice that the laws of mechanical science are founded on the principle, explained at page 16, note, of considering the various properties of bodies (as weight, rigidity, elasticity, &c.) *apart from each other*, before attempting to put them together, as they really exist in natural bodies. Thus, in the above reasonings on bars or levers, we confine our attention at first to one property—viz. their *rigidity*, neglecting the effects of flexibility, &c. ; because these effects can afterwards be separately considered and allowed for. Thus, in order to facilitate the study of Mechanics, and even to render it possible, it is necessary to assume, at first, a perfection which does not exist. The effects of forces, as they

---

* More properly, *mechanical elements*, or *simple machines*, by the combination of which, all other machines are formed.

are modified by machines of various kinds, could not be studied, without some provision of this kind ; thus, cords and rods, or levers, which are machines of the simplest kind, are considered as without weight, the cords perfectly flexible, and the levers perfectly rigid. In short, bodies must be deprived of one or more of their essential properties, or mechanical problems would be too complicated for solution; but having obtained a solution on these terms, we are then in a condition to modify the result by considering the effects of friction, adhesion, weight, elasticity, compressibility, and such like elements, which had been omitted in the first solution of the problem.

30. *The Lever.*—The lever is a bar or rod, supposed to be perfectly rigid, and without weight. It may be *straight* or *bent, simple* or *compound.* We shall confine our attention chiefly to the simple, straight lever, of which there are commonly reckoned three kinds or varieties, depending upon the position of the points of application of the *moving* power, and the *resisting* power, with respect to a certain fixed point called the *fulcrum,* about which the lever is supposed to turn freely. The portions of the lever situated on each side of the fulcrum are called the *arms* of the lever.

31. A lever of the first kind is represented in Fig. 17, I., in which the fulcrum F is situated between the moving power P and the resistance or load w.

Fig. 17, II., is a lever of the second kind, in which the mover P, and the resistance w, act on the same side of the fulcrum ; the load moved being between the fulcrum and the mover.

In a lever of the third kind, Fig. 17, III., the mover and the load also act on the same side of the fulcrum, but the mover P is between the fulcrum F and the load w. Hence, in considering the lever *statically* (or when the two forces are *balanced*), there is no difference between the second and third kind; for, as we are not supposing any motion to be produced, neither force can be regarded as the mover or the moved. To produce motion, it is necessary that one force should prevail, and then the lever will become a lever of the second or the third kind, according as the force *nearer to* or *further from* the fulcrum prevails. Thus Fig. II. is a lever of the second kind, and Fig. III. of the third kind, only while the weight w, in each case, is being *lifted;* but when w is being *lowered,* it becomes the *mover,* and P the *moved,* so that Fig. II. becomes a lever of the third kind, and Fig. III. one of the second kind.

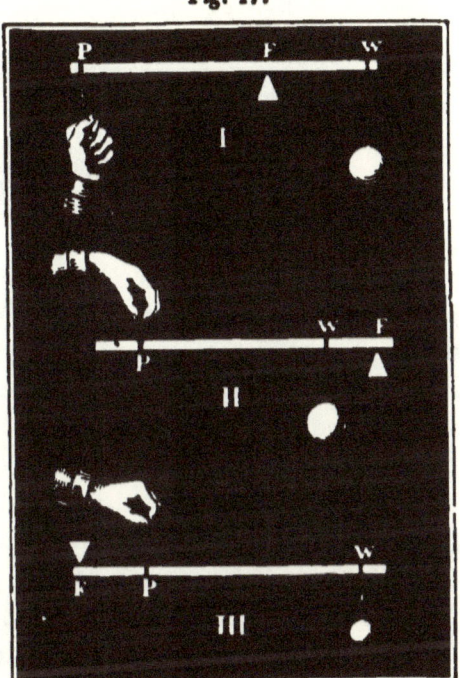

Fig. 17.

32. From what has been already said (25), it is evident that, in all these levers, the power P will sustain the weight w, provided the moment of P be equal to that of the weight. Thus, in the lever of the first or second kind, if w be 12 lbs. at the distance of 3 inches from F, its moment will be 36, and it will be balanced by P=6 lbs. at the distance of 6 inches from F, or by P = 4 lbs. at the distance of 9 inches from F, and so on. Or, if w be 12 lbs., as before, and be situated at the distance of 3 inches from the fulcrum, its moment will be 36; consequently, a power of 3 lbs. at the distance of 12 inches from the fulcrum, or 2 lbs. at the distance of 18 inches, will produce equilibrium.

33. Levers of the first kind are in very common use; such are a crowbar, used for raising stones, and a poker, need for raising the coals in the grate, the bar of the grate being the

fulcrum. The common crowbar is sometimes used as a lever of
the first kind, as in Fig. 18 ; sometimes as a lever of the second
kind, as in Fig. 19. The former is the case whenever we

Fig. 18.   Fig. 19.

press *downwards* to lift the load, and the latter whenever we
press *upwards*. Now, in either figure, a man at P pressing
the long arm of the lever, is able to raise the weight of the
stone A or B, provided that weight do not exceed his pressure
on P, in so great a ratio as the distance P *f* exceeds W *f*.
If a pressure of 50 lbs. at P lift 300 lbs. at W, then P must
move *more* than six times the distance that W rises ; for, if it
move *only* six times that distance, the pressures of 50 lbs. and
300 lbs. would balance each other. Thus, what is gained in
pressure is lost in distance moved through. If the man applied
his power halfway between *f* and P, he need only press through
half the distance, to produce the same effect on the stone, but
he must exert *twice* the pressure.

34. We have an instance of the lever of the second kind
in a chipping-knife, fixed at one end, which is the fulcrum ;
the wood to be cut is placed under it, and is the load, or
resistance to be moved or overcome, and the power is the
hand of the workman at the extremity of the blade. A
wheelbarrow is also a lever of this kind, the wheel being the
fulcrum, the contents of the barrow the weight, and the
man wheeling it the power. In the common form of wheelbarrow, the load is made to incline as much as possible
towards the wheel. This, of course, is an advantage, because
the man bears as much less of the load as its centre of gravity
is nearer to the axle of the wheel than to his hands. An oar

may also be regarded as a lever, but to explain its action fully would lead us far from our present subject.*

35. In a lever of the third kind, as the fishing-rod, in Fig. 20, if w be 12 lbs. at a distance of 9 feet from the fulcrum f, its moment may be expressed by 108. To keep this in equilibrium by a power nearer to the fulcrum than the weight is,

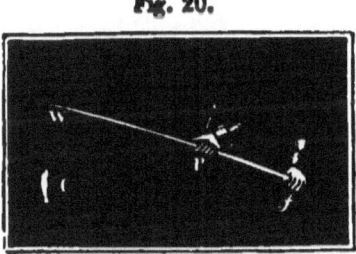

Fig. 20.

such as P at the distance of 3 feet, would require a force of 36 lbs. (because 3 × 36 = 108), or, in other words, the power is, in this case, three times the weight or resistance; and, in all levers of the third kind, the power must exceed the load ; hence they are never used where a great weight is to be lifted, or a great resistance overcome, but only when it is required to move a small weight through a greater distance than it would be convenient to move the hand through. From the principle of virtual velocities, before explained (27), it will be evident that the advantage of this kind of lever is, that it commands speed, rather than force.

36. The symmetry and compactness of the frames of animals depend on the fact, that all their limbs are levers of the third kind. The lifting of our forearm and hand through a considerable space (say a foot), is effected by the power of a

* As there is no fixed fulcrum, the easiest way is to regard the oar as being circumstanced like the rigid line A A' in Fig. 15, which is acted on by three forces, viz. A B, the hand of the rower, A' B', the resistance of the water against the blade, and B P, the resistance of the water against the bow of the boat (transmitted through the boat's side to P) ; but, as this last is not-equal to the sum of the others, it is overcome by them ; and, as its point of application, P, is not situated in their resultant, they do not balance each other, but A B prevails over A' B', as in a lever of the first kind, having its fulcrum at that point between P and A' which remains stationary during the stroke ; and the same point may also be considered as the fulcrum of a lever of the second kind, by which the power at A overcomes the resistance at P.

muscle applied very near the fulcrum, or elbow, and moving through a very much smaller space (say an inch). This muscle must then exert 12 times the force with which the hand is moved; so that when we use a *purchase* (*i. e.* a lever of the first or second kind), in order to lift a great weight through a small space, by the motion of our hand through 12 times that space, this is simply *undoing* what has been done by the natural leverage of the arm. We might have dispensed with the lever, if the muscle had been applied to the *extremity* of our limb, instead of its *origin.* But what a clumsy contrivance would the animal frame have presented, if thus *rigged* with muscles, like a ship! In fact, rigging presents us with an exact inversion of the muscular system of animals. The yards are moved through *small* spaces with *great* force, by the taking in of *much* rope with comparatively *little* force. The limbs, on the contrary, are moved through *great* spaces with *little* force, by the contraction of muscles through very *small* spaces with much *greater* force.

In raising a ladder by the usual method, it is a lever of the second kind, while the centre of gravity is between the hands that raise it and the end on which it rests; and when the hands pass the centre of gravity, it is a lever of the third kind.

37. If the arms of the lever, instead of being straight, are curved or bent, their length must be reckoned by perpendiculars drawn from the fulcrum, upon the directions of the power and weight; and when the lever is straight, if the power and the weight be not parallel in direction, the same rule must be observed. Thus Fig. 21 is a bent lever of the first kind, and Fig. 22 a straight lever of the second ar third kind, according as the flag or the weight preponderates. In either figure, the fulcrum is F, A *a* the direction of the power, and B W the direction of the weight. If the lines A *a* and B W be continued, and perpendiculars F *a* and F *b*, drawn from the fulcrum to those lines, the

moment of the power will be found by multiplying the power by the line F a, and the moment of the weight by multiplying the weight by F b. If these moments be equal, the power will balance the weight.

Fig. 21.

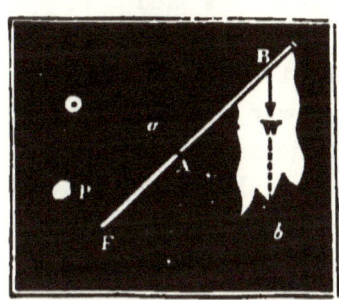

Fig. 22.

38. Many of the most useful implements consist of bent *double* levers, or *pairs* of levers, connected by a joint, which forms their common fulcrum; so that they require no external fulcrum, or resisting point, for each supplies the necessary resistance to the other. Thus scissors, pincers, snuffers, are pairs of levers of the first kind; nutcrackers, of the second kind; and tongs, of the third kind. In the first, when the blades are longer than the handles (as in shears), there is a gain of speed and loss of power; but when the handles are the longer of the two (as in pincers), there is a loss of speed and gain of power. In the second this is always the case, and in the third, on the contrary, power is always lost, and extent of motion gained.

"In drawing a nail with steel forceps, or nippers, we have a good example," says Arnott, "of the advantages of using a tool: 1st, the nail is seized by the teeth of steel, instead of by the soft fingers; 2nd, instead of the griping force of the extreme fingers only, there is the force of the whole hand conveyed through the handles of the nippers; 3rd, the effective force is rendered perhaps six times more effective by the lever length of the handles; and 4th, by making the nippers, in drawing the nail, rest on one shoulder, as a fulcrum, it acquires all the advantages of the lever, or claw-hammer, for the same purpose."

39. When the power is required to be considerable, and it is not convenient to construct a very long lever, a compound lever, or a *composition* of levers, is employed. When a system of this kind is in equilibrium, of course the ratio of the power to the load will be compounded of the ratios subsisting between the arms of each lever; or, in other words, the power multiplied by the continued product of the alternate arms commencing from the power, is equal to the weight multiplied by the continued product of the alternate arms, beginning from the weight. For example, in the following arrangement (Fig. 23) we have three levers, two of the

Fig. 23.

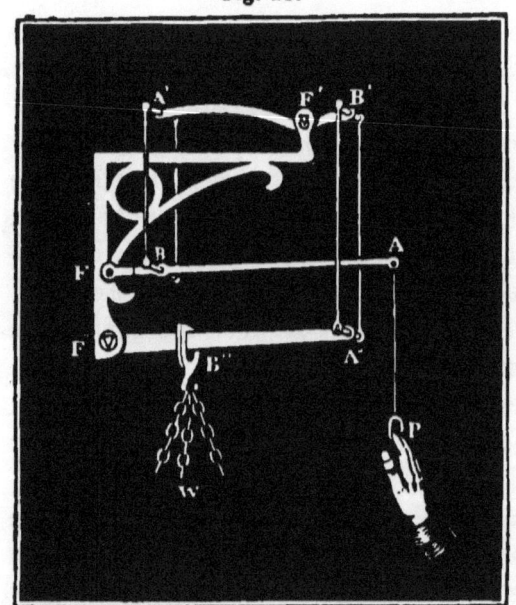

second kind, A F, A″ F″, and one of the first kind, A′ B′; and we will now consider the manner in which the power P is transmitted to the weight W. The power P, acting upon the lever A F, produces a downward force at B, which bears to P the same proportion as A F to B F. Thus, if A F be eight times B F, the force at B is eight times the power P. The arm A′ F′ of the second lever is pulled down by a force equal to eight times the power at P; and this will produce a force at B′, as many times greater than A′, as A′ F′ is greater than B′ F′. Thus, if A′ F′ be 10 times B′ F′, the force at B′ or A″ will be 10 times that at A′ or B; but this last was 8 times the power, and therefore the force exerted at A″ will be 80 times the power. So, also, it may be shown that the weight w is as many times greater than the force at A″, as A″ F″ is greater than B″ F″. If A″ F″ be 6 times B″ F″, the weight w will be 6 times the force at A″. As we know this to be 80 times the power P, the weight, where there is an equilibrium, must be 480 times the power.

The same result might have been obtained more quickly, by dividing the product of A F, A′ F′, and A″ F″, by that of B F, B′ F′, and B″ F″. Thus, if the three former distances were 16 inches, 20 inches, and 18 inches; and the three latter, 2 inches, 2 inches, and 3 inches; then (16 × 20 × 18) ÷ (2 × 2 × 3) = 480. The ratio of 480 : 1 is said to be *compounded* of the three ratios of 8 : 1, 10 : 1, and 6 : 1.

The *weighing-machine* for turnpike-roads is formed of a composition of levers. It is chiefly used for weighing waggons, to ascertain that they are not loaded beyond what is allowed by law to the breadth of their wheels. It consists of a wooden platform, placed over a pit made in the line of the road, and level with its surface ; and so arranged, as to move freely up and down, without touching the walls of the pit. The levers upon which the platform rests are four ; viz. A, B, C, D, Fig. 24, all converging towards the centre, and each moving on a fulcrum, at A, B, C, D, securely fixed in each corner of the pit. The platform rests by its feet, a′ c′ d′, upon steel points, a, b c, d. The four levers are supported at the point F, under the centre of the platform, by a long lever G E resting upon a steel fulcrum at F, while its further end G is carried upwards into the turnpike house, where it is connected with one arm of a balance, while a scale, suspended from the other arm, carries the counterpoise or power, the amount of which, of course, indicates the weight of the waggon on the platform. Now, as the four levers A, B, C, D, are perfectly equal and similar, the effect of the weight distributed amongst them is the same as if the whole weight rested upon any one. In order, therefore, to

ascertain the conditions of equilibrium, we need only consider one of these levers, such as A F. Suppose, then, the
distance from A to F to be 10 times as great as that from A

Fig. 24.

to *a*, a force of 1 lb. at F would balance 10 lbs. at *a*, or on the
platform. So, also, if the distance from E to G be 10 times
greater than the distance from the fulcrum E to F, a force of
1 lb. applied so as to raise up the end of the lever G, would
counterpoise a weight of 10 lbs. on F ; therefore, as we gain
10 times the power by the first levers, and 10 times more by
the lever E G, it is evident that a force of 1 lb. tending to
raise G, would balance 100 lbs. on the platform. If the
weight of 10 lbs. be placed in the opposite arm of the
balance to which G is attached, this 10 lbs. will express
the value of 1,000 lbs. on the platform. When the platform
is not loaded, the levers are counterpoised by a weight
applied to the end of the last lever.

40. *The Balance.*—One of the most useful and interesting
applications of the lever is to the *balance*, which consists
essentially of a lever of the first kind suspended at its centre,
and consequently having the two arms equal. This lever
is called the *beam*, A B, Fig. 25 : the *fulcrum*, or centre of
motion, on which the beam turns, is in the middle ; and the

two extremities of the beam, called the *points of suspension*, serve to sustain the pans or scales : *g* is the centre of gravity of the beam; and this should be situated a little below the fulcrum, for if it were to coincide therewith, that is, if the centre of motion and the centre of gravity were situated in the same point, the beam, as we have seen (22), would rest indifferently in any position. If, on the contrary, the

Fig. 25.

centre of gravity were above the centre of motion, the least disturbance would cause the beam to upset.

The points of suspension should be situated so that a straight line A B joining them is perpendicular to the line of symmetry formed by joining the centre of gravity *g* with the centre of motion *m*.

The direction of the line *m g* is shown by a needle or index attached to the beam, which in delicate balances moves over a graduated arc. This needle may proceed either upwards or downwards, provided it be in the vertical of the centre of gravity. When the needle points to the zero line of the arc, which is of course also in the vertical of the centre of gravity, the beam must be horizontal. But by means of this index we can also ascertain whether equilibrium has been attained, without actually waiting until the beam comes to rest. While the beam is oscillating, if it really be in equilibrium, the needle will describe equal arcs on the graduated scale on each side of the zero point; while, if either scale be overloaded, the needle will move through more degrees on one side of the scale than on the other.

41. In a perfect balance, all the parts must be symmetrical with the centre of gravity ; that is, the parts on either side of this point must be absolutely equal. Such a state of perfection, however, cannot be attained in practice ; the two arms

cannot be made perfectly equal; all that the most skilful maker can do is to render the inequality very small.   When, however, it is necessary to obtain a very exact result, the error occasioned by the inequality of the arms of the balance can be avoided by the ingenious artifice of *double weighing*, invented by Borda.   To weigh a body, is to determine how many times the weight of this body contains another weight, of known value, such as ounces, or portions of ounces. Place the body, which we will call M, in one scale-pan, A, Fig. 25, and produce equilibrium by placing in the other scale-pan, B, some shot, or dry sand, or other substance in a minute state of division, so that very small portions may be added or subtracted, as occasion requires: by this means the needle can be brought exactly to zero, thereby indicating the horizontality of the beam.   This being done, we remove the body M, and substitute for it known weights, such as ounces and portions of ounces, until the beam is again hori- zontal.   The amount of this weight will express exactly the weight of the body M, because these ounces, &c., being placed under exactly the same circumstances of equilibrium as the body M, produce exactly the same effect.

By this method, then, it is not only possible, but easy, to weigh truly with a false balance.   Under ordinary cir- cumstances, an error amounting to a fraction of a grain would be of no consequence; but, in weighing for the purposes of chemical analysis, an error amounting to the thousandth of a grain might be of importance; hence, this method is commonly adopted in such investigations.

42. In ordinary scales, one can readily ascertain whether the point of support is in the middle of the beam, by changing the scale-pans when the balance is in equilibrium.   If the horizontal position is disturbed by this process, the two arms are not of the same length.   A false balance can also be detected by shifting the weights which produce equilibrium : this also will destroy the horizontal position of the arms, if they are sensibly unequal.   But this method also furnishes

the means for ascertaining the true weight of the substance. Some persons are satisfied with taking the arithmetical mean* of the two weights found in this manner; but this is quite erroneous, and will always give too high a result. As the body is over estimated in one weighing *in the same ratio* that it is under estimated in the other weighing, the true weight must plainly be the *geometrical* mean † between the two false estimates.

43. The *stability* of a balance is its tendency to return to, and oscillate about, the position of rest, after being disturbed. The position of the centre of gravity below the point of support determines the stability of a balance. Stability is far more easily attained than *sensibility*, or the tendency of a loaded balance, when poised, to turn when a very small additional weight is placed in either scale. If there were no friction, the scale would turn by the addition of the smallest weight. Friction is diminished as much as possible by placing the beam upon the support by means of knife edges, of hard steel, the support being also of the same material. See Fig. 26.

· Fig. 26.

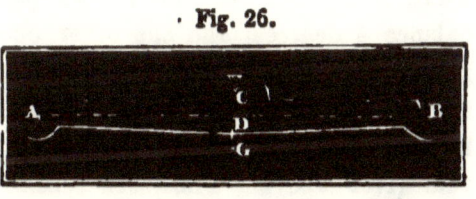

The stability and sensibility of a balance are ascertained by the following means. First, as to the stability of one balance compared with that of another. A small amount of disturbance being given to both, such as one degree, if the force with which the first endeavours to recover its position be double or triple that of the second, the stability of the first is double or triple that of the second. To compare these forces, the weight of both scales, multiplied into C D,

---

* The arithmetical mean of two quantities, *a* and *b*, is half their sum, or $\frac{1}{2}(a+b)$.

† The geometrical mean of two quantities, *a* and *b*, is the square root of their product, or $\sqrt{ab}$.

or the distance between the centre of motion and the intersection of the line drawn through the points of suspension with
the vertical through the centre of motion, must be added to
the weight of the beam, multiplied into c g, or the distance
between the centre of motion and the centre of gravity of the
beam.   For example ; suppose that in two balances these
quantities are as follows :—

	FIRST BALANCE.	SECOND BALANCE.
The arm A D . .	12 inches.	14 inches.
„ C G . .	2 „	3 „
„ C D .	1 „	2 „
Weight of beam	30 ounces.	50 ounces.
Weight of both scales	24 „	30 „

In such case, the stabilities of the first to the second
balance will be as 84 to 210 ; because $24 \times 1 + 30 \times 2 = 84$,
and $30 \times 2 + 50 \times 3 = 210$.

44. The sensibility is ascertained by comparing the angles
through which very small equal weights incline the balances.
Thus, if a grain put into a scale-pan of each inclines one
balance 4 degrees, and the other only 2 degrees, the first
is twice as sensible as the second.   To compare the sensibilities, multiply the length of the arm of each by the
number which represents the stability of the other in the
rule given above.   Thus, the sensibilities of the preceding
balances are as 12×210 to 14×84, or as 2520 to 1176.

The sensibility of a balance is also ascertained by observing
the smallest additional weight that will turn it, and then
comparing this addition with the whole load.   Thus, if a
balance have a troy pound in each scale-pan, and the horizontality of the beam varies by a small quantity, only just
perceptible on the addition of $\frac{1}{100}$th of a grain, the balance is
said to be sensible to $\frac{1}{1152000}$th part of its load, with a pound
in each scale, or that it will determine the weight of a troy
pound within $\frac{1}{576000}$th part of the whole.   Perhaps the most
sensible balance ever constructed, was that employed for
verifying the national standard bushel, the weight of which,
together with the 80 lbs. of water it should contain, was

about 250 lbs. With this weight in each scale, the addition of a single grain occasioned an immediate variation in the index of one-twentieth of an inch, the radius being 50 inches; so that this balance was sensible to $\frac{1}{1750000}$th part of the weight to be determined.

The following are the general rules respecting the sensibility of a balance :—

1. That, all other things being the same, the sensibility is increased by increasing the lengths of its arms.

2. That, all other things being the same, the sensibility is increased by diminishing the weight of the beam.*

3. That the sensibility is increased by diminishing the distance between the centres of gravity and motion.

4. That the sensibility is increased by diminishing the distance of the line joining the points of suspension from the centre of motion.

5. That the sensibility is greater when the load is smaller.

45. In addition to the balance with equal arms, there are various modifications of the lever of the first kind in common use for ascertaining the weights of bodies. Such is the instrument used by the ancient Romans, called the *Roman statera* or *steelyard*. It consists of a beam of iron, resting upon knife-edges or a pivot, with one arm longer than the other. Supposing the shorter arm, with the attached scale, to be sufficiently heavy to balance the longer arm, when the instrument is unloaded, the beam will of course be horizontal.

* It has been already seen that the sensibility of a balance depends on the suspension at the fulcrum, or middle of the beam. It will be perfect, in proportion as friction is diminished between this point and the plane which bears it; for the friction, which results from the superposition of two bodies, is a force which acts in the direction of their surfaces, and which is in opposition to other forces tending to detach these surfaces from each other. Thus, the friction of the knife-edge on its support must oppose the turning of the beam round this point. This rotation cannot take place without detaching some part of the knife-edge and its support from each other. The force required to overcome their adhesion is, as we have seen, a measure of the sensibility of the balance.

The substance to be weighed, w, is suspended from a hook attached to the shorter arm, and a constant weight, P, is made to slide upon the longer arm, until equilibrium is established. Now we know that in the lever the condition of equilibrium is, that the weight w, multiplied by its distance from the fulcrum, is equal to the power or counterpoise P multiplied by its distance from the fulcrum. Now, as the distance of the weight from the fulcrum is constant, and as the counterpoise is also constant, it is evident that in whatever proportion w is increased or diminished, the distance between P and the fulcrum must be increased or diminished in the same proportion; thus, if w be doubled or trebled, the distance of P from the fulcrum must also be doubled or trebled.

Hence the principle upon which this instrument is graduated is sufficiently simple. Suppose the instrument is first to be graduated for weighing pounds. A pound weight

Fig. 27.

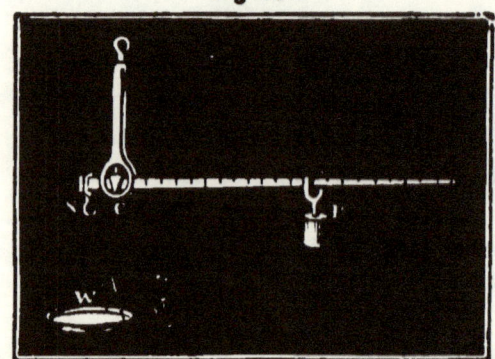

is placed in the scale, and the counterpoise moved towards the centre c, Fig. 27, until the beam is horizontal. A mark is then made with a file at c. A second pound is then placed in the scale, and the counterpoise moved from c, until the beam is again horizontal. A second mark is then made; after which, the whole length of the arm is marked with divisions of the same length as that between the first and second divisions obtained experimentally. Of course the number of any division from c will express the number of pounds which the counterpoise P, resting on that division, will sustain, and this is the weight of the body w.

The above illustration is intended to show the principle of the instrument, rather than to describe that in common use. In an ordinary steelyard, the centre of gravity is not at the fulcrum, so that when the weight P is removed, the longer arm usually preponderates; hence the graduation must be commenced, not from c, but from some point between s and c. These, however, are matters of detail, which will be found treated of fully in larger works. The great convenience of the steelyard is in its requiring only one weight. When the substance to be weighed is heavier than the constant weight, the pressure on the fulcrum is less than in the balance, because with the latter, equilibrium is only produced by a weight equal to that of the body to be weighed; but in the steelyard a less weight will suffice. For example, to balance 10 lbs. in a pair of common scales, we must have a weight of 10 lbs., making together a load of 20 lbs.; but in the steelyard a weight of 10 lbs. may be balanced by only 1 lb., making together a load of only 11 lbs. When, on the contrary, the constant weight exceeds the substance to be weighed, the pressure on the fulcrum is, of course, greater in the steelyard than in the balance; hence the balance is preferable in determining small weights.

When the counterpoise P is moved to the extreme end of the beam, it represents the greatest weight that the instrument, as hitherto described, can determine. There are, however, two methods by which the same beam can be made to determine heavier weights : 1st, by having another point of suspension on the shorter arm, nearer to the fulcrum ; or, 2ndly, by using a heavier counterpoise.

46. *The Danish balance* (Fig. 28) differs from the steelyard, just described, in having the fulcrum F moveable, instead of the counterpoise P, which is fixed at one extremity, while the body to be

Fig. 28.

weighed, w, is suspended from a hook at the other extremity.

If c be the centre of gravity of the unloaded beam and scale-pan, the graduation must commence from that point, since, when the fulcrum-loop is there, it poises the unloaded beam and scale-pan. By suspending from the hook at w, 1, 2, 3, &c. pounds in succession, the divisions may be found to which the fulcrum must be removed in order to produce equilibrium.

47. *The bent-lever balance* is also a convenient form of scale in which the weight is constant. It consists of a bent

Fig. 29.

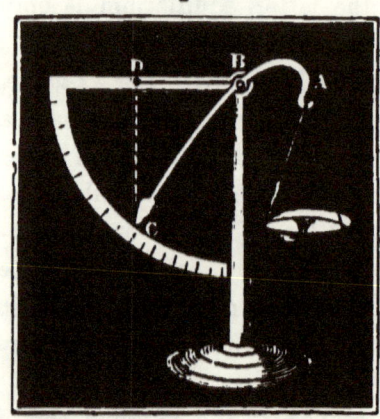

lever A B C, Fig. 29, to one end of which a weight, c, is fixed, and to the other end, A, a hook carrying a scale-pan, w, in which the substance to be weighed is placed. This lever is moveable about an axis, B. As the weight in w depresses the shorter arm B A, its leverage is constantly diminished, while that of the arm C B is constantly increased. When c counterpoises the weight, the division at which it settles on the graduated arc expresses its amount. The graduation of the instrument of course commences at the point where the index settles when there is no load in w. The scale-pan is then successively loaded with 1, 2, 3, &c. ounces or pounds, and the successive positions of the index marked on the arc.

48. Before we conclude this section on the lever, it may be as well to notice a common rule for determining the *mechanical efficacy*, or *power*, of a machine. This is said to be greater or less, according as the ratio of the weight to the power is greater or less. Thus, if the weight be 20 times the power, the mechanical efficacy is said to be 20; if 4 times the weight is equal to 25 times the power, the mechanical efficacy is $\frac{25}{4}$, or 6¼

As the mechanical efficacy of the lever admits of being varied at pleasure by varying the distances of the power and weight from the fulcrum, so we may imagine a lever with a power equal to that of any given machine; such a lever is called an *equivalent lever*, with respect to that machine. As all simple machines may be represented by simple equivalent levers, so the most complex machine may be represented by a compound system of equivalent levers, whose alternate arms, beginning from the power, bear the same proportion to the remaining arms.

49. The principal use of the common lever is for raising weights through small spaces, which is done by a series of short intermitting efforts. After the weight has been raised, it must be supported in its new position while the lever is re-adjusted to repeat the action. The chief defect, therefore, of the common lever is want of range and of the means of supplying continuous motion. This defect would be supplied if the moving power, which in all levers must describe an arc of a circle, could be made to move round the entire circle, and so continue to revolve for any length of time, still producing always the due proportion of effect on the resistance to be overcome. Now, if the resistance be acting always in one straight line (if it be a weight to be lifted, for example), there are many ways in which the

Fig. 30.

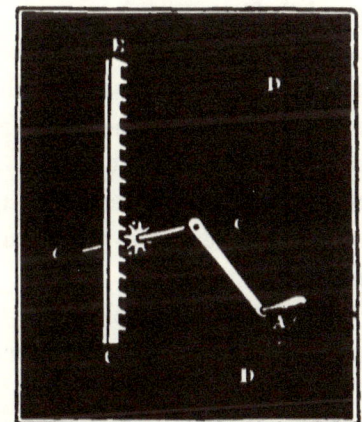

action of the lever may be rendered continuous. Its short arm may be repeated several times as the radii of a circle, and each of these radii in succession may catch and lift some part of the weight, or of a contrivance connected with it. Thus we get the machine called the *rack* and *pinion* (Fig. 30), in which the centre, or axis of motion, $c c$, forms the fulcrum of a lever, whose longer arm c A is called the *winch*, and describes a complete circle; the shorter arm is repeated in the figure 8 times, forming the 8 leaves or teeth of the *pinion*, and there is always one of these employed in lifting by one of its teeth the *rack* B C to which the load or other resistance is applied. Thus, as soon as one of these short arms of the lever has done its work, another is ready to supply its place; and although each lifts the weight through only a very small space, the entire range is limited only by the length of the rack. But in lifting the weight through this range, the hand at A must describe altogether a space much greater, viz. in the proportion that the circumference A D D exceeds the height occupied by 8 teeth of the rack.

50. The flexibility of *cords* affords another still easier means of increasing the range of action of the lever to almost any extent. By filling up the spaces between the leaves of the pinion, in the last example, we may convert it into a *cylinder* or *barrel*, on which if a rope be coiled, and the load be suspended from it, this rope will supply the place of the rack B C, and be wound up in the same manner. This constitutes the common *windlass*, in which the weight hanging on the rope will exceed the force applied to the winch, and just supporting it, in the ratio that the length of the winch, measured from its centre of motion, exceeds the mean radius of a coil of rope, *i. e.* the radius of the barrel + half the thickness of the rope.

51. Thus the efficiency of this machine, the windlass, as a concentrator of force, is augmented either by diminishing the thickness of the barrel, or by increasing the length of the winch; but the barrel would be too much weakened if diminished beyond a certain extent, and the winch becomes useless if lengthened beyond the radius of the circle which the hand and arm can conveniently describe. Hence arises a necessity for multiplying the *long* arm of the lever and making it into several radii, in the same way that the *short* arm was multiplied to form the pinion or the barrel. This repetition of

the longer arm constitutes the *wheel*, which is commonly reckoned as the *second simple machine*, although, as we have seen (49), it is only a particular modification of the *first*, viz. the lever. The advantage of the wheel over the single spoke or winch is, that however long its radius, it can always be turned continuously by a force whose action is confined to a small part only of the circumference. This can be effected in either of the modes above described in the case of the short arm—viz. first, by forming projections on the rim of the wheel, to be successively acted on by the power in the same way that the leaves of the pinion successively act on the resistance ; or secondly, by passing a rope or band round the wheel.

52. The latter affords an easy mode of exhibiting the pro · perties of this most important machine. For this purpose the power is usually represented by a small weight suspended from a cord which is wound on the circumference of the wheel ; and the resistance by a larger weight on a cord that is wound in a contrary direction round the axle.

It will be evident, from an inspection of this machine, that its condition of equilibrium is precisely that of the lever ; only, in this case, the power is multiplied by the radius c b of the wheel, and this will be found equal to the resistance multiplied by the radius of the axle. If, for example, the power be 1 lb. and the radius of the wheel 22 inches, and the load 11 lbs., while the radius of the axle is 2 inches, there will be equilibrium, because the moments are in each case the same. (26.)

We may also prove the same thing by the principle of virtual velocities (27), for in one revolution of the wheel the power descends through a space equal to the circumference of the wheel, and the weight is raised through a space equal to the circumference of the axle. Hence, the moving power, multiplied by the velocity of its motion, is not less than the load moved, multiplied by the velocity of its motion.

· 53. The axle in the wheel is evidently not intermitting in its action, as in the case of the common lever; but the motion which the power communicates to the load, although slow, is constant. Hence it has been called the *continual* or *perpetual lever*, and its mechanical efficacy depends on the ratio of the radius of the wheel to the radius of the axle, or the length of the lever by which the power acts, to the length of that by which the load resists.

54. The power may be applied to the wheel in various ways, such as by pins placed at various distances round its circumference, as in the wheel used to work the rudder of a ship, in which case the hand is used as the power: in some cases the rim of the wheel is dispensed with, and a number of long bars are inserted in the axle, as in the larger kinds of windlass, in which the axle is usually horizontal. In the capstan it is vertical. In either case the wheel consists only of diverging spokes, rendered portable by a number of holes in the axle, into which men insert the ends of these spokes or *hand-spikes*. When the axis is horizontal, each hand-spike is removed from one hole to another, the weight being meanwhile sustained by the action of a *ratchet-wheel*. When the axis is vertical, a number of men may work at it, pushing the bars before them, and thus there need be no intermission of the power. An enormous weight may be raised in this way.

Fig. 31.

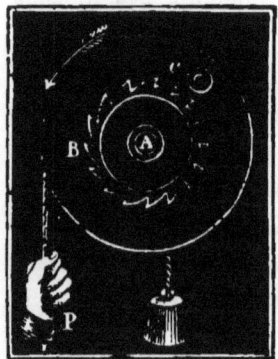

The *ratchet* or *racket-wheel* (Fig. 31) just referred to, is a simple contrivance for preventing a wheel from turning except in one direction. A catch *c* plays into the teeth of the wheel A B, permitting it to revolve in the direction of *c* B, but preventing any recoil on the part of the weight or resistance contrary to the direction of the power.

55. By increasing the size of the wheel in proportion to that of the

axle, forces of very different intensities may be balanced; but as the larger force increases in magnitude, the size of the wheel is increased to an inconvenient extent. Hence the use of a combination or system of wheels and axles. Now, as the wheel and axle is only a modification of the lever, we may expect to find that a system of wheels and axles is only a modification of the compound lever already described (39). Such is the case, and the conditions of equilibrium are also the same. The power being applied to the circumference of the first wheel, transmits its effect to the circumference of the first axle; this acts upon the circumference of the second wheel, which transfers the effect to the circumference of the second axle, which, in its turn, acts upon the circumference of the third wheel, and this transmits its effect to the circumference of the third axle; and thus the force is transmitted until it arrives at the circumference of the last axle, where it encounters the load or resistance.

56. There are various methods by which the circumference of the axles are made to act upon the wheels. Sometimes, by the mere friction of their surfaces, the friction being increased by cutting the wood so that the grains of the opposed surfaces may run in opposite directions; in other cases the surfaces are covered with buff leather; but the most usual method of transmitting power in complex wheelwork is by means of *teeth* or *cogs* raised on the surfaces of the wheels and axles. The word *teeth* is usually applied to the cogs on the surface of the wheel, while those on the surface of the axle are called *leaves*, and the part of the axle from which they project is named a *pinion*, as already noticed (Fig. 30). In a train of wheels thus arranged (Fig. 32), the conditions of the equilibrium are the same as in a train of levers (Fig. 23), that is to say, the power P is to the resistance W, as the continued product of the radii of the pinions *b*, *c*, *d* is to the continued product of the radii of the wheels *a*, *e*, *f*. Thus, if the pinions in Fig. 32 had been respectively 1, 2, and 3 inches radius, and the wheels

respectively 8, 9, and 12 inches radius, then $1 \times 2 \times 3 = 6$, and $8 \times 9 \times 12 = 864$, or, in other words, a power expresssed by 6 would counterbalauce a weight, or overcome a resistance, equal to 864.

When a system thus constructed is in action, the leaves of the pinion must pass in succession between the teeth of the wheel; consequently, the circumferences of the wheels and pinions must bear a certain proportion to the numbers of teeth and leaves; and as the circumferences are as the radii, the numbers of the teeth or leaves must be proportional to the radii. Hence, in assigning the condition of equilibrium, the number of teeth and leaves must be substituted for the radii of the wheels and axles mentioned above, otherwise there might be some doubt as to the real or effective radius of these bodies, viz. to what part of the toothed circumference it should be measured. This is known by dividing the distance between the centres of the wheel and pinion into as many parts as there are teeth in both of them together. Thus, if the wheel have 51, and the pinion 10 teeth, then, the space between their centres being divided into 61 parts, the tenth division from the centre of the pinion, or the fifty-first from the centre of the wheel, will mark the extent of both their effective radii; and two circles drawn with these radii, so as to touch at the said division, are called the *pitch-lines*, or *pitch-circles*, which, as will presently be seen, form the bases for determining the form and size of the teeth. In wheel-work, therefore, the condition of equilibrium is, as expressed by the ratio above, that the power multiplied by the product of the numbers of teeth in all the wheels, is equal to the load multiplied by the product of the number of leaves in all the pinions. If, as in Fig. 32, some of the wheels and axles carry teeth, and others not, then, the effective radii of the former being measured from their centre to their pitch-line, those of the latter must be measured from their centre to the middle of the thickness of the surrounding rope or band.

57. The law of virtual velocities (27) applies also to com-

plex wheel-work. The teeth and leaves being equal, tho circumference (*i. e.* the pitch-line) of each wheel moves with the same velocity as that of the pinion by which it is driven. Now, as each wheel revolves in the same time with its axle, the velocities of their circumferences are as their effective radii or numbers of teeth. Hence the velocity of the power, or the velocity of the circumference of the first wheel, is to that of the first axle as their radii. But the velocity of the circumference of the first pinion is equal to the velocity of the circumference of the second wheel, which is to that of the second pinion as their radii; and by calculating in this way to the end of the train, it will be found that the velocity of the power is to that of the load as the product of the radii of the wheels to the product of the radii of the pinions; or that the power, multiplied by the velocity of the power, is not less than the load multiplied by the velocity of the load.

For example, in Fig. 32, let the number of leaves on the axle *b* of the first wheel *a* be six times less than the number of teeth in the circumference of the second wheel *e*, so that the wheel may be turned only once by every six turns of the axle *b*. In like manner the second wheel *e*, by turning six times, turns the third wheel *f* only once; so that the first wheel turns thirty-six

Fig. 32.

times for only one turn of the third wheel; and as the diameter of the wheel *a* to which the power is applied is

three times as great as that of the axle d, which bears the
weight w or the resistance, $3 \times 36 = 108$. So that $1 : 108$
is in this case the ratio between the velocities w and p
when moving, and consequently between their weights or
pressures when in equilibrium.

58. But as neither this, nor any other system of machinery
(except that of simple levers), is ever used for *weighing*, but
always for communicating *motion*, we must remember that
the conditions of equilibrium only inform us what degree of
force applied to one part of the machine will *balance* a given
resistance at another part. But before motion can be produced, there must, in addition to this, be a redundancy of
one force over the other, sufficient to overcome the *friction*
and other passive resistances, the determination of which, as
well as of the rate of motion produced, belongs to dynamics.
Now, as the levers (in Figs. 20, 22, 24) become levers of the
second or third kind, according as the slower-moving or
quicker-moving force preponderates, so the train of wheels
(Fig. 32) serves to concentrate or diffuse force according as
p or w preponderates; for in one case a weak force, by acting
through a great space, is brought to bear upon a powerful
resistance; in the other, a great force moving through a
small range expends itself in moving weak resistances
through great spaces. Thus, when a heavy weight hanging
from a crane descends, it drags the winch round with extreme
rapidity, but with so little force, that the pressure of a child
may not only keep it from turning, but reverse its motion, and
so raise the weight. Hence power is *concentrated* when the
pinions turn the wheels, but *diffused* when the wheels turn
the pinions. Thus the former arrangement is used in a
crane to gain *power*, the latter in a *clock* or *watch* to gain
extent of *motion*. In one machine, many large turns of the
handle are necessary to lift the weight a few inches; in the
others, the descent of the weight a few feet, or the recoil of
the spring through three or four turns, suffices to carry the
seconds hand through 10,080 or 1,440 revolutions.

59. In machines where this increase of motion is the object, and where no exact proportion between the motions is necessary, the system of teeth or cogs is seldom used, but the communication of motion from a large wheel to a small one is effected in a better as well as cheaper manner by a *strap* or *endless band* passing over them both. They may thus be at any distance apart, and may turn either the same way or contrary ways, according as the strap does or does not *cross* between them; whereas a toothed wheel and its pinion must always turn in contrary directions. The strap may also be conducted over pulleys in any direction.

60. Since wheel-work is used, like other machinery, to transmit and modify force, it is often a matter of nice calculation and contrivance that the precise effect intended should be accomplished, especially in watch and clockwork, where the object is to produce uniform motions of rotation, in times which are exact multiples of each other.

In ordinary wheel-work it is usual, in any wheel and pinion that act on each other, to use numbers of teeth that are *prime* to each other,* so that each tooth of the pinion may encounter every tooth of the wheel in turn; by which means any irregularities will tend to diminish by constant wear, instead of *increasing*, as they must do, in watches and clocks, where the above plan is evidently inapplicable. In these, as well as in all other systems of wheel-work, great attention must be paid to the forms of the teeth and leaves, otherwise there will be a jolting, grinding action, which would end in their mutual destruction. The teeth should be formed in such a manner that those of one wheel press in a direction perpendicular to the radius of the other wheel; that is, the pressure

Fig. 33.

* Numbers *prime* to each other are such as have no common measure, except 1.

should be *tangential* to the wheel, as the line *a b*, Fig. 33, or tangential to the pinion, as the line A B. It is also desirable that during the entire action of one tooth upon another, the direction of the pressure should be the same, so as to produce a uniform effect, by acting with the same leverage. The teeth should be so formed that one may *roll* upon the other, and not rub or scrape.* It is also of importance that as many teeth as possible should be in contact at the same time, so as to distribute the pressure amongst them, and thus to diminish the pressure upon each tooth. Hence pinions of less than 10 or 12 leaves are objectionable; but there is, of course, a limit to the multiplication of teeth, from their becoming too thin to withstand the pressure. It is also desirable that the same teeth in the wheel should be engaged as seldom as possible with the same leaves of the pinion which works it. If, for example, the number of teeth in the wheel were 60, the number of leaves in the pinion 10, each leaf of the pinion would engage every tenth tooth of the wheel, and would always work on the same six teeth with every revolution of the wheel. In clockwork this is, of course, unavoid-

* The complete attainment of all these conditions at the same time is impossible, and very profound analysis has been found necessary to determine what forms of teeth will secure the nearest approach thereto. For some purposes, the *epicycloid* (or curve described by a point in the circumference of a small circle *rolling* round the rim of the wheel) has been proposed; and for others, that the side of each tooth should be an *involute* from the pitch-line (that is, that it should be described by a pencil confined by a thread that is *unwound* from that line). When the teeth are numerous, this curve will approach to a circular arc. In all cases, the teeth should project the same distance *beyond* the pitch-line, that their intervals recede *within* it; and the portions of their sides situated within this circle are usually made straight and radial. The conditions above mentioned are less attainable in pinions than in wheels, and still less in proportion as the leaves are fewer. Hence, the best form of pinion, where great strength is not required, is that called the *trundle* or *lantern* pinion, which consists of two discs, connected near their circumference by 8 or 10 cylindrical rods, which serve instead of leaves; and if these be made to turn freely on their axes, the rolling motion is insured, together with other advantages.

able, *but millwrights generally contrive so that the number of teeth is just one more than a number which is exactly divisible by the number of leaves. This odd tooth is called the hunting-cog.* If, for example, the pinion contain 8 leaves, and the wheel 65 teeth, it is evident that the wheel must revolve 8 times, and the pinion 65 times, before the same leaves and teeth will be again engaged.

61. Toothed wheels are usually divided into three classes, according to the position of the teeth with respect to the axis of the wheel. When the teeth are raised upon the edge of the wheel, as in Fig. 33, they are called *spur-wheels*, or *spur-gear*, which necessarily turn both in the same plane. When raised parallel to the axis, as in Fig. 34, they form a *crown-wheel*, which, by acting on a spur-wheel, turns the latter in a plane at right-angles to itself. When the teeth are raised on a surface inclined to the plane of the wheel, they are called *bevelled wheels*, which are capable of communicating motion in planes inclined at any angle to each other (Fig. 35). Spur-gear is, therefore, used for communicating motion round one axis to another axis parallel to it. See Fig. 32, where the three axes are parallel to each other. Where the axes are at right angles to each other, a crown-wheel, working in a spur-pinion, as in Fig. 34, may be used. The same object may also be

Fig. 34.

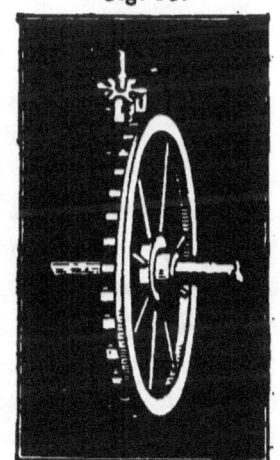

better accomplished by two bevelled wheels. But by bevelled wheels also, a motion round one axis can be communicated to another, inclined to it at any proposed angle. See Fig. 35. In such a case, the surfaces on which the teeth are raised are parts of the surfaces of two cones, and the mode in which they act may be conceived by placing two cones side by side, as *d a e*, *e a d'*. If one be made to revolve,

Fig. 35.

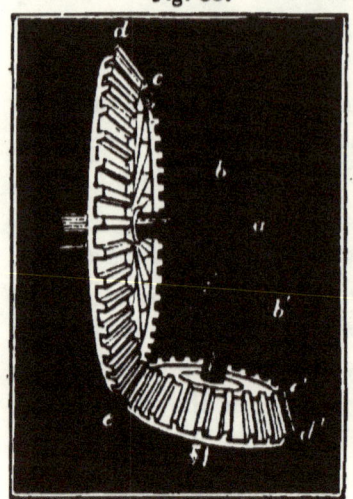

it will cause the other to re-volve also. If the bases of the cones be equal, they will revolve in equal times; if unequal, the number of revolutions will bear the same proportion as the bases. So also the properties which belong to the whole cones will belong to any corresponding parts of them, such as $b\,b'$, $c\,c'$, $d\,d'$, and would therefore apply to wheels, the edges of which are parts, $b\,b'$, $c\,c'$, &c., of the conical surfaces. It is necessary, however, that the vertices of both cones should coincide as at a; therefore the axes of both wheels must be imagined to be prolonged till they meet, and this point will be the common vertex of the cones.

62. The machines which have been hitherto considered are of two kinds, *rigid* and *flexible*. The former owe much of their mechanical advantage to their inflexibility; for if levers were capable of bending, it is obvious that the laws which regulate their action, on the supposition that they are rigid, would no longer apply, or at least would require considerable modification. In the cords, however, used as in Figs. 31, 32, for converting a straight into a circular motion, or one circular motion into another, as in the endless band described in 59, perfect flexibility is as great a desideratum as perfect rigidity was in the former case. Of course it cannot be attained, but, in considering the theory, it is, as already stated (29 and 14 *note*), far more easy to consider such perfection to have been attained, and afterwards to make allowances for whatever interferes therewith, than to attempt, in the first instance, to solve the problem complicated with these extra and varying quantities.

A rope or thread, perfectly flexible and inextensible. is a

machine which enables us to transmit force from one point to another in the direction of its length, as well as by a rigid bar or rod, but with this difference, that the forces which are opposed to each other must always be *divellent*, whereas with a rod they may act either from or towards each other. So far the rigid body appears to present an advantage. But the chief advantage of the rope is, that, from its flexibility, a force acting in one direction may be made to balance an equal force in any other direction.

Fig. 36.

Thus, the weight w, Fig. 36, acting in the direction H w, may, by means of a rope passing through a fixed hook or ring H, be sustained by a power P acting in the direction P H. Assuming the rope to be perfectly flexible and smooth, it would suffer no resistance either from rigidity or friction in passing through the ring, and the cord would be stretched everywhere with the same force which is equal to that of the weight w.

63. We see, then, that the alteration in the direction of the power, by passing the rope through the ring at P, makes no difference in the power; it merely enables us to alter its direction; this, however, supposes the rope to be perfectly smooth and flexible, and the ring to be free from all roughness; but, as it is not possible to fulfil these conditions, the friction arising from the opposite qualities is greatly diminished by substituting for the ring a wheel grooved at the circumference, and turning freely on an axle passing through its centre. Such a wheel is called a *pulley*, and we have already made use of it for altering the directions of forces, in the experiments illustrated by Figs. 7 and 22. We have now to show how, by a different arrangement of pulleys, force may not only be transmitted, but also *concentrated* in degree, thus rendering this machine one of the so-called mechanical powers; and although the *pulley* is commonly called the third of these,

yet it must be remembered, that the *cord* or rope is the efficient agent, no mechanical advantage being gained from the pulley; for the theory of the pulley, as a mechanical power, would be just as complete if the rope were passed through perfectly smooth rings, as in Fig. 36. The real mechanical advantage to be derived from this machine is founded on the fact, that the same flexible cord must always undergo the same tension in every part of its length.

64. Pulleys are called *fixed* or *moveable*, according as their *frame* is fixed or not, for the sheaf or wheel is always moveable on its axis. In fixed pulleys, such as those in Figs. 7 and 22, the power and the load are equal, so that there is no mechanical advantage, but only a convenience in being able to apply the power in any required direction. A *single moveable pulley*, also called a *runner*, is shown at A B, Fig. 37.

Fig. 37.

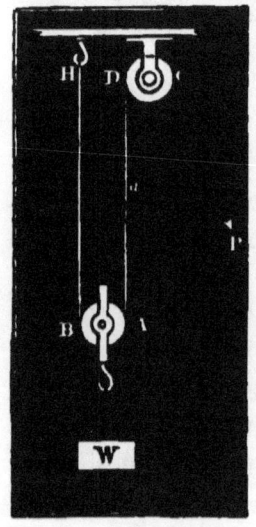

In this example it is evident that the rope must have the same tension everywhere throughout its length, or the system would not be in equilibrium; and, further, in order to be in equilibrium, the tension must be equal to the power P; thus the power P is supported by the tension of that part of the rope which is between C and P. If we call this 1 lb., it will be found that the load W must be 2 lbs., because this is supported by that part of the cord lying between H and B, and also by the part between D and A. In fact, these two portions, B H and A D, of the cord sustain the weight between them. Or we may regard the horizontal diameter of the pulley A B as a lever of the second kind, having its fulcrum at B, the power applied at A, and the load hanging midway between them. In this arrangement, therefore, the power is capable of balancing a weight or opposing a resistance of twice its own amount. It should, however, be observed, that in reckoning the load we must include the weight of the moveable pulley A B, which is also sustained by the power. In Fig. 38 the weight is equal to three times the power, and in Fig. 39 to four times the power. In each of these cases it will be seen that the tension of each part of the rope is equal to the power P. In Fig. 38 the load W is distributed equally among three portions, and in Fig. 39 among four portions of the rope; and as each portion is stretched equally by the power, it follows that in the one case the weight

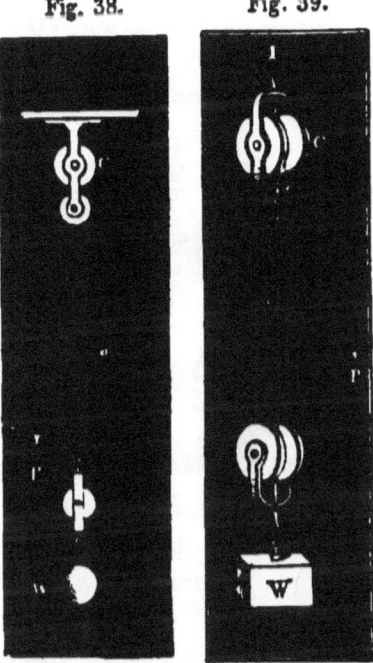

Fig. 38. Fig. 39.

raised is nearly equal to three times, and, in the other case, to four times the power. Hence it appears that in systems of pulleys with one rope and one moveable block,* the load is as many times the power as there are different parts of the rope engaged in supporting the moveable block; and, in general, when the power acts downwards, the number of pulleys required equals the number of times that the power is to be concentrated; but when the power acts upwards, one pulley may be dispensed with, for in the last three figures the power P might have been applied to pull up the cord a.

---

* The *block* is the framework in which the wheels or *sheaves* are secured by means of the pivot or axle. A combination of blocks, sheaves, and ropes, is called a *tackle*. In the pulleys represented in Fig. 38. the sheaves move on separate axles; it is, however, more usual to place them side by side on the same axle, as in Fig. 39.

without the intervention of the fixed pulley c, which adds
nothing to the mechanical effect.

65. In the preceding cases we have supposed the parts
of the rope which support the weight to be parallel, or
nearly so.   When such is not the case, the machine is
greatly deteriorated as a mechanical power; indeed, at
certain obliquities, the
power would require to
be greater than the weight,
in order to produce equi-
librium.   In order to determine the power neces-
sary to support a given
weight when the parts of
the cord B C, B H, Fig. 40,
are not parallel, take the
line B A vertical, and consisting of as many inches (or other
equal parts) as the weight consists of ounces or pounds.   From
A draw A D, parallel to B H; and from E draw A E, parallel to
B C.   The force of the weight represented by the diagonal A B
will, as already stated (9, 10), be equivalent to two forces represented by B D and B E.   The number of inches in these lines
respectively will represent the number of ounces, or pounds,
which are equivalent to the tensions of the parts B C and B H
of the cord; but as these tensions are equal, B D and B E
must be equal, and each will express the amount of power
which stretches the cord at P C.   As each of the four sides
of the parallelogram A E B D equally represents the power,
and as the diagonal A B represents the weight, the latter
must always be *less* than twice the power which is represented by A E, E B, taken together.   But if the angle C B H
exceed 120°, A B will evidently be shorter than E B or B D,
so that the power at P will require to be greater than the
weight W; and this excess may be in any proportion, so that
it is impossible by *any* power applied at P, to pull the
cord C B H mathematically straight, however small the weight

Fig. 40.

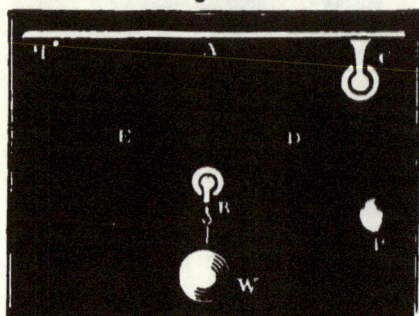

w may be, or even if there be no weight except that of the cord itself. Hence, also, we see the reason that a harp-string, however tightly stretched, can always be pulled aside by a very small transverse force, almost infinitely less than its longitudinal tension.

66. In testing the theory of the pulley dynamically, or by the principle of virtual velocities, we find that in this, as well as in all other machines, whatever is gained in force is lost in velocity. It will be found in all the examples adduced, that the ascent of the weight is as many times less than the descent of the power, as the weight itself is greater than the power. Thus (in Fig. 39), if the power be 1 lb. and the weight 4 lbs., and it be required to raise the weight 1 foot, the power must descend through four feet; for, in order to raise the moveable block 1 foot, each of the four portions of cord by which it hangs must be shortened 1 foot; but as they all form parts of one continued cord, this must on the whole be shortened 4 feet, *i. e.* 4 feet of cord must pass out from the system between the blocks. "What then do we gain by the pulley?" it may be asked: the answer is, "We gain nothing at all;" for, as far as expenditure of power is concerned, we may just as well do without the machine; we gain no power by its means; all we do is to economize it and expend it gradually. In raising a weight of 50 lbs. one foot high, the expenditure of power is obviously the same, whether we accomplish the task by raising 1 lb. through 50 feet, or 50 separate lbs. through 1 foot; and in the pulley, or any other machine, a weight of 50 lbs. cannot be raised a given height with a less expenditure of power than is required to raise 100 lbs. half that height, or 1 lb. 50 times that height.

67. In the common form of block, and when there are several sheaves on the same axle, it is difficult to keep the cords parallel, and the blocks in their respective positions. To remedy this, Smeaton invented the blocks shown in Fig. 41, the action of which will be more intelligible by omitting the rope.

Its course, however, can easily be traced by means of the numbers affixed to the sheaves. One end of the rope is attached to the hook *o*, at the bottom of the upper block; from this point the rope is brought under the wheel marked 1, over 2, under 3, over 4, under 5, and so on, according to the order of the figures, until it is finally passed over the wheel marked 20, on which the power immediately acts. In this arrangement the blocks cannot get deranged, because the power acts directly over the weight. The weight being distributed over 20 parts of the rope, which are equally stretched, it follows that the weight is 20 times the power.

Fig. 41.

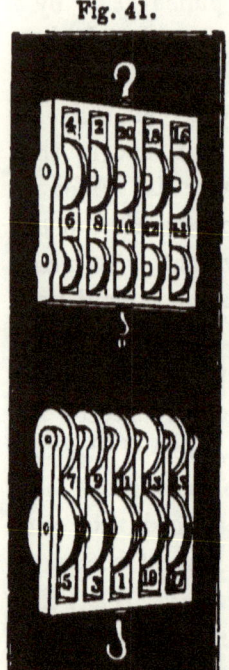

But an arrangement of this kind is accompanied by an enormous amount of friction; each wheel not only having to bear the friction on its axle, but frequently also against the side of the block Another objection arises from the very different velocities with which the sheaves revolve. Suppose that by the action of the power the lower block is raised one foot nearer to the upper one; the several parts of the rope between the two blocks will each be shortened by one foot. One foot of that part of the rope extending from the hook in the upper block to the wheel No. 1, must pass over that wheel, and also over all the succeeding wheels. But that part of the rope extending from No. 1 to No. 2 is *also* shortened by one foot, and this additional foot of rope must also pass over No. 2 and all the succeeding wheels. Hence, one foot of rope passes through No. 1, two feet through No. 2, three feet through No. 3, and so on; and as the velocities with which the wheels revolve are measured by the quantities of rope which pass over them in the same time, it follows, that while No. 1 revolves once, No. 2 revolves twice, No. 3 three times, and so on ; thereby producing an enormous inequality in the wear of the axles.

68. To remedy these defects, it was suggested, that if the wheels were made to differ in size in proportion to the quantity of rope which must pass over them, they would revolve in the same time, and might therefore be all fixed on the same axis, and would require no divisions between the different sheaves of the same block. For this purpose, the sheaves would require to have their diameters in the proportion of the numbers with which they are respectively marked in Fig. 41. By proportioning wheels in this manner, and placing them on the same axle, so that they might revolve in exactly the same time ; or, what is the same thing, by cutting several grooves upon the face of one solid conical wheel, with diameters in the proportion of the odd numbers, 1, 3, 5, &c. for the one pulley ; and corresponding grooves on the face of another solid wheel, in the proportion of the even numbers, 2, 4, 6, &c. for the other pulley ;* on passing the rope successively over the grooves of such wheels, it would be thrown off in the same manner as if each groove were upon a separate wheel, and each wheel on a separate axle. Such is the pulley invented by Mr. James White, and represented in Fig. 42. Its mechanical advantages are very considerable ; and when carefully made, it is found to answer all that was expected of it ; but this very care required in its construction is the chief

Fig. 42.

---

* The end of the rope must be attached to this latter block, whether it be the fixed or the moveable one.

cause of its not getting into general use; for, unless the grooves are proportioned with great nicety, the rope must obviously *slide* upon some of them, *i. e.* move with a different speed from that of their circumferences, thus causing a great increase of friction, and liability to derangement.

69. In the systems of pulleys hitherto described, there is always a fixed point which supports each system, answering to the fulcrum in the lever. It is evident that this fixed point sustains both the power and the weight, as well as the whole tackle. When the system is in equilibrium, the power only supports so much of the weight as is equal to the tension of the cord, the whole remainder of the weight being thrown on the fixed point. In fact, in this, as in all other machines, the power sustains just as much of the weight as is equal to its own force, the remaining part being sustained by the machine. Thus the above system is in equilibrium with a power of 10 lbs. and a weight of 70 lbs. Now, it is obviously impossible for this smaller weight to sustain the larger one: the tension of the cord marked 1 is equal to 10 lbs.; and as the

Fig. 43.

tension is everywhere the same, it follows, that each portion of the cord up to 8 has a tension of 10 lbs.; so that the cord No. 1 sustains the power = 10 lbs.; and the seven other cords (2 to 8 inclusive) sustain between them a weight of 70 lbs.

70. In the pulleys hitherto described, only one rope has been introduced; we have now to consider the effect of several distinct ropes in the same system. Pulleys containing more than one rope are called *Spanish bartons.* Such a system is represented in Fig. 43, containing two ropes. The tension of the rope P B A D is evidently equal to the power; consequently, the portions A B and A D must *each* sustain a portion of the weight equal to the power. The rope C B sustains the tensions

of B P and B A, and therefore the tension of B C A must equal
twice the power. The united tensions of the
ropes which support the pulley A amount,
therefore, to four times the power. The tensions of the respective ropes are marked in
figures, so that the reader will be able to
study the system from the figure itself, which
is an excellent method of impressing mechanical principles on the mind. All verbal descriptions must necessarily be somewhat
complex, and consequently far inferior to the
graphic eloquence of a well-executed diagram.

71. By a slight variation in the last-men-
tioned system, the power of the machine may
be increased (see Fig. 44). The rope which
sustains the power P is here attached to the
block A, and consequently sustains a part of
the weight equal to P. The second rope, B C A D,
acts against the united tensions of P B and
B A, so that the tension of B C, or
C A, or A D, is twice P. Thus the
weight W balances three tensions,
two of which (A C and A D) are
each equal to twice P, and the third
(A B) is equal to P; hence the
weight is five times the power.

Fig. 44.

72. In the system represented
in Fig. 45, four ropes are introduced. The tensions of the several
ropes will be understood from the
numbers, and it will be seen that
in this arrangement the multiplication of the power increases rapidly
with the number of pulleys, being
doubled by every moveable pulley
added; but this advantage over the

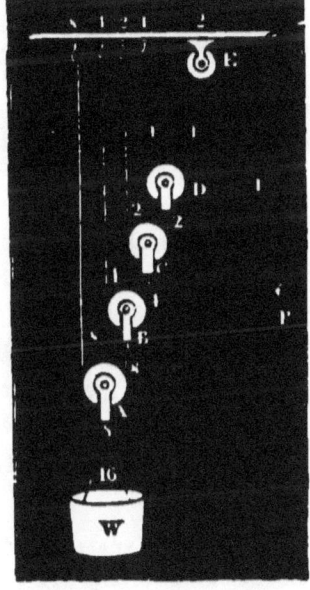

Fig. 45.

common arrangement is more than counterbalanced by the very limited range; for in the common blocks, the motion may be continued till the fixed and the moveable block come into contact; but, in this system, only till D and E come

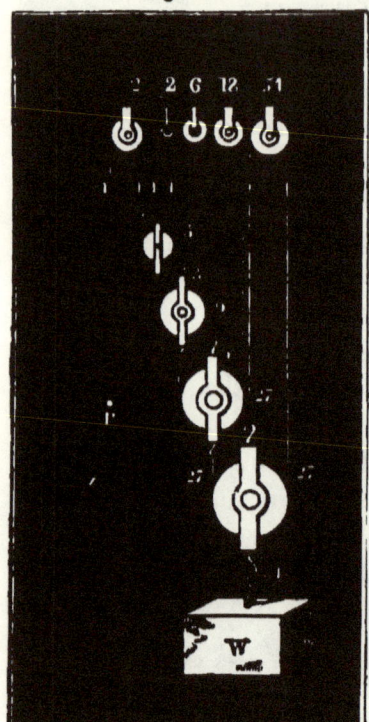

Fig. 46.

together, at which time the other pulleys will be far apart, because c rises only half as fast as D, B only one-fourth, and A only one-eighth as fast. Hence the longest possible range is but a small portion of the whole height occupied by this system, which accordingly entails a great waste of space, and is hardly of any practical use.

73. The mechanical efficiency of this system may be greatly increased by substituting fixed pulleys for the hooks in Fig. 45, the number of ropes remaining the same. In this case, Fig. 46, the tensions of the successive ropes increase in a threefold, instead of a double proportion, as will be evident by tracing the course of each rope in Fig. 46. In such an arrangement one rope would balance three times the power; two ropes 3×3, or 9 times the power; the third rope balances three portions of the second, and consequently its tension would equal 3×9, or 27 times the power; the fourth rope, in like manner, balancing three distinct portions of the third, would have its tension expressed by 3×27 $= 81$, which would be the weight w, the power P being 1.*

---

* The figures at the top of the last four diagrams show the resistances required at the several points of suspension. The reason for these will be

The limited range of this, as of the last system, renders it practically useless.

74. In these cases we have not noticed the effect of the weights of the sheaves and blocks. On examining the figures, it will be found that in some cases their weight acts against the power (Figs. 37, 38, 39, 41, 42, 45, 46); in other cases, they assist the power in supporting the weight (Figs. 43, 44); and there are cases in which the weights of the sheaves and blocks are made to balance each other.

75. The next so-called mechanical power is the *inclined plane*. It is equally simple with the lever; and, like that machine, naturally suggests itself to the mind in raising a load to a moderate height, especially when the load is of such a form as to admit of being rolled. Thus heavy casks are raised into a cart or dray by means of a ladder used as an inclined plane; and are moved out of the cart by the same contrivance. In such a case, the strength of one or two men is sufficient to raise a load of many hundredweight, which, but for this, or some other machine, they could not possibly lift from off the ground.

76. Now, the statical problem of the inclined plane is this:— suppose, for example, it is required to raise a cask weighing 1,000 lbs. into a cart 5 feet high, by means of a ladder or plank 14 feet long, resting against the cart. The question is,—What force must be exerted to prevent the cask rolling down the plank, supposing it to have no friction? The answer is 357¼ lbs.; because the force would have to act through a distance of 14 feet or inches, to raise the weight 5 feet or inches higher, or it would be driven back 14 units of length, by the descent of the cask 5 units lower. Therefore, as 14 : 5 :: 1,000 lbs. : 357¼ lbs. That is, if a man by himself, or two men acting together, exert a power of 357¼ lbs. in

evident on inspecting the ropes hanging from each point; and by adding all these resistances together, it will be seen that in all cases they equal the sum of the power P and the weight W.

the proper direction, they will be able to keep this cask of 1,000 lbs. weight from rolling down, however smooth may be the inclined plane; but as there is always some friction, a *less* power than this will always suffice to produce equilibrium.*

77. This case is clearly analogous to those already noticed in the lever and the pulley, where a small power appears to balance a weight many times greater than itself. But the rigour of mechanical justice requires that for work done there shall always be an equivalent expenditure of force; that for every weight raised there shall always be an equivalent exertion of power; and in the above example, we see that 1,000 lbs. raised through 5 feet, is equivalent to 357¼ lbs. raised through 14 feet, because 1,000 × 5 = 357¼ × 14.

78. The inclined plane is regarded in mechanical science as a perfectly hard, smooth, inflexible surface, inclined obliquely to the weight or resistance. The line A C, Fig. 47, is called the *length* of the inclined plane, B C its *height*, and A B its *base*. If G be a heavy body placed upon it, it will act in the vertical direction G V, of a line passing through its centre of gravity G. Now G V may be made the diagonal of a paral-

Fig. 47.

lelogram G W V X, so that if G V represent the magnitude and direction of the weight, it may be resolved into the two forces represented in direction and magnitude by G W and G X, one of which is parallel, and the other perpendicular to the plane; hence the pressure G V is equivalent to two other pressures, G W and G X; the former of which, G W, is destroyed by the resistance

* The subject of *Friction* is noticed in "The Rudiments of Civil Engineering," Part I. pp. 31—35.

plane, and the latter G X only acts to cause the descent of the body down the plane. Now G X is to V G as B C is to A B; that is to say, a weight placed upon an inclined plane is propelled down the plane by a force bearing such proportion to the weight, as the height of any section of the plane bears to its length. If, therefore, it were required to draw the heavy body G up the plane, any pressure in the direction X G exceeding G X and the friction, would be sufficient to do so; and any pressure in the same direction, which, with the friction, equals G X, would hold the weight in equilibrium.

The same thing may be proved in another way. Let G W be drawn perpendicular to A C, and G V vertical, which is the direction in which the weight acts, while X G or G Y is the direction in which the power acts; and these two forces compose a force equal to the pressure of G on the plane, perpendicular to A B, and forming the diagonal G W of a parallelogram, of which G V, G Y are the sides. Now, we know by the composition of forces (7, 10, 11), that the three lines G V, G Y, and G W,
are proportional to
the forces in those
directions, so that
the power P is to the
weight G as G Y is to
G V, or as A C is to
A B; the triangles

Fig. 48.

G V W, W Y G, and A B C, being all obviously similar. Hence, if two weights balance each other on two inclined planes of the same height (as in Fig. 48), the weights must be directly proportioned to the lengths of the planes on which they rest.

79. In the foregoing examples the power acts in a direction parallel with the surface of the plane, for if the plane be supposed to be without friction, this is the most advantageous way of applying it.* If it act in any other direction, such as W D,

* Because the whole effect of the power is exerted in drawing the weight up the plane; whereas, if the power be directed *above* the plane, as in fig. 49,
Mechanics,

Fig. 49, we get the proportion of the power P to the weight
w by drawing w F perpendicular to the plane A C, W E the

Fig. 49.

vertical of the centre of
gravity of w, and E F parallel
to w D. Now the two forces
P and w must be propor-
tional to the lines w D and
w E, or they will not compound a pressure w F per-
pendicular to the plane,
which is necessary to maintain equilibrium.

If the power act parallel to the base of the plane, as in the
direction w D, Fig. 50, its proportion to the weight will be that
of the height of the plane to the base, for if w E be the vertical
of the centre of gravity of w, and w D parallel to the base in the
direction of the power, then w F will be the resultant of the
weight and power, and must (to preserve equilibrium) be

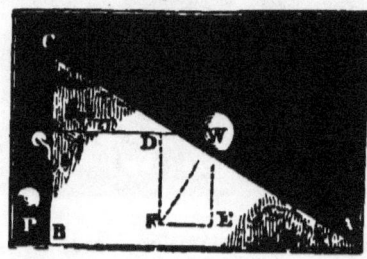

Fig. 50.

perpendicular to the plane ;
but this cannot be the case
unless the triangles D F W,
w F E, be each similar to
the triangle B A C; therefore the power will be represented by the height c B,
the weight by the base B A,
and the pressure by the
length A c.

80. Such are the most important properties of the inclined
plane, to which the principle of virtual velocities is as appli-

it is partly expended in diminishing the pressure, and partly in drawing it
up the plane. If the power be directed below the plane, as in fig. 50, it
is partly expended in increasing the pressure, the remaining part only being
efficient in drawing the weight up the plane. It will be seen hereafter that
if friction be taken into consideration, the direction in which the power acts
with most advantage is altered.

cable as to the other mechanical powers already considered. Let the weight a, Fig. 47, be at the foot of the plane, and the power P at the top; then let P descend until a arrive at the top of the plane. Of course P will have descended through a depth equal to the *length* of the plane, while a will have ascended through a depth equal to its *height;* hence the *perpendicular* spaces through which the weight and power move in the same time are in the proportion of their velocities. The proportion of the weight to the power is that of the length to the height; hence the power and the weight are reciprocally as their virtual velocities. P multiplied by the space through which it moves is equal to w multiplied by the space through which it moves. Hence, if the height of the plane be 2 feet, and its length 50 feet, P will have to descend 50 feet, while w is raised 2 feet in vertical height; and accordingly P must, as we have seen, exceed $\frac{1}{25}$ of the weight of w in order to effect this. In this example we have supposed the power to act parallel to the surface of the plane. If it act in any other direction, the principle of virtual velocities will still be found to apply.

81. Some of the grandest examples of inclined planes are to be found in roads, the inclination of which, when they are not level, is expressed by the height corresponding to a certain length. Thus, when it is said that a certain road has a rise of 1 in 20, &c., it is meant, that if 20 yards or feet, or 20 of any other units, be measured upon the road, the difference in level between the two extremities of the distance measured is 1 such unit.* On a level road the power is expended merely to overcome friction; and on the same road it always bears a constant ratio to the load. This ratio varies on common roads, according to their goodness, from $\frac{1}{18}$ to $\frac{1}{40}$ or $\frac{1}{36}$ of the load;

* The object of road-making is to render the inclined planes (which are naturally short and numerous) as few and long as possible, by throwing several into one. Single planes, however, of any considerable length, can rarely be obtained. There is said to be none longer than that from Lima to Callao, which is about 6 miles and has a descent of 511 feet. or about 1 in 60.

but on an iron railway it is no more than $\frac{1}{150}$ or $\frac{1}{200}$ thereof, according to the dryness or dampness of the rails.*   Now, on a road rising 1 in 20, the power (a horse, for example) has not only to overcome friction, but has really to lift $\frac{1}{20}$ of the load.   So that if the whole force required on a level road were $\frac{1}{18}$ of the load, on this rise it would become $\frac{1}{18} + \frac{1}{20}$, or would be not quite double the force required on the level.   But suppose that, instead of a common road, it were a railway, and that the force required on the level were only $\frac{1}{160}$ of the load, then on the inclined plane we should require $\frac{1}{160} + \frac{1}{20} = \frac{9}{160}$, or eight times the power required on the level.   Hence, the reason that steep planes are so much less admissible on railroads than on common roads; and it is often necessary in road-making, and especially railroad-making, to take a circuitous route rather than carry the road over a steep hill.   So also, a careful driver, in ascending a steep hill, will wind fiom side to side of the road to save his horses, knowing practically that in ascending a certain height the exertion is less by increasing the distance, which is done by this zigzag motion.   The reasons for this practice, however, belong rather to physiology than to Mechanics, because, mechanically, the whole exertion required to lift the load to a given height must be the same, whether the route be long or short; and the exertion required to overcome the friction must be greater, the longer the journey.

It was seen in Fig. 48 that a weight upon one inclined plane may be made to raise or support a weight upon another inclined plane.   It is not necessary that the two inclines should form an angle with each other, as in the figure.   They may be in any position, and be connected by a rope passing over wheels, &c.   Thus, in some railways, loaded waggons are made to descend one incline, and the force of

---

* Hence, a carriage left to itself on an inclined road will not roll down unless the inclination exceed 1 in 20, or 1 in 40 (according to its smoothness), but on a railway it will roll down an inclination of 1 in 150 or 200.   For particulars respecting *sliding* friction, see " Rudiments of Civil Engineering," Part I. pp. 31—35.

their descent serves to draw another set of waggons up another incline.

82. Instead of lifting a load by moving it along an inclined plane, we may effect the same thing by thrusting an inclined plane under the load. A moveable inclined plane is called a *wedge*, and it has sometimes been raised to the dignity of a distinct mechanical power. In its simplest form, as used for raising weights (such as shores placed to support buildings, the centres for arches, &c.), its theory is precisely similar to that of Fig. 50, in which, instead of drawing the load in the direction w D, we may draw the moveable inclined plane (or *wedge*) A B C, in the opposite direction D W; and if w be free to move only vertically up and down, it will obviously be raised through a height equal to B C by the motion of the wedge through a space equal to B A. In the wedge or moveable inclined plane (omitting the consideration of friction), the moving power must bear to the resistance moved, the ratio which the height of the plane bears to its *base*, and not (as in the fixed inclined plane, Fig. 47) the ratio of the height to the *length*. In the fixed plane, therefore, the power always balances a load greater than itself, however steep the slope may be; but in the wedge, the power and the load will be equal if the slope be 45°; and if it be steeper than this, the power will have to exceed the load. Thus, when the centring for an arch descends by displacing the wedges on which it rests, a great power expends itself in overcoming a very small resistance, viz., that arising from the friction of the wedges; and, generally speaking, it is not able to overcome even that resistance.

83. As the wedge is commonly used for separating two surfaces that are pressed together by some force which constitutes the resistance, we must regard it in this case as a *double* wedge, or two inclined planes joined base to base. Such a wedge is generally used for cleaving timber, in which case it is urged by percussion. As regards its efficiency as a machine, the same rule has been applied to it

as to other simple machines; the force acting on the wedge being considered to move through its length $d\,c$, while the resistance yields to the extent of its breadth A B. The force of percussion

(as will presently be explained) differs so completely from continued forces, such as have hitherto been considered, that it admits of no numerical comparison with them; i. e., the proportion between a blow and a pressure cannot be defined; so that the theory of the wedge, as given in scientific mechanics, is of scarcely any practical value; and, besides this, the value of the wedge often depends upon that which is omitted in its theory, namely, the friction between its surfaces and the substance which they divide, as in the case of nails, bolts, and pins, used for binding substances together. Indeed, if it were not for friction, the wedge would recoil after every blow; hence the friction, in this case, has been aptly compared to the ratchet-wheel (Fig. 31). which allows the intermission of the power without loss of effect.

84. The wedge is especially useful where a very great force is required to be exerted through a very small space. A tall chimney, which, through some defect in the foundation, has fallen from the perpendicular, has been restored by means of the wedge. A ship is often raised in dock by wedges driven under its keel. The wedge is the chief power used in the oil-mill, where oil is obtained from seeds by enormous pressure. Masses of timber and stone are also split by means of the wedge. The application of the wedge is most extensive in cutting and piercing instruments, such as razors, knives, chisels, awls, pins, needles, &c. The angle of the wedge is made to vary according to the purpose to which the instrument is to be applied. The mechanical power of the wedge is increased by diminishing its angle, but, in proportion as this is done, the strength of the tool is diminished

Accordingly, the angle of the wedge is made to vary in different tools; in those used for cutting wood it is generally about 30°; for cutting iron, it is from 50° to 60°; and for brass, from 80° to 90°.

85. Another variety of moveable inclined plane, commonly regarded as the sixth and last simple machine, is called the *screw*. In the case of the inclined plane, its mechanical effect is not impaired by giving it a curved instead of a straight course. Whether it be made to wind round a hill, or proceed in a straight line to the summit, is a matter of no consequence, except that the winding incline will be longer and easier than the shorter and steeper one. Now, the screw is nothing more than an inclined plane winding round a cylinder, and bearing the same relation to the ordinary inclined plane, that a circular staircase does to a straight one. The cylinder constitutes the body of the screw, and the inclined plane is called its *worm* or *thread*.

The screw, then, is an inclined plane, constructed upon the surface of a cylinder; and the usual method of forming it is at the turning lathe, in which a cylinder of wood, or metal, is made to revolve upon its axis; and a cutting point being presented to it, is moved in the direction of the length of the cylinder, at such a rate as to be carried through the dis-

Fig. 52.

tance A B between two turns of the thread, while the cylinder revolves once. The shape of the thread may be square or triangular: the former is the stronger, but the latter has least friction, because there is least surface to rub.

86. In the application of the screw, the power is usually transmitted by causing the screw to move through a hollow cylinder, or *nut*, N, on the interior surface of which are a

number of threads, exactly corresponding to those on the screw. The threads of the screw move in the spaces be-tween the threads of the nut, and *vice versâ*. The power is applied, either to turn the nut while the screw is prevented from turning, or to turn the screw while the nut is kept from turning. Neither can be done without producing a longi-tudinal motion of one or the other, whichever meets with least longitudinal resistance ; but this resistance may exceed the turning power, in the proportion that the revolving motion exceeds the longitudinal motion. Thus we gain power by losing motion, as in all other cases where power appears to be increased.

87. In the method of applying the screw shown in the above figure, we get really a compound machine, consisting of the lever and the screw. The power is applied to the end of the lever at P, while the weight or pressure, w, is sustained by the screw, as in the common screw-press. Now, supposing the distance A B, between any two threads of the screw, to be half an inch, and the circumference of the circle described by turning round the end of the lever P to be 5 feet, or 60 inches, or 120 half-inches ; then, a force or pressure of 1 lb. at P would sustain 120 lbs. at w. This is, of course, omit-ting the effect of friction, which in the case of the screw is very great.* The condition of equilibrium, therefore, is, that the power, multiplied by the circumference which it describes, is equal to the weight, or resistance, multiplied by the distance the screw or nut can move longitudinally during one turn, *i. e.*, the distance between the centres, or other cor-responding parts, of two contiguous threads, or rather turns of the same thread,† which distance is called the *pitch* of

* It is almost always sufficient by itself (as in the wedge) to balance the longitudinal force w without any assistance at P. Thus, it generally happens that *no* longitudinal force is sufficient to turn the screw, for its threads would be destroyed rather than turn.

† In Fig. 52 this distance is twice A B, because the screw is *double-threaded*. Screws with more than one thread are occasionally (though

the screw. Or, the power : the weight :: the distance between two contiguous threads : the circumference described by the power; which agrees with the principle of virtual velocities.

It will be seen from this, that we may increase the mechanical efficacy of the screw, either by causing the power to move through a greater space, by increasing the length of the lever; or, secondly, by increasing the number of turns of the thread, the effect of which will be to bring them closer together. Thus, in the above example, if the pitch were $\frac{1}{4}$ instead of $\frac{1}{2}$ an inch, the other conditions remaining the same, the efficacy of the machine would be doubled, and the power of 1 lb. would sustain 240 lbs., instead of 120 lbs.

88. There is, however, a practical difficulty in increasing the number of turns in the thread of a screw, for, as they become crowded into a small space, they become more delicate, and are apt to be torn off under a considerable force, while, if the length of the lever be increased, the machine becomes unwieldy. These objections have been entirely got rid of by the ingenious contrivance of the *differential* screw by Mr. John Hunter, the celebrated surgeon. A B, Fig. 53, is a nut, or plate of metal, in which the screw C D plays. We will suppose the number of threads in this screw to be 10 in every inch. This screw C D is a hollow nut, receiving the smaller screw D E, which contains, we will suppose, 11 threads in every inch; this smaller screw is free to move longitudinally, but is prevented from moving round with the former, by means of the frame-work A F G B of the press. Now

very rarely) made. They are only useful in cases where a longitudinal force is to produce rotary motion. For instance, the interior of a rifle-barrel is a screw, or rather *nut* of this kind, intended to impart to the ball a rotation round the line of its motion; the use of which is, to prevent a rotation round *any other* axis, which usually takes place in other projectiles, and (unless they be perfectly spherical) increases the resistance they encounter.

Fig. 53.

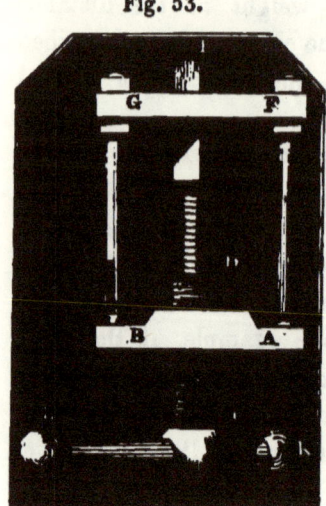

if the handle C K L be turned round 10 times, the screw C D will move 1 inch upwards; and if the smaller screw D E were to move with C D, the point E would advance an inch. If we then turned the screw D E alone 10 times backwards, the point E would move down $\frac{10}{11}$ths of an inch; and the result of both motions would have been to lift the point E $\frac{1}{11}$th of an inch upwards. But if the screw C D is turned 10 times round, while D E is kept from turning, the effect will be the same as if it had moved 10 times round with C D, and then have been turned back again ten times without C D; that is, it will advance $\frac{1}{11}$th of an inch, and at one turn instead of 10 it will advance $\frac{1}{10}$th of $\frac{1}{11}$th, or $\frac{1}{110}$th of an inch. If, therefore, the lever at K move through a whole circumference of a circle, the part E, which acts directly upon the weight, is moved through a space equal to the *difference* between the pitch of the thread of C D and that of D E; whence the name of the arrangement. If we suppose the handle to be only 6 inches long, the power of this machine will be expressed by the number of times the 110th of an inch is contained in the circumference of a circle of 6 inches radius, or 12 inches diameter. Now, by multiplying the diameter of a circle by 3.1416, we get its circumference; and

$$12 \times 3.1416 = 37.6992 \times 110 = 4146.912;$$

so that, by moving the power once round with the force, say of 1 lb., the screw is raised through the 110th part of an inch, with a force of 4147 lbs. nearly; which shows the superiority of this over the common screw; for, in the latter, to gain the same power, there must be 110 threads in an inch, which would render them too weak to resist any considerable force.

In the usual method of applying Hunter's screw, the two threads are cut on different parts of the same cylinder. Upon these are placed nuts, which are capable of moving in the direction of the length, but are not allowed to turn round. It is clear, therefore, that by turning the screw once round, the two nuts will be brought nearer together, or driven farther apart, according to the direction in which the screw is turned, through a space equal to the difference of the pitch of the two threads. In this way, Hunter's screw is well adapted to the purposes of a *micrometer screw*, because it admits of an indefinitely slow motion, without requiring exquisite workmanship in the thread. The uses of the screw as a micrometer have been noticed in our "Introduction to the Study of Natural Philosophy."

89. Fig. 54 is a contrivance usually described, in books on Mechanics, while speaking of the screw. It is called the *endless*, or *perpetual* screw, from having no longitudinal motion, and therefore no limit to its range; but is really a complex machine, being compounded of the screw and the wheel. The thread of the screw is so arranged as to act upon the teeth of the wheel, which are placed obliquely to its

Fig. 54.

axle, like the sails of a windmill; and, in fact, may be regarded as forming exceedingly short portions of the threads of a many-threaded screw, of which the wheel forms a very thin slice, perpendicular to its axis. This wheel bears the same relation to the *nut*, whose place it supplies, that the spur-wheel (Fig. 33) bears to the *rack* (Fig. 30). If the common screw be allowed no motion but that of rotation, its nut must move longitudinally; and the teeth of this wheel move longitudinally with regard to the small cylinder, but the wheel renders this motion circular, and therefore unlimited. The cylinder, on which the screw is cut, being set in motion by a winch, or other means, produces a motion of the wheel upon its own axis, which may be in any direction. The relation between the power and the resistance, supposing the circles which they describe to be *equal*, will be as unity to the number of teeth in the wheel; for each turn of the screw only moves the wheel through the space of one tooth. Hence, if the power and the resistance act with different leverage, or at different distances from their respective axes of motion, the moment of the load, with regard to the axis of the wheel, may exceed the moment of the power, with regard to the axis of the screw, as many times as the wheel has teeth. For instance, let the wheel have 30 teeth : let the power act on a winch 1 foot long, and the load be a weight hanging from a barrel of 3 inches diameter ; then the power applied to the circumference of the wheel must be 8 times the load (for 1 foot $\div$ 1½ inch $=$ 8); but, as there are 30 teeth in the wheel, the load on the winch of the screw may exceed the power 30 times 8 $=$ 240 times. This elegant machine has obviously far less friction than the ordinary screw; and it is, perhaps, the most compact method ever invented for effecting a great change of velocity, and a consequent concentration or diffusion of power, according as the screw is made to turn the wheel, as in a barrel-organ, or the wheel the screw, as in a roasting-jack. It would require a train of 3 or 4 pairs of wheels and pinions to produce the change here effected by *one* wheel of the same size ; for, as a pinion cannot have less than 6 or 8 teeth, it will turn a wheel 6 or 8 times faster than the same wheel would be turned by this screw, which may be regarded as a pinion of only *one* tooth ; and, conversely, the wheel will turn the screw 6 or 8 times, while it would be turning a pinion once. But these advantages are greatly counterbalanced, by the fact that the action between the wheel and the screw is necessarily a *rubbing*, and not a *rolling* action, as that between the wheel and pinion should be (page 58), and thus it leads to far more rapid wear.

The most important applications of Statics to the equilibrium of *fixed* structures are treated of in "Rudiments of Civil Engineering."

90. In concluding this notice of the mechanical powers or elements, we may observe that none of them can be regarded as artificial inventions; they are all copied from Nature's mechanism. The *lever*, as we have seen, is the general machine employed in animal movements. The *wheel*, also, is found in some of the lower infusorial animals. The cord-and-*pulley* principle is employed in our tendons, some of which have their direction changed by passing over fixed pulleys of cartilage, like the ring in Fig. 36.* *Inclined planes* and *wedges* constitute the cutting-teeth, tusks, horns, and other offensive weapons of animals. Some of the smallest animals are furnished with *screws*, or gimlets, by which they pierce the hardest woods, and even stone; and the screw appears to be employed throughout nature, from the huge weapon of the narwhal, down to the minutest microscopic vessels of plants, not as a mechanical power, but as a constructive form, uniting strength with lightness and beauty.† Nor does it seem absent from the inorganic world; for, among the mysterious relations of light, electricity, and magnetism, are found some which point to screw-like properties, or actions, in the elementary molecules of matter. Magnets, and electric currents, exhibit mutual actions comparable to nothing else but those of the screw and its nut; and light is subject, by the action of certain crystals, and (as Faraday has lately discovered, by this same force of magnetism also), to a kind of polarization, called *circular*, which possesses screw-like properties.

* One of the muscles by which the eyeball is moved is called the *trochlearis*, from the *trochlea* or pulley through which the tendon passes.

† Nature presents us with two species of screws, possessing opposite longitudinal motions, when their rotations are alike; or opposite rotations, when their longitudinal motions are alike. Convenience dictates, however, that all artificial screws should be of the same kind, and this kind is called *right-handed*. An example of the contrary, or left-handed screw, occurs in the tendrils of the hop.

PART II.—DYNAMICS.

I. ON DYNAMICAL, OR UNBALANCED FORCES—INSTANTANEOUS FORCES OR IMPACTS.

91. WHEN the forces or pressures which have been considered in the science of Statics cease to be balanced, the body on which they act is set in motion; in which case, other principles become involved in addition to those considered in statics, and the investigation of these constitutes the somewhat more complex science of Dynamics.*

Statics is a deductive science, all the facts which it considers being deducible, like those of arithmetic or geometry, from abstract truths. The only difference between these sciences consists in the number of these abstract truths or ideas which are taken into consideration. In arithmetic, the simplest of them, we admit only the idea of *number ;*† in geometry we add to this the ideas of *space* and *direction ;* and in statics we have to add yet another fundamental idea, that of *force* or *pressure.* In dynamics we have further to introduce the ideas (inseparably dependent on each other) of *time* and *motion ;* but in doing so we have also to depart from the province of pure deduction, and to admit truths which are not perceived by the mind to be necessary, but

---

* This word being derived from δύναμις, *force* or *power*, would properly include all the mechanical sciences, but custom has restricted it to that of motion, and placed it in opposition to Statics, which equally relates to forces.

† In fractional arithmetic, indeed, and still further in algebra, or universal arithmetic, by a gradual extension of this idea, it is converted into the more comprehensive one of *magnitude* or *quantity.*

which depend on what are called *laws of nature*, and can only be proved by an appeal to those laws, *i. e.*, by *experiment*. Thus, dynamics stands at the head of the physical, experimental, or *inductive* sciences, and is, as far as regards its inductive part, the simplest of them all. Indeed, the facts of this science, which had to be established inductively, were so few and simple, that they were all completely established more than two centuries ago, thus leaving the science to be pursued entirely by the method of deduction; while in no other inductive science can it be said that the induction is yet complete, or even likely soon to approach completion.*

92. Of the abstract ideas above mentioned, such as *number*, *space*, *time*, *pressure*, *motion*, it is neither necessary nor possible to give satisfactory definitions. We shall not, therefore, introduce the reader into Dynamics by attempting to define *motion*, any more than on introducing him into Statics we attempted to define *force*.

As the degree or intensity of motion may vary to any extent, this intensity, which is called *velocity*, may be treated like any other magnitude; that is to say, velocities may be compared with each other like pressures (4), so that their ratios may be represented by those of lines, areas, numbers, or any other class of magnitudes. But we must here observe, that in representing velocities by numbers, we have no standard or unit which has been agreed upon, and distinguished by a particular name, as the pound, ounce, &c., for comparing pressures, or the foot, inch, &c., for comparing lengths. Now this seemingly trivial fact leads to more circumlocution, and to the mathematical reader to more unnecessary difficulty in the outset of this subject, than might at first be supposed. For instance, as we cannot form the conception of a motion without associating with it some *time* during which it lasts: the velocity may be constant or *uniform*

---

* Astronomy, or rather that portion of it which may seem an exception to this statement, can only be regarded as a branch of Dynamics.

throughout that time ; or it may be continually *accelerated* or *retarded*, in which cases the velocity at any one moment will be different from that which occurs in the preceding or succeeding moment. Now, as there is no fixed unit of velocity, we must use *two* numbers to express a velocity, for we can only represent it in numbers by using the units of two other kinds of magnitude, *time* and *length*. Thus, we speak of a velocity of 12 miles an hour, or of a mile in 5 minutes; meaning, in the first case, that *if* the motion continued *uniform* for 1 hour, the space described would be 12 miles; or, in the second, that *if* the motion continued uniform through 1 mile, the time elapsed would be 5 minutes. But this evidently applies only to uniform motions; so that, in expressing the velocity of a variable motion at any given instant, though in reality we have nothing to do with any other instant, in which the velocity is different, yet we are obliged to assume that it continues uniform through a certain time or space, and then state what the corresponding space or time would be upon this assumption.

The method of ascertaining the velocity of a motion at one given instant, when it is constantly increasing or diminishing, is a subject into which we cannot now enter. We hope presently to be able to make the reader understand the simplest case of this problem; but we may observe that its general treatment in more complex cases is at once so difficult and so important, as to have been beyond the reach of all the mathematics of the ancients, and to have been the immediate object of the invention of fluxions by Newton, and of the differential calculus by Leibnitz—the two greatest achievements ever made in abstract reasoning, and also the most useful ; for the whole subsequent progress of exact science has depended on them.

93. In statics, force was regarded simply as that which is necessary to oppose or balance force. We are now to regard it, not as it is sometimes defined, *the cause of motion*, but as *the cause of change of motion*. It is to the false idea of

force conveyed in the former definition that we may trace the origin of nearly all the errors in mechanical reasoning committed before the establishment of the true principles of dynamics, and still fallen into when these principles are neglected. The reader must regard it as fully established, that *force*, in the sense in which we have already used it in statics, is not required for the maintenance of motion, but only for its *change*—*i. e.*, for effecting, 1st, a change of *state* from rest to motion, or from motion to rest;* 2nd, a change in the *velocity* of motion, either by accelerating or retarding it; or, 3rd, a change in its *direction*, by deflecting it upwards, downwards, to the right, or to the left. The inertia of matter is only another mode of impressing this idea. And since matter is inert, that is, has no tendency either to rest or motion,† a body impressed with a motion must persist in that motion, in a straight line and with uniform velocity, for ever, unless some new force act upon it, either to change its state, its direction, or its velocity; for it cannot of itself change either its state of rest or its state of motion, its velocity or its direction. This cannot, indeed (like the facts of statics), be discovered by *à priori* reasoning, but is inferred from experiments and observations on all the motions producible by us, or presented to our notice either in the heavens or on the earth, and is known to be true, because any other law which can be substituted for it will be incompatible with some or all of those motions.

94. We are therefore to regard as being in equilibrium, not only such bodies as are at rest, but also such as are performing uniform rectilinear motion; for it is only while their velocity or direction is changing (*i. e.*, while they are being accelerated, retarded, or moving in a curve) that the forces acting on them can be unbalanced, or can produce a resultant

---

* This effect, however, never comes under our observation, because we know of no body in the universe in a state of absolute rest. All the observable effects of force, therefore, are included in the expression *change of motion.*

. † See "Introduction to Natural Philosophy."

pressure; and as long as this pressure remains unbalanced, the motion will continue changing in velocity, or direction, or both; whenever it becomes straight and uniform, the resultant of all the forces acting on the body = 0, or it is not subject to any unbalanced force. Thus, when a train or a steam-boat has been started, its velocity continues for a certain time to increase, because the forces that urge it forward exceed the friction in one case, or the resistance of the water against the bows of the boat in the other; but these opposing forces are dependent on the velocity, and increase because it increases, so that they presently become equal to the forward force imparted by the engines, and then the motion becomes uniform, and the body, although moving at its full speed, is as completely in equilibrium as when it was at rest. Thus, the motive power is required, not to maintain the *motion*, but to maintain *equilibrium* with the opposing friction or resistance. The motion is maintained because the body has been set in motion, and, being inert, has no tendency of itself to alter that state; and also because any alteration of velocity (whether an increase or diminution) would, by increasing or diminishing the resistance, while the steam-power remains unaltered, leave a portion of the former or of the latter unbalanced, and this unbalanced force acting against or with the direction of the motion, would retard or accelerate it till the former velocity was re-established. Thus the equilibrium is stable, or tends, when disturbed, to restore itself.

Similar to this is the case of a parachute or of a drop of rain, which being subject to the constant force of gravity, falls with constantly *increasing* velocity, till the resistance of the air against its fall becomes equal to its weight, which is thenceforth expended in balancing that resistance, so that its velocity continues *uniform*. But in falling bodies generally this equilibrium is never attained, so that their velocity continues to be accelerated throughout their fall.

95. The dynamical effect of force, then, being a change in motion, it will readily be seen that a continued force or

pressure, such as we have hitherto been chiefly considering, must produce a continuous change, whether in velocity or direction (which must in this case be curved). The simpler effect of a sudden change of velocity, or an angular deflection, can only be produced by an *impact*, or instantaneous exertion of force, such as was mentioned when speaking of the wedge (83); and to this kind of force we will, therefore, for the present confine ourselves.

96. The greater part of the forces which impart motion to a body act directly upon only a few of its molecules : thus, when a billiard ball is struck with the cue, we touch only a small portion of its surface; when a bullet is projected from a gun, the gases suddenly evolved from the powder act upon only one hemisphere of the bullet. As all the parts of a body are set in motion by an impulse communicated to a few only of its molecules, it is clear that there must be a diffusion of motion from the parts struck or acted on over all the other parts of the body before it can begin to move. When this is not the case, the part struck is compressed, flattened, or it is chipped off, and performs its journey alone, leaving the mass behind; but when the force has time to be propagated through all the particles, the body is then impressed with a motion common to all its particles. This diffusion of motion from particle to particle requires *time;* the time may be exceedingly short, but not infinitely so; it depends upon the extent of matter to be moved, and also upon its nature, such as whether it be metal, stone, clay, wood, water, air, &c.*

When a force has acted upon a body, and the motion has diffused itself over all the molecules, so as to impress them with a common velocity, the force has done its work ; it has produced its effect, and may be said to have passed from the moving power, or source of motion, into the thing moved. Thus a stone projected by the hand, by a cross-bow, by a sudden blow, or by an explosion, describes a certain path in space in obedience to the force which has acted upon it once

* See " Rudimentary Pneumatics"—Sound.

for all, and then ceased, leaving the force thus impressed to do its work. Now, if the stone in its progress met with no other form of matter, neither with air, nor with water, nor any other fluid, neither with any solid body at rest or in motion—if, in short, no other force acted upon it, it would continue to move with the same velocity and in the same direction for ever.

97. The moving body, then, retains the impression of the force to which it has been subjected, and we may naturally conclude that the same force would not produce the same effects on different bodies. The charge of powder capable of projecting a small shot, for example, may scarcely produce the slightest motion in a cannon-ball. It may be said that the reason for this is, that the ball is so much heavier than the shot; but if this were the true reason, it would follow that if bodies of all kinds were deprived of weight, or had their weight neutralized by being suspended or balanced, they might all be set moving with equal velocity by the same impact. This would certainly not be true, for it is an estab-lished principle in mechanics, that when the same force acts upon different bodies free to move, their velocities are in the inverse ratio of their masses, or of the quantity of matter of which they are composed. Thus the same charge of gun-powder which would project leaden balls whose volumes or masses were as 1, 2, 3, 4, &c., would impart velocities to them as the numbers 1, $\frac{1}{2}$, $\frac{1}{3}$, $\frac{1}{4}$, &c., so that the ball whose mass is 10 would acquire from the same force a velocity of $\frac{1}{10}$th; the mass equal to 100 would have a velocity 100 times less than that of a mass equal to 1, and so on;* hence it will be seen that the mass multiplied into the velocity gives in each case the same number: in the first case, $1 \times 1 = 1$; in the second, $2 \times \frac{1}{2} = 1$, and so on. This product of the mass of a moving body by its velocity, is called the *momen-tum*, or *moving force*, or *quantity of motion*. In speaking of

* When there is no friction, the smallest impact is sufficient to impart motion to the largest mass; but only, of course, a very slow motion.

multiplying a velocity by a weight, we of course mean only
that the units of weight (ounces or pounds, for example)
are to be multiplied by the units of velocity (feet per second,
or miles per hour, for example); and it matters not what
units of each kind are employed, for the product thus obtained means nothing by itself, but only by comparison with
other products similarly obtained by the use of the same
units; and the result of this comparison will be the same,
whatever units are employed. The momenta, or quantities
of motion, in any number of bodies, found in this way, will
bear the same ratios to each other, whether all their weights
be measured in ounces or in tons; their velocities in inches
or in miles, and by the second or by the hour, provided,
always, that they are all measured in the *same* manner. It
appears, then, that the same impact always gives the same
quantity of motion, whatever may be the body which it
impels; so that the true measure and characteristic of an
instantaneous force or impact, is the quantity of motion it is
capable of imparting. Thus, we may describe an impact by
saying that it is equal to 50 lbs. moved 1 foot per second,
or 1 lb. moved 50 feet per second, or 2 lbs. moving 25 feet
per second, &c. &c., all meaning the same thing.

98. In ordinary language, the *force* of any moving body
means its momentum, or the impact required to stop it, or to
impart the same quantity of motion to a body previously at
rest.* Hence, we see:—1. That when equal masses are
in motion, their forces are proportional to their velocities.
2. That when the velocities are equal, the forces are proportional to the masses, or quantities of matter. 3. That
when neither the masses nor velocities are equal, the forces
are in the proportion of both taken jointly, that is, the proportion of their products.

---

* But the useful effect is in most cases proportional not to the *momentum*, but to the *vis viva*, for which see " Rudiments of Civil Engineering,"
Part I. p. 24.

99. These theorems may be illustrated by the apparatus shown in Fig. 55. Two balls of clay, A, B, or of some other comparatively inelastic substance,* are suspended by strings,

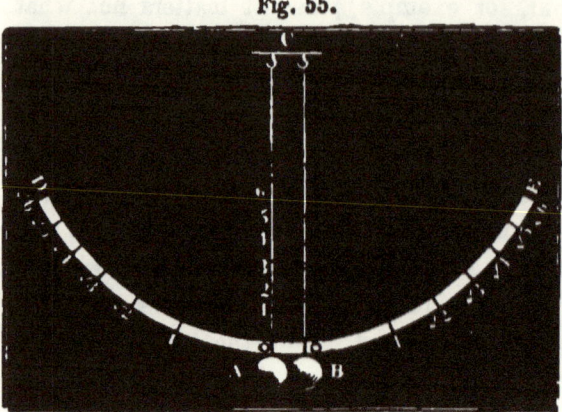

Fig. 55.

so as to hang in contact at the middle of a graduated arc. The arc should be cy-cloidal and di-vided, not in-to equal parts, but as shown in the figure; *viz.*, so that the numbers 1, 2, 3, &c., may be proportional to the perpendicular heights above the level of the point o. Now it will be proved presently, in treating of gravity,—1. That when a ball thus suspended is let fall from any point of the arc, its velocity will be the same whatever may be its mass. 2. That this velocity will continually increase till it reaches the point o. 3. That on arriving there, its velocity will be proportional to the square root of the vertical height which it has descended. 4. That if it start from o with this same velocity, it will ascend to the same height from which it must have fallen to have acquired that velocity, and no higher; because its velocity is, by the action of gravity, constantly diminished, till at this precise height it is destroyed. The velocities of the balls, therefore, at the moment of their arrival at, or departure from, the point o, may be exactly measured by noting the divisions on the scale from which they have descended, or to which they ascend, provided the 4th division be reckoned 2, the 9th division, 3, &c. Now, suppose these balls to be equal in mass, and to be moved in opposite directions,

* Wax softened by the addition of one-fourth its weight of oil answers very well.

A towards D, and B towards E, and then allowed to fall at the same moment: if the balls fall through equal arcs, they will of course impinge upon each other with equal velocities, and each will destroy the force of the other, and remain at rest;* for *equal masses* having *equal velocities* must have *equal forces*.

Let us next suppose that the ball A is double the weight or mass of B; and let A be raised towards D as far as to the first division; and let B be raised towards E as far as the fourth division. When allowed to descend, at such an interval of time as to bring them both at once to the point o,† their velocities will be as $\sqrt{1}$: $\sqrt{4}$, or as 1 : 2; but as their masses are as 2 to 1, their forces will be as 2 × 1 to 1 × 2, or equal. Accordingly, after impact these two bodies will remain at rest, because the equal and opposite forces have destroyed each other. So also, if any balls have their masses inversely as their velocities, their forces will be equal, and they will consequently remain at rest after impact.

Again, suppose A and B to be unequal in mass, but equal in velocity; that A is twice the size of B, and that each is allowed to descend from the same height, at D and E; if the velocity of each be called 6, the quantity of motion in A may be expressed by 2 × 6 = 12, while that in B will be only 1 × 6 = 6. After impact the six parts of motion in B will destroy 6 parts of the 12 in A, leaving only six parts in both bodies. Now the combined mass of both being = 3, and their momentum = 6, their velocity must be $\frac{6}{3}$ = 2; so that both will move on together with a velocity of 2, that

---

* If the experiment be carefully performed with balls of clay, and the arcs be of considerable extent, so as to give a great velocity, the balls on impinging will penetrate each other, and form one ball. If the balls be of lead, they will, under the same circumstances, flatten each other, and then remain at rest.

† The exact adjustment of this interval renders the experiment difficult, unless the balls be made to follow a cycloidal arc, by confining the strings with cycloidal cheeks, in the manner described further on.

is, ⅛ of their velocity before impact; and this will carry them to ⅙ the height from which they descended. Similar results will be obtained when the balls are equal in mass, but have been raised to different divisions.

100. This experiment may be pleasingly varied by using balls of ivory, or some other elastic material; in which case, the quantities of motion which oppose each other are not *destroyed* (as with inelastic bodies), but *reversed;* or at least would be so if the elasticity of the bodies were perfect; but with all natural bodies a portion is destroyed and the rest reversed. The following effects, however, though never exhibited in perfection, may be very nearly imitated by the use of ivory balls. If the balls be equal, on removing A from the vertical up to any division, say $\sqrt{4}$, on the arc, and allowing it to descend and impinge on B, which is at rest, B receives the whole of A's motion, leaving A at rest, and starts off with the force of A, ascending the same number of degrees on the opposite scale that A had descended. Balls of clay or wax thus treated would have moved on both together to the division 1, because the same momentum being shared by twice as much matter, must impart to it half as much velocity. If the ball A has a different mass from B, greater or less, instead of being left quiescent after impact, it moves in the same direction with B if its mass be greater, or it rebounds in an opposite direction if it be less.*

* But in no case will the balls remain together. The quantities of motion gained by one and lost by the other being equal, while their masses are unequal, the velocities gained and lost will be inversely as their masses. When the velocity lost by the striking ball exceeds its whole velocity before the blow, this excess expresses its velocity in the opposite direction; for motion *lost*, or motion *gained in the opposite direction*, are the same thing. If a body moving northward at 10 miles an hour, have its velocity reduced to 3 miles an hour, it matters not whether we say it has lost 7 units of velocity northward, or gained 7 southward; and if its motion had been *reversed*, and become 3 miles an hour, we may either say that it has lost 13 units of northward velocity, or gained 13 of southward.

101. When a number of ivory balls of the same size are suspended, as in Fig. 56, and the first is removed from the vertical, and allowed to impinge upon the others, the last only, No. 7, is moved, and this starts off with the quantity of motion which No. 1 had the moment it struck No. 2. If the balls No. 1 and No. 2 be both raised from the vertical, and allowed to fall together, the last two, Nos. 6 and 7, will be raised.

Fig. 56.

102. In the foregoing cases we have considered the effects resulting from the impact of bodies advancing from opposite directions. Of course, bodies moving in the same direction may impinge if their velocities be different. Thus, if a non-elastic body be overtaken by another, the two bodies after impact will move with a common velocity. If they be equal in mass, half the sum of their velocities will be their common velocity after impact. Since the bodies move in the same direction, there can be no increase or diminution of motion by impact, but only a re-distribution. If before impact A move with the velocity of 5, and B with that of 3, the common velocity of the two bodies, after impact, will be 4, the half of the sum of 5 + 3.

Now suppose A and B to be unequal in mass, as well as in velocity. If the mass of A be 9 and its velocity 12, its quantity of motion will be 108. If the mass of B be 7, and its velocity 9, its quantity of motion will be 63. The sum of the two motions will therefore be 108 + 63 = 171; and this of course will be the whole motion of the united masses after impact. Dividing this, therefore, by the united masses (9 + 7 = 16), we find 171 ÷ 16 = 10$\frac{11}{16}$, the common velocity of the united masses. In general, therefore, when two masses moving in the same direction impinge one upon the other, and after impact move together, their common velocity may be determined by multiplying the numbers expressing the masses by the numbers which express the velocities; the sum of the two products thus obtained, divided by the sum of the numbers expressing the masses, will give a quotient expressing the required velocity.

103. When a moving body comes in contact with a body at rest, it can only continue its motion by pushing this body before it, and consequently communicating to it such a quantity of motion that after impact they move with a common velocity. If the mass of the moving body be equal to that of the body at rest, it is evident that after impact the motion will be equally divided between the two masses, and the velocity will now be only one-half, since the mass has been doubled. It will be only the third of the velocity, if the mass at rest is double that of the moving body; and in general, when a moving body communicates motion to a body at rest, the united velocity of the two bodies is to that of the moving body as the mass of the latter is to the sum of the masses of both. For example, if a musket-ball weigh $\frac{1}{20}$th of a pound, and its velocity on being fired be 1300 feet per second, if it strike a cannon-ball of 48 pounds, suspended as in Fig. 55, it will set it in motion; and the common velocity of the two is to that of the bullet as $\frac{1}{20}$ is to $48 + \frac{1}{20}$, or as 1 is to 961; the common velocity of the two is, therefore, $\frac{1300}{961}$, or about $1\frac{1}{3}$ feet per second.

When a musket-ball strikes against a large stone, or is fired at a mountain, it communicates both to the stone and to the mountain a certain velocity, small indeed, and not measureable unless we could know the mass of the mountain in addition to other particulars. The mass of a large stone, however, is easily found; suppose it to weigh 500 lbs., or that its mass equals 500, its velocity after impact with the musket-ball moving at the rate of 1300 feet per second, and weighing $\frac{1}{20}$th of a pound, will be to 1300 feet as $\frac{1}{20}$ is to $500 + \frac{1}{20}$, or as 1 is to 10001; so that the common velocity of the musket-ball and the stone after impact will be about

1½ inch per second, a motion which is speedily destroyed by resistance and friction: or rather, this motion is speedily absorbed by surrounding bodies, and even by the mass of the earth. Hence it may be said that motion communicates itself among material bodies, and is never lost; when it appears to be so, it in fact only passes from the moving body into other bodies which are at rest, or are endued with a less velocity, and at length it becomes insensible in consequence of its enormous diffusion. In fact, as we have seen, motion can only be destroyed by motion; resistances and friction disperse it, but do not destroy it.

104. The velocity of projectiles is measured on the principles of impact, by a large mass of wood, or of metal, suspended with as little friction as possible, by a bar of iron, and called a *ballistic pendulum* (Fig. 57). The cannon-ball whose velocity is to be determined is fired against the solid block of this pendulum, and the height to which it is made to oscillate by the blow · is shown by an index on a wooden arc, and determines the velocity with which the mass first began to move, when its quantity of motion was equal to that with which the ball struck it. In the next section it will be shown

Fig. 57.

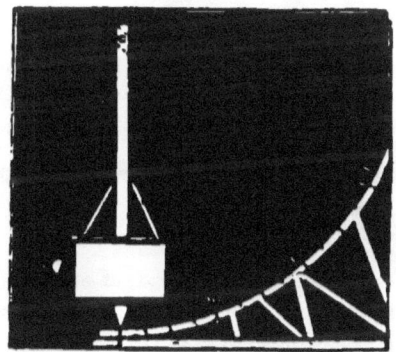

how this is determined, but we may here observe that the velocity at starting is proportional to the square root of the vertical height ascended (99), whatever may be the curve; when that curve is circular, as in this instance, the velocities are as the *chords* of the arcs described; so that if the arc be so graduated that the numbers are proportional to their distances in a straight line from 0, they will correctly express the relative velocities at starting from 0.

Persons who are fond of the marvellous sometimes relate

facts respecting the effects of musket-shots and cannon-balls which are not generally believed, although they are simple consequences of the principles we are now considering. Thus, a musket-ball will pass through a window-pane without cracking the glass, leaving only a clear round hole. If the musket-ball were thrown by hand, the whole pane would be shattered; but with the usual velocity of a musket-ball, that portion of the glass actually struck alone yields to the blow, and the ball has done its work before the surrounding parts have time to share the motion.* If the window-pane were suspended by a silken thread, the shot would only carry away so much of the glass as would allow it space to pass through, without even breaking the thread, or causing it to oscillate. A sheet of paper placed on edge may be perforated by a pistol-ball without being knocked down; and a door half-open may be pierced by a cannon-ball without being shut. M. Pouillet mentions a case where a cannon-ball carried off the extremity of a musket while it was in the soldier's hands without his feeling the stroke, just as the head of a thistle may be struck off by the rapid motion of a stick, without perceptibly bending the stalk. Nay, if the missile be soft, as tallow, it will act with the force of lead, if sufficient velocity be imparted to it. Thus, in the well-known trick of

---

* The *piercing* effects of such bodies are not proportional to their *moving* effects or *momenta*. For suppose two unequal balls (as a 6 and a 12-pounder) to have velocities inversely as their masses; their momenta will be equal (97), so that both will have the same power to move or over-turn an obstacle, but they will not penetrate a soft body to the same depth, that is, overcome a uniform resistance through the same space, for both will overcome the same resistance for *the same length of time*, and during this time the swifter ball will have penetrated twice as far as the other. To have equal piercing effects, therefore, their masses must be inversely as the *squares* of their velocities, so that their momenta multiplied into their velocities may be equal. This mode of estimating the effect by the product of the momentum and velocity, or the product of the mass multiplied *twice* by the velocity, is called the principle of *vis viva*. (See page 93, *note*.)

firing a piece of tallow candle through a board, the parts of the tallow cannot yield until after a certain time; during that time the tallow behaves like a hard solid, and before its particles have had time to yield, the tallow has already passed through the board. So, also, in firing a cannon-ball over the surface of a smooth sea, time is not allowed for the water to yield much, and consequently it behaves like a solid, and reflects the ball. In this way, it is said, that musket-balls have even been flattened.

105. In our Introduction to the Study of Natural Philosophy, some illustrations were given of what are called the laws of motion. It was there explained that every action is accompanied by a corresponding re-action, equal and contrary. In the discharge of a cannon, the elasticity of the gases suddenly liberated by the ignited gunpowder, acts equally in all directions: it acts on the sides with equal and opposite forces, which neutralize each other unless the cannon burst by yielding to one of them; the elasticity of the gases also acts towards the muzzle and the breach, and these two equal and opposite forces would also neutralize each other if the mouth of the cannon were effectually secured; but such not being the case, the ball and the wadding yield: the expansive forces of the gas towards the muzzle and the breach being equal produce an equal effect, the one upon the ball, and the other upon the cannon; the one moves forwards, and the other backwards. This latter motion is called the *recoil* of the gun; and the reason why the recoil produces so much less velocity than the shot receives from the opposite force, is the greater mass of the cannon and its appendages, as compared with the ball. When a sportsman fires a gun, the recoil on his shoulder is equal to that which would be produced by a shot entering the barrel and striking against its solid extremity, with the velocity with which the bullet leaves the same gun. Another proof of the comparative slowness with which motion is propagated through any considerable mass, is, that the recoil does not begin to be felt until the

.bullet has actually left the mouth of the cannon. The experiment in proof of this was performed, for the first time, at Rochelle, in 1667, by order of the Cardinal de Richelieu. A cannon was suspended horizontally, from the end of a very long vertical shaft, or lever, moveable freely about an axis at its other extremity. The ball fired from it under these circumstances struck the object towards which it was directed in precisely the same manner as it did when the cannon was fixed; showing that there could have been no sensible alteration of its position until the ball was discharged from it, otherwise it could not have hit the same point, but a point somewhat lower, depending upon the amount of recoil.

106. The resistance which a moving body meets with in the air, or in the water, is only an effect of the transference of motion. A body moving in water must constantly displace a portion of the fluid equal to its own bulk, and the amount of motion thus communicated to the water is so much lost by the moving body. It is generally admitted in such cases, for air as well as water, that the resistance is in proportion to the square of the velocity of the moving body. When the velocity is doubled, the loss of motion by resistance is quadrupled, because not only is there twice as much fluid to be moved in an equal time, but it has to be moved with twice the velocity. So, also, when the velocity is trebled, the moving body meets three times the number of particles, to which it communicates three times the velocity, thereby occasioning nine times the loss. The resistance to a body moving in water is, therefore, about 800 times greater than if it were moving with the same velocity in air, for it has to move 800 times as much matter in the same time. But if the motion in air were 28 times faster than in water, the resistance would be about the same, for 28 times the velocity generates 28 times 28 times (= 784 times) the resistance.

II.—EFFECTS OF CONTINUED FORCES—UNIFORMLY ACCELE-
RATED MOTION—DESCENT ON INCLINED PLANES AND CURVES
—THE PENDULUM.

107. ONE cannot fail to be struck with the different degrees of rapidity with which bodies fall through the air. A piece of gold falls rapidly, and a dry leaf very slowly; and the popular reason for this difference is, that the gold is heavy and the leaf light; this, however, is not the true reason, for if the gold be beaten out into a thin leaf, neither its absolute nor its specific weight is diminished (indeed, the latter is increased), but the time of its descent through the air is greatly prolonged. The fact is, that every body falling through a fluid is continually subject to two opposite forces, 1st, its *weight*, which is constantly uniform, and acting alone would constantly accelerate the fall, and 2nd, the *fluid resistance*, which, as we have seen, increases with the velocity, so that, however small at first, it must after a certain time (or when a certain velocity is acquired) become equal to the weight of the body, so as to prevent any further acceleration (page 90). Now, the gold presenting a larger surface when beaten out than in the lump, far more resistance is opposed to the leaf than to a thick piece of equal weight, moving with equal velocity. Supposing both to begin to fall at the same instant, when the leaf has attained its maximum and uniform speed, the lump will still continue to be accelerated, for the lump requires a greater speed to generate the same resistance.

108. As the attraction of the earth acts on all bodies in proportion to their quantities of matter,* it is of no consequence, as far as this attraction is concerned, whether a body be in a mass or broken up into small pieces, for each piece will be as strongly attracted as when it was united in one solid mass with the other pieces. The attraction must also be the same on one of these pieces, whether it be in a lump or

* For proof of this see " Natural Philosophy," [40].

beaten out into a thin sheet, since the number of particles remains the same. The difference observable in the time of the fall of these bodies through the air is due to the resistance of that medium ; whence we may fairly conclude that, if the air were altogether absent, and no other resisting medium occupied its place, all bodies, of whatever size and of whatever weight, must descend with the same speed. Under such cir cumstances, a balloon and the smoke of a fire would descend instead of ascending as they now do by the pressure of air, which, bulk for bulk, is heavier than themselves.

The conclusion that in the absence of a resisting medium all bodies would fall with the same speed, is established by a beautiful experiment with the air-pump, in which a piece of metal and a feather are let fall at the same instant from the top of a tall exhausted receiver, when it is found that these two bodies, so dissimilar in weight, strike the table of the air-pump on which the receiver rests at the same instant.*

In vacuo neither the size, weight, density, nor figure of a body, makes any difference in the velocity of its fall ; and all the differences observed in air, are easily explained by its resistance. For instance, a 2-inch shot falls faster than a 1-inch shot, though of the same figure and density. In the larger we have 8 times as much matter to be moved, and also 8 times as much force to move it, and this would give it, in vacuo, the very same velocity (or 8 times the momentum of) the small shot. But it has only 4 times the surface, and is therefore (in a fluid) opposed by only 4 times the resistance. Again, a ball of lead and a ball of cork of the same *weight* fall with equal momenta, but the cork being larger,

---

* A similar experiment may be made without the air-pump, by placing a piece of hot-pressed paper (or even the thinnest tissue-paper), smoothly on a flat piece of polished metal or glass, rather larger than itself, and letting them fall together. Though the light body is uppermost, it will not be left behind, nor will it in the slightest degree retard the fall of the heavier body, as it would if connected with it like a parachute.

encounters more resistance. Now, let them be of equal *size*, their weights of course are unequal, but they both encounter the same resistance, so that the cork, as before, is the most retarded.*

109. Having proved that in reality all bodies tend to fall with the same velocity, the next point is to determine what this common velocity is, and the relation existing between the space fallen through by a body and the time occupied in the fall. This relation will be the law of motion impressed by gravity upon matter.

It would appear at first view that such a question might be determined experimentally by a contrivance similar to that used in the guinea-and-feather experiment (108), only using a very long vertical tube instead of the receiver, and having exhausted it, allowing a heavy body to fall from the top at a given instant, and then marking the point at which it arrives after the lapse of one second, two seconds, three seconds, and

* This equality of speed in the fall of all bodies, when unresisted, proves that their quantities of matter or inertia are exactly proportional to their weights; it proves, for instance, that if a cubic inch of stone weigh three times as much as a cubic inch of water, it contains three times as much matter; for it falls with the same speed, though urged by a triple force, *i. e.*, it requires a triple pressure to impart to it an equal velocity in an equal length of time; and quantities of matter can be estimated in no other way than by comparing the forces required to produce equal dynamical effects on them. These forces may be either *instantaneous* or *continued;* and thus we have two ways of ascertaining the comparative masses of bodies, 1st, by comparing the *impacts* required to impart equal velocity to them, or, 2nd, by comparing the *pressures* required to impart equal velocities in equal lengths of time. This latter condition is necessary, because, as we have seen (95) that every continued force or *pressure* must produce a continually increasing velocity, and as any impact, however small, may move any mass, however great (103), so also any pressure, however small, may impart to any mass any amount of velocity, by acting long enough. A pressure of a single pound might move the largest planet with any number of times its present velocity, and it would be easy to calculate how long it must continue acting to produce this effect.

so on.   But the difficulty in such a mode of observation is, that although a body at the commencement of its fall may move with tolerable slowness, so that the eye can follow it, yet the motion increases so rapidly, that it soon becomes quite impossible to do so.   Accordingly, philosophers have resorted to various contrivances for so modifying the motion of the falling body as to make it appreciable by the senses throughout its whole course.

110. The first philosopher who succeeded in detecting the law of falling bodies was Galileo. When the study of astronomy was no longer for him a safe pursuit, his acute and powerful mind recurred to his earlier mechanical studies, and during his residence at Sienna, after being persecuted by the Inquisition, he published, or at least collected, materials for his "Dialogues on Motion." In this work the following method is given of making experiments on the descent of bodies on inclined planes.*   "In a rule, or rather plank of wood, about 12 yards long, half a yard broad one way and 3 inches the other, we made upon the narrow side or edge a groove a little more than an inch wide: we cut it very straight, and to make it very smooth and sleek, we glued upon it a piece of vellum, polished and smoothed as exactly as possible, and in that we let fall a very hard, round, and smooth brass ball, raising one of the ends of the plank a yard or two at pleasure above the horizontal plane. We observed, in the manner that I shall tell you presently, the time which it spent in running down, and repeated the same observation again and again, to assure ourselves of the time, in which we

* The invention of this method appears, from documents quoted by Venturi and others, to bear date at least as early as 1604.   Descartes insinuates that Galileo first obtained from him the knowledge of the law established in these experiments; but as Descartes was not born until 1596, he must, if his claim be tenable, have been a most astonishing genius at eight years of age.   He also insinuates that Galileo obtained from him the isochronism of the pendulum, which, in fact, was discovered in 1583, thirteen years before Descartes was born.

never found any difference, no, not so much as the tenth part of one beat of the pulse. Having made and settled this experiment, we let the same ball descend through a fourth part only of the length of the groove, and found the measured time to be exactly half the former. Continuing our experiments with other portions of the length, comparing the fall through the whole with the fall through half, two-thirds, three-fourths, in short, with the fall through any part, we found, by many hundred experiments, that the spaces passed over were as the squares of the times, and that this was the case in all inclinations of the plank; during which we also remarked that the times of descent, on different inclinations, observe accurately the proportion assigned to them farther on, and demonstrated by our author. As to the estimation of the time, we hung up a great bucket full of water, which, by a very small hole pierced in the bottom, squirted out a fine thread of water, which we caught in a small glass, during the whole time of the different descents : then weighing from time to time in an exact pair of scales, the quantity of water caught in this way, the differences and proportions of their weights gave the differences and proportions of the times; and this with such exactness, that, as I said before, although the experiments were repeated again and again, they never differed in any degree worth noticing."

111. It will be observed, that as the law first mentioned (that the spaces fallen through from the commencement of the fall are proportional to the squares of the times elapsed, applied equally whatever might be the inclination of the plane, it must apply also when the plane is vertical, or when the body falls freely. The establishment of so important a law by such simple and exquisitely ingenious means may serve to remind the reader that Galileo is not unworthy of the fame which still belongs to his name as a mechanical philosopher, as well as a persecuted astronomer. In later times, the law of falling bodies has received a more complete exposition by the admirable machine invented by Atwood, and which will be

described presently. But first it is necessary to enter a little more fully into the question, in order that the reader may be in a condition fairly to estimate the merits of this machine, and the important law it is intended to illustrate.

112. The fall of a heavy body from a height is a uniformly accelerated motion, because the attraction of the earth, which is the cause of its fall, never ceasing to act, the body gains at each instant of its fall a new impulse, whereby it receives additional velocity, so that its final velocity is the aggregate of all the infinitely small but *equal* increments of velocity thus communicated. Hence, the velocity of a falling body at the end of two seconds is twice that which it had at the end of one; at the end of three seconds three times that which it had at the end of one, and so on. Now, it has been ascertained that a body falling freely through space by the force of gravity acquires at the end of the first second a velocity such as would carry it, without any assistance from gravity, through about 32 feet during the second second. This is the *final velocity* of the body after one second. But during this second, the body passes gradually from a state of rest through various increasing degrees of speed, until it acquires a velocity equal to 32 feet per second. Its *average* speed, therefore, during the whole of the first second will be the arithmetical mean between its starting velocity, which is 0, and its final velocity, which is 32 feet per second. This mean is 16 feet per second; consequently, the space actually fallen through during this one second must be 16 feet. During the second second, the body starting with the velocity of 32 feet acquired during the first second, falls through 32 feet, and also through another 16 feet, due to the action of its weight during this one second only. At the end of the second second the final velocity is twice that at the end of the first second; so that during the third second the body would move through 64 feet, if subject to no force, *i. e.*, if its weight had ceased to act; but as this force continues to act, and would during a second move it through 16 feet (if it

had *no* velocity at starting), the whole space described during this second will be 80 feet, viz., 64 feet by its *previously acquired* velocity, and 16 by that gradually added during this third second.

113. We see, then, that the weight of any body is such a force as will, during one second, impart to that body a velocity of 32 feet per second, in addition to any motion which it may previously have. During any other period it would impart a proportionally greater or less velocity; during two seconds, for instance, a velocity of 64 feet per second; or, during half a second, a velocity of 16 feet per second. Hence, it appears that the time occupied in falling, and the *final* velocity, are proportional to each other; and that an increase in one is necessarily attended by a proportional increase in the other. Now, we have seen that the *average* velocity, during any fall, is exactly half the *final* velocity, for it is the mean between the velocity at starting, viz. 0, and that final velocity; hence, any increase in the time of falling, is attended by a proportional increase in the *average* speed during the whole fall. But the space fallen through is jointly proportional to the time occupied and the average velocity; consequently, when the time is increased in any proportion (say doubled), the body falls, not only twice as long, but also twice as fast, and must therefore fall through *four* times the distance. So, also, if one body falls three times as long as another, it also falls with three times the average speed, and consequently falls, altogether, *nine* times the distance. Thus, the distance fallen must always be proportional to the square of the time occupied; as observed in the experiments of Galileo. It will thus be seen, that though a body fall 16 feet in a second, it will only fall 4 feet in half a second; for it falls with only half as much average speed, viz. a speed of 8 feet per second, or 4 feet per half-second. But it acquires a final velocity of 16 feet per second, which would carry it, in another half-second, through 8 feet, besides the 4 feet due to its acceleration during that half-second, making

altogether 12 feet, and thus accounting for the fall of 16 feet in a second.

We thus get an easy rule for determining the space through which a body has fallen, simply by knowing the time occupied by the fall, and multiplying the square of this by the number of feet through which a body falls in one second. For example :—

The height fallen during one second	= 1 × 16 =	16 feet.
,, ,, two seconds	= 4 × 16 =	64 feet.
,, ,, three seconds	= 9 × 16 =	144 feet.
,, ,, four seconds	= 16 × 16 =	256 feet.
,, ,, five seconds	= 25 × 16 =	400 feet.

And the same rule will apply to any number of seconds, whole or fractional.

114. To show more clearly how this law is derived from the *uniformity* of the accelerating force, we may take the *length* of any figure to represent the *time* of the whole fall, which we may divide into any convenient number of parts ; and we may make the *breadth* of the figure, at each of those divisions, represent the *velocity* at the corresponding instant of the fall. Then the *area* of the figure, or of any portion thereof, will represent the *distance fallen through* during the corresponding part of the time ; for this distance is jointly proportional to the *time* and the *average velocity*, just as the area of a figure is jointly proportional to its *length* and its *average breadth*. Let us draw such a figure, in which the breadth at the commencement is 0, and the increase is uniform, *i. e.* by equal additions, for equal additions to the length. By observing the relations between the breadths of this figure, at different points, and also between the areas of the whole and of different portions thereof, and the areas they *would* have if their breadth continued equal throughout their length, we may learn all that has been stated above, by simply substituting *time* for *length*, *velocity* for *breadth*, and *distance fallen* for *area*. The following is an example :—

A body falling freely during 5½ seconds;

Starting with a velocity of · · · · **0**   **Feet**

Falls during the 1st second · ·   · · · · · · · · · · · **16**
Acquiring a velocity of · · · · · ·   **32** feet per second.

Falls during the 2nd second · ·   · · · · · · · · · **48**
Acquiring a velocity of twice 32, or **64** feet per second.

Falls during the 3rd second · ·   · · · · · · · **80**
Acquiring a velocity of 3 × 32 =   **96** feet per second.

Falls during the 4th second · ·   · · · · · **112**
Acquiring a velocity of 4 × 32 =   **128** feet per second.

Falls during the 5th second · ·   · · · **144**
Acquiring a velocity of 5 × 32 =   **160** ft. per sec.

Falls during the half-second · ·   · · · **84**
Acquiring a final velocity of 5½ times 32 = 176 feet per second.

And falling a total distance of 5½ times 5½ times 16 feet = · · · · **484**

115. These laws are not confined to the motion of *falling*, but apply equally to every uniformly accelerated motion, i. e. every motion produced by a uniform force or pressure. Thus, the rising of a cork through water—the rolling of a ball down an inclined plane—the ascent of the lighter arm of a balance—are motions produced, like that of falling, by the constant and uniform force of gravity, and are therefore uniformly accelerated; i. e. if we abstract the effects of fluid resistance and friction, the above rules, but not the above numbers, will be found applicable. In every such motion, the velocities, at any different instants, are proportional to the times elapsed since the beginning of the motion; the average velocity is half the final velocity; the spaces described during successive equal intervals are as the series of odd numbers, 1, 3, 5, 7, &c.; and the whole spaces described from the beginning of the motion are as the squares of the times taken to describe them. But the numerical data will be different in each case of such motion; that is to say, the

velocity acquired in a given time, or the time occupied in acquiring a given velocity, will vary in each case: and the rate of acceleration will never be so rapid as in the case of a body falling freely, because the force will never be so great in proportion to the quantity of matter moved. All bodies falling freely are accelerated at the same rate, because, in whatever ratio their masses may differ, their accelerating forces preserve exactly the same ratio. If one body gravitate with 10 times as much force as another, it has also 10 times as much matter to be moved; but if we could oppose the weight of *one* lb. to the inertia of *ten* lbs., we should obtain a motion accelerated 10 times more slowly than that of bodies falling freely; *i. e.* a motion that would require 10 seconds to acquire a velocity of 32 feet per second, or in one second would produce only a velocity of 3⅕ feet per second. Now this is exactly what happens when a balance, whose beam and scales weigh 1 lb., is loaded with 5 lbs. in one scale, and 4 lbs. in the other: there is an unbalanced pressure of only 1 lb., but it has to move 10 lbs. of matter.

116. To submit all the laws, which have thus been expounded, to the test of direct experiment, is the object of Atwood's machine. It is obvious that the circumstances attending a heavy body falling freely through the air cannot be observed by any direct method, since a fall during 3 seconds only would require a height of $3^2 \times 16 = 144$ feet, a distance which could not be followed accurately by the eye in so short a time. This difficulty is got over in Atwood's machine by an ingenious artifice. Two weights are attached to the extremities of a fine silken line, which passes over a fixed pulley, or very light wheel, so arranged as to produce very little friction; and the magnitude of these weights is so adjusted that their difference is to their sum in the ratio of unity to any convenient number. For example, suppose one of the weights to be 3.⅓ pennyweights, and the other 32½ pennyweights; their difference will be 1, and their

sum 64; consequently, the accelerating force will be $\frac{1}{64}$ that of a body falling freely. Now, as a body 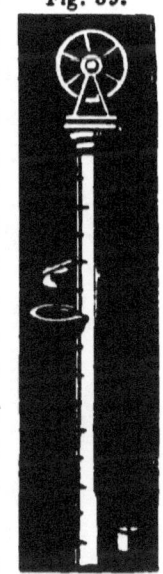 falls 16 feet during the first second, the descent of the preponderating weight will be 16 feet, or 192 inches divided by 64 = 3 inches in 1 second; 12 inches in 2 seconds; 27 inches in 3 seconds, and so on. Hence, by means of a long graduated rod and a pendulum beating seconds, it is easy to follow the weight with the eye, and to notice the descending weight pass over the divisions of the scale; thus furnishing an experimental proof of the laws already explained. By varying the ratio of the two weights, any other degree of acceleration may be obtained; these variations are, of course, only different illustrations of the same laws.

Fig. 59.

117. By means of this apparatus we may also ascertain the degree of velocity acquired at the end of any given time. To do this, the two weights are first taken equal, as, for example, 31½ pennyweights each, when of course equilibrium is produced. In order to produce motion, a small bar about 2 inches long, and weighing 1 pennyweight, is placed upon the weight which is to descend. A brass ring, about 1½ inch in diameter, being previously fixed at any proposed division (as, for example, at 12 inches) in the path of the descending weight; then, as this weight passes through the ring, the bar is left behind, and the accelerating force being thus removed, the velocity will afterwards be uniform (abstracting the effect of friction). In this case we suppose that the body, at the end of two seconds, has descended through 12 inches, and that its final velocity, at the end of that time, is therefore 12 inches per second (being twice its previous average velocity). The uniform motion of the weight would then be at the rate of 12 inches per second, during the third and succeeding seconds, did not the friction of the wheel act as a retarding force, causing it to move slower and slower, until it comes to

rest. It is usual, however, in practice to erect a stage at
some convenient distance from the ring, such as 36 inches,
through which the weight will descend in 3 seconds, the
retardation by friction during that time being insensible, if

Fig. 60.

the wheel be well mounted, in
the way shown in the accom-
panying figure. The axle of
the wheel carrying the thread,
instead of turning in fixed
bearings or holes, rests against
the rims of other wheels, which,
of course, are turned slowly
by the motion of the axle resting on them. By this means,
the friction is diminished so considerably as to have no appreciable effect in using the machine.

118. Galileo's experiments on the descent of bodies on
inclined planes have already been mentioned. It will be
evident from the preceding details, that the rate of acceleration on the inclined plane will be less than that of a body
falling freely, in the proportion that the effective portion of
its weight, acting in the direction of its motion, is less than
its whole weight; that is, as we have seen in Statics (78),
the proportion that the perpendicular height of the plane
bears to its length. Thus, on a plane inclined 1 in 64, the
motion will be the same as that of the weights in the above
example; for the whole mass has to be moved by a force
equal to only $\frac{1}{64}$ of its weight.

119. Hence it appears that (neglecting the effect of friction) the final velocity, on arriving at the bottom of the plane,
is dependent solely on its *height*, and will be the same for all
planes of equal height, however various may be their lengths:
a very remarkable result. From this it also follows, that the
average velocities are the same in descending all planes of
equal height; and hence, that the times of descending them
are exactly proportional to their lengths.

In Fig. 61 are represented four inclined planes of various lengths, but of equal height. The final velocities of bodies rolling down all these planes will be exactly equal to that of a

Fig. 61.

body falling freely down the same height; and the velocity, after descending $\frac{1}{2}$ or $\frac{1}{3}$, or any other portion of one of the planes, will be the same as that acquired in descending a similar portion of the vertical fall. Thus, if the time of descending any of these routes be divided into four equal parts—at the end of the first part, a body will have fallen $\frac{1}{16}$ of the vertical height, or $\frac{1}{16}$ of the length of either plane, viz. as far as the dotted line 1; at the end of half the time, it will (on any plane) have arrived at the dotted line 2, 2, 2; and after $\frac{3}{4}$ of the time, at the dotted line 3, 3, 3; and the velocities at crossing these dotted lines will be the same, whether the body fall vertically or down either of the planes, without friction.

Fig. 62.

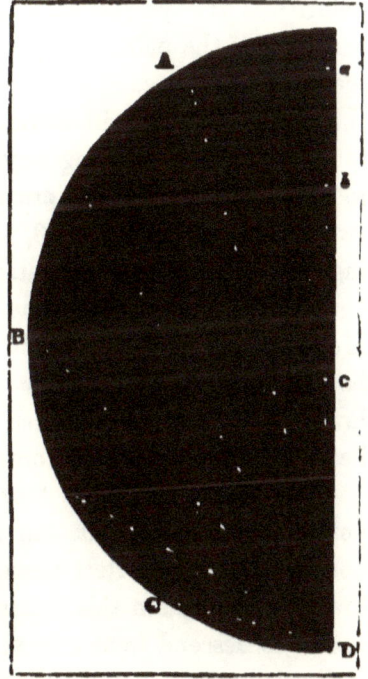

120. Another most remarkable result of these properties of inclined planes is the beautiful experiment in which two or more bodies are placed at different points of a circle, and allowed to descend at the

same instant along as many planes meeting in the lowest
point of the circle: they will arrive there at the same time,
proving that the times of falling through all chords drawn to
the lowest point of a circle are equal. Thus, bodies starting
from A, B, C, Fig. 62, descend in equal times along the chords
A D, B D, and C D. If the bodies start at the same instant,
then at every instant of the fall they will be situated on the
periphery of a smaller circle. Thus, after $\frac{1}{4}$ of the fall, they
will all be crossing the semicircle a; after $\frac{1}{2}$, the semicircle
b; and after $\frac{3}{4}$, the semicircle c.

121. In the descent of bodies upon a curve, the resistance
of the curve neutralizes different portions of the body's gravitating force at different points. Nevertheless, the velocity
acquired is subject to the same law as in the inclined plane,
viz. it is due only to the perpendicular height fallen. Thus,
at whatever point of the curve the body may be arrived, its
velocity is always the same as if it were falling freely from
the level of the point whence it started. For example, in descending the curve drawn in Fig. 61, a body on arriving at
the dotted line 1, will have the same velocity as if it had
fallen vertically, or along any road, straight or curved, down
to the same level. On crossing the level 2 2, it will have
twice, and on crossing 3 3, thrice this velocity. In ascending, its velocity will diminish, and it will cross these lines
again with exactly the same respective velocities as before.
Hence it will be seen, that if there were no friction, it would
be carried over any eminence, or any number of eminences,
lower than that from which it started, and would always
have the same velocity at crossing the same level.

122. Hence it follows that the straight line between two
points at different levels, but not in the same vertical line, is
not the line of shortest descent from the upper point to the
lower. To explain this remarkable fact, let us suppose two
bodies to descend from A to B, Fig. 63, one rolling along the
inclined plane A B, and the other along the circular arc A c B
(or the second body may be suspended like a pendulum,

which will have the same effect). If we divide each of these lines into any number of equal parts, it is obvious that each point of division on the curve will be *lower* than the corresponding point on the straight line; so that, at every instant of the descent, the body on the curve will be lower (and therefore be moving faster) than that on the straight line. Thus its average speed is greater, but

Fig. 63.

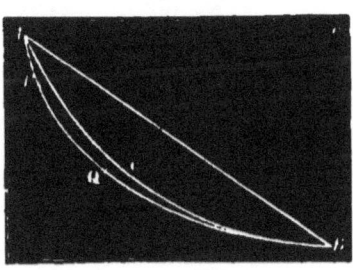

its journey is also longer, and it becomes, therefore, a question, whether its speed, or its length of route, is increased in the greater ratio. In the present case, the speed more than compensates for the increase of length; so that a body will take *less* time to roll down the curve A c B than down the shorter line A B, or down any flatter curve situated between the two. It will be observed, that A c B is the longest *circular* curve that can be drawn from A to B without an ascent towards B; but we may yet give a greater curvature, and consequently a greater length to the descent, without lengthening, but, on the contrary, still diminishing the *time* of descent; and A P Q B represents the extent to which the curvature may be increased before the increase of length will begin to compensate for the increase of speed,—in other words, it represents the *brachystochrone** or *curve of quickest descent.*

Fig. 64.

Mathematicians have determined that this curve is the *cycloid.* or that which is described by a point in the circumference of a carriage-wheel rolling along a plane. Such a point as P.

* From βράχιστος, *shortest,* and χρόνος, *time.*

Fig. 64, describes a series of arch-like curves, each of which is called a cycloid. Now if a slope be made in the form of the half of one of these curves inverted, as A P Q B, Fig. 63, this will be the line of quickest descent from A to B. But a portion of the curve, such as P Q (though described in less time than the straight line P Q), is *not* the line of shortest descent from P to Q. To find this, we must draw a smaller cycloid, of such dimensions, that when its upper extremity is placed at P, it shall pass through Q.

123. But the cycloid possesses a still more remarkable property, called *isochronism,** and which consists in this, that from whatever part of the curve a body may commence its descent, it will always. occupy the same length of time in reaching the bottom. The former property belonged only to arcs extending to the *upper* end of the curve, as A P, A Q, Fig. 63 ; and the present belongs only to such as extend to the *lower* end. Bodies starting from A, P, and Q, at the same instant, will all arrive at B together ; and however near to B a body may start, it will be as long reaching B as if it had descended the whole curve from A ; or if a body suspended

Fig. 65.

from a thread, as A B, Fig. 65, be made to oscillate between cheeks in the form of half-cycloids, A c, a c, in such a way that the thread will just wind over either of the half-cycloids from A to c or c, the body B, in swinging be-

tween these two cheeks, will describe a cycloid c B c ;† so

* From ἴσος, *equal*, and χρόνος, *time*.

† Because it is a mathematical property of the cycloid, that its *evolute*, or the curve described by a thread *unwound* from it, is another cycloid equal and similar to itself.

that from whatever point in this curve the body ε is made to fall, it will arrive at B and pass to its greatest height in the opposite curve in equal times; and however much its oscillations may diminish in extent (by the effects of friction, &c.), they will always be *isochronous*, or *equal-timed*. This, in fact furnishes an *isochronous* or equal-timed pendulum, an instrument which would be invaluable in practice were it not that no substance can be found of sufficient strength and flexibility to form a thread which shall easily wind on the cycloidal cheeks, and of such a nature as that it shall not adhere to them. On this account the cycloidal pendulum, although perfect in theory, is inferior in practice to the simple pendulum, whose valuable and remarkable properties we are now about to describe.* It will be seen that when the common pendulum vibrates in very small arcs of a circle, its vibrations are, for all practical purposes, isochronous, because the circle has the same curvature as the cycloid at its lowest point, and may be confounded with it for a small distance, as seen near B, Fig. 65.

124. The pendulum is one of the simplest of scientific instruments, and also one of the most important, for by its means we are enabled, not only to measure time with precision, but to determine the variation of the force of gravity in different places, whereby data are furnished for determining the figure of the earth, and even the density and arrangement of materials in its interior.

Any weight attached to the end of a flexible thread, and suspended by a fixed point P, Fig. 66, may be said to constitute a pendulum. Its fundamental properties are *first*, to show, when at rest, the exact vertical, or the direction

---

* But the cycloidal cheeks are necessary for properly performing the experiments on impact described in (99). They need not, however, be extensive, for a very small portion of them, as A *d*, *a d*, Fig. 65, will guide the body through a large range of oscillation, viz. from *e* to *e*

in which gravity acts;* *secondly*, to oscillate in a vertical plane when drawn on one side, and then left to itself. If,

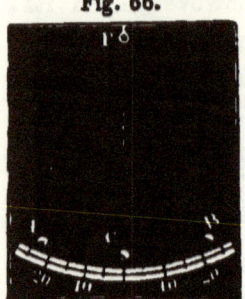

Fig. 66.

for example, the pendulum P C be drawn aside to A and liberated, it will descend to c, and then ascend on the other side as far as B, describing an arc B c, nearly equal to the arc A c.† From the point B it will again descend to c, and then ascend towards A, and so on, for a considerable time. When the weight is descending from A to c, the motion is accelerated, and in ascending from c to B it is retarded.

125. The motion of the pendulum from A to B, or from B to A, is called an *oscillation*, or a *vibration*. Its motion from A to c, or from B to c, is, of course, a *half* vibration or oscillation.

The *amplitude* of each vibration is measured by the arc A B, divided into degrees, minutes, and seconds.

The *duration* of a vibration is the time occupied by the pendulum in describing this arc.

126. If the amplitude of the vibrations of the pendulum does not exceed a certain magnitude, the time of vibration will not sensibly vary, however the amplitude may vary. Thus

---

* When used for this purpose, it is usually called a *plumb-line*.

† It would be *quite* equal to A c were it not for the friction at P, and the resistance of the air; and without these retarding forces the pendulum once moved would never cease to oscillate, the action of gravity being incessant. The proof of this is quite conclusive; for though we cannot remove these retarding forces, we can vary them in a given ratio, *i. e.* we can measure and compare them by other means independently of the pendulum. Now, if we diminish them to one-*half* their former amount, the pendulum will continue oscillating *twice* as long as before; if we diminish them to one-*third*, it will oscillate *thrice* as long, &c.; which is quite sufficient to prove that if the retarding forces were 0, the duration of the motion would be $\frac{1}{0}$ *i. e.* infinite. In a space well exhausted by an air-pump, a pendulum has been known to oscillate for more than twenty hours.

the time of oscillation will be practically the same, whether the angle A P C be 4° or 5°, 2° or 3°, or of so small a magnitude that the eye cannot distinguish it without the aid of a microscope. It is certainly remarkable that the pendulum should require as much time to describe an arc of $\frac{1}{10}$th of a degree, as to describe one of 10 degrees. The reason, however, will be evident when we consider that the effect of gravity in producing motion depends upon the obliquity of the line P A. In the position P C the force of gravity tends to keep the pendulum at rest; the impelling effect of the force of gravity is measured by the distance of the pendulum. from this position; the greater this distance, the greater the average velocity of descent; and any increase of distance within a few degrees (or in the cycloid any increase *whatever*) is exactly compensated by the increased speed of describing it.

127. This remarkable law of isochronism is said to be the earliest mechanical discovery made by Galileo, while pursuing his studies at Pisa, about the year 1581. Being one day in the cathedral of that town, his attention was arrested by the vibrations of a lamp swinging from the roof, which, whether great or small, appeared to the thoughtful young philosopher to recur at equal intervals. The instruments then in use for measuring time being very imperfect, Galileo attempted, before quitting the church, to test this observation by comparing the vibrations of the lamp with the beatings of his own pulse. Being satisfied, by repeated trials, that the oscillations of the lamp were isochronous, he constructed a pendulum with no other object, at first, than that of ascertaining the rate of the pulse and its variations from day to day. In the year 1583, however, we find him recommending the pendulum as a measurer of time. In his first applications of it to astronomical observations, he employed persons to count and register the oscillations, but he soon invented means for effecting this by machinery, and fifty years later, he describes his "time-measurer," or pendulum

clock, "the precision of which is so great, and such, that it will give the exact quantity of hours, minutes, seconds, and even thirds, if their recurrence could be counted; and its constancy is such, that two, four, or six such instruments will go on together so equably, that one will not differ from another so much as the beat of a pulse, not only in an hour but even in a day or a month."

128. Seeing, then, that the vibrations of the pendulum depend upon the force of gravity, which acts upon all bodies with equal effect (108), we may naturally suppose that those vibrations are not influenced by the quantity or quality of the weight suspended. Balls of metal, of ivory, of wood, &c., suspended by strings of the same length, vibrate in the same time; and the same remark would be true with respect to cork and other light substances, were it not that they bear so small a proportion to the resistance of the atmosphere compared with balls of metal. The remark, however, is true of *all* substances suspended in vacuo.

129. Seeing, then, that the time of oscillation of a pendulum vibrating in small arcs, depends neither upon the magnitude of the arc, nor upon the quantity or quality of the substance suspended, let us now inquire what effect will be produced by varying the length of the suspending thread. It can be proved that if the circumference of a circle be regarded as 3.1416 times its diameter, the time of oscillation of a cycloidal pendulum (or of a common pendulum vibrating in very small arcs) will be 3.1416 × the time of falling vertically half the length of the pendulum. Now as the time of oscillation bears a constant ratio to that of falling through the height of the pendulum, and as the times of falling different heights are proportioned to the square roots of those heights,[*] it follows that the times of oscillation of different pendulums are as the square roots of the lengths of the pendulums. For example, if we take three pendulums whose lengths are

---

[*] For the heights fallen are as the *squares* of the times (114).

as the numbers 1, 4, 9, then the times of vibration will be respectively as 1, 2, 3. Three such pendulums are represented in Fig. 67, consisting of three weights suspended in the same vertical line by means of threads, each attached to two points of suspension. It will easily be seen on repeating this experiment, that the pendulum whose length is 1, makes 2 vibrations to every 1 of that whose length is 4, and 3 vibrations to every 1 of that whose length is 9.

Fig. 67.

In determining the above important laws, we have taken what is sometimes called a *simple* or geometrical pendulum, or one in which the weight of the thread is altogether omitted, and the heavy body suspended, supposed to have its whole weight collected into one physical point; or, in other words, the suspended body is supposed to have weight without magnitude.

130. We now take the case of what is sometimes called a *compound* pendulum, in which the effect of weight in the thread and magnitude in the suspended body, are considered. The several parts of such a body will of course be at different distances from the axis of suspension. Now, if each material point of such a body were to be connected with the axis of suspension by a separate thread, and if, while this system were vibrating as a single pendulum, the heavy body were to fall asunder, and each particle were to vibrate by its own separate thread, it is evident that those nearest the point of suspension would vibrate more rapidly than the remoter particles. In a heavy body, such as is used for the bob of a pendulum, all the particles being bound together by the force of cohesion, must vibrate in the same time. Those nearest the point of suspension must be retarded by the slower motion of remoter particles · while these, on the contrary, are

made to vibrate quicker by the tendency of the nearer particles to oscillate in shorter times. Thus, in the annexed figure, it is obvious that the extreme particles at b must be forced to oscillate in shorter times than they would do if left to themselves, while the particles at a must oscillate in longer times than a simple pendulum whose length is A a. There must therefore be some particle between a and b, situated at such a distance from A that the tendency of the particles above it to accelerate its motion, is exactly compensated by the tendency of the particles below it to retard its motion; consequently, the molecule situated at this particular point, viz. o, oscillates in exactly the same time as it would do if liberated from all connection with the other particles above, below, and around, and were set swinging by a thread without weight. This remarkable point is called the *centre of oscillation.* *

Fig. 68.

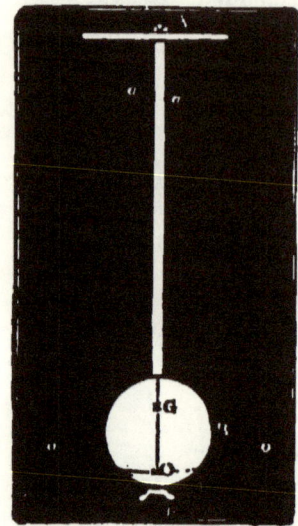

* If the motion of a pendulum is to be completely stopped without producing any pressure on the point of suspension, the opposing force must be applied, not at its *centre of gravity,* but at its *centre of oscillation.* Hence, this point is also named the *centre of percussion.* If a blow be given by a rod of uniform thickness, held by one end, and swung round in a circular arc, the effect of the blow is not so great at the middle, which is its centre of gravity, as at the centre of percussion, which is farther from the hand. This property of the centre of percussion can be ascertained by giving a smart blow with a stick. If we give it motion round the joint of the wrist only, and, holding it at one extremity, strike smartly at a point considerably nearer, or more remote, than two-thirds of its length from the hand, we feel a painful jar or strain in the hand; but if we strike at the point which is precisely two-thirds of its length, no such disagreeable jar will be felt. If we strike the blow at one end of the stick, we must make its centre of motion at

131. The distance of the centre of oscillation from the point of suspension forms what is called the *length* of the pendulum. This length is in effect the length of the simple pendulum, which would oscillate with the same rapidity as the compound pendulum. The position of the centre of oscillation depends on the form and magnitude of the oscillating body, the density of its several parts, and the position of the axis on which it swings. A pendulum of copper with a very thin rod, would have its centre of oscillation at o, Fig. 68 : but if the rod were thicker, its centre of oscillation would be higher ; but it can never be so high as the centre of gravity, G, though whatever raises or lowers the centre of gravity will raise or lower that of oscillation. A small weight added to the lower extremity *b*, causes the centre of oscillation to descend ; if this weight were placed higher than o, it would cause that centre to ascend. Accordingly, in some clocks a small weight is made to slide upon the pendulum-rod, by the adjustment of which the clock may be regulated; it is, however, more common for this purpose to cause the bob to ascend or descend by means of a screw placed beneath it.

132. The addition of matter above the axis of motion, or lengthening the pendulum beyond A, has a very remarkable effect. As the matter above A must be rising whenever the rest of the pendulum is falling, and *vice versâ*, it tends to retard every motion, just as the smaller weight in Atwood's machine retards the fall of the other. Hence the time of oscillation is lengthened, and may be made as long as we please ; for, if the matter above A have its whole moment equal to that of the matter below A, there will be no tendency to oscillate, for A will be the centre of gravity, and

one-third of its length from the other end, and then the strain will be avoided. The convenience of using a hammer, or an axe, depends on the position of its centre of percussion ; and swords have its position marked on the blade, and if they strike at a point very near the centre of percussion of one sword, and very far from that of the other, the latter will be broken but not the former

the body will remain at rest in whatever position it is placed, or if set in motion will tend to rotate continually, and a continual rotation may be regarded as an oscillation of infinite length. Now the nearer we bring the centre of gravity to the axis of motion, the nearer shall we approach this state, and the longer will be the time of oscillation, or the greater will be the virtual length of the pendulum; so that this length may be as great as we please, and when it is greater than the actual length, the centre of oscillation will be *out of* the pendulum, and may be at any distance from it.*

133. Since the virtual length of a pendulum is estimated by the distance of its centre of oscillation from the axis of suspension, it follows from what has been said (129), that the times of vibration of different pendulums are in the same proportion as the square roots of the distances of their centres of oscillation from their axes of suspension. Now it is very remarkable, that whatever may be the positions of these two points, they are always mutually convertible. For example, if A be the axis of suspension, and o the corresponding centre of oscillation, the pendulum will vibrate in the same time if it be removed from its support, inverted, and suspended from o instead of A, for its centre of oscillation will then be at A. This property of the pendulum was made use of by Captain Kater, in his laborious experiments on the length of the seconds pendulum, with a view to furnishing a national standard of weights and measures.

134. The mathematical method of determining the place of the centre of oscillation is somewhat difficult even in pendulums of the simplest forms and of uniform density, and hardly applicable in others. It may be observed, however, that the time of oscillation, and consequently the virtual length, is the same for all positions in which the distance of the axis of suspension from the centre of gravity remains constant; and also, that the centre of gravity is always in

---

* Thus we see that a body may be so held (or have its fixed axis in such a position) as to have *no centre of percussion.*

the straight line joining the centre of oscillation and the axis. Hence, if a sphere be described round the centre of gravity with any radius, another concentric sphere may be found, such that if the axis be a tangent to any point of either the outer or inner sphere, the centre of oscillation will be at the diametrically opposite point of the *other* sphere. It is possible to find such a radius for one of these spheres as shall make the other coincide with it. In this case, that is, when the axis and the centre of oscillation are at equal distances from the centre of gravity, they are as near each other as possible, so that the pendulum then oscillates in the shortest time possible.

135. The determination of the exact virtual length of the pendulum vibrating seconds, or other measurable intervals of time, enables us to ascertain some most important facts respecting the earth and the force of gravity, some of which will be noticed in the next section. But in order to make the pendulum applicable to these delicate observations, it is necessary to determine, *first*, the exact time of a single vibration; and, *secondly*, the exact distance of the centre of oscillation from the point of suspension. The first point is determined by observing the precise number of oscillations made by the pendulum in a certain number of hours, as determined by a good chronometer; and then dividing the time by the number of oscillations, the exact time of one oscillation will be obtained. But as it may be necessary during several hours to count many thousand oscillations, the chances of error are very great: the method of *coincidences*, invented by Borda, may therefore be employed. The pendulum whose motions are to be observed is placed before a pendulum clock, and the two are so adjusted as to oscillate nearly, but not quite in the same time. The two pendulums are set swinging at the same moment, but being slightly unequal in length, they soon cease to swing together; one gains a little upon the other, so that they both cross each other in swinging, until at length one has gained a whole oscillation

upon the other: when this takes place, the two pendulums *coincide* for an instant, and again separate as before. Now, if all these coincidences be observed in a given time, say three hours, the hand of the clock will give the number of vibrations made by its pendulum, and the number of coincidences will show the number of vibrations which the other pendulum has gained or lost upon it. By adding or subtracting the number of coincidences from the number of oscillations shown by the clock, we get the exact number made by the experimental pendulum in three hours. Dividing the number of seconds in the three hours by this number of oscillations, we get the duration in seconds of each oscillation.

The length of the pendulum, that is, the distance of the centre of oscillation from the point of suspension, may be found by the rule already given (133), and by giving to the pendulum a uniform figure and material, it is the more easily determined.

136. The time of vibration and the length of a pendulum being known, it becomes easy, first, to determine the length of a pendulum which shall vibrate a given time; and, secondly, to determine the time of vibration of a pendulum of a given length. In the one case the time of vibration of the known pendulum is to the time of vibration of the required pendulum as the square root of the length of the known pendulum is to the square root of the length of the required pendulum. The second problem may be solved thus:—the length of the known pendulum is to the length of the proposed pendulum as the square of the time of vibration of the known pendulum is to the square of the time of vibration of the proposed pendulum.

III. — UNIFORMLY RETARDED MOTION — COMPOSITION OF MOTIONS—PROJECTILES—HEAVENLY BODIES—CENTRIFUGAL FORCE.

137. WHATEVER has been stated in the last section respecting *uniformly accelerated* motion, as produced by the constant action of a force in the same direction in which a body is moving, will be found equally applicable to the converse case of *uniformly retarded* motion, produced by the constant and uniform action of a force in the contrary direction. As in the former case the velocity increased by equal *additions* in equal times, so in this case it is reduced by equal *losses* in equal times; and if the force be the same, the velocity *lost* in any unit of time, such as a second, will be equal to that *gained* in a similar unit in the former case. Thus, when a body is projected or thrown directly upwards, and then left to the action of gravity, it rises during any second 32 *feet less* than during the previous second, until its velocity is reduced to 0, and then to less than 0, that is, to a motion in the contrary direction, when the same law continues unaltered, for the body gains, like any other falling body, 32 feet of downward motion per second, which is the same thing as losing 32 feet of upward motion. By taking the opposite signs + and — to represent *upward* and *downward* velocity, we may easily determine the motion of a projectile shot upwards with any given velocity, say 100 feet per second. At the end of a second its velocity will be reduced to $100 - 32 = 68$ feet per second; but the average speed during the whole second is the mean between 100 and 68, viz. 84 feet per second.

In the 1st second it rises $100 - 16 =$ 84 feet
In the 2nd „   „ $84 - 32 =$ 52 bringing it to 136 ⎫
In the 3rd „   „ $52 - 32 =$ 20   „   156 ⎪ feet from
In the 4th „   „ $20 - 32 = -$ 12 lowering it to 144 ⎬   the
In the 5th „   „ $-12 - 32 = -$ 44   „   100 ⎪ ground
In the 6th „   „ $-44 - 32 = -$ 76   „·   24 ⎭

And another quarter-second will exactly bring it to the ground, for its velocity at the end of the 6th second is $100 - (6 \times 32) = -92$ feet per second ; and at the end of $6\frac{1}{4}$ seconds it is $100 - (6\frac{1}{4} \times 32) = -100$ feet per second ; and the mean between 92 and 100 is 96, so that the average velocity during the quarter-second is 96 feet per second, or 24 feet per quarter-second.

As the velocity diminishes just as fast during the ascent as it increases during the descent, the body passes any point with the same velocity in rising as in falling, returns to its starting level with its original starting velocity, and takes the same time to perform the whole or any part of its ascent as the whole or the corresponding part of its descent. Hence, having the initial velocity, we can easily find the time of ascent or descent ; thus, as $32 : 100 :: 1$ second, (the time required to gain or lose a velocity of 32) : $3\frac{1}{8}$ seconds (the time required to gain or lose a velocity of 100); whence $6\frac{1}{4}$ seconds are necessary, first to lose and then to gain it. The height attained, then, is $3\frac{1}{8} \times 3\frac{1}{8} \times 16$ feet $= 156$ feet 3 inches.

138. We see by this example, that motions in the same or contrary directions can be *compounded*, like statical forces (6), by mere addition or subtraction ; for, in fact, the place of the body at any moment of its ascent or descent, at 5 seconds after its projection, for instance, is the same as if it had first risen for 5 seconds with the uniform velocity imparted to it at starting, and then fallen for 5 seconds by the free action of gravity. The original velocity continued uniformly during this time would have carried it through $+ 500$ feet ; and the action of gravity, as we have seen (113), would bring it through $- (5 \times 5 \times 16) = -400$ feet ; and, accordingly, the action of both together brings it to $500 - 400 = 100$ feet from the ground. The same process will give its exact height at any other moment of the rise or fall.

139. This composition of motions could not take place were

it not for a physical law of great importance and simplicity, which may be thus expressed, that *the dynamical effects of forces are proportional to their statical effects.* The same force which *balances* another force of twice the amount, will also when unbalanced produce twice as much motion ; that is to say, it will either (I.) impart to *twice* as much matter the *same* velocity in the *same* time; or (II.) it will impart to the *same* matter *twice* the velocity in the *same* time ; or (III.) it will impart to the *same* matter the *same* velocity in *half* the time. It must be distinctly understood, that this is not, as some have supposed, an abstract or necessary truth, but a physical fact, or law of nature,—not a fact to be learnt by *deduction*, but by *induction* from experiments; and it is this which renders dynamics an inductive science. The rules for the composition of statical forces may be deduced without any appeal to nature; but such appeal is necessary before we can apply them to motions, for they would not be so applicable if motions were not proportional to the pressures producing them. For instance, it might have been so ordained that the dynamic effects of forces should be as the *squares* of their statical effects, or *vice versâ*,—that a double pressure should produce a quadruple motion, or a quadruple pressure be required to produce a double motion, in neither of which cases could motions be compounded in the simple manner above explained. One consequence of this would be, that the proper motions of the various objects in a ship, for example, would not be so compounded with the common motion of the whole ship as to produce, with regard to each other, the same effects as if the ship were at rest. For example, to quote a case from Professor Robison, suppose a ship at anchor in a stream, and that one man walks forward on the quarter-deck at the rate of two miles an hour; that another walks from stem to stern at the same rate ; that a third man walks athwart ship, and that a fourth stands still. Now, let the ship be supposed to cut her cable, and to float down the stream at the rate of three miles an hour. We cannot conceive any difference in the change made on each man's motion in absolute space; but their motions are now exceedingly different from what they were: the first man, whom we may suppose to have been walking westward, is now moving eastward one mile per hour; the second is moving eastward four miles per hour; the third is moving in an oblique direction about three points north or south of due east. All have suffered the same change of condition with the man who had been standing still; he has now got a motion eastward at the rate of three miles an hour. In this instance we see very well the circumstance of sameness which obtains in the change of these four conditions. The motion of the ship is blended with the other motions; but this circumstance is equally present whenever the same previous motions are changed into the same new motions. We must ascertain this by considering the manner in which the motion of the ship is blended with each of the men's motions. This kind of combination is called the *composition of motion*, to which the doctrine of the parallelogram of forces is applicable.*

* The importance of this principle, and also that of *experiment* or *active* observation, as distinguished from mere *experience* or *passive* observation, is well shown by the history of an objection once urged against the Copernican system—viz. that if the earth were really moving, a stone dropped from a tower or precipice would be left behind, and fall at a considerable distance westward, just as it would, if dropped from the mast of a ship sailing on a river, be left abaft the foot of the mast. Neither of these experiments was actually tried; they were thought too simple, and their results too obvious, to need a special examination. So the objection was met with learned arguments, answered by others equally satisfactory, till after some years the discussion was suddenly cut short by the simple discovery that the stone *does not* fall abaft the mast, but *accurately* at its foot (if in vacuo or in air that partakes of the ship's motion). Still no one thought of performing with care the other experiment, till, after the complete establishment of the laws of motion, it was seen that this would still, though for a different reason, afford the *experimentum crucis* for deciding whether the earth be in motion or at rest; and now, instead of concluding *against* its motion,

140. But, to take a simpler case than the above, and one which has been already considered statically (8). Suppose the body x, Fig. 69, to be acted on at once by three forces in the directions of the arrows A, B, C; that A acting alone would in one unit of time (such as a second, or an hour) drive the body to a; that B acting alone

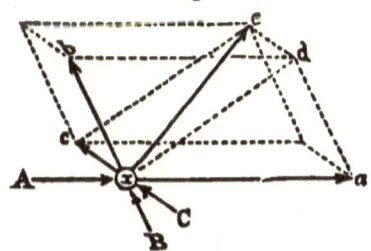

Fig. 69.

(and being weaker than A) would in the same length of time drive the body no further than to b; and that C, in like manner, acting alone, would cause it in the same length of time to reach c. Now, to find the effect of A and B united, complete the parallelogram $x\,a\,d\,b$, and its further angle d is the point to which the body will be sent by the joint action of both A and B, in the *same length of time* that it would have occupied in reaching a by the action of A only, or in reaching b by the action of B only. This will be true, whether the two forces act both in the same manner or in different manners, however varied; but in the latter case, although the body arrive at the point d just as soon, yet it will travel thither by a different route. In order that it may move along the straight line $x\,d$, it is necessary that the two forces act in the same manner; such, for example, as by an instantaneous impulse, which will cause a uniform motion; or both may act continuously and uniformly, so as to produce a uniformly accelerated motion (like that of falling bodies); or both forces may act with a continually varying intensity, both increasing or diminishing at the same rate, and the motion will still be rectilinear. But if one force be instantaneous and the other continuous, or one uniformly continued

because the stone does not fall at a great distance to the *west*, we actually derive a *direct proof* of that motion from the fact that it falls a very minute distance to the *east* of the vertical.—See " Introduction to the Study of Natural Philosophy," (36).

and the other varying in intensity, or both varying by different laws, so as not to preserve constantly the same ratio to each other, then the path of the body will be a curve, still, however, conducting it eventually to the point d, in the same time that the force A would have taken to send it to a, or B to b.

But suppose the third force C to act on the body x, and to be capable of carrying it to c in the same time that A and B jointly would carry it to d. We have only to complete the parallelogram $x\,d\,e\,c$, to find that by the combined action of all three forces the body will be sent in the same unit of time to e. Here it should be observed, that whether we first find the combined effect of A B and then add that of C, or first combine A C and then add B, or first combine B C and then add the effect of A, the result in either case will be the same, and will conduct us to the same point e.

It is another remarkable consequence of this law, that whether we regard the directions of the three forces as being all in one plane, or in different planes; whether we regard the lines of this figure as they really lie flat on the paper, or as the projection or picture of a solid parallelopiped, the law is equally true. The same process is of course capable of being extended to any number of forces or motions.

141. This most important law as regards motions, may therefore be simply expressed in the following terms:—that by any number of forces acting together for a given length of time, a body is brought to the same place as if each of the forces, or one equal and parallel to it, had acted on the body separately and successively for an equal length of time. Thus, by the separate and successive action of the forces A, B, C, or equal and parallel ones, during a certain time, an equal time being allowed to each, the body x will be carried first to a; thence, by a force equal and parallel with B, it will be carried to d, and thence to e, by a force equal and parallel with C. Or if they act in any other order, it is easy to see that x will be carried along three straight lines,

which, though forming a different route in each case, will yet in every case bring it eventually to the same point *e*; which is also the point to which it will be carried when they all act together for the same length of time during which we have supposed each to act separately.

142. Let us now consider the effect of the composition of a *uniform* with a *uniformly accelerated* motion, the two being in different but not opposite directions. In other words, let us observe the effect of a constant and uniform force acting in any way on a body already in motion. We have already considered the particular cases in which the force directly assists or directly opposes the motion,—the former is the case of falling bodies (114), the latter of those shot directly upwards (137). We come now, therefore, to the general case of *projectiles*, *i. e.* bodies thrown horizontally, or obliquely. To simplify the question, let us suppose them to move *in a vacuum*, so that they may be subject to no other force than gravity, which continually *deflects* them out of the straight line which they would otherwise describe (94), and which is called the *line of projection*. Now it matters not whether this line be horizontal, inclining upwards, or inclining downwards, it will constantly be found that the vertical depth of the projectile below this line at any moment, is equal to the depth which it would have fallen during the time which has elapsed since its projection. Thus, if a cannon-ball be shot from A, Fig. 70, in the direction A *b*, and its original velocity be such as would carry it through the space A *a* during one second, then, if not subject to gravity, it would proceed in a straight line and arrive at *a* in one second, at *b* in two seconds, and so on. But gravity alone would cause it during the first second to fall 16 feet, say from A to G. By completing the parallelogram A *a* G *g*, we see that after one second the body will have arrived at *g*, exactly as if it had first been carried by the projectile force during one second to *a*, and then fallen during one second to *g* In the same way, during the next second, the ball

moves in the direction of projection through the space *a b*,
or *g h*, and in the direction of gravity through *h* 2 = 3 times
16 feet.   In the third second it advances as much as before

Fig. 70.

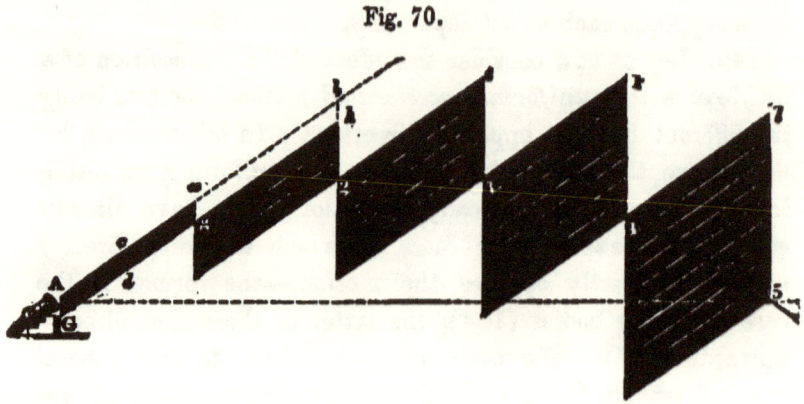

viz. 2 *i*, and falls 5 times 16 feet, bringing it to the point 3
In the fourth and fifth seconds it advances in the direction
3 *k*, or 4 *l*, as much as in the first second, but falls 7 times
and 9 times as much, thus arriving at the points 4 and 5.
Now it results from this, that the points A, *g*, 2, 3, 4, 5, are
necessarily situated on a curved line of that kind called a
parabola, and if the place of the ball at any other moments,
however numerous, be found, all these points will likewise
fall on the same curve.   For instance, at half a second after
projection, the ball will have been shot through half A *a*,
and will consequently be somewhere on the vertical line *c d*,
half-way between A G and *a g ;* but it will not be half-way
between *c* and *d*, and consequently not in the straight line
between A and *g*, for the space fallen through in half a
second is, as we have seen, not 8 but only 4 feet, so that it
will be only 4 feet below c; thus accounting for the continued curvature of its path.*

* As each force produces its whole effect independently of the other,
it will be evident that the flight, however long, must be performed in
the very same time as if the body had been simply shot vertically up

' 143. The same construction will give us the path of a projectile shot horizontally, or obliquely downwards; and in all cases the path will be a portion of a parabola whose axis is vertical, or in the direction of gravity. When the inclination is upwards, as in Fig. 70, the distance from A at which the ball again crosses the horizontal line A 5, is called the *horizontal range*. This will be the greatest possible, with any given velocity of projection, when the body is projected at an angle of 45° with the horizon, which is the reason that mortars are fixed at that angle. In this case the greatest height attained is just one-fourth of the range.* It is also remarkable that the range will be diminished equally by equal deviations from this angle, whether above or below it. Thus a mortar will (with the same charge) carry to the same distance, on a level plain, when it is inclined 40° as when inclined 50°; or the same at 10° as at 80°. A very elementary knowledge of the nature of the parabola will enable the reader to deduce these, and some other singular facts.†

to the highest level which it attains. So also a body shot horizontally with any velocity, will reach any lower level in exactly the same time as if it had been simply dropped.

* So that, as the time of flight is twice the time of falling that height (or the exact time of falling four times that height), the ball arrives at its destination in the same time as if it had fallen a like distance vertically by the action of gravity. Hence the greatest range attainable (in feet) is 16 times the square of the number of seconds in the flight.

† In all this, the resistance of the air has been neglected; and the introduction of this new force, varying as it does both in direction and intensity (being always opposed to the direction of the compound motion, and varying as the square of its velocity), complicates the problem so much as to render it one of the most difficult in dynamics, and one which cannot be said to be even yet reduced to a practical form. The calculations of gunnery are therefore necessarily founded on experiment, rather than exact reasoning. How great an effect the air has in altering the parabolic form, will be obvious from the fact that this curve, if perfect, would be *symmetrical* on each side of its axis; whereas, in the actual path of a projectile, the descending branch is always shorter and steeper than the

144. We have hitherto regarded gravity as a *parallel* force (or as acting everywhere parallel to itself), because the centre towards which it is directed is so distant (nearly 4,000 miles) that the lines converging to such a centre may be considered parallel. But if the range of a projectile amounted to some miles, so as to bear a measurable ratio to the earth's radius, it would be necessary, in finding its path *very exactly*, to allow for the variation in the direction of gravity; or in other words, to regard it as a *central* force, by making the lines A G, *a g*, *b* 2, *i* 3, *k* 4, *l* 5, Fig. 70, no longer parallel, but such as would, if continued, meet at the earth's centre.

145. A moderate acquaintance with the conic sections will enable the reader to imagine the effect of this change, viz. to

Fig. 71.

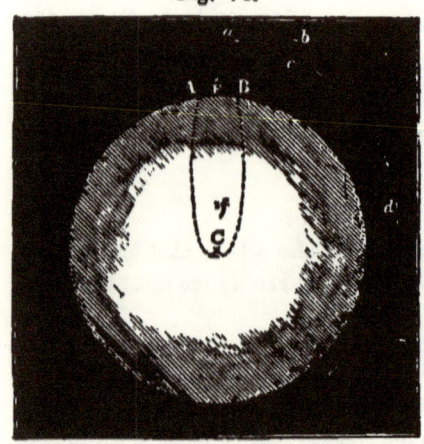

convert the parabola into one extremity of a very long and narrow *ellipse*, whose other extremity passes round the earth's centre, and has its focus at that centre. Such, indeed, is the curve described by every projectile. Thus, in Fig. 71, a body thrown from A to B does not strictly describe a parabola whose focus is at F, but an ellipse, of which *one* focus is at F and the *other* at C. It is prevented, indeed, by impinging on the earth's surface at B, from describing more than a very small part of

ascending one. If a cricket-ball described a parabola, it would fall to the ground as obliquely as it originally rose from the bat, but it is easily seen that it falls more perpendicularly. The want of symmetry will be more obvious in throwing a body of less density, such as cork; but it increases so greatly with the velocity of projection, that a cannon-ball will describe a less symmetrical curve than a ball of cork thrown by hand.

the curve;* but if we suppose all obstacles to be removed—if we imagine, for instance, the whole mass of the earth to be concentrated at the point c—the body would proceed round the entire oval, and (if encountering no resistance) return to the point A whence it started, and continue to revolve perpetually in the same orbit, which would exactly resemble that of a comet round the sun. Or, supposing the earth to retain its actual dimensions, if a body were projected horizontally from a with such a velocity as could carry it through the space a b, in the time of falling through no greater space than b c, such body, though perpetually *deflected* by gravity, could never be brought to the ground by gravity alone; but (if meeting with no other matter to be moved, such as air) would continue in the elliptical curve a c d, which, after approaching within a certain distance of the earth, again recedes therefrom, attains its greatest distance at the point diametrically opposite to its least distance, and has, like the former ellipse, one of its foci at c, the other being in this case at f. By a nice adjustment of the velocity and direc-

---

* If it be asked, What becomes of its motion? (for it has been stated (103) that motion is never lost), the reply is, that it is absorbed by (*i. e.* produces its effect on) the mass of the earth, by checking and destroying the equal and contrary motion which was imparted thereto by the *recoil of the gun.* Thus, were it not for the quality of action and reaction, even the puny motions produced by human agency would gradually drive the earth out of her orbit, and derange the mechanism of the universe. A child jumping pushes the earth from him, as well as himself from the earth; and then attracts it *as much* as he is attracted, *i. e.* with as much *momentum.* As the spaces moved through by each are inversely as their masses, it follows that their common centre of gravity remains unmoved: and this *conservation of the centre of gravity* is a principle of the utmost importance. It must be constantly borne in mind, that no actions, however violent, between two or more bodies, can possibly move or disturb the motion of their common centre of gravity,—*that* can only be affected by forces from without the system. Even in the meeting of two cannon-balls, or the bursting of a bomb in the air, the common centre of gravity of all the fragments will continue its previous course, perfectly undisturbed by the shock

tion of projection, the eccentricity of the ellipse might become 0, or the path circular and concentric with the earth.

146. It is in this manner, then, that the *moon* revolves in an ellipse of small eccentricity, of which one focus is occupied by the earth's centre. Her deflection from the straight line, indeed, during a second, does not amount to anything approaching 16 feet; but, nevertheless, it is due to a force exactly identical with that which deflects a projectile. To prove this, we have only to observe that the distance of the moon from the centre of the earth is found by triangulation * to vary within certain limits, which, for the sake of simplicity, we will call 58 and 62 terrestrial radii; *i. e.* 58 and 62 times *our* distance from the same centre. Now the moon's deflection, when at the former distance, amounts, during any given time, to $\frac{1}{3364}$ of the deflection or fall of a terrestrial body during the same length of time. But when at the latter-named distance, her deflection is only $\frac{1}{3844}$ of that of a terrestrial body during an equal time. These numbers, 3364 and 3844, will be observed to be the squares of 58 and 62, whence it appears that the force which deflects the moon, varies in intensity *inversely* as the *square* of her *distance from the earth's centre* varies; and this is confirmed by observing her deflection at all other intermediate distances. Hence we may easily calculate at what rate she would be deflected or attracted if placed at any other distance not comprised within these limits. Now, if we calculate in this manner her deflection or fall, supposing her situated at *our own* distance from the earth's centre, we shall find it would be exactly 16 feet in a second, 64 feet in two seconds, &c. &c., like that of our projectiles or falling bodies.†

---

* See " Introduction to the Study of Natural Philosophy," (22).

† The identity of the force is further placed beyond all doubt by finding that the same variation of intensity, according to the distance from the earth's centre, applies also to terrestrial bodies; for the distance fallen by them in the first second is found to be rather less upon

147. This calculation is celebrated as having laid the foundation of that magnificent discovery which forms the most memorable epoch in the whole history of science. But the reader must not suppose that the merit of this grand generalization consisted merely, or indeed at all, in a bold and fortunate conjecture, supported by a few such calculations as this. Such a conjecture was not even new; but in order to remove it from the barren region of conjecture into that of rigid and useful demonstration, Newton had not merely to calculate, but to invent *new methods* of calculation (those previously known being wholly inadequate to solve such questions); not merely to demonstrate, but to invent new modes of demonstration, such as, though never before heard of, should yet command universal assent. He had, moreover, to show how this simple idea, when fully carried out, represented *exactly*, in *number*, *weight*, and *measure*, not only the main features of planetary motion, but all its minutest details;—not only the *mean* motions, or such as are observable without actual measurement, and reconcileable with the simple notions of *circular* and uniform motion,—not only the inequalities detected by a more attentive observation, and still designated by the term *anomaly* (though Kepler had just then reduced them to perfect order, and shown their dependence on the *ellipticity* of the orbits),—not only the still smaller, and till then unaccountable and seemingly capricious deviations from these laws of Kepler,—but also

high mountains than at the sea-level, and to be diminished exactly as the *square* of the *distance from the earth's centre* is increased. This has been proved by comparing the oscillations of a pendulum at both stations, for the times of these oscillations can be compared, with any degree of exactness, by counting the number of them made in a day, or any number of days; and we have seen that these times bear a constant ratio to that of falling half the height of the pendulum. A pendulum beating exact seconds at Chamouni, would lose upwards of 120 beats per day at the top of Mont Blanc; the depth fallen by a body in the first second being nearly two-sevenths of an inch more in the valley than on the mountain.

numerous other variations, too slow or too minute to be
detected by the instruments then in use, but which improved
means of observation have since rendered appreciable, thus
affording continually, as the observations become more
exact, new confirmations of this wonderful theory; which,
among all the multifarious phenomena of falling bodies, pendulums, the earth, moon, sun, tides, planets, satellites, comets,
double stars, leaves not *one* fact imperfectly explained, either
as regards kind or *quantity;* whether it be a cosmical
movement, perceptible only in the lapse of many ages, or the
rising of one spring-tide an inch higher than another, or the
gain or loss of a few beats per month by a pendulum placed
in a new situation.

148. Not content, like many theorists, with proving that his
assumed force would be sufficient to produce all the observed
effects, Newton undertook to prove that no other force could
possibly explain them; no other being reconcileable with the
laws which had just been established by the indefatigable
labours of Kepler. This philosopher had devoted his life to
the work of ascertaining the laws which regulate (I.) the relative velocities of a planet in different parts of its orbit; (II.)
the form of that orbit; and (III.) the relative velocities of the
different planets; and he had succeeded in all three objects.

149. First, with regard to the variations in the velocity of
the same planet, he had found, that in the case of Mars (and
it has since been amply confirmed in every other case), the
imaginary line drawn from the planet to the sun's centre
(called the *radius vector*) moves always in the same plane,
and in such a way as to pass over equal *areas* in equal *times.*
Thus in Fig. 72 (which represents the most eccentric of the
known planetary orbits), if the areas of the sectors 1, 2, 3,
4, 5, be all equal, the planet will employ an equal time in
moving through each of these portions of its orbit. It can be
demonstrated from this, that the force which deflects it is
never directed otherwise than towards the point s; and,
indeed, that a force so directed will necessarily produce this

effect, may be easily proved* thus:—Let the body be at a, and moving with such velocity as would in a unit of time carry it to b, while the attraction towards s would, in the same unit, draw it to g. Let us first suppose the attraction to act only for an instant, but to impart, in that instant, such a velocity as would carry the body in a unit of time to g. By drawing the parallelogram $a\,g\,b\,c$, it will be seen that, at the end of this time,

Fig. 72.

the body will be found at c; and as both the component motions are, for the present, supposed to be uniform, the path of the body will be the straight line $a\,c$ (140). Now let the attraction again act for an instant only, imparting such a velocity towards s as would, in another unit of time, carry the body, if previously at rest, through the space $c\,g'$, which

* However simple this and the other *results* of Kepler's labours may appear, they could not be elicited without a degree of perseverance almost unparalleled, and of which we can hardly form an idea. He had neither the *sextant*, which has been called "a portable observatory," nor *logarithms*, by which a few lines of simple addition are made to serve instead of sheets of complex calculations. Yet thousands of observations had to be made and compared, not only to ascertain the truth of each of Kepler's laws, but the falsehood of each of his unsuccessful guesses—and these amounted, in the present case alone, to *seventeen*. His contemporaries regarded him as a useless dreamer; but without these discoveries we should have had no *Nautical Almanac*. Merchants, underwriters, the most practical men of the present day, stake their fortunes upon the results of these dreamy speculations of Kepler.

may be greater or less than *a g* in any proportion.   But the
previously acquired motion of the body would carry it in this
second unit through the space *c d* equal to *a c*, and in a
straight line with it.   We draw, therefore, the parallelogram
c g' d e, and find that the body will describe in this time the
straight line *c e*.   Now, by the well-known rules respecting
the areas of triangles (Euclid, Book I. Prop. 37), because *d e*
and *c s* are parallel, the triangles *e c s*, *d c s* are equal, and
(Prop. 38) because *a c* and *c d* are equal, the triangles *a c s*,
d c s are equal; so that *e c s* is equal to *c a* s, or the area
described by the radius vector in the second unit, to that
described in the first; and therefore, if the attraction continue
to act by instantaneous impulses (whether equal or not),
repeated at equal intervals of time, the body (having its
motion changed by each impulse, but uniform during the
intervals) will describe a series of straight lines, such that the
area described in each interval will be equal.   Now, however
short and numerous we suppose these equal intervals to be, the
law will still obtain; therefore it will obtain when they are
infinitely short, *i. e.* when the force acts continuously; in which
case the series of straight lines becomes a *curve*.   To whatever
point, then, the deflecting force (or attraction) may be directed,
the radius drawn from this point passes over areas proportional
to the times of describing them; and conversely, when this
uniform description of areas is observed, with regard to any
point s, it proves that the deflecting force is constantly directed
towards that point.   This remains true, in whatever way the
magnitude of the force may vary.

150. The second law observed by Kepler, is, that every planet
describes an *elliptical* orbit, having the sun's centre in one of
its foci.*   As the former law enabled Newton to deduce the

---

* Strictly speaking, however, neither this nor the former law applies
exactly to the *sun's centre*, but to that point near it which is the common
centre of gravity of himself and all his planets, and which point is, as
we have seen, immoveable by any action between the bodies of the
system.

manner in which the *direction* of the force varies; so the
present enabled him to prove how its *magnitude* varies; viz.
inversely as the square of the body's distance from the centre
of attraction; so that if the distance be doubled, the force is
diminished 4 times. It has been thought by some that this
is a *necessary* property of every force directed to or from a
centre, because anything spreading in all directions from a
centre,—light from a candle, for instance,—becomes, at a double
distance, spread over a quadruple space (twice as long, and
twice as broad); but it has been doubted whether this argument can be extended to forces in general, and the great
philosopher himself certainly regarded the law as an *experimental* one. It applies so universally, however, to central
forces, that this may be considered useful as a method of
impressing it on the memory.* The proof that it applies to
terrestrial gravity has already been mentioned. (See note,
page 140.)

151. Kepler's third great discovery, instead of relating to
the motion of each planet separately, indicates a relation
between them all; thus binding the whole into one har-
monious system, and enabling Newton to prove that the forces
deflecting them towards the sun are not merely *similar*, but
identical. Kepler found that the *periodic times* of any two
planets (*i. e.* the times occupied in revolving round their whole
orbits) are proportional to the *square roots of the cubes* of
the *longest diameters* of those orbits; or, as it is commonly
stated, "the squares of the times are as the cubes of the mean
distances;" for it will be observed that the *mean* distance of
a planet from the sun is half the *major axis* (or longest
diameter) of its orbit, for it comes to its *greatest* and *least*
distances at the two extremities of this line, which is, accordingly, equal to the sum of these distances, or twice their mean.

152. From this law, Newton proved that the deflections in
equal times of two *different* planets were connected in the very

* This is more fully explained by a figure in " Introduction to Natural
Philosophy," (55).

same manner as those of the *same* planet in different parts
of its orbit; viz. that they were inversely as the squares of
the distances from the sun's centre. Thus the same sort of
connexion is established between the *sunward* deflections of
different planets, as between the *earthward* deflections of the
moon and of a projectile. Moreover, it follows, that as all
the planets are deflected inversely as the squares of their
distances, they would all be deflected *equally* if *at the same
distance,* i. e. they would all fall sunward with equal velocities; just as we have seen that all terrestrial bodies (at the
same place) fall earthward with equal velocities; and that
the moon would do the same at the same distance. Thus we
have another point of resemblance between solar and terrestrial attraction ; that each pulls all bodies at the same distance
with equal velocities, and therefore with forces exactly proportioned to the masses of the bodies pulled.

153. The observance of exactly the same laws in the motions of the satellites of the great planets, shows that a force
of the same kind is exerted towards *their* centres. Moreover,
at equal distances, the largest body attracts with most force
in every case; for the deflection towards Jupiter is 340
times,—towards Saturn 101 times,—and towards the Sun
354,936 times—greater than that towards the Earth at an
equal distance, and in equal times. That these numbers are
only *in the order of* (but not *proportional to*) the sizes of the
respective bodies, need not surprise us, for it simply indicates
a difference of *density*, by no means greater than that existing
between some of the commonest substances around us, such
as marble and wood.

154. So far we find nothing to contradict the idea that this
force of attraction is a peculiar virtue inherent in certain
points, viz. the centres of these great bodies. But Newton's
generalization went a great deal further than this. Having
first proved that all these effects would be exactly the same,
on the supposition of a similar force exerted by *each particle*
of matter composing them, he then showed that there were

certain other phenomena not explicable on the former suppo·
sition, for though a *sphere* composed of attractive particles
will produce on every other body exactly the same effects as
if its attraction resided in its centre alone, this is not the case
with a *spheroid* or *orange-like* body, such as Jupiter; and
accordingly there are certain variations observable in the
motions of his satellites, which show that they are attracted
not merely by his centre, but by every part of his mass.*
Other inequalites in their motions also prove that they
attract each other, and Jupiter himself, with forces exactly
proportioned to their masses; and similar reactions between
all, even the smallest, bodies of the solar system, account, in
exact measure, for all the minutest deviations from Kepler's
laws; so that at length—to place the crowning stone upon
this wondrous edifice—we have in our own day seen the
inverse problem of perturbation solved.   By the comparison
of certain deviations, not exactly explained by the action of
the *known* bodies, theory boldly referred them to the influence
of a body previously *unknown*, and even pointed out its place
in the trackless and infinite void; so that when the telescope

---

* The lunar inequalities prove the same thing with regard to the
matter of the earth.   But a more satisfactory proof perhaps is derived
from the fact that, notwithstanding the diminution of gravity in ascending
mountains, it diminishes also in descending mines, because the stratum
of earth above us then *opposes* instead of *assists* the attraction of that
below.   This experiment was first tried by Messrs. Airy and Whewell by
swinging a pendulum at the bottom of Dolcoath Mine.   That all protu-
berances also share the attractive power, is shown by the deflection of
the plumb-line near the foot of mountains, which was first observed by
Bouguer and La Condamine at the foot of the Andes, and afterwards,
with great precision, by Maskelyne, in 1774, at the mountain Schehallien,
in Perthshire.   The plumb-line deviated about 6″ from the vertical direction.   It was ascertained from this experiment, and from a careful measurement of the mountain and examination of the density of its materials,
that the mass of the terrestrial globe is about 5 times greater than that
of a globe of water of the same dimensions: Cavendish made it 5.4, and
the recent repetition of the Cavendish experiment by the Astronomical
Society has made it 5.6.

was pointed to that assigned spot, the feeble glimmering of the planet was at once detected. This may be regarded as one of the greatest triumphs which modern science has achieved.

155. It appears, then, that attraction or gravity is a universal property, common to all matter, every particle in the universe* attracting every other particle; but the attraction between two bodies *both* of moderate size, is too feeble to be observed under common circumstances. The attraction of a ship for boats very near it, however, is well known; and Cavendish distinctly observed, and even measured, that of leaden globes delicately suspended in an air-tight room, and viewed from a distance through a telescope.

156. The force which we call the *weight* of any body is, therefore, the *resultant* of the forces with which it is attracted by all the other bodies in the universe, all their forces being proportional to their masses divided by the squares of their distances. Such, at least, is a correct definition of the weight of any body at *rest* or in rectilinear motion; but in the case of bodies describing curves, we have seen that some *centripetal*, or centreward, force is necessarily employed in deflecting them from the straight line which their inertia would otherwise cause them to describe. In a wheel or a pendulum this force is supplied by the *cohesion* of the spokes or the pendulum-rod, but in a projectile or a planet it is supplied by *gravity*. Now, in the case of all bodies resting on the earth's surface, a portion of their earthward gravity must be employed in thus deflecting them from a straight line into the circle which they describe by the earth's daily rotation and we must restrict the term *weight* to that portion of their gravity which is not so employed, for this is the only portion which causes them to fall or press downwards. If their gravity were only just sufficient to deflect them (as is the case with a planet), they would have no downward pressure, that is, no *weight*. This is what actually occurs on the

* It has been established by the joint labours of the two Herschels, that the same force regulates the motions of the immeasurably distant *double stars*.

outer edge of Saturn's ring, and is in all probability necessary to the very existence of that stupendous arch.* The same thing would occur on the earth's equator if her rotation were only 17 times more rapid than it is, for the deflection from a straight line would then amount to 16 feet in 1 second, 64 feet in 2 seconds, &c., or would be as much as gravity could produce. At present, however, the deflection of a body at the equator during a second is only about $\frac{2}{3}$ of an inch, so that a body deprived of weight would, in consequence of its inertia, pursue a straight line, or *tangent* to the equator, which would in 1 second lift it $\frac{2}{3}$ of an inch above the surface. Now this *tendency*, which the inertia of bodies gives them, to recede from the centre of their motion, may be regarded as a *force*, under the name of *centrifugal* force. The *weight* of a body, then, is the resultant of its *gravity* towards all the other bodies of the universe, compounded with its *centrifugal force*.

157. When different bodies revolve round the same axis in equal times, as the different parts of a wheel or of the earth, their centrifugal forces are evidently proportional to their distances from that axis. Hence, in receding from the equator,

---

* As there is a limit to the cohesion and rigidity of all solids, how-ever hard, such vast masses as the planets could not (if at rest) deviate beyond a certain extent from the spherical figure, for their prominent parts could not support their own weight, but would sink and spread, as the Pyramids would do if composed of jelly, or the Andes if composed of freestone; and this limit to the height of mountains would be *less* in a *larger* planet, so that perhaps *no* substance in a mass as large as the Sun could behave differently from a fluid. So also with arches: as Chester bridge could not have been built of jelly, so there would be a limit to the span even of an arch of steel. What, then, must be the adamantine texture of an arch encircling a world! and not *this*, but the thousandfold greater world of Saturn! We may conclude that this wondrous structure could not subsist by cohesion alone, unassisted by its centrifugal force.

For a practical view of the subject of cohesion, and tables of its amount in different solids, see "Rudiments of Civil Engineering," Part I. chap. iii.

our centrifugal force diminishes, because we approach nearer the earth's axis. But besides being diminished, it ceases to be directly opposed to gravity, because the latter acts *towards* the earth's *centre*, while the former acts *from*, and at right angles with, her *axis*. Thus, in London, it acts not directly upward, but upward and *southward*, at an angle of $51\frac{1}{2}°$ from the vertical. (By the vertical we here mean the earth's radius, and by up and down, to and from her centre.) The whole effect of centrifugal force in this latitude during a second would be about 0.415 of an inch, viz. 0.259 upward, and 0.325 southward. Compounding this, then, with the effect of gravity, which is 193.403 inches[*] downward, we find that their combined effect, or that of *weight*, will be only 193.145 inches downward, and 0.325 of an inch southward. A body, then, does not fall, nor a plumb-line hang, truly vertical, or towards the earth's centre, but deviates towards the south by about $\frac{1}{594}$ of its length. Hence, a surface which we call level or horizontal, as that of a liquid, is not equidistant at all its points from the earth's centre, but may be said to have a rise toward the south of 1 in 594 (as compared with a *spherical* surface concentric with the earth). By extending the same argument to every part of the earth's surface, it will appear, that if it were covered with a fluid, the surface of that fluid would be a spheroid 26 miles thicker across the equator than from pole to pole; so that if the earth were a solid sphere, water might be poured on till it stood 13 miles high at the equator, still leaving the poles dry. But as some land is exposed, and some covered, in every latitude, we thus see that the earth has been designedly formed with a shape nearer this spheroid than the sphere, and with a view to her

---

* This number is obtained thus exactly by means of pendulum observations; for we have seen that as the time of one vibration : the time of falling half the pendulum's length :: the circumference of a circle, : its diameter (129). Whence it follows, that the height fallen in one second is 3.1416 × 3.1416 × half the length of a seconds pendulum at the same place.

rotation with this particular velocity.* The same applies to the other planets, the rapid rotation of Jupiter, for instance, explaining his great deviation from the spherical figure.

158. We need not multiply instances of the more familiar effects of centrifugal force,—the destructive violence with which grinding-stones have flown in pieces when too rapidly turned, or the useful application of the same force to regulate the supply of steam to an engine by the *conical pendulum*, or *governor*. Some beautiful illustrations, however, are afforded by the feats of horsemanship in the ring of an amphitheatre. It may not be generally known that the circular form is absolutely necessary to the success of these performances. It would probably be impossible for the horseman even to stand on his saddle while the horse is moving in a straight line, still less to perform the elegant and surprising evolutions which we so much admire, because it would be impossible for the rider so to alter the position of his body with each motion of the horse as to keep the centre of gravity of his body constantly within the narrow base of his feet. "But if," as Professor Moseley remarks, "instead of riding in a straight line, he rides in a *curve*, a new force is lent to him to support his weight—acting, too, as if it acted at the same point where his weight may be supposed to act, viz. his centre of gravity; this new force is his centri-

---

* Thus we see, that on approaching the equator, not only must the centrifugal force increase, because we are farther from the axis, but also the force of gravity must slightly diminish, because we are a little farther from the centre. For both reasons, therefore, *weight* must diminish; and this will be detected by opposing a weight to some constant force (as the elasticity of a spring), or more exactly by the vibrations of the pendulum. The first observations for this purpose were made by Richter in 1672, at Cayenne, where he found the seconds pendulum to be about $\frac{1}{9}$ inch shorter than at Paris. The London seconds pendulum has been made the standard of our measures, as already noticed (note, p. 3). The pendulum observations, measurements of degrees ("Introduction to Natural Philosophy," sec. 22), and lunar perturbations, though perfectly independent, all concur in making the difference of the earth's greatest and least diameters = about $\frac{1}{300}$ of either.

fugal force. His centre of gravity has now no longer any occasion to be brought over the base of his feet, another horizontal force joins in supporting it, and poised between the horizontal force and the resistance of his feet, its equilibrium is easily found. To the action of the centrifugal force, which would otherwise overthrow him *outwards*, the horseman slightly opposes the weight of his body by leaning inwards ; and does he find his inclination too great, he urges on his horse, and his centrifugal force, thus increased, raises him up again. By thus varying his velocity and the inclination of his body, the conditions of his equilibrium are placed completely under his control, and he can perform a thousand evolutions that moving in a straight line he could not ; he can leap upon his horse, stand upon his head or his hands whilst he is performing his gyrations, or jump from his horse upon the ground, and, running to accompany its motion, vault again upon his saddle. The conditions of his stability, and even the force of his gravity, appear to be mastered. There is in fact given to him a third invisible power, by the act of his revolution, which is a certain modification of the force of his onward motion ; this acts with him in all the evolutions he makes, and is the secret of all his feats."

THE conditions of equilibrium in liquids, and the pressures exerted by them, are considered in the science of Hydrostatics, the third of the four great divisions which form the subject of general Mechanics.

159. The properties of liquids are always modified by the action of two forces; viz. that of weight, or the attraction of gravitation, to which they, in common with matter of all kinds, are subject; and, secondly, molecular attraction, which must act differently in liquids and solids, although we have no means of determining in what this difference consists. We can readily form an idea of the distinct action of each of these forces, for we can imagine a mass of water ceasing to be heavy without ceasing to be liquid; such a mass would neither fall nor flow when turned out of the vessel containing it, and indeed it would not require for its equilibrium to be sustained by the ground, or even by a vessel; and yet such a mass of weightless fluid would display a number of remarkable properties, the most important of which would be equality of pressure in all directions; that is to say, the liquid would transmit equally, and in all directions, any pressure exerted on its surface. For example, let *a b c d e f*, Fig. 73, be a vessel containing a liquid supposed to be without weight, and P a solid piston, which exactly covers its surface. If the piston is also without weight, it is clear that the liquid experiences no pressure; and that if a hole were made in the

vessel no portion of the liquid would flow out. Now, suppose that the piston be loaded with any given weight, say 100 pounds, it will of course tend to sink down into the liquid, and it would do so unless the liquid itself opposed such a tendency. Whether the liquid be compressible or not, the result is the same, for the liquid must either become annihilated, or it must bear up the weight of 100 lbs. If we divide the liquid into any number of layers, the uppermost layer, which is in contact with the piston, and sustains it, also sustains the whole of the weight, and would of course descend unless supported by the layer immediately beneath, which receives from the one above it as much pressure as that one receives from the piston. So also the second layer presses upon the third, and in this way we may go on until we arrive at the bottom of the vessel, which we shall find has to sustain the pressure of the 100 lbs. exactly as if the weight and piston were placed there instead of being transmitted by the liquid. Now, as this pressure of 100 lbs. is borne by the whole of the base of the vessel, it is evident that one-half of the base sustains only 50 lbs., and that one-hundredth part of the base sustains only 1 lb. We see, then, from this illustration, 1st, That the pressure is transmitted by horizontal surfaces from the top to the bottom of the vessel without any loss of effect; 2nd, That the pressure is equal at each point; 3rd, That it is proportional to the extent of the surface under consideration.

Fig. 73.

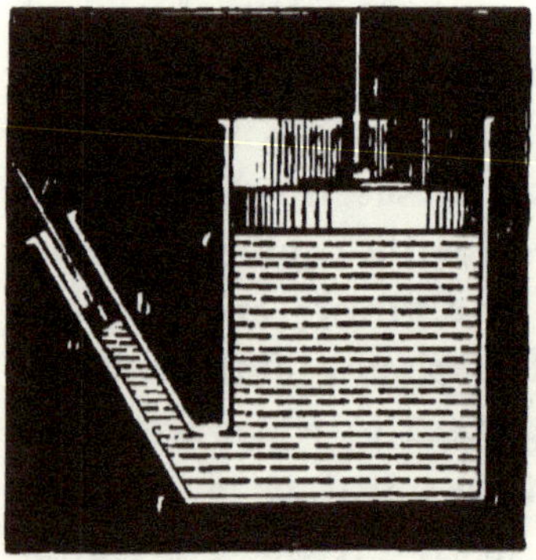

160. So far we find no difference between a liquid and a solid; but the peculiar characteristic of liquids is, that the same effects are produced on the *sides* of the vessel as on the base. If a lateral opening be made in any direction, as at *a b*, the liquid will spirt out; and if the opening thus made be of the

same size as the piston P, it will require a force equal to
100 lbs. to prevent the water from spirting out; if this side
opening be only one-hundredth of the area of the piston, the
water may be kept back with the force of 1 lb. If a hole be
made in the piston, the liquid will spirt upwards, proving
that the piston also sustains a pressure similar to that on the
base and sides of the vessel. Indeed, this necessarily arises
from the principle of action and reaction. It will be seen
that liquids transmit equally, and in all directions, the pressures exerted on any part of them, so that every surface
which they touch receives (and must return) a pressure proportioned to its area. Thus, if the area of the piston P be, as
we have supposed, 100 times that of the piston p, it will
require a pressure of 100 lbs. on P to balance 1 lb. on p. Thus
we have another simple machine, like those commonly called
mechanical powers, and described in Statics (IV.). And this
hydrostatic power, no less than the others, depends on the
principle of virtual velocities; for it is evident that if the
piston p be pushed in through any given distance, the piston
P, which is 100 times larger, will be thrust out only $\frac{1}{100}$ of
that distance, so that whatever may be the gain of power, it
is procured by an equivalent loss of motion. Used as a press
(Bramah's press), this machine has some great advantages
over the wedge or the screw, as its mechanical efficacy can
evidently be increased to almost any extent without any pro-
portionate increase of friction or complication of parts.

161. Now it must be evident that this property can be in
no way altered by conferring weight on the liquids under consideration, except that additional forces arising from the
mutual weight and pressure of the particles have to be taken
into account. Whence it follows, that in order for a liquid to
be in equilibrium, first every point of its surface must be
perpendicular or normal to the force which acts upon it;
and, secondly, each individual particle of the liquid must
experience equal pressures in all directions

162. With respect to the first condition of equilibrium, let

us suppose that the surface is not perpendicular to the force which acts upon the liquid particles; that this surface follows the direction $a\,c\,d\,e$, Fig. 74, while the force

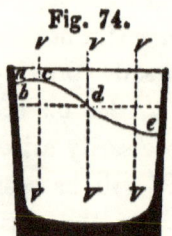

Fig. 74.

acts in the direction of the vertical lines v v. In such case a horizontal layer $b\ d$ must be pressed by the weight of all the particles above it; and this pressure being, as we have seen, transmitted laterally, the molecule d, for example, would be thrust out by this lateral pressure, since there is no counterbalancing pressure on the opposite side; it is thrust aside, and another particle occupies its place, which, in its turn, is also thrust aside, until at length the particles forming the curve $a\,c\,d$ have fallen into the depression $d\ e$, and the whole surface has become horizontal. The same process would take place with any other portion of the liquid above the horizontal surface, and there can be no equilibrium until there are no more particles to descend; when such is the case, they are all ranged in a plane normal to the force.*

* From this law arises not only the generally level or horizontal surface of liquids at rest, but also all the deviations from such a level. Thus the surface of water commonly rises with a concave slope where it meets the side of the vessel, because the particles very near the solid are attracted by *it* as well as by the earth; and the resultant of the two attractions is therefore not vertical, but more and more inclined in approaching the solid wall; and the liquid surface is everywhere at right angles with this resultant. If, however, the solid be *less than half* as dense as the liquid, the extreme particles will be more attracted by the liquid on one side than by the solid on the other, so that the resultant will incline the contrary way, and the surface will be *depressed* instead of being *raised*, and *convex* instead of *concave*, as happens with mercury resting against glass, or water against a dry cork; but if the cork be previously wetted, the liquid film adhering to it will have the same effect as a denser solid. Many other curious effects of this kind are classed under the term *capillarity*. (See "Introduction to Natural Philosophy," sec. 39.) Widely contrasted in scale, but similar in principle to these, are the effects mentioned in our last section. The general surface of the ocean, acted on at once by two forces (gravity towards the earth's centre, and centrifugal force from her axis), must, at every point, be

163. From the principle of equal pressures, as well as from the first condition of equilibrium in liquids, many important consequences are obtained. For example, the pressure of water and other liquids upon a given surface, is in proportion jointly to the magnitude of that surface and to the mean height of the liquid above that surface.* This truth is readily understood in the case of a cylindrical vessel, such as No. 1, in Fig. 75, but it is not so evident in the vessels No. 2 and No. 3. All three vessels contain very unequal quantities of water; they differ in every respect ex-

Fig. 75.

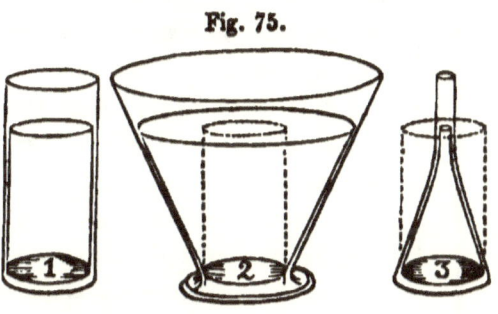

cept being of equal height and base; and in each case the same amount of pressure is exerted on the base without any regard to the bulk of the water. Hence we may estimate the pressure of a fluid upon the base of the containing vessel by multiplying its height into the area of the base, and this product by the density of the fluid. In the vessel No. 2 it will be seen that the bottom bears only the column of fluid denoted by the dotted lines, and which is exactly equal to the whole fluid in No. 1. But however paradoxical it may

perpendicular to their resultant (*i. e.* to the direction of the plumb-line), and hence becomes a spheroid, flattened towards the poles. So also in the sides of a whirlpool the liquid surface is sloping, because the resultant of gravity and centrifugal force is sloping, as would be shown by a plumb-line in a vessel carried round the whirl. The moon's attraction, too, combines with that of the earth to produce a resultant which is not always vertical; and thus the mobile surface of the ocean, constantly seeking an equilibrium which it cannot find on account of the moon's motion, is alternately raised and depressed, and produces the periodical oscillations of the tides.

* That is, its height above the *centre of gravity* of the surface.

appear, it is no less true, that the base of No. 3 bears a pressure exactly equal to this same weight of fluid, although the
whole vessel does not contain so much.

164. Some curious results may be obtained by the operation of this law. Let a vessel A, Fig. 76, full

Fig. 76.

of water, have a slender tube B screwed into it;
on filling the tube with water to a certain height,
the vessel will immediately burst; and the height
of the fluid necessary to effect this result will be
exactly the same, however large or however small
the tube may be; so that the weight of a single
ounce of water, if piled high enough, may burst
the strongest vessel. Suppose the bore of the tube
to be one-twentieth of an inch, then whatever pressure is transmitted through it, an equal pressure
will be borne by every space one-twentieth of an
inch in diameter throughout the interior of A.
Now a square inch contains about 530 such spaces;
so that an ounce of water poured into such a tube
would exert a pressure of 530 ounces, or 33 pounds,
on every square inch of A; a force which few
vessels, except steam-boilers, are made capable of
resisting.

165. Thus the whole interior surface of a vessel
is subject to an enormous pressure in consequence
of the manner in which liquid pressure is transmitted. And not only the interior surface, but
the liquid particles also in every part of the
vessel, are subject to corresponding pressures.
In the interior of the liquid mass contained in
the vessel shown in Fig. 77, let us imagine a
layer *l l* parallel to the surface s s. All the particles of this
layer are evidently pressed by the mass of liquid above
them; they are, as it were, under the pressure of a liquid
cylinder s s *l l*. But it is important to observe that this
pressure from above, downwards, is, by the principle of

action and reaction, exactly equal to that
from below, upwards; and the separate
molecules of this layer *l l* are held in
equilibrium by these equal and opposite
pressures. Now, in limiting our attention
to a portion only of this layer, *a b*, it will
be seen that the surface *a b* is at once
pressed from above, downwards, by the
liquid column *c d b a*, and from below,

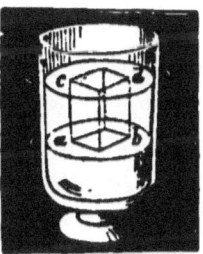

upwards, by a precisely equal force; so that if a solid were
plunged into the water whose base exactly occupied *a b*,
this pressure would act upon the solid from below, upwards,
tending to drive it out of the liquid.

166. This will be clear from the following experiment:—
A tolerably large glass tube *t*, Fig. 78, ground flat at its lower
extremity, is closed by means of a glass plate or valve *v v*,
from the centre of which proceeds a string
up to the top of the tube. If the surfaces
be tolerably smooth, the valve will close the
tube water-tight on pulling the string. On
lowering the tube thus closed into the vessel of water A B C D, the thread can be let
go, because the valve will be upheld by the
upward pressure of the water; and that
this pressure is equal to that which it
would sustain at that depth from a column
of water acting from the surface, down-

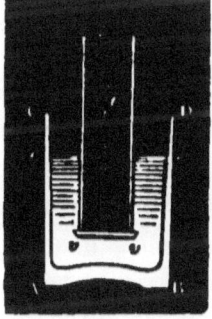

Fig. 78.

wards, is proved by pouring water into the tube. As soon
as the interior level approaches the exterior *a a*, the glass
valve is pressed from above as much as it was before pressed
from below, and it then falls to the bottom of the vessel
by its own weight.*

* Or rather by the difference between its weight and that of an equal
bulk of water, for it cannot descend without raising such a quantity of
water, just as the heavy arm of a balance cannot descend without raising
the lighter arm.

167. The pressure, then, upon a given surface, is the same, whether it face upwards or downwards; and may also be proved to be the same in whatever direction it be turned, provided its centre of gravity remain at the same depth below the liquid surface; for this pressure is equal to the weight of a column of liquid whose base is the given surface, and whose length equals the depth of its centre of gravity.

168. In water, the pressure on any surface at the depth of 1 foot is equal to nearly half a pound on the square inch. At 2 feet deep it is about 1 lb. At 3 feet $= 1\frac{1}{2}$ lb. At 4 feet $=$ 2 lbs. At 5 feet $= 2\frac{1}{2}$ lbs. In a cubical vessel full of a liquid, the pressure on any one side is equal one-half the pressure on the base; for the bottom sustains a pressure equal to the whole weight of the fluid, and the pressure sustained by each side is equal to the weight of a mass as long and broad as that surface, and as deep as its centre, and, consequently, equal to half the contents of the vessel. Hence we get the remarkable result that, in a cubical vessel, a liquid produces a total amount of pressure 3 times as great as its own weight; for if this equal 1, and the pressure upon each of the 4 sides be equal to half that upon the base, $4 \times \frac{1}{2} = 2$, and $2 + 1 = 3$.

169. In any surface which sustains the pressure of a mass of fluid, there is a point called the *centre of pressure*, at which the whole pressure of the mass may be conceived to act, and to which, if a single sufficient force were applied, the mass of fluid would be supported, and the surface kept at rest. In any vertical surface extending to the top of the fluid, this point is at one-third the depth of the fluid from the bottom, and at the middle of the breadth of the surface. The determination of this point is of the highest importance in all works made to resist fluid pressure.

170. When a number of vessels communicate with each other, whatever be their form or size, the same conditions of equilibrium apply to the fluid contained in them as to a single vessel. In the first place, the surfaces of the fluid in the vessels are all *level;* and, secondly, they are all *at the same*

level, provided the same fluid be used. Thus, on filling the large vessel A with water, or mercury, or any other fluid, it will exert a pressure on the side tube, near the bottom, equal to the area of the tube × by the height, × by the density of the fluid; and on opening the stop-cock *c*, this pressure will cause the fluid to ascend into the small vessel B until it attains the same level as in A, when equilibrium will be established, because the water in A, as well as the water in B, presses upon the same space at *c*, and both are of the same height.

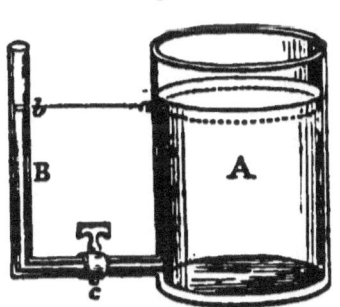

Fig. 79.

171. After what has been said, it is scarcely possible for the reader to ask a not uncommon question: " If water presses equally in all directions, why does not the large mass in A cause the small mass in B to overflow?" A man who was seeking a solution of the absurd. mechanical problem of perpetual motion, once asked himself this very question, and constructed a vessel of the form shown in Fig. 80, supposing that the large mass of water in the vessel would force the water along the narrow tube and raise it to its extremity, where it would flow back into the larger division perpetually. He was, however, greatly surprised to see the fluid in both divisions settle at the same level.

Fig. 80.

172. If fluids of different densities, such as water and mercury, be made to communicate, the height to which they will rise in the limbs of a vessel such as A B, Fig. 81, will be respectively in the inverse ratio of their densities. If the bend be first filled with mercury, and water be then poured into A, a column of that fluid, 13.6 inches high, will be necessary

Fig. 81.

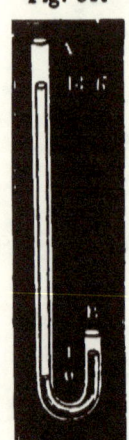

to balance 1 inch of mercury in B, mercury being 13$\frac{6}{10}$ times denser than water. It matters not how unequal in bore may be the two branches of the tube: if the experiment be repeated in such an apparatus as Fig. 79, the result will be the same, whether the mercury be in A or in B; the whole height of water will always be 13.6 times that of the higher mercurial level above the lower. This affords an easy illustration of the principle of the *barometer*, for which see " Rudimentary Pneumatics."

173. The *densities* or *specific gravities* of different bodies are usually compared with water as a standard on what is sometimes called the *principle of Archimedes*, namely, that when a solid is immersed in a fluid, it displaces a quantity of the fluid exactly equal to its own bulk. If the quantity of fluid thus displaced be lighter than the solid, the solid will sink in the fluid; if it be of the same weight, it will rest indifferently in any part of the fluid; if heavier, it will float in such a manner as to displace only as much fluid as may equal its own *weight*. But confining our attention to the first case (of a body that sinks), the body thus immersed in the fluid apparently loses a portion of its weight exactly equal to that of the fluid displaced, as the following experiment will prove. A solid cylinder of copper s, Fig. 82, exactly fitting into a hollow cylinder c of the same material, are both suspended from an arm of a balance, and brought into equilibrium by weights in the opposite scale-pan P. The solid cylinder is allowed to dip into an empty glass. On filling up this glass with water, so as completely to immerse the solid cylinder, the scale-pan P will sink down in consequence of the apparent loss of weight in the cylinder s. Now, on filling up the hollow cylinder c with water, the balance is restored. The fluid support which is given to s is represented by the weight of the water in c required to restore the equilibrium of the balance; and as s

exactly fits into c, the bulk
of water poured into c must
be exactly equal to that
displaced by s. And this
would be true, whatever
might be the material of s,
whether gold or cork. If it
were cork, it would appear
to lose more than its whole
weight, or to acquire, when
immersed, a levity or up-
ward tendency, which, however, is still found to be
neutralized, and its exact
weight restored, by filling
c. It is scarcely necessary
to observe, that all apparent

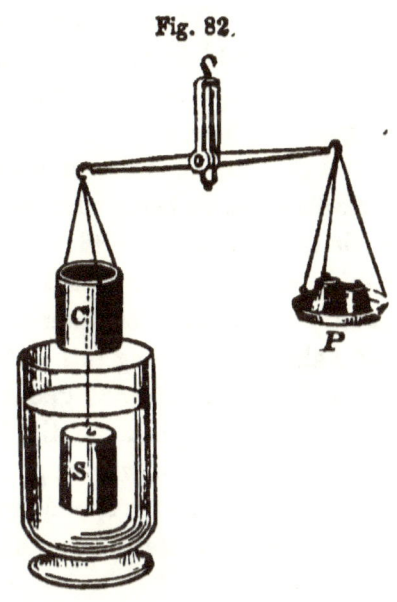

Fig. 82.

instances of a tendency the reverse of gravity, as in smoke,
balloons, &c. are only effects of this kind depending on the
pressure of the surrounding fluid, which must be denser than
the rising body.

174. In ascertaining the specific gravity or density of a
solid denser than water, it is first weighed in air and then in
water. By subtracting the weight of the substance in water
from its weight in air, and dividing the latter by the difference, the product will be the specific gravity required. For
example, a piece of gold weighs in air 77 grains, and in water
73 grains; then $77 - 73 = 4$; and $\frac{77}{4} = 19\frac{1}{4}$. The proportion, therefore, of the weights of equal bulks of the metal and
the water, is 77 to 4, or $19\frac{1}{4}$ to 1. So that gold is $19\frac{1}{4}$ times
heavier than its own bulk of water; and this number is
called the specific gravity or density of gold. It is obviously
unimportant how much or how little be taken,—the specific
gravity will be the same. It is equally unimportant whether
the standard of comparison be taken as 1 or 1000. It is
usual, however, to write the value of the standard decimally,

thus—1.000. When, therefore, we say that the specific gravity of gold is 19¼, or 19.25, we mean that a quantity of water weighing 1 is exactly equal in bulk to a mass of gold weighing 19¼. The specific gravity of cork is only 0.24; that is, the mass of water which any given bulk of cork displaces on being plunged into it, is rather more than 4 times heavier than the cork. The specific gravities of liquids are taken by means of a bottle capable of holding exactly 1,000 grains of water at a given temperature (such as 60° Fahr.). On filling this bottle with proof spirit, it will be found to contain only 837 grains; so that .837 is the specific gravity of proof spirit. If the bottle be filled with sulphuric acid of commerce, it will weigh about 1845 grains; and hence 1.845 is said to be the specific gravity of this acid. In taking the specific gravities of gases and vapours, atmospheric air is the standard.

175. When a body *floats* on a fluid, it displaces a quantity equal in *weight* to itself; when it *sinks*, it displaces a quantity equal in *bulk*. Hence the conditions of equilibrium in floating bodies are two:—1st. That the portion immersed : the whole bulk :: the density of the solid : that of the fluid. 2nd. That the centre of gravity of the solid, and that of the fluid displaced, are in the same vertical line. The equilibrium, however, may be stable or unstable; and if stable, the body will, on being disturbed, return to its former position by a number of oscillations which are isochronous, like those of the pendulum; and their times depend on the position of a point called the *metacentre*, which has the properties of the *point of suspension* in pendulums. When the metacentre is *lower* than the centre of gravity of the whole body, the equilibrium is *unstable;* otherwise it is stable.

176. THE principles which regulate the motions of fluids are considered in the fourth division of Mechanics, called *Hydrodynamics*, or *Hydraulics*. This subject is one of great complexity, on account of the facility with which a fluid mass is set in motion by the disturbance of a few only of its particles; and the resulting motions are modified, either in their velocity or in their direction, by so many causes, that it is difficult to anticipate or explain the various phenomena which arise. There are, however, in this science certain fundamental laws which go far to generalize the phenomena.

177. The sides of a vessel containing a fluid are subject to two opposite forces—one arising from the hydrostatic pressure of the fluid, tending to burst the vessel outwards; the other, the atmospheric pressure, or that of any other medium surrounding the vessel, tending to burst the vessel inwards. If an opening be made in the side or base of the vessel, the liquid will flow out, provided the interior pressure be greater than the exterior. In the common trick of covering a glass quite full of water with a piece of paper, and inverting the glass without spilling the water, the atmospheric pressure is greater than that of the water, and would continue to be so if the glass were 32 feet in depth. If the mouth of the glass be small, as in a narrow-necked phial, no paper need be used, for, on inverting it, the pressure of the air on the mobile but narrow surface of the fluid will prevent it from flowing out without dividing, which its cohesion prevents it from doing. If the neck be enlarged, the air, being so much lighter than the water, will force a passage up through it, and break up the liquid column. But if an opening be made in the top of the vessel, the liquid will flow smoothly, as if no air were present; for the atmospheric pressure, together with that of the fluid *within*, is opposed to the atmospheric pressure alone *without;* and the motion is produced by the difference of these pressures, viz. that of the liquid alone.

178. In the examples which we are about to consider of liquids escaping from an orifice, the flow will result from excess of pressure, and not from the breaking up of the liquid column. But, in order that results may be comparable, it is necessary that the surface of the liquid in the containing vessel be maintained at the same height by some contrivance which shall add to the vessel the same amount of liquid as flows from it. In such case, neglecting all mechanical obstacles arising from friction and other causes, the flow of liquids from orifices in vessels obeys the force of gravitation, and their motion becomes accelerated, according to the law already noticed for falling bodies (114). The expression of this law, known as *Torricelli's theorem*, is, That particles of fluid, on escaping from an orifice, possess the same velocity as if they had fallen freely *in vacuo* from a height equal to that of the fluid surface above the centre of the orifice.

179. Now, as we have already seen (112), that all bodies falling from the same height *in vacuo*, acquire the same velocity; the flow of liquids from an orifice does not depend upon their densities, but only on the depth of the orifice below the level of the fluid. Mercury and water, for example, flow with the same velocity when they escape by similar orifices at the same depth below their levels; for although the pressure of the mercury is 13½ times greater than that of the water, it has 13½ times as much matter to move.

180. We have seen (115) that the velocities acquired by falling bodies are as the square roots of the heights; that in order to produce a twofold velocity, a fourfold height is necessary, &c.; so also in the escape of liquids from an orifice, the velocities are as the square roots of the depths of the orifices below the surface of the fluid; so that, if we wish to double the velocity of discharge from the same orifice, a fourfold depth is required; to obtain a threefold velocity, a ninefold pressure is necessary, and so on.*

* Because, in an equal time, *thrice* as much matter has to be moved with *thrice* as much velocity.

181. When a vessel with vertical sides is allowed to empty itself by an orifice in the bottom, the quantities flowing out in successive equal intervals are as a diminishing series of odd numbers (as 9, 7, 5, 3, 1), or as the spaces described in equal intervals by a falling body, *taken backwards.*

182. In such cases there forms, after a certain time, a hollow depression on the surface immediately over the orifice; this increases until it becomes a cone or funnel, the centre or lowest point of which is in the orifice, and the liquid flows in lines directed towards this centre.* Of course, the issuing stream or vein is vertical if the orifice is at the bottom of the vessel, or it describes a parabolic curve if the orifice is at the side. In either case it moulds itself, as it were, to the form of the orifice, and extends to a considerable distance before it scatters and divides into drops. Between the mouth of the orifice and the point where it begins to divide, the liquid vein has a permanent form, and a polished surface; and notwith-standing the rapid motion of the liquid particles which succeed each other incessantly, the jet has the appearance of a per-fectly motionless rod of glass. At the commencement of its course, the vein is of the same diameter as the orifice, but for a short distance its diameter grows less, forming what is called the *vena contracta,* or contracted vein of fluid (Fig. 83). The reason for this contraction appears to be, that as the liquid particles approach the orifice, they converge to a point beyond it, so that the liquid column in escaping must neces-sarily be narrower or more contracted at the point towards which the motion of the liquid converges, than it is either before it arrives at that point, or after it has passed it. The greatest contraction of this fluid vein is at a distance from the orifice equal to half its diameter; the diameter of the con-

---

* In this state of the liquid a rotary motion is imparted to it, and rapidly increases, because all the particles are approaching the centre; and by virtue of their inertia they tend to maintain the same velocity which they had in a larger circle, so that their angular velocity (or the number of revolutions in a given time) is constantly increased.

tracted portion being to that of the orifice as 5 : 7.   Hence
the real discharge of fluid is only $\frac{25}{49}$, or
about half of the theoretic discharge, or
that which would take place if the whole
orifice transmitted fluid with the velocity of
a body that had fallen from the surface.[*]

Fig. 83.

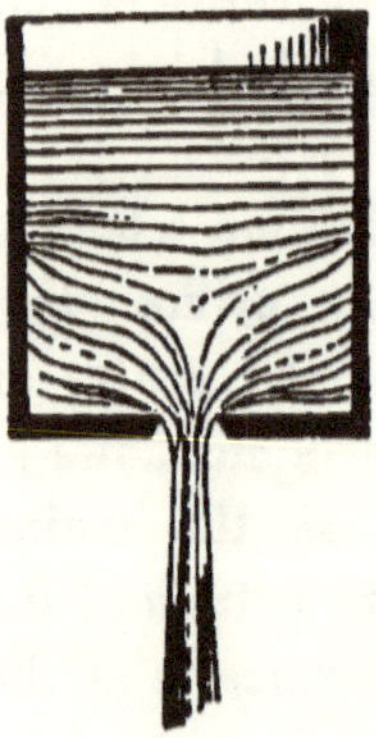

183. The division of the vein at a certain
distance from the orifice is not produced
only by the presence of the air, it takes
place *in vacuo,* and is the result of the
acceleration due to gravity.   The effect of
this acceleration is best seen in a stream of
treacle, which tapers downwards, because
the flow (or quantity passing in a given time) must be equal
at all points of the stream, so that wherever the *velocity* is
greater than at another point, the size (or *sectional area*) of
the stream must be diminished in the same proportion.   In
water, however, the cohesion is not of such a kind as to
admit of this tapering; but each portion, when it has acquired a certain velocity, tears itself away from the stream,
forming a drop, and leaving the stream, which has been
forcibly elongated, to contract again, till another drop is
detached.   Thus each drop is subject during its fall to certain periodic vibrations, by which it alternately elongates
and contracts.   A series of pulsations, also, occurs at the
orifice, the number of which is in the direct ratio of the
rapidity of the current, and in the inverse ratio of the diameter of the orifice; they are often sufficiently rapid to
produce a distinct musical sound.   If a note in unison with
this be played on a musical instrument at such a distance as

* It is evident that only those particles which are vertically above the
centre of the orifice can descend through it in a straight line. All others
coming from the sides of the vessel must move in lines more or less inclined.   Hence the particles on the outside of the effluent stream are
retarded, and move more slowly than those in its centre.   Hence also
arises the difference between the *mean velocity* of the escape and the
velocity due to gravity (180).

to be scarcely audible, the aërial pulses thus produced have a marked effect on the vein in shortening the limpid part.

184. When a tube is added to the orifice, the flow is accelerated if air be present, for the reason explained in "Rudimentary Pneumatics;" but, *in vacuo*, no such acceleration takes place. The most remarkable and useful result, however, of the experiments on the flow of water through pipes, is the discovery that it may be accelerated by merely giving particular forms to the commencement and termination of the pipe, without altering its general capacity. A 4-inch pipe (of any length) may be made to deliver considerably more water, if its first 3 inches and last yard be enlarged conically, than if they were cylindrical like the rest of the pipe.

185. One of the most intricate subjects to which the laws of motion have yet been applied deductively, is that of *liquid waves*. When any portion of a liquid surface is raised above or depressed below the rest, we have already seen (162) that it will return to the general level, but in doing so it acquires a velocity which necessarily carries it beyond the position of equilibrium, and thus produces a series of oscillations, which are communicated in every direction over the liquid surface, each portion receiving its motion from that preceding it, and therefore arriving at each phase of its oscillation a little later than the preceding portion; whence arises the appearance of a form travelling along the surface, which form we call a *wave*. Each wave contains, at any one moment, particles in all possible stages of their oscillation, some rising, some falling, some at the top of their range, some at the bottom; and the distance from any row of particles to the next row that are in precisely the same stage of their oscillation, is called the *breadth of a wave*. Now as these oscillations are caused by the force of gravity, we may expect some analogy between their laws and those of the pendulum, and accordingly, when the depth of the liquid is disregarded, or considered as unlimited, the wave-breadth (like the pendulum-length) varied as the square of the time of oscillation; so that the time which

elapses between the arrival of the crests of two successive
waves at a fixed point, is as the square root of the distance
between them, or the distance which either of them travels
over in the said time; hence it is easy to see that their
velocity varies inversely as the square root of their breadth.
For instance, if a certain buoy be observed to rise and fall
twice as often as another, the waves which pass it must be
four times as broad as those which pass the other, but as they
travel over this *quadruple* distance in only *double* the time,
they must evidently move with a double velocity.* When
the water, however, is so shallow that the waves are affected
by the form of the bottom, the simplicity of these results gives
place to an extreme degree of complexity. The use of these
investigations lies in their application to the *tides*, which may
be regarded as waves of moderate height, but enormous breadth
and velocity, the time of oscillation being half a lunar day,
and the velocity sometimes 1,000 miles an hour.

186. To hydrodynamics belongs, also, the theory of such
machines for raising water as do not depend on atmospheric
pressure. Such are the water-screw, invented by Archimedes, the endless chain of buckets, the water-ram, the
hydraulic belt,† &c.; but perhaps the most ingenious of these

---

* The velocity of waves that run in the same or the opposite direction
with a ship, may be ascertained by means of the log, or any other floating
body, attached to a known length of cord. By noticing the time that elapses
between the lifting of this body, and that of the ship's stern, by the same
wave, and adding or subtracting the way made by the ship during that
interval, we find the time which the wave takes to travel the length of the
cord. In this way it has been found, that in the open ocean, some waves
travel at the rate of 80 miles an hour · the breadth of such waves is sometimes a quarter of a mile. The utmost difference of level is found by measuring how high above the ship's water-line an eye must be raised to have an
uninterrupted view of the horizon. No authentic observations of this kind
give more than 25 feet, even in the greatest storms.

† This machine, the use of which has been revived within a few years, is
one of the most efficient of water elevators, yet the most inexplicable in its
action. In its ancient form it consisted of a number of hair-ropes, for which
a band of flannel, or felt, is now substituted, passing over two rollers, one at

is the *water-ram*, by which a stream of water descending a small depth is made alternately to open and close a valve, at each shutting of which, a portion of the water is driven up another tube, to a level considerably higher than that from which it originally descended, and is then retained there by a valve.

187. To this science also belongs the application of the power of streams and waterfalls to useful purposes. The chief means of effecting this, are, the *undershot* wheel, the *overshot* wheel, the *breast* wheel, the *horizontal* water-wheel, the *hydraulic engine*, the *Tourbine*, and *Barker's mill*. The first two are too well known to require a description, but we may observe, that the overshot wheel is always the most advantageous where the height of the fall is sufficient to admit of its use. The smallest rill may be applied in this manner, but the undershot wheel requires a considerable body of water. The breast wheel unites, in some measure, the advantages of both, and is applicable to falls of a medium height, as it requires only a fall equal to its *radius*, and not to its *diameter*, as is the case with the overshot wheel. This wheel is formed with plain floats, but the water enters at the level of its axle, and descends round one quadrant of its circumference, which is enclosed for this purpose in a sort of box of masonry. The horizontal water-wheel is used in some parts of France, and is the most applicable to a small fall, and a small quantity of water. Its floats are set diagonally, and may receive the water at one or at several points of its circumference at once. In the hydraulic engine, the pressure of a column of water is applied as the motive power, by means of a piston and cylinder, like those of the steam-engine. The Tourbine has been principally used in France, in cases where the fall of

the top, and the other at the bottom of the well. By means of the upper roller, it is set in very rapid motion, when the water adheres to its surface in a layer which is thicker the more rapidly it moves, and becomes nearly half an inch thick when the velocity is 1,000 feet per minute. It follows the band to any height, and is thrown off by centrifugal force, in turning over the upper roller.

water is very considerable. Barker's mill acts on a different principle from any of these, and has not yet been applied on a large scale, though experiments made on models have shown it to be the least wasteful of all modes of applying the power of a waterfall. It consists of an upright tube, from the lower end of which proceed two horizontal branches closed at their ends, and giving the whole the form of an inverted ⊥. This apparatus is moveable on a vertical axis, and water is admitted at the top through a funnel; of course, this will produce no motion, because the pressures against all parts of the interior balance each other: but suppose a hole to be made in one side of one of the horizontal arms, the water flows out, and the pressure on that surface which the hole occupies is removed. Hence the pressure on the opposite side of the tube is unbalanced, and causes it to recede in the direction contrary to that of the issuing stream. A similar hole in the other arm doubles the effect.

188. In all water-wheels it is a constant rule that the greatest mechanical effect will be produced when the velocity of the parts driven is just *half* that of the stream driving them; and this is a most important principle, applicable also to the sails of windmills and ships, and the paddles of steamers. It is obvious that the pressure of the wind or water on any of these bodies diminishes as their velocity approaches that of the current, so that if it were possible for a water-wheel to revolve with exactly the velocity of the stream, there would be no pressure on its floats, and, consequently, no power to drive any other machinery. On the other hand, the pressure is at a maximum when the wheel is standing still, but then having no velocity, it is also powerless. As the power then is proportional to the *product* of the pressure and velocity, it is greatest when they have each their mean value, that is, in the exact medium between these two states—*rest* and *motion with the current*,—in other words, it is greatest when the velocity is *half* that of the current.

INDEX.

PRINTED BY H. VIRTUE AND COMPANY, LIMITED, CITY ROAD, LONDON.

CROSBY LOCKWOOD & SON'S

LIST OF WORKS

ON

CIVIL, MECHANICAL, MARINE AND ELECTRICAL ENGINEERING.

A Complete Catalogue of NEW and STANDARD WORKS on MINING and COLLIERY WORK-ING; ARCHITECTURE and BUILDING; The INDUSTRIAL ARTS, TRADES and MANU-FACTURES; CHEMISTRY and CHEMICAL MANUFACTURES; AGRICULTURE, FARM-ING, GARDENING, AUCTIONEERING, LAND AGENCY, &c. Post Free on Application.

LONDON:

7, STATIONERS' HALL COURT, LUDGATE HILL, E.C.,

AND

121a, Victoria Street, Westminster, S.W.

1909.

LIST OF WORKS

ON

CIVIL, MECHANICAL, ELECTRICAL

AND MARINE ENGINEERING.

ACETYLENE, LIGHTING BY. Generators, Burners, and Electric Furances. By WILLIAM E. GIBBS, M.E. With 66 Illustrations. Crown 8vo, cloth **7/6**

AËRIAL NAVIGATION. A Practical Handbook on the Construction of Dirigible Balloons, Aërostats, Aëroplanes, and Aëromotors. By FREDERICK WALKER, C.E., Associate Member of the Aëronautic Institute. With 104 Illustrations. Large Crown 8vo, cloth . . . *Net* **7/6**

AËRIAL OR WIRE-ROPE TRAMWAYS. Their Construction and Management. By A. J. WALLIS-TAYLER, A.M.Inst.C.E. With 81 Illustrations. Crown 8vo, cloth **7/6**

AIR GAS LIGHTING SYSTEMS. See PETROL AIR GAS.

ALTERNATING CURRENTS, THE PRINCIPLES OF. For Students of Electrical Engineering. By E. T. LARNER, A.I.E.E., of the Engineering Department, G.P.O., London. 144 pages, with 69 Illustrations. Crown 8vo, cloth. [*Just published. Net* **3/6** COMPARISON OF CONTINUOUS AND ALTERNATING CURRENTS—SIMPLE HARMONIC MOTION—VECTORIAL REPRESENTATION—ALTERNATING CURRENT THEORY—CIRCUITS IN SERIES—CIRCUITS IN PARALLEL—ALTERNATING CURRENT POWER.

ARMATURE WINDINGS OF DIRECT CURRENT DYNAMOS. Extension and Application of a General Winding Rule. By E. ARNOLD, Engineer, Assistant Professor in Electro-Technics and Machine Design at the Riga Polytechnic School. Translated from the original German by FRANCIS B. DE GRESS, M.E., Chief of Testing Department, Crocker-Wheeler Company. Medium 8vo, 120 pp., with over 140 Illustrations *Net* **12/0**

BEAMS. EXPERIMENTS ON THEIR FLEXURE. Resulting in the Discovery of New Laws of Failure by Buckling. By ALBERT E. GUY. Medium 8vo, cloth . . . . *Net* **9/0**

BLAST FURNACE CALCULATIONS AND TABLES FOR FURNACE MANAGERS AND ENGINEERS. Containing Rules and Formulæ for Finding the Dimensions and Output Capacity of any Furnace, as well as the regular Outfit of Stoves, Heating Surface, Volume of Air, Tuyere Area, &c., per ton of Iron per day of 24 hours. By JOHN L. STEVENSON. F'cap. 8vo, leather . . . . *Net* **5/0**

BOILER AND FACTORY CHIMNEYS. Their Draught-Power and Stability. With a chapter on "Lightning Conductors." By ROBERT WILSON, A.I.C.E., Author of "A Treatise on Steam Boilers," &c. Crown 8vo, cloth **3/6**

BOILER CONSTRUCTION. A Practical Handbook for Engineers, Boiler-Makers, and Steam Users. Containing a large Collection of Rules and Data relating to Recent Practice in the Design, Construction, and Working of all Kinds of Stationary, Locomotive, and Marine Steam-Boilers. By WALTER S. HUTTON, Civil and Mechanical Engineer. With upwards of 500 Illustrations. Fourth Edition, carefully Revised, and Enlarged. Medium 8vo, over 680 pages, cloth, strongly bound 18/0

HEAT, RADIATION, AND CONDUCTION—NON-CONDUCTING MATERIALS AND COVERINGS FOR STEAM-BOILERS—COMPOSITION, CALORIFIC-POWER AND EVAPORATIVE-POWER OF FUELS—COMBUSTION, FIRING STEAM-BOILERS, PRODUCTS OF COMBUSTION, ETC., CHIMNEYS FOR STEAM-BOILERS—STEAM BLAST—FORCED DRAUGHT—FEED-WATER—EFFECT OF HEAT ON WATER—EXPANSION OF WATER BY HEAT—WEIGHT OF WATER AT DIFFERENT TEMPERATURES—CONVECTION—CIRCULATION—EVAPORATION—PROPERTIES OF SATURATED STEAM—EVAPORATIVE POWER OF BOILERS—PRIMING, ETC.—WATER-HEATING SURFACES OF STEAM-BOILERS—TRANSMISSION OF HEAT—SMOKE TUBES—EVAPORATIVE POWER AND EFFICIENCY OF BOILERS—WATER-CAPACITY AND STEAM-CAPACITY OF BOILERS—FIRE-GRATES, FIRE BRIDGES, AND FIRE-BARS—POWER OF BOILERS—CYLINDRICAL SHELLS AND FURNACE-TUBES OF BOILERS, ETC.—TESTS OF MATERIALS—STRENGTH AND WEIGHT OF BOILER-PLATES—EFFECT OF TEMPERATURE ON METALS—RIVET HOLES—RIVETS—RIVETED JOINTS OF STEAM-BOILERS—CAULKING ENDS OF CYLINDRICAL SHELLS—STAYS FOR BOILERS, ETC.—STEAM GENERATORS—DESCRIPTION AND PROPORTIONS OF CORNISH, LANCASHIRE, AND OTHER TYPES OF STATIONARY BOILERS—BOILER-SETTING—MULTI-TUBULAR, LOCOMOTIVE, PORTABLE, MARINE, VERTICAL, AND WATER-TUBE BOILERS—SUPER-HEATERS—COST OF STEAM PRODUCTION—FURNACES FOR REFUSE-FUELS—DESTRUCTORS, ETC.—SAFETY-VALVES—STEAM PIPES—STOP-VALVES AND OTHER MOUNTINGS FOR BOILERS—FEED-PUMPS—STEAM PUMPS—FEED-WATER CONSUMPTION—INJECTORS—INCRUSTATION AND CORROSION—FEED-WATER HEATERS—EVAPORATORS—TESTING BOILERS—EVAPORATIVE PERFORMANCES OF STEAM BOILERS; STEAM-BOILER EXPLOSIONS, ETC.

" There has long been room for a modern handbook on steam boilers; there is not that room now, because Mr. Hutton has filled it. It is a thoroughly practical book for those who are occupied in the construction, design, selection, or use of boilers."—*Engineer.*

BOILERMAKER'S ASSISTANT. In Drawing, Templating, and Calculating Boiler Work, &c. By J. COURTNEY, Practical Boilermaker. Edited by D. K. CLARK, C.E. Eighth Edition. Crown 8vo, cloth . 2/0

BOILERMAKER'S READY RECKONER. With Examples of Practical Geometry and Templating for the Use of Platers, Smiths, and Riveters. By John COURTNEY. Edited by D. K. CLARK, M.Inst.C.E. Crown 8vo, cloth 4/0

BOILERMAKER'S READY RECKONER & ASSISTANT, being the two previous mentioned volumes bound together in one volume. With Examples of Practical Geometry and Templating, for the Use of Platers, Smiths, and Riveters. By JOHN COURTNEY. Edited by D. K. CLARK, M.Inst.C.E. Fifth Edition, 480 pp., with 140 Illustrations. Crown 8vo, half bound 7/0

"No workman or apprentice should be without this book."—*Iron Trade Circular.*

BOILER MAKING AND PLATING. A Practical Handbook for Workshop Operations, including an Appendix of Tables. By JOSEPH G. HORNER, A.M.I.M.E. Second Edition. Thoroughly revised and enlarged. 380 pp., with 351 Illustrations. Crown 8vo, cloth.
[*Just published. Net* 9/0

BOILERS (STEAM). Their Construction and Management. By R. ARMSTRONG, C.E. Illustrated. Crown 8vo, cloth . . . 1/6

BOILERS. Their Strength, Construction, and Economical Working. By R. WILSON, C.E. Fifth Edition. 12mo, cloth . . . 6/0

BRIDGE CONSTRUCTION IN CAST AND WROUGHT
IRON. A Complete and Practical Treatise on, including Iron Foundations. In Three Parts.—Theoretical, Practical, and Descriptive. By WILLIAM HUMBER. A.M.Inst.C.E., and M.Inst.M.E. Third Edition, revised and much improved, with 115 Double Plates (so of which now first appear in this edition), and numerous Additions to the Text. In 2 vols., imp. 4to, half-bound in morocco . . . . **£6 16s. 6d.**

"In addition to elevations, plans, and sections, large scale details are given, which very much enhance the instructive work of these illustrations."—*Civil Engineer and Architect's Journal.*

BRIDGES AND VIADUCTS, IRON AND STEEL. A
Practical Treatise upon their Construction. For the use of Engineers, Draughtsmen, and Students. By FRANCIS CAMPIN, C.E. Crown 8vo, cloth **3/6**

BRIDGES (IRON) OF MODERATE SPAN: Their Con-
struction and Erection. By H. W. PENDRED. With 40 illustrations. Crown 8vo, cloth **2/0**

BRIDGES, OBLIQUE. A Practical and Theoretical Essay.
With 13 large Plates. By the late GEORGE WATSON BUCK, M.Inst.C.E. Fourth Edition, revised by his Son, J. H. WATSON BUCK, M.Inst.C.E. ; and with the addition of Description to Diagrams for Facilitating the Construction of Oblique Bridges, by W. H. BARLOW, M.Inst.C.E. Royal 8vo, cloth **12/0**

"As a guide to the engineer and architect, on a confessedly difficult subject, Mr. Buck's work is unsurpassed."—*Building News.*

BRIDGES, TUBULAR AND OTHER IRON GIRDER.
Describing the Britannia and Conway Tubular Bridges. With a Sketch of Iron Bridges, &c. By G. D. DEMPSEY, C.E. Crown 8vo, cloth . **2/0**

CALCULATOR (NUMBER, WEIGHT, AND FRACTIONAL).
Containing upwards of 250,000 Separate Calculations, showing at a Glance the Value at 422 Different Rates, ranging from $\frac{1}{16}$th of a Penny to 20s. each, or per cwt., and £20 per ton, of any number of articles consecutively, from 1 to 470. Any number of cwts., qrs., and lbs., from 1 cwt. to 470 cwts. Any number of tons, cwts., qrs., and lbs., from 1 to 1,000 tons. By WILLIAM CHADWICK, Public Accountant. Fourth Edition, Revised and Improved. 8vo, strongly bound **18/0**

CALCULATOR (WEIGHT). Being a Series of Tables upon a
New and Comprehensive Plan, exhibiting at one Reference the exact Value of any Weight from 1 lb. to 15 tons, at 300 Progressive Rates, from 1d. to 168s. per cwt., and containing 186,000 Direct Answers, which, with their Combinations, consisting of a single addition (mostly to be performed at sight), will afford an aggregate of 10,266,000 Answers ; the whole being calculated and designed to ensure correctness and promote despatch. By HENRY HARBEN, Accountant. Sixth Edition, carefully Corrected. Royal 8vo, strongly half-bound . . . . **£1 5s.**

CHAIN CABLES AND CHAINS. Comprising Sizes and Curves
of Links, Studs, etc., Iron for Cables and Chains, Chain Cable and Chain
Making, Forming and Welding Links, Strength of Cables and Chains,
Certificates for Cables, Marking Cables, Prices of Chain Cables and Chains,
Historical Notes, Acts of Parliament, Statutory Tests, Charges for Testing,
List of Manufacturers of Cables, etc., etc.   By THOMAS W. TRAILL,
F.E.R.N., M.Inst.C.E., Engineer-Surveyor-in-Chief, Board of Trade, Inspec-
tor of Chain Cable and Anchor Proving Establishments, and General Super-
intendent, Lloyd's Committee on Proving Establishments.   With numerous
Tables, Illustrations, and Lithographic Drawings. Folio, cloth **£2 2s.**

CIVIL ENGINEERING. By HENRY LAW, M.Inst.C.E.   In-
cluding a Treatise on Hydraulic Engineering by G. R. BURNELL,
M.Inst.C.E.   Seventh Edition, revised, with Large Additions on Recent
Practice by D. KINNEAR CLARK, M.Inst.C.E.   Crown 8vo, cloth   **6/6**

CONDUCTORS FOR ELECTRICAL DISTRIBUTION.
Their Materials and Manufacture, The Calculation of Circuits, Pole-Line
Construction, Underground Working, and other Uses. By F. A. C. PERRINE,
A.M., D.Sc. ; formerly Professor of Electrical Engineering, Leland Stanford,
Jr., University ; M.Amer.I.E.E.   Medium 8vo, 300 pp., fully illustrated,
including Folding Plates and Diagrams . . . . . *Net* **20/0**

CONTINUOUS RAILWAY BRAKES. A Practical Treatise
on the several Systems in Use in the United Kingdom, their Construction
and Performance.   By M. REYNOLDS. 8vo, cloth **9/0**

CRANES, the Construction of, and other Machinery for Raising
Heavy Bodies for the Erection of Buildings, &c. By J. GLYNN, F.R.S.
Crown 8vo, cloth **1/6**

CURVES, TABLES OF TANGENTIAL ANGLES AND
MULTIPLES.   For Setting-out Curves from 5 to 200 Radius. By A.
BEAZELEY, M.Inst.C.E.   7th Edition, Revised.   With an Appendix on
the use of the Tables for Measuring up Curves.   Printed on 50 Cards, and
sold in a cloth box, waistcoat-pocket size **3/6**

" Each table is printed on a small card, which, placed on the theodolite, leaves the hands free
to manipulate the instrument—no small advantage as regards the rapidity of work."—*Engineer*.

DRAINAGE OF LANDS, TOWNS AND BUILDINGS.
By G. D. DEMPSEY, C.E.   Revised, with large Additions on Recent Practice
in Drainage Engineering by D. KINNEAR CLARK, M.Inst.C.E.   Fourth
Edition.   Crown 8vo, cloth **4/6**

DYNAMIC ELECTRICITY AND MAGNETISM, ELE-
MENTS OF.   A Handbook for Students and Electrical Engineers.   By
PHILIP ATKINSON, A.M., Ph.D.   Crown 8vo, cloth, 417 pp., with 120
Illustrations **10/6**

DYNAMO BUILDING.   HOW TO MAKE A DYNAMO.
A Practical Treatise for Amateurs.   By ALFRED CROFTS.   Crown 8vo,
cloth **2/0**

DYNAMO ELECTRIC MACHINERY. By SAMUEL SHELDON,
A.M., Ph.D., Professor of Physics and Electrical Engineering at the Polytechnic Institute of Brooklyn, etc., assisted by HOBART MASON, B.S., E.E.

In two volumes (sold separately).

Vol. I.—DIRECT CURRENT MACHINES. Sixth Edition, Revised. 202 Illustrations . . . . *Net* **12/0**

Vol. II.—ALTERNATING CURRENT MACHINES. Fifth Edition. With 184 Illustrations . . . . *Net* **12/0**

DYNAMO MANAGEMENT. A Handybook of Theory and
Practice for the Use of Mechanics, Engineers, Students, and others in Charge of Dynamos. By G. W. LUMMIS-PATERSON, Electrical Engineer. Fourth Edition, Revised and Enlarged. 300 pp., with 117 Illustrations. Crown 8vo, cloth . . . . *[Just published.* Net **4/6**

ELECTRICAL UNITS—MAGNETIC PRINCIPLES—THEORY OF THE DYNAMO—ARMATURES—ARMATURES IN PRACTICE—FIELD MAGNETS—FIELD MAGNETS IN PRACTICE—REGULATION DYNAMOS — COUPLING DYNAMOS — INSTALLATION, RUNNING AND MAINTENANCE OF DYNAMOS—FAULTS IN DYNAMOS—FAULTS IN ARMATURES—MOTORS.

" The book may be confidently recommended."—*Engineer.*

DYNAMO, MOTOR AND SWITCHBOARD CIRCUITS
FOR ELECTRICAL ENGINEERS. A Practical Book dealing with the subject of Direct, Alternating and Polyphase Currents. By WILLIAM R. BOWKER, Consulting Electrical and Street Railway Engineer, Professor of Physics in the University of Southern California, Los Angeles. Second Edition, revised and greatly enlarged. 180 pages, with 130 illustrations. Medium 8vo, cloth. . . . . *[Just published.* Net **7/6**

DYNAMO AND MOTOR CIRCUITS—STARTING AND STOPPING OF SAME—METHODS OF CHANGING DIRECTION OF ROTATION—SYNCHRONISM—PARALLELING OF ALTERNATORS, ETC.—POLYPHASE CIRCUITS—POLYPHASE TRANSMISSION OF POWER—DIPHASE AND TRIPHASE CIRCUITS, ETC. — BOOSTERS — EQUALISERS—REVERSIBLE BOOSTERS—STORAGE BATTERIES—END-CELL SWITCHES, ETC.—ELECTRIC TRACTION MOTORS — SERIES — PARALLEL CONTROLLERS — CAR WIRING DIAGRAMS — MOTOR VEHICLE CIRCUITS — CANAL HAULAGE ROTARY CONVERTERS — SWITCHBOARD CIRCUITS, ETC.

DYNAMOS (ALTERNATING AND DIRECT CURRENT).
A Text-book on their Construction for Students, Engineer-Constructors and Electricians-in-Charge. By TYSON SEWELL, A.M.I.E.E., Lecturer and Demonstrator in Electrical Engineering at the Polytechnic, Regent Street, London, author of " The Elements of Electrical Engineering." 328 pp., with over 230 Illustrations. Large crown 8vo, cloth . . . . *Net* **7/6**

FUNDAMENTAL PRINCIPLES OF DIRECT CURRENTS—THE MAGNETIC FIELD—THE PRODUCTION OF AN ELECTRO-MOTIVE FORCE—FUNDAMENTAL PRINCIPLES OF ALTERNATING CURRENTS—THE ALTERNATING MAGNETIC FIELD—THE CAPACITY OF THE CIRCUIT—BIPOLAR DYNAMO CONSTRUCTION—THEORY OF BIPOLAR MACHINES—BIPOLAR DYNAMO DESIGN — MULTIPOLAR DYNAMO CONSTRUCTION — MULTIPOLAR DYNAMO DESIGN—SINGLE PHASE ALTERNATORS—CONSTRUCTION OF ALTERNATORS—POLYPHASE ALTERNATORS — EXCITING, COMPOUNDING AND SYNCHRONISING OF ALTERNATORS.

EARTHWORK DIAGRAMS. Giving graphically the Cubic
Contents for different Heights of Banks and Cuttings, either 66 ft. or 100 ft. Chains. By R. A. ERSKINE-MURRAY, A.M.Inst.C.E., and Y. D. KIRTON, A.M.Can.Soc.C.E. On a sheet in a roll.

5/0 *Net*, or mounted on card, *Net* **7/6**

These Diagrams or Scales have been designed with the intention of reducing the labour connected with the computation of earthwork quantities, and especially those of railways and roads. It has been found in the Authors' practice that they are much quicker, and at the same time as accurate and much more complete than most of the tables heretofore published.

EARTHWORK MANUAL. By ALEX. J. GRAHAM, C.E. With numerous Diagrams. Second Edition. 18mo, cloth **2/6**

EARTHWORK TABLES. Showing the Contents in Cubic Yards of Embankments, Cuttings, &c., of Heights or Depths up to an average of 80 feet. By JOSEPH BROADBENT, C.E., and FRANCIS CAMPIN, C.E. Crown 8vo, cloth **5/0**

EARTHWORK TABLES, HANDY GENERAL. Giving the Contents in Cubic Yards of Centre and Slopes of Cuttings and Embankments from 3 inches to 80 feet in Depth or Height, for use with either 66 feet Chain or 100 feet Chain. By J. H. WATSON BUCK, M.Inst.C.E. On a Sheet mounted in cloth case **3/6**

ELECTRIC LIGHT. Its Production and Use. By J. W. URQUHART. Crown 8vo, cloth **7/6**

ELECTRIC LIGHT FITTING. A Handbook for Working Electrical Engineers. By J. W. URQUHART. Crown 8vo, cloth . . **5/0**

ELECTRIC LIGHT FOR COUNTRY HOUSES. A Practical Handbook, including Particulars of the Cost of Plant, and Working. By J. H. KNIGHT. Crown 8vo, wrapper **1/0**

ELECTRIC LIGHTING. By ALAN A. CAMPBELL SWINTON, M.Inst.C.E., M.I.E.E. Crown 8vo, cloth **1/6**

ELECTRIC LIGHTING AND HEATING POCKET BOOK. Comprising useful Formulæ, Tables, Data, and Particulars of Apparatus and Appliances for the use of Central Stations, Engineers, Contractors, and Engineers-in-Charge. By SYDNEY F. WALKER, R.N., M.I.E.E., M.I.M.E., A.M.Inst.C.E., Etc. F'cap 8vo, 448 pp., 270 Diagrams, and 240 Tables. *Net* **7/6**

DEFINITIONS—DIFFERENT UNITS EMPLOYED—LAWS OF ELECTRIC CIRCUITS—DIFFERENCES BETWEEN WORKING OF CONTINUOUS AND ALTERNATING CURRENTS—LAWS OF ELECTRO-MAGNETIC AND ELECTRO-STATIC INDUCTION—ELECTRICITY GENERATORS—ACCUMULATORS—SWITCHBOARDS—SWITCHES, CIRCUIT-BREAKERS, ETC. —CABLES—METHODS OF INSULATION—SIZES AND INSULATION OF CABLES MADE BY LEADING MAKERS—CONDUITS—LEADING WIRES AND OTHER ACCESSORIES—MEASURING INSTRUMENTS OF ALL KINDS AND APPARATUS FOR TESTING LAMPS AND ACCESSORIES—APPARATUS FOR HEATING BY ELECTRICITY.

ELECTRIC SHIP-LIGHTING. A Handbook on the Practical Fitting and Running of Ships' Electrical Plant. By J. W. URQUHART. Crown 8vo, cloth **7/6**

ELECTRIC-WIRING, DIAGRAMS & SWITCH-BOARDS. By NEWTON HARRISON, E.E., Instructor of Electrical Engineering in the Newark Technical School. Crown 8vo, cloth . . . . *Net* **5/0**

THE BEGINNING OF WIRING—CALCULATING THE SIZE OF WIRE—A SIMPLE ELECTRIC LIGHT CIRCUIT CALCULATED—ESTIMATING THE MAINS, FEEDERS, AND BRANCHES—USING THE BRIDGE FOR TESTING—THE INSULATION RESISTANCE—WIRING FOR MOTORS—WIRING WITH CLEATS, MOULDING AND CONDUIT—LAYING-OUT A CONDUIT SYSTEM—POWER REQUIRED FOR LAMPS—LIGHTING OF A ROOM—SWITCHBOARDS AND THEIR PURPOSE—SWITCHBOARDS DESIGNED FOR SHUNT AND COMPOUND-WOUND DYNAMOS—PANEL SWITCHBOARDS, STREET RAILWAY SWITCH-BOARDS, LIGHTNING ARRESTERS—THE GROUND DETECTOR—LOCATING GROUNDS—ALTERNATING CURRENT CIRCUITS—THE POWER FACTOR IN CIRCUITS—CALCULATION OF SIZES OF WIRE FOR SINGLE, TWO AND THREE-PHASE CIRCUITS.

ELECTRICAL AND MAGNETIC CALCULATIONS. For the Use of Electrical Engineers and Artisans, Teachers, Students, and all others interested in the Theory and Application of Electricity and Magnetism. By A. A. ATKINSON, M.S., Professor of Physics and Electricity in Ohio University, Athens, Ohio. Crown 8vo, cloth . . . . *Net* **9/0**

ELECTRICAL DICTIONARY. A Popular Encyclopædia of Words and Terms Used in the Practice of Electrical Engineering. By T. O'CONOR SLOANE, A.M., E.M., Ph.D., Author of " Arithmetic of Electricity," " Electricity Simplified," " Electric Toy Making," etc. Fourth Edition, with Appendix. 690 pages and nearly 400 Illustrations. Large Crown 8vo, cloth
Net **7/6**
" The work has many attractive features in it, and is, beyond doubt, a well put together and useful publication. The amount of ground covered may be gathered from the fact that in the index about 5,000 references will be found."—*Electrical Review.*

ELECTRICAL ENGINEERING. A First-Year's Course for Students. By TYSON SEWELL, A.I.E.E., Lecturer and Demonstrator in Electrical Engineering at the Polytechnic, Regent Street, London. Fourth Edition, Revised, with additions. Large Crown 8vo, cloth. 466 pp., with 277 Illustrations . . . . *Net* **5/0**
OHM'S LAW—UNITS EMPLOYED IN ELECTRICAL ENGINEERING—SERIES AND PARALLEL CIRCUITS — CURRENT DENSITY AND POTENTIAL DROP IN THE CIRCUIT—THE HEATING EFFECT OF THE ELECTRIC CURRENT—THE MAGNETIC EFFECT OF AN ELECTRIC CURRENT—THE MAGNETISATION OF IRON—ELECTRO-CHEMISTRY—PRIMARY BATTERIES— ACCUMULATORS—INDICATING INSTRUMENTS—AMMETERS, VOLTMETERS, OHMMETERS—ELECTRICITY SUPPLY METERS—MEASURING INSTRUMENTS, AND THE MEASUREMENT OF ELECTRICAL RESISTANCE — MEASUREMENT OF POTENTIAL DIF-FERENCE, CAPACITY, CURRENT STRENGTH, AND PERMEABILITY—ARC LAMPS—INCAN-DESCENT LAMPS — MANUFACTURE AND INSTALLATION—PHOTOMETRY — THE CON-TINUOUS CURRENT DYNAMO—DIRECT CURRENT MOTORS—ALTERNATING CURRENTS —TRANSFORMERS, ALTERNATORS, SYNCHRONOUS MOTORS—POLYPHASE WORKING—APPENDIX I., THE THREE-WIRE SYSTEM—APPENDIX II., QUESTIONS AND ANSWERS.
" Distinctly one of the best books for those commencing the study of electrical engineering. Everything is explained in simple language which even a beginner cannot fail to understand."—*The Engineer.*

ELECTRICAL ENGINEERING (ELEMENTARY). In Theory and Practice. A Class Book for Junior and Senior Students and Working Electricians. By J. H. ALEXANDER. With nearly 200 Illustrations. Crown 8vo, cloth . . . . *Net* **3/6**
FUNDAMENTAL PRINCIPLES—ELECTRICAL CURRENTS—SOLENOID COILS, GALVANO-METERS—VOLT-METERS—MEASURING INSTRUMENTS—ALTERNATING CURRENTS—DYNAMO ELECTRIC MACHINES—CONTINUOUS CURRENT DYNAMOS—INDUCTION, STATIC TRANSFORMERS, CONVERTERS—MOTORS—PRIMARY AND STORAGE CELLS—ARC LAMPS—INCANDESCENT LAMPS—SWITCHES, FUSES, ETC.—CONDUCTORS AND CABLES—ELEC-TRICAL ENERGY METERS—SPECIFICATIONS—GENERATION AND TRANSMISSION OF ELECTRICAL ENERGY—GENERATING STATIONS.

ELECTRICAL ENGINEERING. See ALTERNATING CURRENTS.

ELECTRICAL TRANSMISSION OF ENERGY. A Manual for the Design of Electrical Circuits. By ARTHUR VAUGHAN ABBOTT, C.E., Member American Institute of Electrical Engineers, Member American Institute of Mining Engineers, Member American Society of Civil Engineers, Member American Society of Mechanical Engineers, etc. Fourth Edition, entirely Re-Written and Enlarged, with numerous Tables, 16 Plates, and nearly 400 other Illustrations. Royal 8vo, 700 pages. Strongly bound in cloth . . . . *Net* **30/0**
INTRODUCTION—THE PROPERTIES OF WIRE—THE CONSTRUCTION OF AERIAL CIRCUITS—GENERAL LINE WORK—ELECTRIC RAILWAY CIRCUITS—PROTECTION—THE CONSTRUCTION OF UNDERGROUND CIRCUITS—CONDUITS—CABLES AND CONDUIT CON-DUCTORS—SPECIAL RAILWAY CIRCUIT—THE INTERURBAN TRANSMISSION LINE—THE THIRD RAIL—THE URBAN CONDUIT—ELECTRICAL INSTRUMENTS—METHODS OF ELEC-TRICAL MEASUREMENT — CONTINUOUS-CURRENT CONDUCTORS — THE HEATING OF CONDUCTORS—CONDUCTORS FOR ALTERNATING CURRENTS—SERIES DISTRIBUTION—PARALLEL DISTRIBUTION—MISCELLANEOUS METHODS—POLYPHASE TRANSMISSION—THE COST OF PRODUCTION AND DISTRIBUTION.
NOTE.—This Volume forms an indispensable Work for Electrical Engineers, Railway and Tramway Managers and Directors, and all interested in Electric Traction.

ELECTRICITY AS APPLIED TO MINING. By ARNOLD

LUPTON, M.Inst.C.E., M.I.Mech.E., M.I.E.E., late Professor of Coal Mining at the Yorkshire College, Victoria University, Mining Engineer and Colliery Manager; G. D. ASPINALL PARR, M.I.E.E., A.M.I.Mech.E., Associate of the Central Technical College, City and Guilds of London, Head of the Electrical Engineering Department, Yorkshire College, Victoria University; and HERBERT PERKIN, M.I.M.E., Certificated Colliery Manager, Assistant Lecturer in the Mining Department of the Yorkshire College, Victoria University. Second Edition, Revised and Enlarged. Medium 8vo, cloth, 300 pp., with about 170 Illustrations . . . . . *Net* **12/0**

INTRODUCTORY—DYNAMIC ELECTRICITY—DRIVING OF THE DYNAMO—THE STEAM TURBINE—DISTRIBUTION OF ELECTRICAL ENERGY—STARTING AND STOPPING ELECTRICAL GENERATORS AND MOTORS—ELECTRIC CABLES—CENTRAL ELECTRICAL PLANTS —ELECTRICITY APPLIED TO PUMPING AND HAULING—ELECTRICITY APPLIED TO COAL CUTTING—TYPICAL ELECTRIC PLANTS RECENTLY ERECTED—ELECTRIC LIGHTING BY ARC AND GLOW LAMPS—MISCELLANEOUS APPLICATIONS OF ELECTRICITY—ELECTRICITY AS COMPARED WITH OTHER MODES OF TRANSMITTING POWER—DANGERS OF ELECTRICITY.

" The book is a good attempt to meet a growing want, and is well worthy of a place in the mining engineer's library."—*The Electrician.*

ELECTRICITY IN FACTORIES: ITS COST AND CON-

VENIENCE. A Handbook for Power Producers and Power Users. By A. P. HASLAM, M.I.E.E. About 300 pp., fully illustrated. Demy 8vo.
[*In the Press.*

ELECTRICITY. A STUDENT'S TEXT-BOOK. By H.

M. NOAD, F.R.S. 650 pp., with 470 Illustrations. Crown 8vo . . **9/0**

ELECTRICITY, POWER TRANSMITTED BY, AND

APPLIED BY THE ELECTRIC MOTOR, including Electric Railway Construction. By PHILIP ATKINSON, A.M., Ph.D., author of " Elements of Static Electricity." Fourth Edition, Enlarged, Crown 8vo, cloth, 224 pp., with over 90 Illustrations . . . . *Net* **9/0**

ELECTRO - PLATING AND ELECTRO - REFINING OF

METALS. Being a new edition of Alexander Watt's " Electro-Deposition." Revised and Largely Re-written by ARNOLD PHILIP, Assoc. R.S.M., B.Sc., A.I.E.E., F.I.C., Principal Assistant to the Admiralty Chemist, formerly Chief Chemist to the Engineering Departments of the India Office, and sometime Assistant Professor of Electrical Engineering and Applied Physics at the Heriot-Watt College, Edinburgh. 700 pp., with numerous Illustrations, Large Crown 8vo, cloth . . . . *Net* **12/6**

ENGINE-DRIVING LIFE. Stirring Adventures and Incidents

in the Lives of Locomotive Engine-Drivers. By MICHAEL REYNOLDS. Third Edition. Crown 8vo, cloth **1/6**

ENGINEERING DRAWING. A WORKMAN'S MANUAL.

By JOHN MAXTON, Instructor in Engineering Drawing, Royal Naval College, Greenwich. Eighth Edition. 300 Plates and Diagrams. Crown 8vo, cloth **3/6**

" A copy of it should be kept for reference in every drawing office."—*Engineering.*

ENGINEERING ESTIMATES, COSTS, AND ACCOUNTS.

A Guide to Commercial Engineering. With numerous examples of Estimates and Costs of Millwright Work, Miscellaneous Productions, Steam Engines and Steam Boilers; and a Section on the Preparation of Costs Accounts. By A GENERAL MANAGER. Second Edition. 8vo, cloth **12/0**

" The information is given in a plain, straightforward manner, and bears throughout evidence of the intimate practical acquaintance of the author with every phase of commercial engineering.' —*Mechanical World.*

ENGINEERING PROGRESS (1863-6). By WM. HUMBER,
A.M.Inst.C.E. Complete in Four Vols. Containing 148 Double Plates, with Portraits and Copious Descriptive Letterpress. Impl. 4to, half-morocco. Price, complete, **£12 12s.**; or each Volume sold separately at **£3 3s.** per Volume. *Descriptive List of Contents on application.*

ENGINEER'S AND MILLWRIGHT'S ASSISTANT. A
Collection of Useful Tables, Rules, and Data. By WILLIAM TEMPLETON. Eighth Edition, with Additions. 18mo, cloth **2/6**

"A deservedly popular work. It should be in the 'drawer' of every mechanic. —*English Mechanic.*

ENGINEER'S HANDBOOK. A Practical Treatise on Modern
Engines and Boilers, Marine, Locomotive, and Stationary. And containing a large collection of Rules and Practical Data relating to Recent Practice in Designing and Constructing all kinds of Engines, Boilers, and other Engineering work. The whole constituting a comprehensive Key to the Board of Trade and other Examinations for Certificates of Competency in Modern Mechanical Engineering. By WALTER S. HUTTON, Civil and Mechanical Engineer, Author of "The Works' Manager's Handbook for Engineers," &c. With upwards of 420 Illustrations. Sixth Edition, Revised and Enlarged. Medium 8vo, nearly 560 pp., strongly bound **18/0**

"A mass of information set down in simple language, and in such a form that it can be easily referred to at any time. The matter is uniformly good and well chosen, and is greatly elucidated by the illustrations. The book will find its way on to most engineers' shelves, where it will rank as one of the most useful books of reference."—*Practical Engineer.*

"Full of useful information, and should be found on the office shelf of all practical engineers.' —*English Mechanic.*

ENGINEER'S, MECHANIC'S, ARCHITECT'S,
BUILDER'S, ETC. TABLES AND MEMORANDA. Selected and Arranged by FRANCIS SMITH. Seventh Edition, Revised, including ELECTRICAL TABLES, FORMULÆ, and MEMORANDA. Waistcoat-pocket size, limp leather **1/6**

"The best example we have ever seen of 270 pages of useful matter packed into the dimensions of a card-case."—*Building News.*

ENGINEER'S YEAR-BOOK FOR 1909. Comprising
Formulæ, Rules, Tables, Data and Memoranda in Civil, Mechanical, Electrical, Marine and Mine Engineering. By H. R. KEMPE, M.Inst.C.E., Electrician to the Post Office, Formerly Principal Staff Engineer, Engineer-in-Chief's Office, General Post Office, London, Author of "A Handbook of Electrical Testing," "The Electrical Engineer's Pocket-Book," &c. With 1,000 Illustrations, specially Engraved for the work. Crown 8vo, 950 pp., leather . . . . [*Just Published.* **8/0**

"Kempe's Year-Book really requires no commendation. Its sphere of usefulness is widely known, and it is used by engineers the world over."—*The Engineer.*

"The volume is distinctly in advance of most similar publications in this country."—*Engineering.*

ENGINEMAN'S POCKET COMPANION, and Practical Edu-
cator for Enginemen, Boiler Attendants, and Mechanics. By MICHAEL REYNOLDS. With 45 Illustrations and numerous Diagrams. Fifth Edition. Royal 18mo, strongly bound for pocket wear **3/6**

EXCAVATION (EARTH AND ROCK). A Practical Treatise, by CHARLES PRELINI, C.E. 365 pp., with Tables, many Diagrams and Engravings. Royal 8vo, cloth . . . . *Net* **16/0**

FACTORY ACCOUNTS: their PRINCIPLES & PRACTICE. A Handbook for Accountants and Manufacturers. By E. GARCKE and J. M. FELLS. Crown 8vo, cloth **7/6**

FIRES, FIRE-ENGINES, AND FIRE BRIGADES. With a History of Fire-Engines, their Construction, Use, and Management. Hints on Fire-Brigades, &c. By C. F. T. YOUNG, C.E. 8vo, cloth, **£1 4s.**

FOUNDATIONS AND CONCRETE WORKS. With Practical Remarks on Footings, Planking, Sand and Concrete, Béton, Pile-driving, Caissons, and Cofferdams. By E. DOBSON. Crown 8vo . . . **1/6**

FUEL, ITS COMBUSTION AND ECONOMY. Consisting of an Abridgment of "A Treatise on the Combustion of Coal and the Prevention of Smoke." By C. W. WILLIAMS, A.Inst.C.E. With extensive Additions by D. KINNEAR CLARK, M.Inst.C.E. Fourth Edition. Crown 8vo, cloth **3/6**

FUELS: SOLID, LIQUID, AND GASEOUS. Their Analysis and Valuation. For the use of Chemists and Engineers. By H. J. PHILLIPS, F.C.S., formerly Analytical and Consulting Chemist to the Great Eastern Railway. Fourth Edition. Crown 8vo, cloth **2/0**

GAS AND OIL ENGINE MANAGEMENT. A Practical Guide for Users and Attendants, being Notes on Selection, Construction, and Management. By M. POWIS BALE, M.Inst.C.E., M.I.Mech.E. Author of "Woodworking Machinery," &c. Second Edition, with an additional Chapter on Gas Producers. Crown 8vo, cloth . . . . . . *Net* **3/6**

SELECTING AND FIXING A GAS ENGINE—PRINCIPLES OF WORKING, ETC.—FAILURES AND DEFECTS—VALVES, IGNITION, PISTON RINGS, ETC.—OIL ENGINES—GAS PRODUCERS —RULES, TABLES, ETC.

GAS ENGINEER'S POCKET-BOOK. Comprising Tables, Notes and Memoranda relating to the Manufacture, Distribution, and Use of Coal Gas and the Construction of Gas Works. By H. O'CONNOR, A.M.Inst. C.E. Third Edition, Revised. Crown 8vo, leather . . *Net* **10/6**

"The book contains a vast amount of information."—*Gas World.*

GAS-ENGINE HANDBOOK. A Manual of Useful Information for the Designer and the Engineer. By E. W. ROBERTS, M.E. With Forty Full-page Engravings. Small Fcap. 8vo, leather . . *Net* **8/6**

GAS ENGINES. With Appendix describing a Recent Engine with Tube Igniter. By T. M. GOODEVE, M.A. Crown 8vo, cloth . **2/6**

GAS ENGINES. See INTERNAL COMBUSTION ENGINES.

GAS-ENGINES AND PRODUCER-GAS PLANTS. A
Treatise setting forth the Principles of Gas Engines and Producer Design, the Selection and Installation of an Engine, the Care of Gas Engines and Producer-Gas Plants, with a Chapter on Volatile Hydrocarbon and Oil Engines. By R. E. MATHOT, M.E. Translated from the French. With a Preface by DUGALD CLERK, M.Inst.C.E., F.C.S. Medium 8vo, cloth, 310 pages, with about 150 Illustrations . . . . *Net* **12/0**

MOTIVE POWER AND COST OF INSTALLATION—SELECTION OF AN ENGINE—INSTALLATION OF AN ENGINE—FOUNDATION AND EXHAUST—WATER CIRCULATION—LUBRICATION—CONDITIONS OF PERFECT OPERATION—HOW TO START AN ENGINE—PRECAUTIONS—PERTURBATIONS IN THE OPERATION OF ENGINES—PRODUCER-GAS ENGINES—PRODUCER-GAS—PRESSURE GAS-PRODUCERS—SUCTION GAS-PRODUCERS—OIL AND VOLATILE HYDROCARBON ENGINES—THE SELECTION OF AN ENGINE.

GAS LIGHTING. See ACETYLENE.

GAS LIGHTING FOR COUNTRY HOUSES. See PETROL
AIR GAS.

GAS MANUFACTURE, CHEMISTRY OF. A Practical
Manual for the Use of Gas Engineers, Gas Managers and Students. By HAROLD M. ROYLE, F.C.S., Chief Chemical Assistant at the Becton Gas Works. Demy 8vo, cloth. 340 pages, with numerous Illustrations and Coloured Plate . . . . *Net* **12/6**

PREPARATION OF STANDARD SOLUTIONS—ANALYSIS OF COALS—DESCRIPTION OF VARIOUS TYPES OF FURNACES—PRODUCTS OF CARBONISATION AT VARIOUS TEMPERATURES—ANALYSIS OF CRUDE GAS—ANALYSIS OF LIME—ANALYSIS OF AMMONIACAL LIQUOR—ANALYTICAL VALUATION OF OXIDE OF IRON—ESTIMATION OF NAPTHALIN—ANALYSIS OF FIRE-BRICKS AND FIRE-CLAY—ART OF PHOTOMETRY—CARBURETTED WATER GAS—APPENDIX CONTAINING STATUTORY AND OFFICIAL REGULATIONS FOR TESTING GAS, VALUABLE EXCERPTS FROM VARIOUS IMPORTANT PAPERS ON GAS CHEMISTRY, USEFUL TABLES, MEMORANDA, ETC.

"It should prove a useful book of instruction and reference both to students in the technical colleges and to practical engineers and managers in their daily duties."—*Scotsman.*

GAS WORKS. Their Construction and arrangement, and the
Manufacture and Distribution of Coal Gas. By S. HUGHES, C.E. Ninth Edition. Revised, with Notices of Recent Improvements by HENRY O'CONNOR, A.M.Inst.C.E. Crown 8vo, cloth **6/0**

GEOMETRY. For the Architect, Engineer, and Mechanic. By
E. W. TARN, M.A., Architect. 8vo, cloth **9/0**

GEOMETRY FOR TECHNICAL STUDENTS. By E.
H. SPRAGUE, A.M.Inst.C.E. Crown 8vo, cloth . . . . *Net* **1/0**

GEOMETRY OF COMPASSES. By OLIVER BYRNE. Coloured
Plates. Crown 8vo, cloth **3/6**

HEAT, EXPANSION OF STRUCTURES BY. By JOHN
KEILY, C.E. Crown 8vo, cloth **3/6**

HOISTING MACHINERY. Including the Elements of Crane
Construction and Descriptions of the Various Types of Cranes in Use. By JOSEPH HORNER, A.M.I.M.E. Crown 8vo, cloth, with 215 Illustrations, including Folding Plates . . . . *Net* **7/6**

HYDRAULIC MANUAL. Consisting of Working Tables and
Explanatory Text. Intended as a Guide in Hydraulic Calculations and Field Operations. By Lowis D'A. JACKSON. Fourth Edition, Enlarged. Large crown 8vo, cloth **16/0**

HYDRAULIC POWER ENGINEERING. A Practical Manual
on the Concentration and Transmission of Power by Hydraulic Machinery.
By G. CROYDON MARKS, A.M.Inst.C.E. Second Edition, Enlarged, with
about 240 Illustrations. 8vo, cloth . . . . . *Net* 10/6
SUMMARY OF CONTENTS:—PRINCIPLES OF HYDRAULICS—THE FLOW OF WATER—
HYDRAULIC PRESSURES—MATERIAL—TEST LOAD—PACKING FOR SLIDING SURFACES
—PIPE JOINTS—CONTROLLING VALVES—PLATFORM LIFTS—WORKSHOP AND FOUNDRY
CRANES—WAREHOUSE AND DOCK CRANES—HYDRAULIC ACCUMULATORS—PRESSES
FOR BALING AND OTHER PURPOSES—SHEET METAL WORKING AND FORGING MACHINERY
—HYDRAULIC RIVETERS—HAND AND POWER PUMPS—STEAM PUMPS—TURBINES—
IMPULSE TURBINES—REACTION TURBINES—DESIGN OF TURBINES IN DETAIL—WATER
WHEELS—HYDRAULIC ENGINES—RECENT ACHIEVEMENTS—PRESSURE OF WATER—
ACTION OF PUMPS, &c.
"Can be unhesitatingly recommended as a useful and up-to-date manual on hydraulic trans-
mission and utilisation of power."—*Mechanical World.*

HYDRAULIC TABLES, CO-EFFICIENTS, & FORMULÆ.
For Finding the Discharge of Water from Orifices, Notches, Weirs, Pipes, and
Rivers. With New Formulæ, Tables, and General Information on Rain-fall,
Catchment-Basins, Drainage, Sewerage, Water Supply for Towns and Mill
Power. By JOHN NEVILLE, C.E., M.R.I.A. Third Edition, revised, with
additions. Numerous Illustrations. Crown 8vo, cloth . . . 14/0

INTERNAL COMBUSTION ENGINES. Their Theory, Con-
struction, and Operation. By ROLLA C. CARPENTER, M.M.E., LL.D., and
H. DIEDERICHS, M.E., Professors of Experimental Engineering, Sibley
College, Cornell University. 610 pages, with 373 Illustrations. Medium
8vo, cloth . . . . [*Just published.* Net 21/0
INTRODUCTION, DEFINITIONS AND CLASSIFICATIONS, INDICATED AND BRAKE
HORSE-POWER—THERMODYNAMICS OF THE GAS ENGINE—THEORETICAL COMPARISON
OF VARIOUS TYPES OF INTERNAL COMBUSTION ENGINES—THE VARIOUS EVENTS OF THE
CONSTANT VOLUME AND CONSTANT-PRESSURE CYCLE AS MODIFIED BY PRACTICAL
CONDITIONS—THE TEMPERATURE ENTROPY DIAGRAM APPLIED TO THE GAS ENGINE—
COMBUSTION—GAS ENGINE FUELS, THE SOLID FUELS, GAS PRODUCERS—THE GAS-
ENGINE FUELS, LIQUID FUELS, CARBURETERS AND VAPORISERS—GAS ENGINE FUELS,
THE GAS FUELS, THE FUEL MIXTURE EXPLOSIBILITY, PRESSURE, AND TEMPERATURE
—THE HISTORY OF THE GAS ENGINE—MODERN TYPES OF INTERNAL COMBUSTION
ENGINES—GAS ENGINE AUXILIARIES, IGNITION, MUFFLERS, AND STARTING APPARATUS
—REGULATION OF INTERNAL COMBUSTION ENGINES—THE ESTIMATION OF POWER OF
GAS ENGINES—METHODS OF TESTING INTERNAL COMBUSTION ENGINES—THE PER-
FORMANCE OF GAS ENGINES AND GAS PRODUCERS—COST OF INSTALLATION AND OF
OPERATION.

IRON AND METAL TRADES' COMPANION. For Ex-
peditiously Ascertaining the Value of any Goods bought or sold by Weight,
from 1s. per cwt. to 112s. per cwt., and from one farthing per pound to one
shilling per pound. By THOMAS DOWNIE. Strongly bound in leather,
396 pp. 9/0

IRON AND STEEL. A Work for the Forge, Foundry, Factory,
and Office. Containing ready, useful, and trustworthy Information for Iron-
masters and their Stock-takers; Managers of Bar, Rail, Plate, and Sheet
Rolling Mills; Iron and Metal Founders; Iron Ship and Bridge Builders;
Mechanical, Mining, and Consulting Engineers; Architects, Contractors,
Builders, &c. By CHARLES HOARE, Author of "The Slide Rule," &c. Ninth
Edition. 32mo, leather 6/0

IRON AND STEEL CONSTRUCTIONAL WORK, as applied
to Public, Private, and Domestic Buildings. By FRANCIS CAMPIN, C.E.
Crown 8vo, cloth 3/6

IRON & STEEL GIRDERS. A Graphic Table for facilitating
the Computation of the Weights of Wrought Iron and Steel Girders, &c.,
for Parliamentary and other Estimates. By J. H. WATSON BUCK, M.Inst.C.E.
On a Sheet. 2/6

IRON-PLATE WEIGHT TABLES. For Iron Shipbuilders,

Engineers, and Iron Merchants. Containing the Calculated Weights of upwards of 150,000 different sizes of Iron Plates from 1 foot by 6 in. by ¼ in. to 10 feet by 5 feet by 1 in. Worked out on the Basis of 40 lbs. to the square foot of Iron of 1 inch in thickness. By H. BURLINSON and W H SIMPSON. 4to, half-bound . . . . **£1 5s.**

IRRIGATION (PIONEER). A Manual of Information for

Farmers in the Colonies. By E. O. MAWSON, M.Inst.C.E., Executive Engineer, Public Works Department, Bombay. With Chapters on Light Railways by E. R. CALTHROP, M.Inst.C.E., M.I.M.E. With Plates and Diagrams. Demy 8vo, cloth . . . . *Net* **10/6**

VALUE OF IRRIGATION, AND SOURCES OF WATER SUPPLY—DAMS AND WEIRS—CANALS—UNDERGROUND WATER—METHODS OF IRRIGATION—SEWAGE IRRIGATION—IMPERIAL AUTOMATIC SLUICE GATES—THE CULTIVATION OF IRRIGATED CROPS, VEGETABLES, AND FRUIT TREES—LIGHT RAILWAYS FOR HEAVY TRAFFIC—USEFUL MEMORANDA AND DATA.

LATHE PRACTICE. A Complete and Practical Work on the

Modern American Lathe. By OSCAR E. PERRIGO, M.E., Author of "Modern Machine Shop Construction, Equipment, and Management," etc. Medium 8vo, 424 pp., 315 illustrations. Cloth . . . *Net* **12/0**

HISTORY OF THE LATHE UP TO THE INTRODUCTION OF SCREW THREADS—ITS DEVELOPMENT SINCE THE INTRODUCTION OF SCREW THREADS—CLASSIFICATION OF LATHES—LATHE DESIGN: THE BED AND ITS SUPPORTS—THE HEAD-STOCK CASTING, THE SPINDLE, AND SPINDLE-CONE—THE SPINDLE BEARINGS, THE BACK GEARS, AND THE TRIPLE-GEAR MECHANISM—THE TAIL STOCK, THE CARRIAGE, THE APRON, ETC.—TURNING RESTS, SUPPORTING RESTS, SHAFT STRAIGHTENERS, ETC.—LATHE ATTACHMENTS—RAPID CHANGE GEAR MECHANISM—LATHE TOOLS, HIGH-SPEED STEEL, SPEEDS AND FEEDS, POWER FOR CUTTING TOOLS, ETC.—TESTING A LATHE—LATHE WORK—ENGINE LATHES—HEAVY LATHES—HIGH-SPEED LATHES—SPECIAL LATHES—REGULAR TURRET LATHES—SPECIAL TURRET LATHES—ELECTRICALLY-DRIVEN LATHES.

LATHE-WORK. A Practical Treatise on the Tools, Appliances,

and Processes employed in the Art of Turning. By PAUL N. HASLUCK. Eighth Edition. Crown 8vo, cloth **5/0**

" We can safely recommend the work to young engineers. To the amateur it will simply be invaluable."—*Engineer.*

LAW FOR ENGINEERS AND MANUFACTURERS.

See EVERY MAN'S OWN LAWYER. A Handybook of the Principles of Law and Equity. By a Barrister.' Forty-sixth (1909) Edition, Revised and Enlarged, including Abstracts of the Legislation of 1907-8 of especial interest to Engineering Firms and Manufacturers, such as the Workmen's Compensation Act, 1906 ; the Prevention of Corruption Act, 1906 ; the Trades Disputes Act, 1906 ; the Census of Production Act, 1906 ; the New Companies Act, 1907 ; the Limited Partnerships Act, 1907 ; the Patents and Designs Act, 1907 ; and many other recent Acts. Large crown 8vo, cloth, 838 pages.

[*Just published. Net* **6/8**

" No Englishman ought to be without this book."—*Engineer.*

"Ought to be in every business establishment and all libraries."—*Sheffield Post.*

" It is a complete code of English Law written in plain language, which all can understand. . . . Should be in the hands of every business man, and all who wish to abolish lawyers' bills."—*Weekly Times.*

" A useful and concise epitome of the law, compiled with considerable care."—*Law Magazine.*

LEVELLING, PRINCIPLES AND PRACTICE OF. Show-

ing its Application to Purposes of Railway and Civil Engineering in the Construction of Roads ; with Mr. TELFORD'S Rules for the same. By FREDERICK W. SIMMS, M.Inst.C.E. Ninth Edition, with LAW'S Practical Examples for Setting-out Railway Curves, and TRAUTWINE'S Field Practice of Laying-out Circular Curves. With 7 Plates and numerous Woodcuts. 8vo **8/6**

" The publishers have rendered a substantial service to the profession, especially to the younger members, by bringing out the present edition of Mr. Simms's useful work."—*Engineering.*

LOCOMOTIVE ENGINE. The Autobiography of an old Locomotive Engine. By ROBERT WEATHERBURN, M.I.M.E. With Illustrations
and Portraits of GEORGE and ROBERT STEPHENSON. Crown 8vo, cloth.
Net **2/6**

LOCOMOTIVE ENGINE DEVELOPMENT. A Popular
Treatise on the Gradual Improvements made in Railway Engines between
1803 and 1903. By CLEMENT C. STRETTON, C.E. Sixth Edition, Revised
and Enlarged. Crown 8vo, cloth . . . . *Net* **4/6**

LOCOMOTIVE ENGINE DRIVING. A Practical Manual for
Engineers in Charge of Locomotive Engines. By MICHAEL REYNOLDS,
M.S.E. Twelfth Edition. Crown 8vo, cloth, **3/6** ; cloth boards **4/6**

LOCOMOTIVE ENGINES. A Rudimentary Treatise on. By
G. D. DEMPSEY, C.E. With large Additions treating of the Modern Locomotive, by D. K. CLARK, M.Inst.C.E. With Illustrations. Crown 8vo, cloth
3/0

LOCOMOTIVE (MODEL) ENGINEER, Fireman and Engine
Boy. Comprising a Historical Notice of the Pioneer Locomotive Engine
and their Inventors. By MICHAEL REYNOLDS. Crown 8vo, cloth, **3/6**
cloth boards **4/6**

**LOCOMOTIVES, THE APPLICATION OF HIGHLY
SUPERHEATED STEAM TO.** See STEAM.

MACHINERY, DETAILS OF. Comprising Instructions for
the Execution of various Works in Iron in the Fitting Shop, Foundry, and
Boiler Yard. By FRANCIS CAMPIN, C.E. Crown 8vo, cloth . . **3/0**

MACHINE SHOP TOOLS. A Practical Treatise describing
in every detail the Construction, Operation and Manipulation of both Hand
and Machine Tools ; being a work of Practical Instruction in all Classes of
Modern Machine Shop Practice, including Chapters on Filing, Fitting and
Scraping Surfaces ; on Drills, Reamers, Taps and Dies ; the Lathe and its
Tools ; Planers, Shapers and their Tools ; Milling Machines and Cutters ; Gear
Cutters and Gear Cutting ; Drilling Machines and Drill Work ; Grinding
Machines and their Work ; Hardening and Tempering, Gearing, Belting,
and Transmission Machinery ; Useful Data and Tables. By W. H. VAN
DERVOORT, M.E. Illustrated by 673 Engravings. Medium 8vo.
Net **21/0**

MAGNETOS FOR AUTOMOBILISTS: How made and How
used. A handybook on their Construction and Management. By S. R.
BOTTONE. Crown 8vo, cloth . . . . *Net* **2/0**

MARINE ENGINEERING. An Elementary Manual for Young
Marine Engineers and Apprentices. By J. S. BREWER. Crown 8vo, cloth.
1/6

MARINE ENGINEER'S GUIDE to Board of Trade Exam-
inations for Certificates of Competency. Containing all Latest Questions to
Date, with Simple, Clear, and Correct Solutions ; 302 Elementary Questions
with Illustrated Answers, and Verbal Questions and Answers ; complete Set
of Drawings with Statements completed. By A. C. WANNAN, C.E., Consulting Engineer, and E. W. I. WANNAN, M.I.M.E., Certificated First Class
Marine Engineer. With numerous Engravings. Fourth Edition, Enlarged.
500 pages. Large crown 8vo, cloth . . . . . . *Net* **10/6**

MARINE ENGINEER'S POCKET-BOOK. Containing latest
Board of Trade Rules and Data for Marine Engineers. By A. C. WANNAN.
Fourth Edition, Revised, Enlarged, and Brought up to Date. Square 18mo,
with thumb Index, leather . . . . **5'0**

MARINE ENGINES AND BOILERS. Their Design and
Construction. A Handbook for the Use of Students, Engineers, and Naval
Constructors. Based on the Work "Berechnung und Konstruktion der
Schiffsmaschinen und Kessel," by Dr. G. BAUER, Engineer-in-Chief of the
Vulcan Shipbuilding Yard, Stettin. Translated from the Second German
Edition by E. M. DONKIN, and S. BRYAN DONKIN, A.M.I.C.E. Edited
by LESLIE S. ROBERTSON, Secretary to the Engineering Standards Com-
mittee, M.I.C.E., M.I.M.E., M.I.N.A., &c. With numerous Illustrations
and Tables. Medium 8vo, cloth . . . . *Net* **25/-**

SUMMARY OF CONTENTS:—PART I.—MAIN ENGINES—DETERMINATION OF CYLIN-
DER DIMENSIONS—THE UTILISATION OF STEAM IN THE ENGINE—STROKE OF PISTON
—NUMBER OF REVOLUTIONS—TURNING MOMENT—BALANCING OF THE MOVING PARTS
—ARRANGEMENT OF MAIN ENGINES—DETAILS OF MAIN ENGINES—THE CYLINDER—
VALVES—VARIOUS KINDS OF VALVE GEAR—PISTON RODS—PISTONS—CONNECTING
ROD AND CROSSHEAD—VALVE GEAR RODS—BED PLATES—ENGINE COLUMNS—
REVERSING AND TURNING GEAR. PART II.—PUMPS—AIR, CIRCULATING FEED, AND
AUXILIARY PUMPS. PART III.—SHAFTING, RESISTANCE OF SHIPS, PROPELLERS
—THRUST SHAFT AND THRUST BLOCK—TUNNEL SHAFTS AND PLUMMER BLOCKS—
SHAFT COUPLINGS—STERN TUBE—THE SCREW PROPELLER—CONSTRUCTION OF THE
SCREW. PART IV.—PIPES AND CONNECTIONS—GENERAL REMARKS, FLANGES,
VALVES, &c.—UNDER WATER FITTINGS—MAIN STEAM, AUXILIARY STEAM, AND
EXHAUST PIPING—FEED WATER, BILGE, BALLAST AND CIRCULATING PIPES. PART V.—
STEAM BOILERS—FIRING AND THE GENERATION OF STEAM—CYLINDRICAL BOILERS.
— LOCOMOTIVE BOILERS—WATER-TUBE BOILERS—SMALL TUBE WATER-TUBE
BOILERS—SMOKE BOX—FUNNEL AND BOILER LAGGING—FORCED DRAUGHT—BOILER
FITTINGS AND MOUNTINGS. PART VI.—MEASURING INSTRUMENTS. PART VII.—
VARIOUS DETAILS—BOLTS, NUTS, SCREW THREADS, &c.—PLATFORMS, GRATINGS,
LADDERS — FOUNDATIONS—SEATINGS — LUBRICATION — VENTILATION OF ENGINE
ROOMS—RULES FOR SPARE GEAR. PART VIII.—ADDITIONAL TABLES.

"An excellent specimen of the best class of German technical handbooks ; it is clear and
systematic in arrangement ; perfectly sound on theoretical matters ; and very complete, detailed,
and distinct in descriptions of construction and directions for calculations, with fully-detailed
numerical and graphical examples."—*Engineer.*

"The book covers very completely the whole range of subjects embraced by the title.
Dr. Bauer has produced a volume which forms a most useful and important addition to our
practical text-books on marine engineering, and he has been most fortunate in securing translators
and editor who have been able to place his views before English readers in such an eminently
satisfactory form."—*Engineering*

". . . All who wish to know the principles on which this principal branch of science is
based should be in possession of a copy of this work. There is nothing but solid matter in it."—
Marine Engineer.

"The book is one of the best we have ever seen on the subject. It will be welcomed both
by the designer and the student of marine engineering, and no marine engineer who wishes to be
up-to-date can afford to be without it."—*Steamship.*

MARINE ENGINES AND STEAM VESSELS. By R.
MURRAY, C.E. Eighth Edition, thoroughly Revised, with Additions by
the Author and by GEORGE CARLISLE, C.E. Crown 8vo, cloth . . **4/6**

MASONRY DAMS FROM INCEPTION TO COMPLETION.
Including numerous Formulæ, Forms of Specification and Tender, Pocket
Diagram of Forces, &c. For the use of Civil and Mining Engineers. By
C. F. COURTNEY, M.Inst.C.E. 8vo, cloth **9/0**

MASTING, MAST-MAKING, AND RIGGING OF SHIPS.
Also Tables of Spars, Rigging, Blocks; Chain, Wire, and Hemp Ropes, &c.,
relative to every class of vessels. By R. KIPPING. Crown 8vo, cloth **2/0**

MATERIALS AND CONSTRUCTION. A Theoretical and
Practical Treatise on the Strains, Designing, and Erection of Works of Construction. By F. CAMPIN. Crown 8vo, cloth **3/0**

MATERIALS, A TREATISE ON THE STRENGTH OF.
By P. BARLOW, F.R.S., P. W. BARLOW, F.R.S., and W. H. BARLOW, F.R.S.
Edited by WM. HUMBER, A.M.Inst.C.E. 8vo, cloth **18/0**
" The standard treatise on that particular subject."—*Engineer.*

MATHEMATICAL TABLES. For Trigonometrical, Astronomical, and Nautical Calculations; to which is prefixed a Treatise on Logarithms, by H. LAW, C.E. With Tables for Navigation and Nautical Astronomy. By Prof. J. R. YOUNG. Crown 8vo, cloth . . . **4/0**

MEASURES: BRITISH AND AMERICAN CUSTOMARY AND METRIC LEGAL MEASURES. For Commercial and Technical Purposes, forming the Measure Section of Part I. of "The Mechanical Engineer's Reference Book." By NELSON FOLEY, M.I.N.A. Folio, cloth.
[Just Ready.
MEASURES : LEGAL STANDARDS—LINEAL—SQUARE—CUBIC AND CAPACITY—WEIGHT—COMPOUND UNITS—VELOCITY AND SPEED—MEASURES OF GRAVITY—MASS—FORCE—WORK—POWER—ELECTRICAL—HEAT—MOMENTS—ENERGY—MOMENTUM—CENTRIFUGAL FORCE—ANGLES—EQUIVALENTS : CUSTOMARY MEASURES TO METRIC, AND *vice versa*—LINEAL—SQUARE—CUBIC AND CAPACITY—WEIGHTS.

MECHANICAL ENGINEERING. Comprising Metallurgy, Moulding, Casting, Forging, Tools, Workshop Machinery, Mechanical Manipulation, Manufacture of the Steam Engine, &c. By FRANCIS CAMPIN, C.E. Third Edition. Crown 8vo, cloth **2/6**

MECHANICAL ENGINEERING TERMS. (Lockwood's Dictionary). Embracing terms current in the Drawing Office, Pattern Shop, Foundry, Fitting, Turning, Smiths', and Boiler Shops, &c. Comprising upwards of 6,000 Definitions. Edited by J. G. HORNER, A.M.I.M.E. Third Edition, Revised, with Additions. Crown 8vo, cloth . . . *Net* **7/6**

MECHANICAL ENGINEER'S COMPANION. Areas, Circumferences, Decimal Equivalents, in inches and feet, millimetres, squares, cubes, roots, &c. ; Strength of Bolts, Weight of Iron, &c. ; Weights, Measures, and other Data. Also Practical Rules for Engine Proportions. By R. EDWARDS, M.Inst.C.E. Fcap. 8vo, cloth **3/6**

MECHANICAL ENGINEER'S POCKET-BOOK. Comprising Tables, Formulæ, Rules, and Data: A Handy Book of Reference for Daily Use in Engineering Practice. By D. KINNEAR CLARK, M.Inst.C.E., Sixth Edition, thoroughly Revised and Enlarged. By H. H. P. POWLES, A.M.Inst.C.E., M.I.M.E. Small 8vo, 700 pp., Leather . . *Net* **6/0**
MATHEMATICAL TABLES—MEASUREMENT OF SURFACES AND SOLIDS—ENGLISH WEIGHTS AND MEASURES—FRENCH METRIC WEIGHTS AND MEASURES—FOREIGN WEIGHTS AND MEASURES—MONEYS—SPECIFIC GRAVITY, WEIGHT, AND VOLUME — MANUFACTURED METALS — STEEL PIPES — BOLTS AND NUTS — SUNDRY ARTICLES IN WROUGHT AND CAST IRON, COPPER, BRASS, LEAD, TIN, ZINC—STRENGTH OF MATERIALS—STRENGTH OF TIMBER—STRENGTH OF CAST IRON—STRENGTH OF WROUGHT IRON—STRENGTH OF STEEL—TENSILE STRENGTH OF COPPER, LEAD, &c.—RESISTANCE OF STONES AND OTHER BUILDING MATERIALS—RIVETED JOINTS IN BOILER PLATES—BOILER SHELLS—WIRE ROPES AND HEMP ROPES — CHAINS AND CHAIN CABLES—FRAMING—HARDNESS OF METALS, ALLOYS, AND STONES—LABOUR OF ANIMALS—MECHANICAL PRINCIPLES—GRAVITY AND FALL OF BODIES—ACCELERATING AND RETARDING FORCES—MILL GEARING, SHAFTING, &c.—TRANSMISSION OF MOTIVE POWER — HEAT—COMBUSTION: FUELS—WARMING, VENTILATION, COOKING STOVES—STEAM—STEAM ENGINES AND BOILERS—RAILWAYS—TRAMWAYS — STEAM SHIPS — PUMPING STEAM ENGINES AND PUMPS—COAL GAS—GAS ENGINES, &c.—AIR IN MOTION —COMPRESSED AIR—HOT AIR ENGINES—WATER POWER—SPEED OF CUTTING TOOLS —COLOURS—ELECTRICAL ENGINEERING.

"It would be found difficult to compress more matter within a similar compass, or produce a book of 700 pages which should be more compact or convenient for pocket reference. . . . Will be appreciated by mechanical engineers of all classes."—*Practical Engineer.*

MECHANICAL ENGINEER'S REFERENCE BOOK. For Machine and Boiler Construction. By NELSON FOLEY, M.I.N.A. New Edition, Revised throughout and much Enlarged. To be issued in parts.
[In Preparation.
The Measure Section of Part I.—**BRITISH AND AMERICAN CUSTOMARY AND METRIC LEGAL MEASURES**—now ready. *See* under MEASURES.

MECHANICAL HANDLING OF MATERIAL. A
Treatise on the Handling of Material such as Coal, Ore, Timber, &c., by Automatic or Semi-Automatic Machinery, together with the Various Accessories used in the Manipulation of such Plant, and Dealing fully with the Handling, Storing, and Warehousing of Grain. By G. F. ZIMMER, A.M.Inst.C.E. 528 pages Royal 8vo, cloth, with 550 Illustrations (including Folding Plates) specially prepared for the Work . . . *Net* **25/0**
"It is an essentially practical work written by a practical man, who is not only thoroughly acquainted with his subject theoretically, but who also has the knowledge that can only be obtained by actual experience in working and planning installations for the mechanical handling of raw material."—*The Times.*

MECHANICS. Being a concise Exposition of the General
Principles of Mechanical Science and their Applications. By C. TOMLINSON, F.R.S. Crown 8vo, cloth **1/6**

MECHANICS: CONDENSED. A Selection of Formulæ, Rules,
Tables, and Data for the Use of Engineering Students, &c. By W. G. C. HUGHES, A.M.I.C.E. Crown 8vo, cloth **2/6**

MECHANICS OF AIR MACHINERY. By Dr. J. WIESBACH
and PROF. G. HERRMANN. Authorized Translation with an Appendix on American Practice by A. TROWBRIDGE, Ph.B., Adjunct Professor of Mechanical Engineering, Columbia University. Royal 8vo, cloth . . *Net* **18/0**

MECHANICS' WORKSHOP COMPANION. Comprising a
great variety of the most useful Rules and Formulæ in Mechanical Science, with numerous Tables of Practical Data and Calculated Results for Facilitating Mechanical Operations. By WILLIAM TEMPLETON, Author of "The Engineer's Practical Assistant," &c., &c. Eighteenth Edition, Revised, Modernised, and considerably Enlarged by W. S. HUTTON, C.E., Author of "The Works' Manager's Handbook," &c. Fcap. 8vo, nearly 500 pp., with 8 Plates and upwards of 250 Diagrams, leather **8/0**
"This well-known and largely-used book contains information, brought up to date, of the sort so useful to the foreman and draughtsman. So much fresh information has been introduced as to constitute it practically a new book."—*Mechanical World.*

MECHANISM AND MACHINE TOOLS. By T. BAKER,
C.E. With Remarks on Tools and Machinery by J. NASMYTH, C.E. Crown 8vo, cloth **2/6**

MENSURATION AND MEASURING. With the Mensuration
and Levelling of Land for the purposes of Modern Engineering. By T. BAKER, C.E. New Edition by E. NUGENT, C.E. Crown 8vo, cloth **1/6**

METAL-TURNING. A Practical Handbook for Engineers,
Technical Students, and Amateurs. By JOSEPH HORNER, A.M.I.Mech.E. Author of "Pattern Making," &c. Large Crown 8vo, cloth, with 488 Illustrations . . . . *Net* **9/0**
SUMMARY OF CONTENTS:—INTRODUCTION—RELATIONS OF TURNERY AND MACHINE SHOP—SEC. I. THE LATHE, ITS WORK, AND TOOLS—FORMS AND FUNCTIONS OF TOOLS—REMARKS ON TURNING IN GENERAL.—SEC. II. TURNING BETWEEN CENTRES—CENTRING AND DRIVING—USE OF STEADIES—EXAMPLES OF TURNING INVOLVING LINING-OUT FOR CENTRES—MANDREL WORK.—SEC. III. WORK SUPPORTED AT ONE END—FACE PLATE TURNING—ANGLE PLATE TURNING—INDEPENDENT JAW CHUCKS—CONCENTRIC, UNIVERSAL, TOGGLE, AND APPLIED CHUCKS.—SEC. IV. INTERNAL WORK—DRILLING, BORING, AND ALLIED OPERATIONS.—SEC. V. SCREW CUTTINGS AND TURRET WORK. —SEC. VI. MISCELLANEOUS — SPECIAL WORK — MEASUREMENT, GRINDING — TOOL HOLDERS—SPEED AND FEEDS, TOOL STEELS—STEEL MAKERS' INSTRUCTIONS.

METRIC TABLES. In which the British Standard Measures
and Weights are compared with those of the Metric System at present in Use on the Continent. By C. H. DOWLING, C.E. 8vo, cloth . . . **10/6**

MILLING MACHINES; their Design, Construction, and Work-
ing. A Handbook for Practical Men and Engineering Students. By JOSEPH HORNER, A.M.I.Mech.E., Author of "Pattern Making," &c. With 269 Illustrations. Medium 8vo, cloth . . . . . . *Net* **12/6**
LEADING ELEMENTS OF MILLING MACHINE DESIGN AND CONSTRUCTION—PLAIN AND UNIVERSAL MACHINES — ATTACHMENTS AND BRACINGS — VERTICAL SPINDLES MACHINES—PLANO-MILLERS OR SLABBING MACHINES—SPECIAL MACHINES—CUTTERS—MILLING OPERATIONS—INDEXING, SPIRAL WORK, AND WORM, SPUR, AND BEVEL GEARS, ETC.—SPUR AND BEVEL GEARS—FEEDS AND SPEEDS.

MOTOR CAR CATECHISM. Containing about 320 Questions and Answers Explaining the Construction and Working of a Modern Motor Car. For the Use of Owners, Drivers, and Students. By JOHN HENRY KNIGHT. Second edition, revised and enlarged, with an additional chapter on Motor Cycles. Crown 8vo, with Illustrations.   [*Just Published.* Net **1/6**

THE PETROL ENGINE—TRANSMISSION AND THE CHASSIS—TYRES—DUTIES OF A CAR DRIVER—MOTOR CYCLES—LAWS AND REGULATIONS.

MOTOR CAR ENGINEERING. Practical Lectures on the Motor Car. By ROBERT W. A. BREWER, A.M.Inst.C.E., M.I.M.E., M.I.A.E. With numerous Illustrations. Demy 8vo .   .   .   .   [*In the Press.*

MOTOR CARS FOR COMMON ROADS. By A. J. WALLIS-TAYLER, A.M.Inst.C.E.   212 pp., with 76 Illustrations. Crown 8vo, cloth **4/6**

MOTOR VEHICLES FOR BUSINESS PURPOSES. A Practical Handbook for those interested in the Transport of Passengers and Goods. By A. J. WALLIS-TAYLER, A.M.Inst.C.E. With 134 Illustrations. Demy 8vo, cloth .   .   .   . *Net* **9/0**

NAVAL ARCHITECT'S AND SHIPBUILDER'S POCKET BOOK. Of Formulæ, Rules, and Tables, and Marine Engineer's and Surveyor's Handy Book of Reference. By CLEMENT MACKROW. M.I.N.A. Ninth Edition, Fcap., leather .   .   .   .   .   . *Net* **12/6**

SIGNS AND SYMBOLS, DECIMAL FRACTIONS—TRIGONOMETRY—PRACTICAL GEOMETRY—MENSURATION—CENTRES AND MOMENTS OF FIGURES—MOMENTS OF INERTIA AND RADII GYRATION—ALGEBRAICAL EXPRESSIONS FOR SIMPSON'S RULES—MECHANICAL PRINCIPLES—CENTRE OF GRAVITY—LAWS OF MOTION—DISPLACEMENT, CENTRE OF BUOYANCY—CENTRE OF GRAVITY OF SHIP'S HULL—STABILITY CURVES AND METACENTRES—SEA AND SHALLOW-WATER WAVES—ROLLING OF SHIPS—PROPULSION AND RESISTANCE OF VESSELS—SPEED TRIALS—SAILING, CENTRE OF EFFORT—DISTANCES DOWN RIVERS, COAST LINES—STEERING AND RUDDERS OF VESSELS—LAUNCHING CALCULATIONS AND VELOCITIES—WEIGHT OF MATERIAL AND GEAR—GUN PARTICULARS AND WEIGHT—STANDARD GAUGES—RIVETED JOINTS AND RIVETING—STRENGTH AND TESTS OF MATERIALS—BINDING AND SHEARING STRESSES—STRENGTH OF SHAFTING, PILLARS, WHEELS, &c.—HYDRAULIC DATA, &c.—CONIC SECTIONS, CATENARIAN CURVES—MECHANICAL POWERS, WORK—BOARD OF TRADE REGULATIONS FOR BOILERS AND ENGINES—BOARD OF TRADE REGULATIONS FOR SHIPS—LLOYD'S RULES FOR BOILERS—LLOYD'S WEIGHT OF CHAINS—LLOYD'S SCANTLINGS FOR SHIPS—DATA OF ENGINES AND VESSELS—SHIPS' FITTINGS AND TESTS—SEASONING PRESERVING TIMBER—MEASUREMENT OF TIMBER—ALLOYS, PAINTS, VARNISHES—DATA FOR STOWAGE—ADMIRALTY TRANSPORT REGULATIONS—RULES FOR HORSE-POWER, SCREW PROPELLERS, &c.—PERCENTAGES FOR BUTT STRAPS—PARTICULARS OF YACHTS—MASTING AND RIGGING—DISTANCES OF FOREIGN PORTS—TONNAGE TABLES—VOCABULARY OF FRENCH AND ENGLISH TERMS—ENGLISH WEIGHTS AND MEASURES—FOREIGN WEIGHTS AND MEASURES—DECIMAL EQUIVALENTS—USEFUL NUMBERS—CIRCULAR MEASURES—AREAS OF AND CIRCUMFERENCES OF CIRCLES—AREAS OF SEGMENTS OF CIRCLES—TABLES OF SQUARES AND CUBES AND ROOTS OF NUMBERS—TABLES OF LOGARITHMS OF NUMBERS—TABLES OF HYPERBOLIC LOGARITHMS—TABLES OF NATURAL SINES, TANGENTS—TABLES OF LOGARITHMIC SINES, TANGENTS, &c.

" In these days of advanced knowledge a work like this is of the greatest value. It contains a vast amount of information. We unhesitatingly say that it is the most valuable compilation for its specific purpose that has ever been printed. No naval architect, engineer, surveyor, seaman, wood or iron shipbuilder, can afford to be without this work."—*Nautical Magazine.*

NAVAL ARCHITECTURE. An Exposition of the Elementary Principles. By J. PEAKE. Crown 8vo, cloth **3/6**

NAVIGATION AND NAUTICAL ASTRONOMY, In Theory and Practice. By Prof. J. R. YOUNG. Crown 8vo, cloth .   .   . **2/6**
"A very complete, thorough, and useful manual for the young navigator."—*Observatory.*

NAVIGATION, PRACTICAL. Consisting of the Sailor's Sea Book, by J. GREENWOOD and W. H. ROSSER; together with Mathematical and Nautical Tables for the Working of the Problems, by H. LAW, C.E., and Prof. J. R. YOUNG **7/0**

PATTERN MAKING. Embracing the Main Types of Engineering Construction, and including Gearing, Engine Work, Sheaves and Pulleys, Pipes and Columns, Screws, Machine Parts, Pumps and Cocks, the Moulding of Patterns in Loam and Greensand, Weight of Castings, &c. By J. G. HORNER, A.M.I.M.E. Third Edition, Enlarged. With 486 Illustrations. Crown 8vo, cloth . . . . *Net* **7/6**

"A well-written technical guide, evidently written by a man who understands and has practised what he has written about."—*Builder.*

PATTERN MAKING. A Practical Work on the Art of Making Patterns for Engineering and Foundry Work, including (among other matter) Materials and Tools, Wood Patterns, Metal Patterns, Pattern Shop Mathematics, Cost, Care, &c., of Patterns. By F. W. BARROWS. Fully Illustrated by Engravings made from Special Drawings by the Author. Crown 8vo, cloth.

Net **6/0**

PATTERN MAKERS AND PATTERN MAKING—MATERIALS AND TOOLS—EXAMPLES OF PATTERN WORK—METAL PATTERNS—PATTERN SHOP MATHEMATICS—COST, CARE, AND INVENTORY OF PATTERNS—MARKING AND RECORD OF PATTERNS—PATTERN ACCOUNTS.

PETROL AIR GAS. A Practical Hand-book on the Installation and Working of Air Gas Lighting Systems for Country Houses. By HENRY O'CONNOR, F.R.S.E., A.M.Inst.C.E., &c., Author of "The Gas Engineer's Pocket-Book." Crown 8vo . . *[In the Press. Price about* **1/6** *Net.*

PIONEER ENGINEERING. A Treatise on the Engineering Operations connected with the Settlement of Waste Lands in New Countries. By E. DOBSON, M.Inst.C.E. Second Edition. Crown 8vo, cloth **4/6**

PNEUMATICS, Including Acoustics and the Phenomena of Wind Currents, for the use of Beginners. By CHARLES TOMLINSON, F.R.S. Crown 8vo, cloth **1/6**

PUMPS AND PUMPING. A Handbook for Pump Users. Being Notes on Selection, Construction, and Management. By M. POWIS BALE, M.Inst.C.E., M.I.Mech.E. Fifth Edition. Crown 8vo, cloth . **3/6**

"The matter is set forth as concisely as possible. In fact, condensation rather than diffuseness has been the author's aim throughout; yet he does not seem to have omitted anything likely to be of use."—*Journal of Gas Lighting.*

PUNCHES, DIES, AND TOOLS FOR MANUFACTURING IN PRESSES. By JOSEPH V. WOODWORTH. Medium 8vo, cloth. 482 pages with 700 Illustrations . . . . *Net* **16/0**

SIMPLE BENDING AND FORMING DIES, THEIR CONSTRUCTION, USE AND OPERATION—INTRICATE COMBINATION, BENDING AND FORMING DIES, FOR ACCURATE AND RAPID PRODUCTION—AUTOMATIC FORMING, BENDING AND TWISTING DIES AND PUNCHES, FOR DIFFICULT AND NOVEL SHAPING—CUT, CARRY, AND FOLLOW DIES, TOGETHER WITH TOOL COMBINATIONS FOR PROGRESSIVE SHEET METAL WORKING—NOTCHING PERFORATING AND PIERCING PUNCHES, DIES AND TOOLS—COMPOSITE, SECTIONAL, COMPOUND AND ARMATURE DISK AND SEGMENT PUNCHES AND DIES—PROCESSES AND TOOLS FOR MAKING RIFLE CARTRIDGES, CARTRIDGE CASES OF QUICK-FIRING GUNS, AND NICKEL BULLET JACKETS—THE MANUFACTURE AND USE OF DIES FOR DRAWING WIRE AND BAR STEEL—PENS, PINS, AND NEEDLES, THEIR EVOLUTION AND MANUFACTURE—PUNCHES, DIES, AND PROCESSES FOR MAKING HYDRAULIC PACKING LEATHERS, TOGETHER WITH TOOLS FOR PAINT AND CHEMICAL TABLETS—DRAWING, RE-DRAWING, REDUCING, FLANGING, FORMING, REVERSING, AND CUPPING PROCESSES, PUNCHES AND DIES FOR CIRCULAR AND RECTANGULAR AND SHEET-METAL ARTICLES—BEADING, WIRING, CURLING AND SEAMING PUNCHES AND DIES FOR CLOSING AND ASSEMBLING OF METAL PARTS—JEWELLERY DIE-MAKING, EYE GLASS, LENS AND MEDAL DIES, AND CONSTRUCTION OF SPOON AND FORK-MAKING TOOLS—DESIGN, CONSTRUCTION AND USE OF SUB-PRESSES AND SUB-PRESS DIES FOR WATCH AND CLOCK WORK AND ACCURATE PIERCING AND PUNCHING—DROP FORGING AND DIE SINKING, TOGETHER WITH MAKING OF DROP DIES, STEAM-HAMMER DIES, NUMBER-PLATE TOOLS AND DIES FOR BOLT MACHINES—METHODS, DESIGNS, WAYS, KINKS, FORMULAS AND TOOLS FOR SPECIAL WORK, TOGETHER WITH MISCELLANEOUS INFORMATION OF VALUE TO TOOL AND DIE MAKERS AND SHEET-METAL GOODS MANUFACTURERS—SPECIAL AND NOVEL PROCESSES, PRESSES AND FEEDS FOR WORKING SHEET METAL IN DIES.

RECLAMATION OF LAND FROM TIDAL WATERS.
A Handbook for Engineers, Landed Proprietors, and others interested in Works of Reclamation. By A. BEAZELEY, M.Inst.C.E.   8vo, cloth.   *Net* 10/6

"The work contains a great deal of practical and useful information which cannot fail to be of service to engineers entrusted with the enclosure of salt marshes, and to land-owners intending to reclaim land from the sea."—*The Engineer.*

REFRIGERATING AND ICE-MAKING MACHINERY.
A Descriptive Treatise for the Use of Persons Employing Refrigerating and Ice-Making Installations, and others.   By A. J. WALLIS-TAYLER, A.M.Inst.C.E.   Third Edition, Enlarged.   Crown 8vo, cloth   .   . 7/6

"May be recommended as a useful description of the machinery, the processes, and of the facts, figures, and tabulated physics of refrigerating."—*Engineer.*

REFRIGERATION AND ICE-MAKING POCKET BOOK.
By A. J. WALLIS-TAYLER, A.M.Inst.C.E.   Author of " Refrigerating and Ice-making Machinery," &c.   Fourth Edition.   Crown 8vo, cloth.   *Net* 3/6

REFRIGERATION, COLD STORAGE, & ICE-MAKING :
A Practical Treatise on the Art and Science of Refrigeration.   By A. J. WALLIS-TAYLER, A.M.Inst.C.E., Author of " Refrigerating and Ice-Making Machinery."   600 pp., with 360 Illustrations.   Medium 8vo, cloth.   *Net* 15/0

"The author has to be congratulated on the completion and production of such an important work and it cannot fail to have a large body of readers, for it leaves out nothing that would in any way be of value to those interested in the subject."—*Steamship.*

RIVER BARS.   The Causes of their Formation, and their
Treatment by " Induced Tidal Scour"; with a Description of the Successful Reduction by this Method of the Bar at Dublin. By I. J. MANN, Assist. Eng. to the Dublin Port and Docks Board.   Royal 8vo, cloth   .   . 7/6

"We recommend all interested in harbour works—and, indeed, those concerned in the improvement of rivers generally—to read Mr. Mann's interesting work."—*Engineer.*

ROADS AND STREETS.   By H. LAW, C.E., and D. K. CLARK,
C.E.   Revised, with Additional Chapters by A. J. WALLIS-TAYLER, A.M.Inst.C.E.   Seventh Edition.   Crown 8vo, cloth 6/0

"A book which every borough surveyor and engineer must possess, and which will be of considerable service to architects, builders, and property owners generally."—*Building News.*

ROOFS OF WOOD AND IRON.   Deduced chiefly from the
Works of Robison, Tredgold, and Humber.   By E. W. TARN, M.A., Architect.   Fifth Edition.   Crown 8vo, cloth 1/6

SAFE RAILWAY WORKING.   A Treatise on Railway Acci-
dents, their Cause and Prevention; with a Description of Modern Appliances and Systems.   By CLEMENT E. STRETTON, C.E.   Third Edition, Enlarged. Crown 8vo, cloth 3/6

SAFE USE OF STEAM.   Containing Rules for Unprofes-
sional Steam Users.   By an ENGINEER.   Eighth Edition.   Sewed   . 6D.

"If steam-users would but learn this little book by heart, boiler explosions would become sensations by their rarity."—*English Mechanic.*

SAILMAKING. By SAMUEL B. SADLER, Practical Sailmaker,
late in the employment of Messrs. Ratsey and Lapthorne, of Cowes and
Gosport. Second Edition. Revised and Enlarged. Plates. 4to, cloth
Net **12/6**

SAILOR'S SEA BOOK. A Rudimentary Treatise on Naviga-
tion. By JAMES GREENWOOD, B.A. With numerous Woodcuts and
Coloured Plates. New and Enlarged Edition. By W. H. ROSSER.
Crown 8vo, cloth **2/6**

SAILS AND SAIL-MAKING. With Draughting, and the
Centre of Effort of the Sails. Weights and Sizes of Ropes; Masting,
Rigging, and Sails of Steam Vessels, etc. By R. KIPPING, N.A. Crown
8vo, cloth **2/6**

SCREW-THREADS, and Methods of Producing Them. With
numerous Tables and complete Directions for using Screw-Cutting
Lathes. By PAUL N. HASLUCK, Author of "Lathe-Work," etc. Sixth
Edition. Waistcoat-pocket size **1/6**
" Full of useful information, hints and practical criticism. Taps, dies, and screwing tools
generally are illustrated and their action described."—*Mechanical World.*

SEA TERMS, PHRASES, AND WORDS; Technical Dic-
tionary (French-English, English-French), used in the English and French
Languages. For the Use of Seamen, Engineers, Pilots, Shipbuilders, Ship-
owners, and Shipbrokers. Compiled by W. PIRRIE, late of the African
Steamship Company. F'cap. 8vo, cloth **5/0**

SHIPBUILDING INDUSTRY OF GERMANY. Compiled
and Edited by G. LEHMANN-FELSKOWSKI. With Coloured Prints, Art
Supplements, and numerous Illustrations throughout the text. Super-royal
4to, cloth . . . . *Net* **10/6**

SHIPS AND BOATS. By W. BLAND. With numerous Illustrations and Models. Tenth Edition. Crown 8vo, cloth . . **1/6**

SHIPS FOR OCEAN AND RIVER SERVICE. Principles
of the Construction of. By H. A. SOMMERFELDT. Crown 8vo . . **1/6**
ATLAS OF ENGRAVINGS to illustrate the above. Twelve large folding
Plates. Royal 4to, cloth **7/6**

SMITHY AND FORGE. Including the Farrier's Art and
Coach Smithing. By W. J. E. CRANE. Crown 8vo, cloth . . **2/6**

STATICS, GRAPHIC AND ANALYTIC. In their Practical
Application to the Treatment of Stresses in Roofs, Solid Girders, Lattice,
Bowstring, and Suspension Bridges, Braced Iron Arches and Piers, and other
Frameworks. By R. HUDSON GRAHAM, C.E. Containing Diagrams and
Plates to Scale. With numerous Examples, many taken from existing
Structures. Specially arranged for Class-work in Colleges and Universities.
Second Edition, Revised and Enlarged. 8vo, cloth **16/0**
" Mr. Graham's book will find a place wherever graphic and analytic statics are used or
studied."—*Engineer.*

STATIONARY ENGINE DRIVING. A Practical Manual for
Engineers in Charge of Stationary Engines. By MICHAEL REYNOLDS
M.S.E. Eighth Edition. Crown 8vo, cloth, 3/6; cloth boards . 4/6
"The author is thoroughly acquainted with his subjects, and has produced a manual which is
an exceedingly useful one for the class for whom it is specially intended."—*Engineering.*

STATIONARY ENGINES. A Practical Handbook of their
Care and Management for Men-in-charge. By C. HURST. Crown 8vo. *Net* 1/0

STEAM : THE APPLICATION OF HIGHLY SUPER-
HEATED STEAM TO LOCOMOTIVES. Being a reprint from a Series
of Articles appearing in the *Engineer.* By ROBERT GARBE. Privy Councillor,
Prussian State Railways. Translated from the German. Edited by LESLIE
S. ROBERTSON, Secretary of the Engineering Standards Committee,
M.Inst.C.E., M.I.Mech.E., M.Inst.N.A., etc. Medium 8vo, cloth
[*Just Published.* 7/6

STEAM AND THE STEAM ENGINE. Stationary and
Portable. Being an Extension of the Treatise on the Steam Engine of
Mr. J. SEWELL. By D. K. CLARK, C.E. Fourth Edition. Crown 8vo,
cloth 3/6
"Every essential part of the subject is treated of competently, and in a popular style."—*Iron.*

STEAM AND MACHINERY MANAGEMENT. A Guide
to the Arrangement and Economical Management of Machinery, with
Hints on Construction and Selection. By M. POWIS BALE, M.Inst.M.E.
Crown 8vo, cloth 2/6
"Gives the results of wide experience."—*Lloyd's Newspaper.*

STEAM ENGINE. A Practical Handbook compiled with
especial Reference to Small and Medium-sized Engines. For the Use of
Engine Makers, Mechanical Draughtsmen, Engineering Students, and users
of Steam Power. By HERMAN HAEDER, C.E. Translated from the German
with additions and alterations, by H. H. P. POWLES, A.M.I.C.E., M.I.M.E.
Third Edition, Revised. With nearly 1,100 Illustrations. Crown 8vo,
cloth . . . . *Net* 7/6
"This is an excellent book, and should be in the hands of all who are interested in the construction and design of medium-sized stationary engines. . . . A careful study of its contents and
the arrangement of the sections leads to the conclusion that there is probably no other book like it
in this country. The volume aims at showing the results of practical experience, and it certainly
may claim a complete achievement of this idea."—*Nature.*

STEAM ENGINE. A Treatise on the Mathematical Theory of,
with Rules and Examples for Practical Men. By T. BAKER, C.E. Crown
8vo, cloth 1/6
"Teems with scientific information with reference to the steam-engine."—*Design and Work.*

STEAM ENGINE. For the Use of Beginners. By Dr. LARDNER.
Crown 8vo, cloth 1/6

STEAM ENGINE. A Text-Book on the Steam Engine, with a
Supplement on GAS ENGINES and PART II. on HEAT ENGINES. By T.
M. GOODEVE, M.A., Barrister-at-Law, Professor of Mechanics at the Royal
College of Science, London ; Author of "The Principles of Mechanics," "The
Elements of Mechanism," etc. Fourteenth Edition. Crown 8vo, cloth . 6/0
"Professor Goodeve has given us a treatise on the steam engine, which will bear comparison
with anything written by Huxley or Maxwell, and we can award it no higher praise."—*Engineer.*
"Mr. Goodeve's text-book is a work of which every young engineer should possess himself."
Mining Journal.

STEAM ENGINE (PORTABLE). A Practical Manual on
its Construction and Management. For the use of Owners and Users of
Steam Engines generally. By WILLIAM DYSON WANSBROUGH. Crown
8vo, cloth **3/6**

" This is a work of value to those who use steam machinery. . . . Should be ead by every
one who has a steam engine, on a farm or elsewhere."—*Mark Lane Express.*

STEAM ENGINEERING IN THEORY AND PRACTICE.
By GARDNER D. HISCOX, M.E. With Chapters on Electrical Engineering.
By NEWTON HARRISON, E.E., Author of " Electric Wiring, Diagrams, and
Switchboards." 450 Pages. Over 400 Detailed Engravings. *Net* **12/6**

HISTORICAL—STEAM AND ITS PROPERTIES—APPLIANCES FOR THE GENERATION
OF STEAM—TYPES OF BOILERS—CHIMNEY AND ITS WORK—HEAT ECONOMY OF THE
FEED WATER—STEAM PUMPS AND THEIR WORK—INCRUSTATION AND ITS WORK—
STEAM ABOVE ATMOSPHERIC PRESSURE—FLOW OF STEAM FROM NOZZLES—SUPER-
HEATED STEAM AND ITS WORK—ADIABATIC EXPANSION OF STEAM—INDICATOR AND
ITS WORK—STEAM ENGINE PROPORTIONS—SLIDE VALVE ENGINES AND VALVE MOTION
—CORLISS ENGINE AND ITS VALVE GEAR—COMPOUND ENGINE AND ITS THEORY—
TRIPLE AND MULTIPLE EXPANSION ENGINE—STEAM TURBINE—REFRIGERATION—
ELEVATORS AND THEIR MANAGEMENT—COST OF POWER—STEAM ENGINE TROUBLES
—ELECTRIC POWER AND ELECTRIC PLANTS.

STONE BLASTING AND QUARRYING. For Building and
other Purposes. With Remarks on the Blowing up of Bridges. By Gen.
Sir J. BURGOYNE, K.C.B. Crown 8vo, cloth **1/6**

STONE-WORKING MACHINERY. A Manual dealing with
the Rapid and Economical Conversion of Stone. With Hints on the Arrangement and Management of Stone Works. By M. POWIS BALE, M.Inst.C.E.
Crown 8vo, cloth **9/0**

" Should be in the hands of every mason or student of stonework."—*Colliery Guardian.*

STRAINS, HANDY BOOK FOR THE CALCULATION OF.
In Girders and Similar Structures and their Strength. Consisting of Formulæ
and Corresponding Diagrams, with numerous details for Practical Application, &c. By WILLIAM HUMBER, A. M.Inst.C.E., &c. Sixth Edition.
Crown 8vo, with nearly 100 Woodcuts and 3 Plates, cloth . . . **7/6**

" We heartily commend this really *handy* book to our engineer and architect readers."—
English Mechanic.

STRAINS ON STRUCTURES OF IRONWORK. With
Practical Remarks on Iron Construction. By F. W. SHEILDS, M.Inst.C.E.
8vo, cloth **5/0**

SUBMARINE TELEGRAPHS. Their History, Construction,
and Working. Founded in part on WÜNSCHENDORFF'S " Traité de Télé-
graphie Sous-Marine," and Compiled from Authoritative and Exclusive
Sources. By CHARLES BRIGHT, F.R.S.E., A.M.Inst.C.E., M.I.Mech.E.
M.I.E.E. Super royal 8vo, nearly 800 pages, fully Illustrated, including
a large number of Maps and Folding Plates, strongly bound in cloth
Net **£3 3s.**

"Mr. Bright's interestingly written and admirably illustrated book will meet with a welcome
reception from cable men."—*Electrician.*

SUPERHEATED STEAM, THE APPLICATION OF, TO LOCOMOTIVES. See STEAM.

SURVEYING AS PRACTISED BY CIVIL ENGINEERS AND SURVEYORS.

Including the Setting-out of Works for Construction and Surveys Abroad, with many Examples taken from Actual Practice. A Handbook for use in the Field and the Office, intended also as a Text-book for Students. By JOHN WHITELAW, Jun., A.M.Inst.C.E., Author of "Points and Crossings." With about 260 Illustrations. Second Edition. Demy 8vo, cloth . . . . *Net* **10/6**

SURVEYING WITH THE CHAIN ONLY—SURVEYING WITH THE AID OF ANGULAR INSTRUMENTS—LEVELLING—ADJUSTMENT OF INSTRUMENTS—RAILWAY (INCLUDING ROAD) SURVEYS AND SETTING OUT—TACHEOMETRY OR STADIA SURVEYING—TUNNEL ALIGNMENT AND SETTING OUT—SURVEYS FOR WATER SUPPLY WORKS—HYDROGRA-PHICAL OR MARINE SURVEYING—ASTRONOMICAL OBSERVATIONS USED IN SURVEYING—EXPLANATIONS OF ASTRONOMICAL TERMS—SURVEYS ABROAD IN JUNGLE, DENSE FOREST, AND UNMAPPED OPEN COUNTRY—TRIGONOMETRICAL OR GEODETIC SURVEYS.

"This work is written with admirable lucidity, and will certainly be found of distinct value both to students and to those engaged in actual practice."—*The Builder.*

SURVEYING, LAND AND ENGINEERING. For Students

and Practical Use. By T. BAKER, C.E. Twentieth Edition, by F. E. DIXON, A.M.Inst.C.E. With Plates and Diagrams. Crown 8vo, cloth

2/0

SURVEYING, LAND AND MARINE. In Reference to the

Preparation of Plans for Roads and Railways; Canals, Rivers, Towns, Water Supplies; Docks and Harbours. With Description and Use of Surveying Instruments. By W. DAVIS HASKOLL, C.E. Second Edition, Revised with Additions. Large crown 8vo, cloth **9/0**

"This book must prove of great value to the student. We have no hesitation in recommending it, feeling assured that it will more than repay a careful study."—*Mechanical World.*

SURVEYING, PRACTICAL. A Text-book for Students Pre-

paring for Examinations or for Survey Work in the Colonies. By GEORGE W. USILL, A.M.Inst.C.E. Eighth Edition, thoroughly Revised and Enlarged by ALEX. BEAZELEY, M.Inst C.E. With 4 Lithographic Plates and 360 Illustrations. Large crown 8vo, **7/6** cloth; or, on thin paper, leather, gilt edges, rounded corners, for pocket use **12/6**

ORDINARY SURVEYING—SURVEYING INSTRUMENTS—TRIGONOMETRY REQUIRED IN SURVEYING—CHAIN SURVEYING—THEODOLITE SURVEYING—TRAVERSING—TOWN-SURVEYING—LEVELLING—CONTOURING—SETTING OUT CURVES—OFFICE WORK—LAND QUANTITIES—COLONIAL LICENSING REGULATIONS—HYPSOMETER TABLES—INTRODUCTION TO TABLES OF NATURAL SINES, ETC.—NATURAL SINES AND CO-SINES—NATURAL TANGENTS AND CO-TANGENTS—NATURAL SECANTS AND CO-SECANTS.

"The first book which should be put in the hands of a pupil of civil engineering."—*Architect.*

SURVEYING TRIGONOMETRICAL. An outline of the

Method of Conducting a Trigonometrical Survey. For the Formation of Geographical and Topographical Maps and Plans, Military Reconnaissance. Levelling, &c., with Useful Problems, Formulæ, and Tables. By Lieut.-General FROME, R.E. Fourth Edition, Revised and partly Re-written by Major-General Sir CHARLES WARREN, G.C.M.G., R.E. With 19 Plates and 115 Woodcuts, royal 8vo, cloth **16/0**

SURVEYING WITH THE TACHEOMETER. A Practical

Manual for the use of Civil and Military Engineers and Surveyors, including two series of Tables specially computed for the Reduction of Readings in Sexagesimal and in Centesimal Degrees. By NEIL KENNEDY, M.Inst.C.E., With Diagrams and Plates. Second Edition. Demy 8vo, cloth *Net* **10/6**

"The work is very clearly written, and should remove all difficulties in the way of any surveyor desirous of making use of this useful and rapid instrument."—*Nature.*

SURVEY PRACTICE. For Reference in Surveying, Levelling, and Setting-out ; and in Route Surveys of Travellers by Land and Sea. With Tables, Illustrations, and Records. By L. D'A. JACKSON, A.M.Inst.C.E. Second Edition. 8vo, cloth **12/6**

SURVEYOR'S FIELD BOOK FOR ENGINEERS AND MINING SURVEYORS. Consisting of a Series of Tables, with Rules, Explanations of Systems, and use of Theodolite for Traverse Surveying and plotting the work with minute accuracy by means of Straight Edge and Set Square only ; Levelling with the Theodolite, Setting-out Curves with and without the Theodolite, Earthwork Tables, &c. By W. DAVIS HASKOLL, C.E. With numerous Woodcuts. Fifth Edition, Enlarged. Crown 8vo, cloth **12/0**

"The book is very handy ; the separate tables of sines and tangents to every minute will make it useful for many other purposes, the genuine traverse tables existing all the same."—*Athenæum.*

TECHNICAL TERMS, English-French, French-English : A Pocket Glossary ; with Tables suitable for the Architectural, Engineering, Manufacturing, and Nautical Professions. By JOHN JAMES FLETCHER. Fourth Edition, 200 pp. Waistcoat-pocket size, limp leather . . . **1/6**

"The glossary of terms is very complete, and many of the Tables are new and well arranged. We cordially commend the book." —*Mechanical World.*

TECHNICAL TERMS, Eng.-Spanish, Spanish-Eng : A Pocket Glossary of Engineering, Technical, Nautical and Mining Terms. By R. D. MONTEVERDE, B.A. (Madrid).

[In Preparation. Price about **2/0** *Net.*

TELEPHONES : THEIR CONSTRUCTION, INSTALLATION, WIRING, OPERATION AND MAINTENANCE. A Practical Reference Book and Guide for Electricians, Wiremen, Engineers, Contractors, Architects, and others interested in Standard Telephone Practice. By W. H. RADCLIFFE and H. C. CUSHING, JR. 180 pages. With 125 Illustrations. Fcap 8vo, cloth . . . . *[Just published. Net* **4/6**

TELEPHONES : FIELD TELEPHONES FOR ARMY USE : INCLUDING AN ELEMENTARY COURSE IN ELECTRICITY AND MAGNETISM. By Lieut. E. J. STEVENS, D.O., R.A., A.M.I.E.E., Instructor in Electricity, Ordnance College, Woolwich. Crown 8vo, cloth. With Illustrations . . . . . . *[Just Published. Net* **2/0**
BATTERIES—ELECTRICAL CIRCUITS—MAGNETISM—INDUCTION—MICROPHONES AND RECEIVERS—PORTABLE AND FIELD TELEPHONE SETS—SELF-INDUCTION, INDUCTIVE CAPACITY, ETC.

TELEPHONY. See WIRELESS TELEPHONY and WIRELESS TELEGRAPHY.

TOOLS FOR ENGINEERS AND WOODWORKERS. Including Modern Instruments of Measurement. By JOSEPH HORNER, A.M.Inst.M.E., Author of "Pattern Making," &c. Demy 8vo, with 456 Illustrations . . . . *Net* **9/0**
SUMMARY OF CONTENTS :—INTRODUCTION—GENERAL SURVEY OF TOOLS—TOOL ANGLES.—SEC. I. CHISEL GROUP—CHISELS AND APPLIED FORMS FOR WOODWORKERS —PLANES—HAND CHISELS AND APPLIED FORMS FOR METAL WORKING—CHISEL-LIKE TOOLS FOR METAL TURNING, PLANING, &c—SHEARING ACTION AND SHEARING TOOLS—SEC. II. EXAMPLES OF SCRAPING TOOLS.—SEC. III. TOOLS—RELATING TO CHISELS AND SCRAPES—SAWS—FILES—MILLING CUTTERS—BORING TOOLS FOR WOOD AND METAL —TAPS AND DIES.—SEC. IV. PERCUSSIVE AND MOULDING TOOLS—PUNCHES, HAMMERS AND CAULKING TOOLS—MOULDING AND MODELLING TOOLS—MISCELLANEOUS TOOLS. —SEC. V. HARDENING, TEMPERING, GRINDING AND SHARPENING.—SEC. VI. TOOLS FOR MEASUREMENT AND TEST—STANDARDS OF MEASUREMENT—SQUARES, SURFACE PLATES, LEVELS, BEVELS, PROTRACTORS, &c.—SURFACE GAUGES OR SCRIBING BLOCKS —COMPASSES AND DIVIDERS—CALIPERS, VERNIER CALIPERS, AND RELATED FORMS— —MICROMETER CALIPERS—DEPTH GAUGES AND ROD GAUGES—SNAP CYLINDRICAL AND LIMIT GAUGES—SCREW THREAD, WIRE AND REFERENCE GAUGES—INDICATORS, ETC.

"As an all-round practical work on tools it is more comprehensive than any with which we are acquainted, and we have no doubt it will meet with the large measure of success to which its merits fully entitle it."—*Mechanical World.*

TOOTHED GEARING. A Practical Handbook for Offices, and Workshops. By J. HORNER. A.M.I.M.E. Second Edition, with a New Chapter on Recent Practice. With 184 Illustrations. Crown 8vo, cloth **6/0**

TRAMWAYS: THEIR CONSTRUCTION AND WORKING. Embracing a Comprehensive History of the System; with an exhaustive Analysis of the Various Modes of Traction, including Horse Power, Steam Cable Traction, Electric Traction, &c.; a Description of the Varieties of Rolling Stock; and ample Details of Cost and Working Expenses. New Edition, Thoroughly Revised, and Including the Progress recently made in Tramway Construction, &c. By D. KINNEAR CLARK, M.Inst.C.E. With 400 Illustrations. 8vo, 780 pp., buckram **28/0**

TRUSSES OF WOOD AND IRON. Practical Applications of Science in Determining the Stresses, Breaking Weights, Safe Loads, Scantlings, and Details of Construction. With Complete Working Drawings. By W. GRIFFITHS, Surveyor. Oblong 8vo, cloth **4/6**
"This handy little book enters so minutely into every detail connected with the construction of roof trusses that no student need be ignorant of these matters."—*Practical Engineer.*

TUNNELLING. A Practical Treatise. By CHARLES PRELINI, C.E. With additions by CHARLES S. HILL, C.E. With 150 Diagrams and Illustrations. Royal 8vo, cloth . . . . *Net* **16/0**

TUNNELLING, PRACTICAL. Explaining in detail the Setting-out the Works, Shaft-sinking, and Heading-driving, Ranging the Lines and Levelling underground, Sub-Excavating, Timbering and the Construction of the Brickwork of Tunnels. By F. W. SIMMS, M.Inst.C.E. Fourth Edition, Revised and Further Extended, including the most recent (1895) Examples of Sub-aqueous and other Tunnels, by D. KINNEAR CLARK, M.Inst.C.E. With 34 Folding Plates. Imperial 8vo, cloth . . . . . **£2 2s.**

TUNNEL SHAFTS. A Practical and Theoretical Essay on the construction of large Tunnel Shafts. By J. H. WATSON BUCK, M.Inst.C.E., Resident Engineer, L. and N. W. R. With Folding Plates, 8vo, cloth **12/0**
"Will be regarded by civil engineers as of the utmost value and calculated to save much time and obviate many mistakes."—*Colliery Guardian.*

WAGES TABLES. At 54, 52, 50, and 48 Hours per Week. Showing the Amounts of Wages from One quarter of an hour to Sixty-four hours, in each case at Rates of Wages advancing by One Shilling from 4s. to 55s. per week. By THOS. GARBUTT, Accountant. Square crown 8vo, half-bound **6/0**

WATER ENGINEERING. A Practical Treatise on the Measurement, Storage, Conveyance, and Utilization of Water for the Supply of Towns, for Mill Power, and for other Purposes. By CHARLES SLAGG, A.M.Inst.C.E. Second Edition. Crown 8vo, cloth **7/6**

WATER, POWER OF. As Applied to Drive Flour Mills and to give motion to Turbines and other Hydrostatic Engines. By JOSEPH GLYNN, F.R.S., &c. New Edition. Illustrated. Crown 8vo, cloth **2/0**

WATER SUPPLY OF CITIES AND TOWNS. By WIL-
LIAM HUMBER, A.M.Inst. C.E., and M.Inst.M.E., Author of "Cast and
Wrought Iron Bridge Construction," &c., &c. Illustrated with 50 Double
Plates, 1 Single Plate, Coloured Frontispiece, and upwards of 250 Woodcuts,
and containing 400 pp. of Text. Imp. 4to, elegantly and substantially
half-bound in morocco . . . . *Net* **£6 6s.**

LIST OF CONTENTS:—I. HISTORICAL SKETCH OF SOME OF THE MEANS THAT HAVE
BEEN ADOPTED FOR THE SUPPLY OF WATER TO CITIES AND TOWNS.—II. WATER AND
THE FOREIGN MATTER USUALLY ASSOCIATED WITH IT.—III. RAINFALL AND EVAPORA-
TION.—IV. SPRINGS AND THE WATER-BEARING FORMATIONS OF VARIOUS DISTRICTS.
—V. MEASUREMENT AND ESTIMATION OF THE FLOW OF WATER.—VI. ON THE SELECTION
OF THE SOURCE OF SUPPLY.—VII. WELLS.—VIII. RESERVOIRS.—IX. THE PURIFICATION
OF WATER.—X. PUMPS.—XI. PUMPING MACHINERY.—XII. CONDUITS.—XIII. DISTRIBU-
TION OF WATER.—XIV. METERS, SERVICE PIPES, AND HOUSE FITTINGS.—XV. THE LAW
AND ECONOMY OF WATER-WORKS.—XVI. CONSTANT AND INTERMITTENT SUPPLY.—
XVII. DESCRIPTION OF PLATES.—APPENDICES, GIVING TABLES OF RATES OF SUPPLY,
VELOCITIES, &c., &c., TOGETHER WITH SPECIFICATIONS OF SEVERAL WORKS ILLUS-
TRATED, AMONG WHICH WILL BE FOUND: ABERDEEN, BIDEFORD, CANTERBURY,
DUNDEE, HALIFAX, LAMBETH, ROTHERHAM, DUBLIN, AND OTHERS.

"The most systematic and valuable work upon water supply hitherto produced in English, or
in any other language. Mr. Humber's work is characterised almost throughout by an
exhaustiveness much more distinctive of French and German than of English technical treatises."
—*Engineer.*

WATER SUPPLY OF TOWNS AND THE CONSTRUC-
TION OF WATER-WORKS. A Practical Treatise for the Use of
Engineers and Students of Engineering. By W. K. BURTON, A. M.Inst.C.E.,
Consulting Engineer to the Tokyo Water-works. Third Edition, Revised.
Edited by ALLAN GREENWELL, F.G.S., A.M.Inst.C.E., with numerous
Plates and Illustrations. Super-royal 8vo, buckram . . . **25/0**

I. INTRODUCTORY. — II. DIFFERENT QUALITIES OF WATER. — III. QUANTITY OF
WATER TO BE PROVIDED.—IV. ON ASCERTAINING WHETHER A PROPOSED SOURCE OF
SUPPLY IS SUFFICIENT.—V. ON ESTIMATING THE STORAGE CAPACITY REQUIRED
TO BE PROVIDED.—VI. CLASSIFICATION OF WATER-WORKS.—VII. IMPOUNDING RESER-
VOIRS.—VIII. EARTHWORK DAMS.—IX. MASONRY DAMS.—X. THE PURIFICATION OF
WATER.—XI. SETTLING RESERVOIRS.—XII. SAND FILTRATION.—XIII. PURIFICATION
OF WATER BY ACTION OF IRON, SOFTENING OF WATER BY ACTION OF LIME, NATURAL
FILTRATION.—XIV. SERVICE OR CLEAN WATER RESERVOIRS—WATER TOWERS—STAND
PIPES.—XV. THE CONNECTION OF SETTLING RESERVOIRS, FILTER BEDS AND SERVICE
RESERVOIRS.—XVI. PUMPING MACHINERY.—XVII. FLOW OF WATER IN CONDUITS—
PIPES AND OPEN CHANNELS.—XVIII. DISTRIBUTION SYSTEMS.—XIX. SPECIAL PRO-
VISIONS FOR THE EXTINCTION OF FIRES.—XX. PIPES FOR WATER-WORKS.—XXI. PRE-
VENTION OF WASTE OF WATER.—XXII. VARIOUS APPLIANCES USED IN CONNECTION
WITH WATER-WORKS.

APPENDIX I. By PROF. JOHN MILNE, F.R.S.—CONSIDERATIONS CONCERNING THE
PROBABLE EFFECTS OF EARTHQUAKES ON WATER-WORKS, AND THE SPECIAL PRE-
CAUTIONS TO BE TAKEN IN EARTHQUAKE COUNTRIES.

APPENDIX II. By JOHN DE RIJKE, C.E.—ON SAND DUNES AND DUNE SANDS AS
A SOURCE OF WATER SUPPLY.

"We congratulate the author upon the practical commonsense shown in the preparation of
this work. . . . The plates and diagrams have evidently been prepared with great care, and
cannot fail to be of great assistance to the student."—*Builder.*

WATER SUPPLY, RURAL. A Practical Handbook on the
Supply of Water and Construction of Water works for small Country Districts.
By ALLAN GREENWELL, A.M.Inst.C.E., and W. T. CURRY, A.M.Inst.C.E.,
F.G.S. With Illustrations. Second Edition, Revised. Crown 8vo, cloth **5/0**

"The volume contains valuable information upon all matters connected with water supply
It is full of details on points which are continually before water-works engineers."—*Nature.*

WELLS AND WELL-SINKING. By J. G. SWINDELL,
A.R.I.B.A., and G. R. BURNELL, C.E. Revised Edition. Crown 8vo,
cloth **2/0**

WIRELESS TELEGRAPHY: ITS THEORY AND PRAC-
TICE. A Handbook for the use of Electrical Engineers, Students, and Operators. By JAMES ERSKINE-MURRAY, D.Sc., Fellow of the Royal Society of Edinburgh, Member of the Institution of Electrical Engineers. Demy 8vo, 338 pages, with over 130 Diagrams a..d Illustrations. *Net* **10/6**

ADAPTATIONS OF THE ELECTRIC CURRENT TO TELEGRAPHY—EARLIER ATTEMPTS AT WIRELESS TELEGRAPHY—APPARATUS USED IN THE PRODUCTION OF HIGH FRE-QUENCY CURRENTS—DETECTION OF SHORT-LIVED CURRENTS OF HIGH FREQUENCY BY MEANS OF IMPERFECT ELECTRICAL CONTACTS—DETECTION OF OSCILLATORY CURRENTS OF HIGH FREQUENCY BY THEIR EFFECTS ON MAGNETISED IRON—THERMOMETRIC DE-TECTORS OF OSCILLATORY CURRENTS OF HIGH FREQUENCY—ELECTROLYTIC DETECTORS —THE MARCONI SYSTEM—THE LODGE-MUIRHEAD SYSTEM—THE FESSENDEN SYSTEM—THE HOZIER-BROWN SYSTEM—WIRELESS TELEGRAPHY IN ALASKA—THE DE FOREST SYSTEM—THE POULSEN SYSTEM—THE TELEFUNKEN SYSTEM—DIRECTED SYSTEMS—SOME POINTS IN THE THEORY OF JIGS AND JIGGERS—ON THEORIES OF TRANSMISSION—WORLD-WAVE TELEGRAPHY—ADJUSTMENTS, ELECTRICAL MEASUREMENTS AND FAULT FINDING—ON THE CALCULATION OF A SYNTONIC WIRELESS TELEGRAPH STATION—TABLES AND NOTES.

" . . . A serious and meritorious contribution to the literature on this subject. The Author brings to bear not only great practical knowledge, gained by experience in the operation of wireless telegraph stations, but also a very sound knowledge of the principles and phenomena of physical science. His work is thoroughly scientific in its treatment, shows much originality throughout, and merits the close attention of all students of the subject."—*Engineering*.

WIRELESS TELEPHONY IN THEORY AND PRACTICE.
By ERNST RUHMER. Translated from the German by J. ERSKINE-MURRAY, D.Sc., M.I.E.E., &c. Author of "A Handbook of Wireless Telegraphy." With an Appendix on Recent Advances by the Translator, and numerous Illustrations. Demy 8vo, cloth .   .   .   [*Just published.* *Net* **10/6**

"A very full descriptive acc·unt of the experim ntal work which has been carried out on Wireless Telephony is to be found in Professor Ruhmer's book. . . . The volume is profusely illustrated by both photographs and drawings, and should prove a useful refere ce Work for those directly or in..irectly interested in the subject."—*Nature*.

"The explanations and discussions are all clear and simple, and the whole volume is a very readable record of important and interesting work."—*Engineering*.

"The translator is to be congratulated upon the selection of his task, and upon the excellent manner in which he has accomplished it: for this is a book that marks an era in the progress of applied science."—*Times*.

"The book is well written and contains much interesting information on a subject which promises great developments."—*Glasgow Herald*.

WORKSHOP PRACTICE. As applied to Marine, Land, and
Locomotive Engines, Floating Docks, Dredging Machines, Bridges, Ship building, &c. By J. G. WINTON. Fourth Edition, Illustrated. Crown 8vo, cloth **3/6**

WORKS' MANAGER'S HANDBOOK. Comprising Modern
Rules, Tables, and Data. For Engineers, Millwrights, and Boiler Makers ; Tool Makers, Machinists, and Metal Workers ; Iron and Brass Founders, &c. By W. S. HUTTON, Civil and Mechanical Engineer, Author of "The Practical Engineer's Handbook." Seventh Edition, carefully Revised, and Enlarged. Medium 8vo, strongly bound **15/0**

STATIONARY AND LOCOMOTIVE STEAM-ENGINES, GAS PRODUCERS, GAS-ENGINES, OIL-ENGINES, ETC.—HYDRAULIC MEMORANDA: PIPES, PUMPS, WATER-POWER, ETC.—MILLWORK: SHAFTING, GEARING, PULLEYS, ETC.—STEAM BOILERS, SAFETY VALVES, FACTORY CHIMNEYS, ETC.—HEAT, WARMING, AND VENTILATION—MELTING, CUTTING, AND FINISHING METALS—ALLOYS AND CASTING—WHEEL-CUTTING, SCREW-CUTTING, ETC.—STRENGTH AND WEIGHT OF MATERIALS—WORKSHOP DATA, ETC.

"The volume is an exceedingly useful one, brimful with engineer's notes, memoranda, and rules, and well worthy of being on every mechanical engineer's bookshelf."—*Mechanical World*.

PUBLICATIONS OF THE ENGINEERING STANDARDS COMMITTEE.

M ESSRS. CROSBY LOCKWOOD and SON, having been appointed OFFICIAL PUBLISHERS to the ENGINEERING STANDARDS COMMITTEE, beg to invite attention to the List given below of the Publications already issued by the Committee, and will be prepared to supply copies thereof and of all Subsequent Publications as issued.

THE ENGINEERING STANDARDS COMMITTEE is the outcome of a Committee appointed by the Institution of Civil Engineers at the instance of Sir John Wolfe Barry, K.C.B., to inquire into the advisability of Standardising Rolled Iron and Steel Sections.

The Committee as now constituted is supported by the Institution of Civil Engineers, the Institution of Mechanical Engineers, the Institution of Naval Architects, the Iron and Steel Institute, and the Institution of Electrical Engineers ; and the value and importance of its labours—not only to the Engineering profession, but to the country at large—has been emphatically recognised by His Majesty's Government, who have made a liberal grant from the Public Funds by way of contribution to the financial resources of the Committee, and have placed at its disposal the services (on the several Sub-Committees) of public officials of the highest standing selected from various Government Departments.

The subjects already dealt with, or under consideration by the Committee, include not only Rolled Iron and Steel Sections, but Tests for Iron and Steel Material used in the Construction of Ships and their Machinery, Bridges and General Building Construction, Railway Rolling Stock, Underframes, Component Parts of Locomotives, Railway and Tramway Rails, Electrical Plant, Insulating Materials, Screw Threads and Limit Gauges, Pipe Flanges, Cement, etc.

These particulars will be sufficient to show the importance to the Trade and Industries of the Empire of the work the Committee has undertaken.

Reports already Published :—

1. **BRITISH STANDARD SECTIONS** (9 lists).—ANGLES, EQUAL AND UNEQUAL.—BULB ANGLES, TEES AND PLATES.—Z AND T BARS.—CHANNELS.—BEAMS, *Net* 1/0
2. **TRAMWAY RAILS AND FISH-PLATES.** *Net* 21/0
3. **REPORT ON THE INFLUENCE OF GAUGE LENGTH.** By Professor W. C. UNWIN, F.R.S. *Net* 2/6
4. **PROPERTIES OF STANDARD BEAMS.** (*Included in No.* 6.) *Net* 1/0
5. **STANDARD LOCOMOTIVES FOR INDIAN RAILWAYS.** *Net* 10/6
6. **PROPERTIES OF BRITISH STANDARD SECTIONS.** Diagrams, Definitions, Tables, and Formulæ. *Net* 5/0
7. **TABLES OF COPPER CONDUCTORS AND THICKNESSES OF DI-ELECTRIC.** *Net* 2/6
8. **TUBULAR TRAMWAY POLES.** *Net* 5/0
9. **BULL-HEADED RAILWAY RAILS.** *Net* 10/6
10. **TABLES OF PIPE FLANGES.** *Net* 2/6
11. **FLAT-BOTTOMED RAILWAY RAILS.** *Net* 10/6
12. **SPECIFICATION FOR PORTLAND CEMENT.** *Net* 2/6
13. **STRUCTURAL STEEL FOR SHIPBUILDING.** *Net* 2/6

PUBLICATIONS OF THE ENGINEERING STANDARDS COMMITTEE—(*continued*).

14. STRUCTURAL STEEL FOR MARINE BOILERS. *Net* 2/6
15. STRUCTURAL STEEL FOR BRIDGES AND GENERAL BUILDING CONSTRUCTION . . . *Net* 2/6
16. SPECIFICATIONS AND TABLES FOR TELEGRAPH MATERIALS. *Net* 10/6
17. INTERIM REPORT ON ELECTRICAL MACHINERY. *Net* 2/6
19. REPORT ON TEMPERATURE EXPERIMENTS ON FIELD COILS OF ELECTRICAL MACHINES. *Net* 5/0
20. BRITISH STANDARD SCREW THREADS. *Net* 2/6
21. BRITISH STANDARD PIPE THREADS. *Net* 2/6
22. THE EFFECT OF TEMPERATURE ON INSULATING MATERIALS. *Net* 5/0
23. STANDARDS FOR TROLLEY GROOVE AND WIRE. *Net* 1/0
24. MATERIAL USED IN THE CONSTRUCTION OF RAILWAY ROLLING STOCK. *Net* 10/6
25. ERRORS IN WORKMANSHIP. Based on Measurements carried out by the National Physical Laboratory. *Net* 10/6
26. SECOND REPORT ON LOCOMOTIVES FOR INDIAN RAILWAYS. *Net* 10/6
27. STANDARD SYSTEMS FOR LIMIT GAUGES. (Running Fits). *Net* 2/6
28. NUTS, BOLT-HEADS, AND SPANNERS. *Net* 2/6
29. INGOT STEEL FORGINGS FOR MARINE PURPOSES. *Net* 2/6
30. INGOT STEEL CASTINGS FOR MARINE PURPOSES. *Net* 2/6
31. STEEL CONDUITS FOR ELECTRICAL WIRING. *Net* 2/6
32. STEEL BARS (for use in automatic Machines). *Net* 2/6
33. CARBON FILAMENT GLOW LAMPS. *Net* 5/0
34. WHITWORTH, FINE, AND PIPE THREADS. (Mounted on Card and varnished.) *Net* 6d.
35. COPPER ALLOY BARS (for use in Automatic Machines). *Net* 2/6
36. STANDARDS FOR ELECTRICAL MACHINERY. 2nd Report. *Net* 1/0
37. CONSUMERS' ELECTRIC SUPPLY METERS (Motor Type for Continuous and Single-Phase Circuits). *Net* 2/6
38. LIMIT GAUGES FOR SCREW THREADS. *Net* 1/0
39. COMBINED REPORTS ON SCREW THREADS (containing Nos. 20, 28, 38). *Net* 3/6
40. CAST IRON SPIGOT AND SOCKET LOW PRESSURE HEATING PIPES. *Net* 2/6
41. CAST IRON SPIGOT AND SOCKET FLUE OR SMOKE PIPES. *Net* 2/6

London : Crosby Lockwood & Son,

7, STATIONERS' HALL COURT, LUDGATE HILL, E.C.,

and 121a, Victoria Street, Westminster, S.W.

BRADBURY, AGNEW, & CO. LD., PRINTERS, LONDON AND TONBRIDGE.   (15-11-08.)

WEALE'S SCIENTIFIC & TECHNICAL SERIES.

MATHEMATICS, ARITHMETIC, &c.

CROSBY LOCKWOOD & SON, 7, Stationers' Hall Court, E.C.

WEALE'S SCIENTIFIC & TECHNICAL SERIES.

BUILDING & ARCHITECTURE.

CROSBY LOCKWOOD & SON, 7, Stationers' Hall Court, E.C.